THE DARK LORD

OF

DERKHOLM

Diana Wynne Jones' first children's book was published in 1973. Her magical, humorous stories have enthralled children and adults ever since, and she has inspired many of today's children's and fantasy authors. Among Diana's best loved books for older children are the *Chrestomanci* series and the *Howl* books. Her novel *Howl's Moving Castle* was made into an award-winning film. She was described by Neil Gaiman as "the best children's writer of the last 40 years".

Titles by Diana Wynne Jones

Chrestomanci Series
Charmed Life
The Magicians of Caprona
Witch Week
The Lives of Christopher Chant
Mixed Magics
Conrad's Fate
The Pinhoe Egg

Howl Series
Howl's Moving Castle
Castle in the Air
House of Many Ways

Archer's Goon
Black Maria
Dogsbody
Eight Days of Luke
Enchanted Glass
The Homeward Bounders
The Merlin Conspiracy
Deep Secret
The Ogre Downstairs
Power of Three
A Tale of Time City
Wilkin's Tooth
The Game

For older readers
Fire and Hemlock
Hexwood
The Time of the Ghost

For younger readers
Wild Robert
Earwig and the Witch
Vile Visitors

THE DARK LORD

OF
DERKHOLM

HarperCollins *Children's Books*

First published in Great Britain by Victor Gollancz in 1998
This edition first published in Great Britain by
HarperCollins *Children's Books* in 2013
HarperCollins *Children's Books* is a division of HarperCollins*Publishers* Ltd,
77-85 Fulham Palace Road, Hammersmith, London, W6 8JB.

www.harpercollins.co.uk

1

Text copyright © Diana Wynne Jones 1998

The author and illustrator assert the moral right to be identified as the author and
illustrator of this work.

ISBN 978-0-00-750757-3

Printed and bound in England by Clays Ltd, St Ives plc.

To Robin McKinley

CHAPTER ONE

*

"Will you all be quiet!" hissed High Chancellor Querida. She pouched up her eyes and glared round the table.

"I was only trying to say—" a king, an emperor and several wizards began.

"At once," said Querida, "or the next person to speak spends the rest of his life as a snake!"

This shut most of the University Emergency Committee up. Querida was the most powerful wizard in the world and she had a special feeling for snakes. She looked like a snake herself, small and glossy-skinned and greenish, and very, very old. Nobody doubted she meant what she said. But two people went on talking anyway.

Gloomy King Luther murmured from the end of the table, "Being a snake might be a relief." And when Querida's eyes darted round at him, he stared glumly back, daring her to do it.

And Wizard Barnabas, who was Vice-Chancellor of University, simply went on talking "...trying to say, Querida, that you don't understand what it's like. You're a woman. You only have to be the Glamorous Enchantress. Mr Chesney won't let women do the Dark Lord." Querida's eyes snapped round at him with no effect at all. Barnabas gave her a cheerful smile and puffed a little. His face seemed designed for good humour. His hair and beard romped round his face in grey curls. He looked into Querida's pouched eyes with his blue, bloodshot ones and added, "We're all worn out, the lot of us."

"Hear, hear!" a number of people round the table muttered cautiously.

"I know that!" Querida snapped. "And if you'd listen, instead of all complaining at once, you'd hear me saying that I've called this meeting to discuss how to put a stop to Mr Chesney's Pilgrim Parties for good."

This produced an astonished silence.

A bitter little smile put folds in Querida's cheeks. "Yes," she said. "I'm well aware that you elected me High Chancellor because you thought I was the only person ruthless enough to oppose Mr Chesney and that you've all been very disappointed that I didn't immediately leap at his throat. I have, of course, been studying the situation.

It is not easy to plan a campaign against a man who lives in another world and organises his tours from there." Her small green-white hands moved to the piles of paper, bark and parchment in front of her and she began stacking them in new heaps with little dry rustling movements. "But it is clear to me," she said, "that things have gone from bad, to intolerable, to crisis point and that something must be done. Here I have forty-six petitions from all the male wizards attached to the University and twenty-two from other male magic users, each pleading chronic overwork. This pile is three letters signed by over a hundred female wizards, who claim they are being denied equal rights. They are accurate. Mr Chesney does not think females can be wizards." Her hands moved on to a mighty stack of parchments with large red seals dangling off them. "This," she said, "is from the kings. Every monarch in the world has written to me at least once protesting at what the tours do to their kingdoms. It is probably only necessary to quote from one. King Luther, perhaps you would care to give us the gist of the letter I receive from you once a month?"

"Yes, I would," said King Luther. He leant forward and gripped the table with powerful blue-knuckled hands. "My kingdom is being ravaged," he said. "I have been selected as Evil King fifteen times in the last twenty years, with the result that I have a tour through once a week, invading my court and trying to kill me or my courtiers. My wife has left me and taken the children with her for safety. The towns and countryside are being devastated. If the army of the Dark Lord doesn't march through and sack my city, then the Forces of Good do it next time. I admit I'm being paid quite well for this, but the money I earn is so urgently needed to repair the capital for the next Pilgrim Party that there is almost none to spare for helping the farmers. They grow hardly anything these days. You must be aware, High Chancellor—"

Querida's hand went to the next pile, which was of paper, in various shapes and sizes. "I am aware, thank you, Your Majesty. These letters are a selection of those I get from farmers and ordinary citizens. They all state that what with magical weather-conditions, armies marching over crops, soldiers rustling cattle, fires set by Dark Lord's Minions and other hazards, they are likely to starve for the foreseeable future." She picked up another smallish pile of paper. "Almost the only people who seem to be prospering are the innkeepers and they complain that the lack of barley is making it hard to brew sufficient ale."

"My heart bleeds," King Luther said sourly. "Where would we be if a Pilgrim Party arrived at an inn with no beer?"

"Mr Chesney would not be pleased," murmured a High Priest. "May the gods defend us, Anscher preserve us from that!"

"Chesney's only a man," muttered the delegate from the Thieves' Guild.

"Don't let him hear you say that!" Barnabas said warningly.

"Of course he's only a man," snapped Querida. "He just happens to be the most powerful man in the world, and I've taken steps to ensure that he cannot hear us inside this council chamber. Now may I go on? Thank you. We are being pressured to find a solution by several bodies. Here" – she picked up a large and beautifully lettered parchment with paintings in the margins – "is an ultimatum from Bardic College. They say that Mr Chesney and his agents appear to regard all bards with the tours as expendable. Rather than lose any more promising musicians, they say here, they are refusing to take part in any tours this year, unless we can guarantee the safety of—"

"But we can't!" protested a wizard two places down from Barnabas.

"True," said Querida. "I fear the bards are going to have to explain themselves to Mr Chesney. I also have here similar but more moderate letters from the seers and the healers. The seers complain that they have to foresee imaginary events and that this is against the articles of their guild, and the healers, like the wizards, complain of chronic overwork. At least they only threaten not to work this year. And here—" she lifted up a small ragged pile of paper, "here are letters from the mercenary captains. Most of them say that replacements to manpower, equipment and armour cost them more than the fees they earn from the Pilgrim Parties, and this one on top from – Black Gauntlet, I think the man's name is – also very feelingly remarks that he wants to retire to a farm, but he has not in twenty years earned enough for one coo—"

"One what?" said King Luther.

"Cow. He can't spell," said Barnabas.

"—even if there were any farms where he would be safe from the tours," said Querida. She shuffled more papers, saying as she shuffled, "Pathetic letters from nuns, monks, werewolves. Where are—? Oh yes, here." She picked up a white sheet which glowed faintly and a large pearly slice of what seemed to be shell, covered with faint marks. "Probably one of their old scales," she remarked. "These are protests from the Elves and the dragons."

"What have they got to complain of?" another wizard asked irritably.

"Both put it rather obscurely," Querida confessed. "I think the Elfking is talking about blackmail and the dragons seem to be bewailing the shrinking of their hoards of treasure, but both of them seem to be talking about their birthrate too, so one cannot be sure. You can all read them in a short while, if you wish, along with any other letters you want. For now, have I made my point?" Her pouchy eyes darted to look at everyone around the long table. "I have asked everyone I can think of to tell me how the tours affect them. I have received over a million replies. My study is overflowing with them and I invite you all to go and inspect it. What I have here are only the most important. And the important thing is that they all, in different ways, say the same thing. They want an end to Mr Chesney's Pilgrim Parties."

"And have you thought of a way to stop them?" Barnabas asked eagerly.

"No," said Querida. "There is no way."

"What?" shouted almost everyone round the table.

"There is no way," Querida repeated, "that I can think of. Perhaps I should remind you that Mr Chesney's decisions are supported by an extremely powerful demon. All the signs are that he made a pact with it when he first started the tours."

"Yes, but that was forty years ago," objected the young Emperor of the South. "Some of us weren't born then. Why should I have to keep on doing what that demon made my grandfather do?"

"Don't be foolish," Querida snapped. "Demons are immortal."

"But Mr Chesney isn't," argued the young Emperor.

"Possibly he isn't, but I've heard he has children being groomed to take over after him," Barnabas said sadly.

Querida's eyes darted to the Emperor in venomous warning. "Don't speak like that outside this room. Mr Chesney does not like to hear anyone being less than enthusiastic about his Pilgrims, and we do not mention the demon. Have I made myself plain?" The young Emperor swallowed and sat back. "Good," said Querida. "Now, to business. The tour agents have been in this world for over a month and the arrangements for this year's tours are almost complete. Mr Chesney is due here himself tomorrow to give the Dark Lord and the Wizard Guides their final briefings. The purpose of this meeting is supposed to be to appoint this year's Dark Lord."

Heavy sighs ran round the table. "All right," said one of the wizards, out of the general dejection. "Who is it to be? Not me. I did it last year."

Querida gave her sour little smile, folded her hands and sat back. "I have no idea," she said blandly. "I have no more idea who is to be Dark Lord than I have about how to stop the tours. I propose that we consult the Oracles."

There was a long, thoughtful silence. Relieved shiftings began around the table as even the slowest of the people there realised that Querida was, after all, trying to find a way out. At last, the High Priest said dubiously, "Madam Chancellor, I understood that the Oracles were set up for Mr Chesney by wizards of the University—"

"And by a former High Priest, who asked the gods to speak through the Oracles," Querida agreed. "Is that any reason why they shouldn't work, Reverend Umru?"

"Well," said the High Priest. "Er. Mightn't the Oracles, in that case, be – well – biased?"

"Probably," said Querida. "For that reason, I propose to ask both the White Oracle and the Black Oracle. They will say two different things and we will do them both."

"Er," said High Priest Umru. "Two Dark Lords?"

"If necessary," said Querida. "Anything it takes." She pushed back her chair and stood up. Because she was so small, this kept her head at exactly the same height. Her small lizard-like chin jutted as she looked round the table. "We can't all go to the Oracles," she said, "and some of you look far too tired. I shall take a representative body. King Luther, I think, and Barnabas, you come. And you, High Priest Umru—"

Umru stood up and bowed, with his hands clasped across his large belly. "Madam Chancellor, I would hate to be selected on false pretences. I am probably one of the few people here who does not object to the Pilgrim Parties. My temple has prospered exceedingly out of them over the years."

"I know," said Querida. "You people keep taking me for a fool. I want you as a representative of the other point of view, of course. And I'll take you too, for the same reason." Her hand darted out like a snake's tongue to point at the delegate from the Thieves' Guild.

He was a young man, thin and fair and clever-looking. He was extremely surprised. "Me?" he said. "Are you sure?"

"What a silly question," Querida said. "Your Guild must have made a mint from the Pilgrims, one way and another."

A strange expression crossed the face of the thief, but he got up without a word. His clothing was as rich as that of the High Priest. His long silk sleeves swirled as he walked gracefully round the table. "Aren't the Oracles in the Distant Desert?" he asked. "How do we go?"

"By a translocation spell I have already set up," Querida said. "Come over here, the four of you." She led the way to the empty part of the room, where one of the large flagstones in the floor could be seen to have faint marks round its edges. "The rest of you can start reading those letters while we're away," she said. "And I'll need a name for you," she told the young thief.

"Oh – Regin," he said.

"Stand here," Querida said, pushing him to one corner of the flagstone. She pushed King Luther, Barnabas and High Priest Umru to each of the other corners and slithered between Umru and King Luther to stand in the centre of the stone herself. From the point of view of the people still sitting at the table, she disappeared entirely behind Umru's belly. Then, quietly and without warning, all five of them vanished and the flagstone was bare.

From the point of view of the four people with Querida, it was like suddenly stepping into an oven – an oven that was probably on fire, King Luther thought, shielding his eyes with his stout woollen sleeve. Sweat ran out from under Barnabas's curls. Umru gasped and staggered and then tried wretchedly to get sand out of his embroidered slippers and loosen his vestments at the same time.

Only Querida was perfectly happy. She said "Ah!"

and stretched, turning her face up to the raging sun with a blissful smile. Her eyes, the young thief noticed, were wide open and looking straight into the sun. Wizards! he thought. He was as uncomfortable as the other three, but he had been trained to seem cool and keep his wits about him. He looked around. The Oracles were only a few yards away. They were two small domed buildings, the one on the left so black that it looked like a hole in the universe, and the one on the right so dazzlingly white that sweat ran stinging into his eyes and he had to look away from it.

While they waited for the other three to recover, Querida took Regin's arm and pulled him across the sand, towards the white building. "Why did you look so oddly when I said your guild must have made a mint from the tours?" she hissed up at him. "Does that mean you want the tours stopped too?"

Trust her to notice! the thief thought ruefully. "Not exactly, Madam Chancellor. But if you think about it, you'll see that after forty years we haven't got much else to steal. We're debating stealing from one another – and even if we did, there's nothing much left to spend what we steal on. Actually, I was sent to ask whether it was permissible to steal from the Pilgrims."

"Don't you steal from tourists?" Querida asked. When he shook his head, another blissful grin spread over Querida's little lizard face. "Do you know, I believe that must be one thing that Mr Chesney forgot to put in his rules. By all means start stealing from tourists." Her face darted round towards Umru, who was now mopping his head with his embroidered cape. "Come along, man! Don't just stand there! Come along, all of you, before you fry. We'll begin with the White Oracle."

She led the way to the white building. Regin followed, stepping lightly in his soft boots, although sweat trickled past his ears. King Luther and Barnabas trudged glumly after them. Umru floundered behind and had some trouble fitting through the narrow white doorway.

Inside, it was dark and beautifully cool. They stood in a row looking into a complete darkness that seemed to take up much more space than such a small building could hold.

"What do we do?" King Luther asked.

"Wait," said Querida. "Watch."

They waited. After a while, as happens when you stare into total darkness, they all thought they could see dots, blobs and twirling patterns. Sun dazzle, King Luther thought. Trick of the eyeballs, Regin thought. Take no notice. Means nothing.

All at once the seeming dazzles gathered purposefully together. It was impossible to think they meant nothing. In a second or so, they definitely formed the shape of something that might have been human, though swirling and too tall, composed of dim reds and sullen blues and small flashes of green. A soft hollow voice, with a lot of echoes behind it, said, *Speak your question, mortals.*

"Thank you," Querida said briskly. "Our question is this: What do we do to abolish the Pilgrim Parties and get rid of Mr Chesney for good?"

The swirling shape dived, mounted to something twenty feet high and then shrank to something Querida's size, weaving this way and that. It seemed agitated. But the hollow voice, when it spoke, was the same as before. *You must appoint as Dark Lord the first person you see on leaving here.*

"Much obliged," said Querida.

Quite suddenly, the little temple was not dark at all. It was a very small space, hardly big enough for the five of them, with bare white walls and a floor of drifted sand in which bits of rubbish could be seen, evidently dropped by other people who had been to consult the White Oracle. There were scraps of paper, a small shoe, buckles, straps and plumstones. Something flashed, half-buried in the sand by the toes of Regin's boots. While everyone was turning to go out, he stooped and picked it deftly up, and then paused in surprise with the rest of them, because the doorway was no longer narrow. It was now wide enough for all five of them to walk out side by side. They stepped forward into the heat again, blinking at empty miles of glaring desert.

"No one here," said Querida.

"I suppose it'll be the first person we see when we get back then," Barnabas said.

Regin looked at what he had picked up. It was a strip

of cloth. There were black letters printed on it that read: *Be careful what you ask for: you may get it.* He passed it silently to King Luther, who was nearest.

"Now it warns us!" said King Luther, and passed it to Umru.

"This is something I often tell my flock," Umru said.

"Wizards know it too," Barnabas said. He took the cloth and passed it to Querida. "We've been warned, Querida. Do you still want to consult the Black Oracle as well?"

"Of course I do. And I am always very careful what I ask for," Querida retorted. She led the way across the short distance to the black temple. The others looked at one another, shrugged, and followed.

The black building breathed out cold from its surface. Umru sighed with relief as he came under its walls, but his teeth were actually chattering slightly by the time it was his turn to squeeze through the narrow entrance. Inside, he moaned miserably, because it was as hot in there as the desert outside. He stood puffing and panting in deep darkness while, just as before, dazzles and blobs gathered in front of their eyes.

We wait for them to gather, Regin thought wisely. But this time, instead of gathering, the twirling dazzles retreated, swirling away to the sides and glowing more and more strongly. It took all the watchers a full minute to realise that the darkness left behind was now the shape of a huge nearly-human figure.

"Oh, I see!" muttered Querida.

You do? said a great hollow voice. It was deep as a coalmine. *Then ask.*

"Thank you," said Querida and, just as before, she asked, "What do we do to abolish the Pilgrim Parties and get rid of Mr Chesney for good?"

There was a long, long silence. The darkness remained absolutely still while the silence lasted, and then abruptly quivered and broke up, with shoots of light rushing through it from either side. When it spoke again, the deep voice shook a little.

You must appoint as Wizard Guide to the last tour the second person you see on leaving here.

Then, as in the white temple, the space was small and empty and they were crowded together, standing among rubbish. It was slightly less hot.

"I swear that thing was laughing!" Barnabas said as they turned to go and found, as before, that the doorway was now wide enough to take all of them.

Something glittered in the sand by Regin's boot. This time he did not pick it up. He put his toe under it and nudged it until he could see that it was a scrap of paper with one gold edge. Sure enough, it had written on it: *Be careful what you ask for: you may get it.* He decided not to mention it to the others.

"Well, the desert's still empty," said King Luther. "Oh!"

A man was just coming out of the temple of the

White Oracle. He was a tall, fattish, mild-faced man, dressed in the kind of clothes farmers wore. He was edging sideways out of the narrow entrance with one arm up to shade his eyes, but they could all see his face quite clearly.

Barnabas said, "Oh no!" and King Luther said, "I'll be damned!" Umru shook his head. "Be careful what you ask for," he sighed. Querida drew in a little hiss of breath.

"What's the matter?" asked Regin. "Who is he? Who are they, I mean?" he added as someone else squeezed out of the white doorway behind the wide man. This person was a boy of about fourteen who looked rather like the man, except that he was skinny where the man was wide. As he asked, the man rounded on the boy.

"There," he said. "You're answered. Satisfied?"

"No I am not!" said the boy. "I've never heard of this person. Who is he?"

"Goodness knows," replied the man. "But he's no one at the University, so it's quite clear you're not going to the University to learn your wizardry anyway. I was right."

The boy's chin bunched angrily. "There's no need to look so pleased. You always try to stop me doing what I want!"

And the two of them stood in the sand and shouted at one another.

"Who are they?" Regin asked again.

"I don't know the boy," Querida said, "but I know the man all right. His name is Derk. And he did once qualify at the University as a wizard. There is no doubt Mr Chesney would accept him as Dark Lord."

"The boy's his son," Barnabas said. "His name's Blade. Querida, I don't want to do this. Derk is a nice man and a friend of mine. He's actually very gifted—"

"There are two opinions about that," Querida snapped. "Has the boy any talent?"

"Bags of it," Barnabas said miserably. "Takes after his mother."

"Oh – Mara, I remember," Querida said. "I must talk to Mara. That's settled then. We have our Dark Lord and our Wizard Guide according to both the Oracles."

"We could always pretend we hadn't seen them and choose the next two people we see," King Luther suggested.

"The gods forfend!" Umru gasped, mopping his face with his undercape.

Querida shot King Luther her snakiest look and marched over to the two outside the white temple. As she reached them, Derk was leaning forward to bawl into his son's face, with a wholly reasonable air, as if he were simply discussing something quietly, "I tell you, the University's not a place to learn anything these days. They haven't had a new idea for thirty years. All they do is crawl to Mr Chesney."

Querida could easily pretend not to hear this, because Blade was at the same time screaming, "I don't want to hear! It's just excuses to stop me doing what I want! You let Shona go to Bardic College, so why don't you let me learn magic?"

"ER – HEM!" said Querida, loudly enlarged by magic.

Derk and Blade both whirled round. "Tyrant!" Blade screamed in her face and then bowed over, consumed with embarrassment.

Derk surveyed the tiny glistening lady in the robes of High Chancellor. His eyes travelled on to the tall glum sweaty figure of King Luther and the huge shape of Umru and the blisters of sweat popping out on his vast red-blotched cheeks. He nodded to them and smiled at Barnabas, whose curls were wet and whose face was even redder than Umru's. Finally he looked at the young man in the rear who was a stranger to him and only pretending not to be hot. "Oh hallo," he said. "What are you all doing here? Is there some reason you aren't using a refrigeration spell?"

"No, I forgot, bother it!" said Querida. "I like the heat."

Derk nudged Blade. Blade recovered from his embarrassment enough to make a slight gesture. Incredible, blessed coolness spread over the four men. "Bags of talent indeed," Regin murmured.

"Thank you, young man," Umru said gratefully.

Blade was clearly intending to demonstrate that it was not usual for him to scream into people's faces. He bowed. "You're welcome, Your Reverence," he said with great politeness. "And – excuse me – do any of you know a wizard called Deucalion?" He looked round them anxiously as they all shrugged and shook their heads. "Magic user then?" he asked, with his voice dropping hopelessly.

"Never heard of anyone of that name, Blade," said Barnabas. "Why?"

"He's the one the White Oracle says is going to train me as a wizard," Blade explained. "Dad's never heard of him either." He sighed.

Querida swept this aside. "We, as it happens, have consulted the Oracles also," she said. "They have named you, Wizard Derk, as this year's Dark Lord and you, young Blade, as Wizard Guide to the last tour."

"Now listen—" said Derk.

"No arguing with the Oracles, Derk," Barnabas said quietly.

"But—" said Blade.

"Nor you, young man," said Querida. "Both of you are going to be very busy for the next six months."

At this Derk stirred himself, powerfully but a little uncertainly, and stood over Querida. "I don't think you can do this," he said.

"Oh yes I can," she said. "Go home and make ready. Tomorrow at midday sharp, Mr Chesney and all the

Wizard Guides and I will be arriving at your house to brief you on this year's plans." When Derk still stood there, she gazed up at him like a cobra ready to strike and added, "In case you are planning to be away from home tomorrow, I must point out you are in a very poor position, Wizard Derk. You have not paid your wizard's dues to the University for fifteen years. This gives me the right to exact penalties."

"I sent you a griffin's egg," Derk said.

"It was addled," said Querida. "As I am sure you knew."

"And I couldn't send you anything else," Derk went on seriously. "All the products of my wizardry are alive. It would be criminal to shut them up in the University dues-vault. You'd want to kill them and embalm them first. Besides, my wife has paid dues enough for the two of us."

"Mara's miniature universes are quite irrelevant to Mr Chesney," Querida stated. "Be warned, Wizard Derk. Either you present yourself at Derkholm to Mr Chesney and the rest of us tomorrow, or you have every magic user in this world looking for you to make you be Dark Lord. Do I make myself clear?"

Blade pulled his father's arm. "Better go, Dad."

"And you, young man," said Querida. "You're to be there too."

Blade succeeded in pulling his father round sideways, but Derk still looked down at Querida across his own shoulder. "No one should have this kind of power," he said.

"To whom do you refer, Wizard?" she asked, still in her cobra stance.

"Chesney, of course," Derk said rather hastily.

Here Blade pulled harder and the two of them disappeared in a stinging cloud of blown sand.

"Phew!" said Barnabas. "Poor old Derk!"

"Let us go home more slowly," said Querida. "I feel a little tired."

The return journey was more like a lingering walk, in which they trod now on a patch of hot sand, now on wiry dead grass, now on rocks or moss. Regin put himself beside Querida as they went. "Who is this Wizard Derk?" he asked.

Querida sighed. "A shambles of a man. The world's worst wizard, to my mind."

"Oh come now, Querida," said Barnabas. "He's excellent at what he does – just a little unconventional, you know. When we were students together I always thought he was twice as bright as me."

Querida shuddered. "Unconventional is a kind word for it. I was Senior Instructor then. Of all the things he did wrong, my worst memories are of being dragged up in the middle of the night to deal with that vast blue demon that Derk had called up and couldn't put down. You remember?"

Barnabas nodded and bit his lip in order not to laugh.

"Nobody knew its name, so none of the usual exorcisms worked. It took the entire staff of the University to get rid of it in the end. All through the night. Derk was never much good at conventional wizardry, I admit. But you use him a lot, don't you, Reverend?"

Umru smiled sweetly, his fat comfortable cool self again. "I pay for Wizard Derk's services almost every time my temple has a tour party through. No one but Wizard Derk can make a convincing human corpse out of a dead donkey." Regin stared. Umru smiled ever more sweetly. "Or a sheep," he said. "We are always chosen as an evil priesthood, and the Pilgrims expect us to have a vilely tortured sacrifice to display. Wizard Derk saves us the necessity of using people."

"Oh," said Regin. He turned to where King Luther was trudging grimly in the rear. "And you, Your Majesty? You know this wizard too?"

"We use him for hangings and heads on spikes occasionally," King Luther said, "But I hire him most often for the feast when the damn Pilgrims have gone. He has performing animals. Pigs mostly."

"Pigs?" said Regin.

"Yes, pigs," said King Luther. "They fly."

"Oh," Regin said again. As he said it, they arrived back on the flagstone in the council room again. Regin's teeth chattered, Barnabas was shivering, Umru was juddering all over. Querida was unaffected. So was King Luther, whose northern kingdom was never warm.

"What is the matter?" Umru cried out. People turned from reading the heaps of letters on the table to stare at him. He held his hands out piteously. "Look. Blue!"

"Oh. Um," said Barnabas. "It's young Blade's fault, I'm afraid. Boys of that age never know their own strength. I'll do what I can, but it may take an hour or so."

CHAPTER TWO

✳

*D*erkholm was in an uproar. Blade's sister Shona was by the stables, saddling two of the horses so that Derk could take her to Bardic College as soon as he got home from the Oracle, when Elda came galloping up with her wings spread, rowing herself along for extra speed, screaming that Derk was going to be Dark Lord. Elda was squawking with excitement, according to Don, who had been galloping after Elda to try to calm things down, and Shona either did not understand her or did not believe her straight away. When she did, Shona instantly unsaddled the horses and turned them back into the paddock.

According to Don, Shona then struck a fine pose (it was something Shona had been doing ever since she was enrolled as a trainee bard, and it annoyed Don particularly and Kit almost as much) and declared, "I'll put off going to college for as long as Dad needs me. We have to show family solidarity over this."

Shona, despite the pose, was highly excited by the news. As she raced back to the house carrying her saddlebags and violin case, with Don and Elda bounding ahead, all the animals caught it, even the Friendly Cows, and the rest of the day was loud with honks, squawks, moos and the galloping of variously shaped feet.

Otherwise, Blade thought sourly, there was not much family solidarity around. When Shona burst in, flushed and looking violently pretty, their parents were having a row. Derk was roaring, "There *must* be a way to get out of it! I *refuse* to touch Chesney's money!" Though he was not much given to wizardly displays, Derk was feeling so strongly that he was venting magefire in all directions. One of the hall carpets was in flames.

"Dad!" Shona cried out. "You'll set the house on fire!"

Neither of their parents attended, though Mara shot Shona an angry look. Mara was enclosed in the steel-blue light of a wizard's shields and she seemed quite as excited as Shona. "Stop being a fool, Derk!" she was shouting. "If the Oracle says you're to be Dark Lord, then there's nothing you can do!"

Magefire fizzed on Mara's shields as Derk howled back, "Sod the Oracle! I'm not going to stand for it! And you should be helping me find a way out of it, not standing there backing the whole rotten system up!"

"I'm doing no such *thing*!" Mara screamed. "I'm merely trying to tell you it's inevitable. You'd know that too if you weren't in such a tantrum!"

Blade was trying to stamp out the flames on the rugs when the big griffin Callette lumbered calmly through the front door carrying the rainwater butt and upended it over the carpet. The hall hissed and steamed and smelt horrible.

Shona hastily snatched her luggage out of the water. "Dad," she said, "be reasonable. We'll all help you. We'll get you through it somehow. Think of it. You've got five griffins, two wizards and a bard, who are all going to look after you while you do it. I bet none of the other Dark Lords has ever had help like you've got."

You had to hand it to Shona, Blade thought. She was far better at getting on with Dad than he was. Within minutes, Derk was calm enough simply to go striding about the house with his face all puzzled and drooping, saying over and over, "There *has* to be a way out of it!" while Shona followed him, coaxing. Elda did her bit by following Derk too, looking sweet and golden and cuddly.

Blade managed to talk to his mother at last.

He found her sitting at the kitchen table, pale but relieved-seeming, while Lydda made supper. Lydda was the only one of the griffins who really liked cooked food. And she not only liked it, she was passionate about it.

She was always inventing new dishes. Blade found it very hard to understand. In Lydda's place, he would have felt like Cinderella, but it was clear Lydda felt nothing of the kind. She said, turning her yellow beak and one large bright eye towards Blade, "Do you *have* to come and get under my feet in here?"

Mara looked up at Blade's face. "Yes," she said. "He does."

Lydda's tail lashed, but she said nothing. The golden feathers of her wings and crest were loud with No Comment.

"What did the Oracle say?" Mara asked Blade.

"*Your teacher will be Deucalion*," Blade quoted glumly. He saw his mother's fine, fair eyebrows draw together. "Don't tell me. You haven't heard of him either."

"No – o," Mara said. "The name rings a bell somewhere, but I certainly don't remember any wizard of that name. It must be some other magic user. Be patient. He – or she – *will* turn up, Blade. The White Oracle is always right."

Blade sighed.

"And what else?" asked his mother.

"Why doesn't Dad *understand*?" Blade burst out. "He let Shona go to bard college. *Why* is he so set against me going to University? I've told him and *told* him that I need to get there and get some training *now* in the junior section if I'm going to be properly grounded – and all he says is that he'll teach me himself. And he *can't*, Mum! *You* can't. The things I can do are all quite different from yours or Dad's. So *why*?"

"Well, there are two reasons," Mara said. "The first is that the University didn't understand Derk, or treat him at all well, when he was there. I was there with him, so I know what a miserable time he had. Your father was full of new ideas – like creating the griffins – and he wanted nothing so much as to be helped to find out how to make those ideas work. But instead of helping him, they tried to force him to do things *their* way. It didn't matter to them at all that he was brilliant in *his* way. They went on at him about how wizardry these days had to be directed towards things that made the tours better, and they told him contemptuously that pure research was no use. I found him in tears more than once, Blade."

"Yes, but that was *him*," Blade objected. "I'm different. I've got lots of ideas but I don't want to try them out yet. I want to know the *normal* things first."

"Fair enough," said Mara. "I didn't share my ideas about micro-universes in those days. But you can surely understand the second reason Derk doesn't want you at the University. They really do nothing there these days that isn't going to help the tours. They haven't time to look beyond. They probably don't dare to. And your father thinks, rightly or wrongly, that you'll end up as miserable as he was, or that you'll find yourself doing nothing but look after the tours like the rest of them. And that would break his heart, Blade."

Blade found himself wanting to say whole numbers of things – everything from *I do understand* to *But this is not his life, it's mine*! – and could only manage, rather sulkily, "Well, it turns out we're both having to look after the tours anyway."

Before Mara could reply, Lydda cut in with, "This Mr Chesney – does he eat the same stuff as us? He's from a different world, isn't he?"

Mara sprang up. "Oh – yes. I'm sure he does. That reminds me—"

"Good," said Lydda. "I'm planning godlike snacks."

"And I must get us organised," said Mara. "Let me see – there'll be eighty-odd wizards, plus two people with Mr Chesney, and us. Blade, come and help me see if we can turn the dining room into a Great Hall. And there's your father's clothes—"

From then on it was all a mighty bustle. Derk, for the most part, strode through it muttering "There *must* be a way out!" and doing all his usual things, like feeding and exercising the animals, turning the sprinkler on his coffee bushes, milking the Friendly Cows and checking his experiments, while everyone else raced about. Blade thought rather angrily that Dad seemed to have taken Shona's offer of help far too literally. Derk did not come near the house until Blade and Mara were trying to move the garden.

It was almost dark by then. Before that, Blade and Mara had tried to stretch the house out to make room for a Great Hall in the middle. Shona decided that they needed marble stairs, too, leading into the Hall, and sat on the ordinary wooden stairs making drawings of sculptured bannisters and sketches of the sort of clothes Derk should wear. But before the house was even half long enough, there were alarming creakings and crunchings from all over it. Kit roared a warning, and Don and Elda dashed indoors to say the middle of the roof was dipping downwards, spreading the tiles like scales on a fircone. At the same time, Lydda shrieked that the kitchen was falling in and Shona shouted that the new marble stairs were *swaying*. Blade and Mara had to prop the house up and think again.

"Put everyone out on the terrace," Kit suggested, "and make sure it doesn't rain. That way, the griffins can help hand round the food."

This was almost the only help Kit had offered, Blade thought morosely, and he knew it was only because Kit was far too big to be comfortable indoors these days. At least Don and Elda were helping in the kitchen. Or no, Blade knew he was being unfair to Kit really. After Blade and Mara had expanded the terrace into a large stone platform reaching halfway to the front gates, Kit got busy hauling all the tables and chairs in the house out there. Blade's annoyance with Kit was because he *knew* the griffins were up to something. He had seen all five of them, even Lydda – *and* Callette, who almost never, on principle, did anything Kit wanted – gathered in a secretive cluster round Kit in the twilight. It made Blade feel hurt and left out. The griffins were, after all, his brothers and sisters. Most of the time, it worked like that. But there were times – like this, and almost always under Kit's leadership – when the griffins shut the rest of them out. Blade *hated* it.

So much for family solidarity! he thought, and turned to help Mara to bend and push the shrubberies and all the flowerbeds into some kind of shape around the new, huge terrace. "If we shunt the little forest up to this corner—" Mara said to him. "No, even if we do, we'll *have* to straighten the drive. I know your father hates straight lines in a garden, but there simply isn't *room*."

Here Don backed out on to the terrace carrying one end of the piano stool, with Shona attached to the other end of it, screaming, "I said give it *back*! I need it to do my practice on!"

Kit slammed down the kitchen table and gave voice like six out-of-tune bugles. "LET HIM TAKE IT. WE NEED IT. YOU CAN PRACTISE AT COLLEGE."

"No I *can't*! I'm not *going* to college until this is over! I promised Dad!" Shona shrilled.

"You're still going to give it here." Kit dropped to all fours, tail slashing, and advanced on Shona. Even on all fours, he towered over her.

"You big bully," Shona said, not in the least impressed. "Do you *want* me to poke you in the eye?"

"I think I'd better break that up," Mara said.

But at that point Derk appeared, rushing across the acre of terrace to stare down at the twilit garden in horror. "What do you think you're *doing*, woman?"

"Trying to make it *fit* – what did you *think*?" Mara said, while behind Derk, Kit and Shona hastily pretended to be having a friendly discussion.

"Leave it. I'll do it," said Derk. "Why is it that no one but me has the *slightest* artistic sense when it comes to gardening?"

Everyone went to bed exhausted.

CHAPTER THREE

✳

Wizards began arriving from about eleven the next morning. When Querida and Barnabas reached the gates of Derkholm, they found themselves met by a silent pair of griffins. These were Don and Lydda. Kit, for some reason, had insisted on a matched pair. Don and Lydda were the same age – thirteen – and almost the same handsome golden-to-brown colours, and they were the same size, if you allowed for the fact that Lydda's shape was – to put it politely – chunky, while Don's was spare. Under the big gold-tinted brown feathers of his wings, his ribs always showed and always worried Mara.

The two of them preceded Querida and Barnabas up the straight drive (for, despite working until after midnight,

Derk had not found room to make the drive wander as he wanted) and to the enormous terrace, where they politely bowed the two wizards up the steps. It was perhaps unfortunate that the moving around of the garden had resulted in the clump of man-eating orchids arriving at a bed just beside these steps. They made a dart at Querida as she passed, all several dozen yellow blooms at once. Querida turned and *looked* at them. The orchids drew back hastily.

On the terrace, the various tables had been converted into one long one, covered with a white cloth – which had been two dozen tea towels an hour before – and the assorted chairs had become identical graceful gold seats. Mara felt rather proud of the effect as she came forward wearing a rich brocade dress – Shona had stylishly sewn together two aprons and a tablecloth to make the basis of the dress – to show the newcomers to their seats.

Derk was beside Mara in clothes Shona and Mara had worked on late into the night. They were indigo velvet – Callette's idea – with a cloak that swirled to reveal a starry night sky. It was real sky and real stars, as if seen small and distant. Querida naturally ignored this wondrous lining. "I'm glad to see you're being sensible about this, Wizard Derk," she said.

"Not sensible," he said. "Resigned." While he worked on the garden in the dark, it had come to Derk that the only way to go through with this was to promise himself that, as soon as it was over, he would start work at once on a completely new kind of animal.

Barnabas, like every other wizard to arrive, was captivated by the lining of that cloak. "Is that real sky?" he asked. "How?"

Derk annoyed Mara, as he had annoyed her when every single other wizard had asked about it, by lifting one arm to peer at the miraculous lining she had worked so hard to fix there, and saying, "Oh, it's just one of Mara's clever little universes, you know." He saw Mara turn away in irritation and lead Querida to the chair reserved for her. She and Querida seemed to have a lot to say to one another. He cursed the Oracle. It was not just that he did not like Querida. This Dark Lord business was already putting differences between himself and Mara, and he had a feeling it could end by separating them entirely. He said glumly to Barnabas, "We've put you and Querida at the end where Mr Chesney's going to sit."

As Barnabas sat in a golden chair that was in fact Shona's piano stool, Callette tramped up the steps and thumped down another barrel of beer. Barnabas eyed it gladly. "Ah!" he said. "Is that some of Derk's own brew?" Callette inspected him with one large grey and black eye and nodded briefly before she went away.

Why aren't they talking? Blade wondered as he came on to the terrace carrying their biggest coffee pot. Elda was in front of him, pushing a trolley loaded with wine, glasses and mugs. She had been in the kitchen with him for half an hour and nothing would possess her to utter a word. He supposed it was something to do with Kit's plan. Stupid. He felt tired and nervous. And he had been woken far too early this morning by groanings and creakings from the overstretched roof. No one had had time to put it right. And there was no time now. Blade's job was to make sure that every one of the eighty or so wizards round the table had the drinks they preferred. They did look tired, he thought, as he went his rounds with coffee pot and trolley. The fact that they were all in formal robes, red or white or black, made their faces look really pale and tired. And the beards did not help. Wizards he had met without beards had suddenly got them now.

"Oh, it's the rules," one of the younger ones, a wizard called Finn, told him. "Mr Chesney won't hear of a wizard guiding a Pilgrim Party without a beard. Coffee, please. How do you come by your coffee? I can only get it from the tours. I asked to be paid in coffee last year, I love it so much."

"My father grows it," Blade said.

"Really?" Finn said eagerly. "Will he sell me any?"

"I should think so," said Blade. "Look – does that mean I'll have to wear a beard? I'm supposed to be a Wizard Guide."

Finn gave him a startled look. "We-ell," he said. "You'd look a bit odd – see what Mr Chesney says."

I can't wait! thought Blade. You'd think Mr Chesney rules the universe.

Once every wizard was in a seat and supplied with a drink, Shona stepped out through the windows at the end of the terrace, carrying her violin and wearing her green bardic robes. They made her look lovely. Shona's hair was darker than Mara's, dark, glossy and wavy. Otherwise she had inherited her mother's good looks. Several wizards made admiring noises as she set the violin under her chin. Shona's colour became lovelier than ever. She struck an attitude and, very conscious of admiring stares, began to play divinely.

"Can't you stop her showing off?" Derk murmured to Mara as he went round with a bottle of wine.

"She'll grow out of it," Mara whispered back.

"She's *seventeen*!" Derk hissed angrily. "It's about time she did."

"She's beautiful. She plays wonderfully. She's *entitled*!" Mara whispered forcefully.

"Bah!" said Derk. Another disagreement already. What kind of animal would he create when this was over? He hadn't done much with insects up to now.

As he considered insects, he felt the magics of Derkholm reacting with someone else's. It felt like Barnabas. He gave Barnabas a puzzled look.

"It's all right," Barnabas said. "I made Mr Chesney a horseless carriage – thing with a sort of motor in front – years ago. He always uses it to get around in. That'll be him coming now."

Here we go then, Derk thought. He stared, along with

everyone else, anxiously at the gates. You could see nothing but sky beyond the gates from the terrace, but he felt the other magics travel up the valley towards Derkholm, and then stop. Shortly Lydda and Don came pacing up the driveway, tails sedately swinging, and behind them strode a gaggle of purposeful-looking people, four of them, in tight dark clothes. Four! Derk looked anxiously at Mara and Mara hastily stood up, leaving an extra chair free. She picked up a bottle of wine and joined Blade by the trolley.

"Go and get the snacks now," she whispered.

"In a second." Blade was frankly fascinated by the people striding up the drive. All had their hair cut painfully short, even the one at the back, who was a woman in a tight striped skirt. The smallest man strode in front, not carrying anything. The other two men were large and they both carried little cases. The woman carried both a case and a board with papers clipped to it. On they came, looking neither right nor left, busy expressions on their faces. Blade, suddenly and unexpectedly, found he was hurt and quite angry that they did not bother even to glance at the garden that his father had worked so hard on last night. Derk had got it looking marvellous. They were not bothering to notice Don and Lydda, either, and they were looking quite as marvellous. Their coats shone with brushing and their feathers gleamed gold against the reds and greens and blues lining the drive.

Perhaps I have got some family solidarity after all!

Blade thought, and he hoped the orchids would take a bite out of one of these people. He could tell Shona was feeling much the same. She was playing a marching tune, harshly, in time to the four pairs of striding feet.

They swept on up the steps. To Blade's disappointment, something seemed to intimidate the orchids. They only made a half-hearted snap at the woman, and she did not notice. She just followed the others. The man in front behaved as if he had eighty wizards waiting for him round a huge table every day. He marched straight to the empty seat at the head of the table and sat in it, as if it was obvious where he would sit. The two other men took chairs on either side of him. The woman took Mara's empty chair and moved it back so that she could sit almost behind the first man. He put out a hand and she put the little case into it without his needing to look. He slapped the case down on the table and clicked the locks back with a fierce *snap*.

"Good afternoon," he said, in a flat, chilly voice.

"Good afternoon, Mr Chesney," said nearly every wizard there.

Shona changed from a march to a sentimental ballad, full of treacly swooping.

Mr Chesney had greyish mouse-coloured lank hair and a bald patch half hidden by the lank hair combed severely across it. His face was small and white and seemed ordinary, until you noticed that his mouth was upside-down compared with most people's. It sat in a grim downward curve under his pointed nose and above his small rocklike chin, like the opening to a man-trap. Once you had noticed that, you noticed that his eyes were like cold grey marbles.

Widow spiders, Derk thought desperately, if I gave them transparent green wings.

Lydda loped past Blade before he could observe any more, glaring at him. He and Elda both jumped guiltily and hurried away to the kitchen. They came back carrying large plates fragrantly piled with Lydda's godlike snacks, in time to hear Mr Chesney's flat voice saying, "Someone silence that slavegirl with the fiddle, please."

There was a loud twang as one of Shona's strings snapped. Her face went white and then flooded bright red.

Ants, thought Derk, with all sorts of interesting new habits. "You mean my daughter, Mr Chesney?" he asked pleasantly.

"Is she?" said Mr Chesney. "Then you should control her. I object to noise in a business meeting. And while I'm on the subject of control, I must say I am not at all pleased with that village at the end of your valley. You've allowed it to be far too prosperous. Some of the houses even look to have electric light. You must order it pulled down."

"But—" Derk swallowed and thought the ants might have outsize stings. He did not say that he had no right to pull down the village, or add that everyone there was a friend of his. He could see there was no point. "Wouldn't an illusion do just as well?"

"Settle it how you want," said Mr Chesney. "Just remember that when the Pilgrim Parties arrive there, they will expect to see hovels, abject poverty and heaps of squalor, and that I expect them to get it. I also expect you to do something about this house of yours. A Dark Lord's Citadel must always be a black castle with a labyrinthine interior lit by baleful fires – you will find our specifications in the guide Mr Addis will give you – and it would be helpful if you could introduce emaciated prisoners and some grim servitors to solemnise the frivolous effect of these monsters of yours."

Perhaps the antstings could spread diseases, Derk thought. "You mean the griffins?"

"If that's what the creatures are," said Mr Chesney. "You are also required to supply a pack of hounds, black with red eyes, a few iron-fanged horses, leathery-winged avians etcetera – again, the guidebook will give you the details. Our Pilgrims will be paying for the very greatest evil, Wizard, and they must not be disappointed. By the same token, you must plough up these gardens and replace them with a gloomy forecourt and pits of balefire. And you'll need the place to be guarded by a suitable demon."

"I'll supply the demon," Querida put in quickly.

Derk remembered the blue demon as well as Querida did. He turned to give her a grateful look and caught sight of Mara, standing behind Querida, looking delighted.

Now what? he thought. She knows I can't summon demons. What makes her so happy about it? He thought hard of six different diseases an ant might spread and asked Mr Chesney, "Is there anything else?"

"Yes. You yourself," Mr Chesney said. "Your appearance is far too pleasantly human. You will have to take steps to appear as a black shadow nine feet high, although, as our Pilgrims will only expect to meet you at the end of their tour, you need not appear very often. When they do meet you, however, they require to be suitably terrified. Your present appearance is quite inadequate."

Diseases! Derk thought. But he could not resist saying, "Isn't there a case for the Dark Lord appearing to have a divine and sickly beauty?"

"Not," said Mr Chesney, "to any Pilgrim Party. Besides, this would interfere with our choice for this year's novelty. This year, I have decided that one of your gods must manifest at least once to every party."

An anxious rustle ran round the entire table.

Mr Chesney's head came up and his mouth clamped like a man-trap round someone's leg. "Is there some problem with that?"

Querida was the only person brave enough to answer. "There certainly is, Mr Chesney. Gods don't appear just like that. And I don't think *any* god has appeared to anyone for at least forty years."

"I see no problem there," Mr Chesney told her. He turned to Derk. "You must have a word with High Priest

Umru. Tell him I insist on his deity appearing." He picked a sheaf of crisp blue papers out of his little case and flicked the pages over. "Failure to supply this year's novelty is covered by article twenty-nine of our original contract. Yes, here it is. I quote. 'In the event of such failure all monies otherwise accruing as payment for services rendered over the tour or tours will be withheld by Chesney Pilgrim Parties for that year and the individuals responsible will be fined in addition a sum not exceeding one hundred gold coins.' This means that no one will get paid unless a god appears. Yes, I think there's no problem here," Mr Chesney said. He put the papers away and sat back. "I shall now let Mr Addis take over the meeting."

In the silence that followed, the large man on Mr Chesney's right put his briefcase on the table and smiled jovially round at everyone. Mr Chesney meanwhile refused wine from Mara and beer from Elda, but accepted a cup of coffee from Blade, which he pushed to one side without tasting. He took a snack from the plate Lydda offered him, sniffed at it and, with a look of slight distaste, laid it beside the coffee. The woman behind him refused everything. At least, Blade thought, the wizards were eating and drinking heartily enough. The beer barrel was empty when he tested it.

"Tell Callette to bring another one," he whispered to Elda in the dreadful silence.

Ants needn't sting people to spread the diseases, Derk

thought. They could do it just by crawling between people's toes.

The large Mr Addis was fetching wads of different coloured pamphlets out of his case. Such was the silence that Blade could clearly hear the shiftings and creakings from the place where the stretched roof dipped down. He looked up anxiously. He saw a row of round snouts and interested little eyes peering over the bent gutter. So *that* was what the noise was! Blade nearly laughed. The pigs had discovered that the dip in the roof was beautifully warm and gave them an excellent view of the terrace. It looked as if the whole herd was up there. Some of the sounds were definitely those of a porker blissfully scratching its back against a loose tile. Blade longed to point the pigs out to Mara at least, but everyone was looking so shocked and solemn that he did not dare.

"Well, folks," Mr Addis said cheerfully, "this year we have one hundred and twenty-six Pilgrim Parties booked. They'll be starting a fortnight from now and going off daily in threes, from three different locations, for the next two months. In view of the unusual numbers, we're confining the tours just to this continent, but that still gives us plenty of scope. It means that some of you Wizard Guides are going to have to do double tours, but you should get round that easily by aiming to get your first party of Pilgrims through in a snappy six weeks or so. We'll be starting from the three inns in Gna'ash, Bil'umra and Slaz'in—"

"*Where?*" said Derk.

"—so apportion yourselves accordingly," said Mr Addis.

"Pardon?"

"I've never heard of these places," said Derk.

"They're all marked down on our map," said Mr Addis. "Here." He picked up the top one of his papers, a cream one, and handed it to Derk. Barnabas made a tired, practised gesture on the other side of the table, and there was a map in front of everyone. There was even one for Blade, on top of the plate of snacks he was holding. He put the plate on the table and unfolded the map. To his slight alarm, it meant nothing to him.

"Oh, I see," said Derk. "You mean Greynash, Billingham and Sleane."

"We like to rename our places, Mr Dark Lord, to give the right exotic touch," Mr Addis explained kindly. "Now, as you'll see, in order to get the Pilgrim Parties through all their scheduled adventures, we have to route them in a number of ways, colour-coded on your map. Note that some of you will have your temple episode early, some in the middle and some late, and that the same applies to the exotic eastern adventure. We then split the tours into two for the enslavement episode. Half of you will go north to be captured by pirates and half south to Costamara to be taken as gladiators. Because of this division, we have selected ten cities for sacking this year. Mr Dark Lord, please negotiate with your Dark Elves on this point and make sure they allow the Pilgrims to escape before the cities are burnt. And after this, all Pilgrim Parties come together again for the regular weekly battle in Umru's lands. Wizard Guides must take care here that each party is unaware of the presence of other parties. We like our customers to believe that their own tour is unique. You'll find all the tour-plans laid out in the pink schedule."

He picked up a pink pamphlet. Barnabas made another gesture, and everyone had one of those too. Blade unfolded page after page of lists and swallowed unhappily. "And here are your colour-coded copies," said Mr Addis. This time, Blade received a green paper that looked slightly simpler. The other wizards got blue or yellow or green lists.

In a fuzz of bewilderment, Blade heard Mr Addis continue, "Please take note that this year's tour is choreographed around the one weakness of the Dark Lord. Each party will pick up clues to the Dark Lord's weak point as it goes round, ending in the retrieval of an object that contains this weakness – this is to be guarded by a dragon in the north – and then going on, after the battle, to kill the Dark Lord. Mr Dark Lord, I'm sure I can count on you to lay one hundred and twenty-six clues at each spot marked with an asterisk on the map. And you will, of course need the same number of objects for the dragon to guard."

Derk thought vehemently of ants crawling between people's toes to spread disease. Otherwise, he thought he might cry. "What kind of objects have you in mind?" he asked.

"Any object, at your discretion," smiled Mr Addis, "though we tend to prefer something with a romantic bias, such as a goblet or an orb. But basically it should be capable of containing the weakness of your choice."

"Athlete's foot?" asked Derk, with his mind on ants.

"We prefer it to be a magical weakness, or even a moral one," Mr Addis corrected him, with a kindly smile.

Derk stared at him, unable to concentrate. It was not just that he was thinking of ants while being deluged with instructions and coloured papers. Mara was up to something. He could feel her working magic and it worried him acutely. "Moral weakness?" he said. "You mean sloth or something? Callette likes making objects. I suppose I could ask—"

And here was Callette herself, with her back talons grating the terrace as she heaved along another beer barrel. She set it down with an enormous thump, in the wrong place, between Mr Chesney and the woman with the clipboard. *Whump.* The top was open. Bright red stuff splashed in all directions, smelling rather nasty.

Chairs scraped as everyone but Mr Chesney got out of the way. The woman sprang up with a scream. "Oh, Mr Chesney! It's blood!"

Blood was running down one side of Mr Chesney's face and dripping on his suit. He turned and stared reprovingly at the barrel while he got out his handkerchief.

Derk wondered how Callette had come to be so stupid. Callette's mind was always a mystery to him, but still—! "Callette," he said. "That's not beer."

Callette's huge head pecked forward. She stared down into the rippling red liquid in the utmost surprise. Every innocent line of her said *How is it not beer?*

"It just isn't," Derk told her. "It's one of the vats from my workroom and I know it was sealed by a stasis spell. I can't think why it's open. I'm terribly sorry," he said to the woman. She was still standing up, whimpering and dabbing at red spots on her tight pin-striped skirt with a paper hanky. "I'll get it off for you – for both of you. It's only pigs' blood."

The pigs on the roof heard him. At the words *pigs' blood*, there was an instant outcry, squeals, grunts and yells of protest. Pink bodies surged about up there and trotters clattered on tiles.

"Oh, shut up!" Derk yelled up at them. "It's a pig from the village. Your ancestors came from the marshes."

This did nothing to soothe the pigs. They continued to surge about, yelling their protest, until Ringlet, one of the larger sows, slipped, overbalanced, and toppled off the roof. As her heavy round body came plummeting down, squealing fearsomely, she looked certain to land splat in the middle of the table. Half the wizards prudently ducked underneath. Several vanished. Chairs fell over, and cups and mugs. Even Mr Addis put his hands nervously over his head. But Ringlet, still squealing mightily, struggled about in the air and managed to right herself in time to spread her stubby little white wings. Violently flapping, and squealing hysterically, she got control inches from the table and flew screaming down the length of it, just rising in time to miss Mr Chesney, and then rising again to swoop up to the roof. The whole herd took off from the tiles joyfully to meet her, flapping, grunting and bawling like a disturbed pink rookery.

Shona dashed past Blade and fled in through the front door. He could see her there, and Elda with her, inside the hall, clutching one another and shaking with laughter. He marvelled that Callette could sit there on her haunches looking so solemnly innocent – he took his hat off to her. He wanted badly to giggle himself, until he looked at Mr Chesney. Mr Chesney had not moved, except to wipe the blood off himself. He was just sitting there, waiting for the interruption to stop.

"Take it away and get a proper barrel of beer," Derk told Callette. She heaved the vat up and tramped away with it without a word. "I'm sorry," Derk said, as wizards began cautiously reappearing from under the table or out of thin air and setting chairs upright again.

"Accepted, but don't let it occur again," said Mr Chesney. "Mr Addis."

"Right." Mr Addis switched on his friendly smile again. "I'm now going on to the update of our rules, which you will find in this black book." He passed a heavy little volume to Barnabas.

Barnabas raised his hand. Then he paused, puffing a little from his recent dive under the table. "I think," he said, "that as we have a new Dark Lord this year, I'd better appoint myself his Chief Minion, as the most experienced wizard here. Is that agreed?"

A sigh ran round the table as the wizards saw the favourite job go out of their reach, but most of them nodded. "It won't be the usual cushy post this year anyway," someone murmured.

Barnabas smiled ruefully and gestured. Blade and Derk each found themselves holding a thick shiny book labelled in gold, *Wizards' Bible*.

"Keep this by you and consult it at all times," Mr Addis said, "and please note that the rules are here to be kept. We had a few slip-ups last year, which have resulted in changes. This year, we require all Wizard Guides to make sure that a healer stays within a day's trek of them. Healers have been instructed about this. And Wizard Guides are now officially required to ensure that all Pilgrims marked *expendable* on their list meet with a brave and honourable end and have that end properly witnessed by other Pilgrims. Last year we had someone return home alive. And in another case, lack of witnesses caused searching enquiries from the Missing Persons Bureau. Let's do better this year, shall we? And now I hand you over to my financial colleague, Mr Bennet."

Callette came back and boomed another barrel down

on the terrace. Everyone looked at it nervously, but when Blade opened the tap, it was beer.

Mr Bennet cleared his throat and opened his briefcase.

It was hard to listen to Mr Bennet. He had that boring kind of voice you shut your mind to. Derk sat leafing through the black book, wondering how he would ever learn all these rules. Ants that built real cities perhaps? Blade was busy handing out fresh beer and being surprised at how many wizards leant forward and attended eagerly to Mr Bennet. The word *bonus* seemed to interest them particularly. But all Blade gathered was that the Dark Lord was allowed a bonus if he thought up any interesting new evils, and Dad did not seem to be attending. After quite a long while, Mr Bennet was saying, "With the usual proviso that Chesney Pilgrim Parties will query extravagant claims, will you please use these calculators to record your expenses."

Barnabas gestured and Blade found a flat little case covered with buttons in his hand. He was examining it dubiously when Callette silently reappeared from the other end of the terrace and took hold of the case in two powerful talons.

"All right, as long as you give it back," Blade said automatically. "And explain how it works," he added as Callette took it away. Callette always understood gadgets. She nodded at him over one brown-barred wing as she padded off.

Then, for a moment, Blade was sure the meeting was

over. Mr Addis and Mr Bennet stood up. The wizards relaxed. But Mr Chesney passed his briefcase back to the woman without looking at her and said, "One more thing."

Everyone stiffened, including Mr Addis and Mr Bennet.

"Wizard Derk," said Mr Chesney, "since you owe me for this suit, which your monster has ruined, I propose that instead of the usual fine we appoint your lady wife as this year's Glamorous Enchantress. Without fee, of course."

Derk spun in his chair and saw Mara standing there, glowing with a glamour and looking absolutely delighted. She doesn't *need* the glamour, he thought. She's still beautiful. So this was what she had been working on.

"You agree?" asked Mr Chesney and, before Derk could say a word, he turned to Querida. "You will be standing down from the post this year."

"Glad to," Querida said dryly. But Derk kept his eye on her, and on Mara, and saw Querida was truly pleased. She and Mara were exchanging looks and all but hugging themselves.

What's going *on*? Derk wondered angrily.

He was taken by surprise to find that Mr Chesney and the others were actually leaving. They went clattering down the terrace steps, with Mr Chesney in front again. This time the orchids cringed away as the four strode off down the driveway. Derk started after them, but not very fast. He was not sure if he should show them politely to the gate, as he would have done for normal people. He was only halfway down the drive when they reached the gate.

And Kit was suddenly there, several tons of him, parked in the gateway, sitting like a cat and blocking the way entirely. He towered over Mr Chesney and his three helpers. From where Derk was, he could have sworn Kit was as tall as the house. Funny, he thought. I didn't think even Kit was that big.

"Out of my way, creature," Mr Chesney said in his flat colourless voice.

Kit's answer was to spread his wings, which made him look even larger. As Kit was mainly black these days and his wing feathers were jetty, the effect was very menacing indeed. Even Mr Chesney took half a step backwards. As soon as he did, Kit bent forward and peered very intently into Mr Chesney's face.

Mr Chesney stared at that wickedly large sharp buff-coloured beak pointing between his eyes. "I said get out of my way, creature," he said, his voice grating a little. "If you don't, you'll regret it."

At this, Mr Addis and Mr Bennet each dropped their briefcases and reached under their coats in a way that looked meaningful. The girl threw down her board and fumbled at her waist. Derk broke into a run, with the starry cloak billowing behind and holding him back. "Kit!" he yelled. "Stop it, Kit!"

But as soon as Mr Chesney's followers moved, Kit leapt into the air. His enormous wings clapped once, twice, causing a wind that made the four people stagger about, and then he was sailing above them, uttering squawks of sheer derision. He sailed low above Derk, almost burying Derk in the windblown cloak. "*Kit!*" Derk bawled angrily.

"Squa-squa-squiii-squa-squa!" Kit said and sailed on, up into the dip in the roof, where the pigs erupted again in a frenzy of flapping and squealing, trying to get out of Kit's way before Kit landed on them.

Most of them made it, Derk thought. He felt the thump of Kit's landing even from beside the gate. "I do apologise," he said to Mr Chesney. "Kit's only fifteen—"

"Consider yourself fined a hundred gold, wizard," Mr Chesney said coldly, and marched away to his horseless carriage.

CHAPTER FOUR

*

After that, Derk badly wanted to be alone. He wanted to visit his animals, scratch backs and rub noses in peace. But he knew he must talk to Querida, much as he disliked her. "Would you like me to show you my animals?" he asked her, by way of doing both things at once.

Querida looked along the table. Most of the wizards were still there, eating and drinking and chatting cheerfully. She nodded and stood up. She barely came up to Derk's elbow. "On the understanding that I don't offer to embalm any of the creatures, I suppose," she said. "Although I think I'd hesitate before I tried embalming a griffin." She jerked her chin in the direction of the roof. All that could be seen there was a ruffled lump of black feathers where Kit was, after a fashion, lying low.

"I'll talk to *you* when I come back!" Derk shouted up at the lump. "If I have to get on a ladder to do it!"

Kit gave no sign that he had heard. Derk gave up on him and led Querida across the terrace and round to the back of the house. She remarked as they went, "Dealing with an adolescent griffin must be even worse than dealing with an adolescent human."

"Hm," said Derk, Remembering some of the things Blade had said to him yesterday, he was not sure that was true. But there was no doubt that Kit had been very difficult lately. He sighed, because he had sudden piercing, overwhelming memories of Kit when he was first hatched, memories of a small, scrawny, golden bundle of down and fine fur; of his own pride in his very first successfully hatched griffin; of himself and Mara lovingly bundling Kit from one to the other; of two-year-old Shona and Kit rolling on the floor together, rubbing beak to nose and laughing. Kit had been so small and thin and fluffy that they had called him their Kitten. No one had expected him to grow so very big. Or so difficult.

They came round the back of the house where the pens and plantations stretched away uphill. "What a lot of space you have here!" Querida exclaimed.

"The whole end of the valley," Derk said.

The animals knew Derk was there. Most of them came rushing towards the ends of their pens to meet him. Derk fed Big Hen a corncob – she was about the size of an ostrich and he had used the shells of her eggs as eggs for the griffins – and then suffered himself to be slobbered on and gazed at by the Friendly Cows. He began to feel soothed. Bother ants! he thought. He had done bees after all. What he needed was an animal that no one had thought of before.

"Cows?" asked Querida, looking up at the big sticky noses and the great moony eyes.

"Er – sort of," Derk admitted. "I bred them to be very stupid. Animals know, you see – you saw the pigs' opinion of that blood – and I wanted a cow that wouldn't know when we needed her for the griffins to eat. But they turned out so very friendly that it's quite difficult at times."

"Indeed." Querida moved on to the next pen, full of very small sheep. "What's your opinion of the great Mr Chesney?"

"If I ever bred a piranha with a hyena, I'd call it a Chesney," Derk said.

"That's right," said Querida. "We're just like your Friendly Cows to him, you know."

"I know," said Derk.

"And he means every word he says. You did understand that, did you?"

"I understood," Derk said sombrely. If he ever bred a Chesney, he thought, it would have to have gills and be amphibious.

"Good," said Querida. "You aren't a fool, whatever

else you are. Did you know those sheep eat meat? There's one over there munching a sparrow."

"They do," Derk admitted. "I got them a bit wrong somewhere."

They moved on to the next enclosure, whose occupants stood in a row with their long necks stretched, honking sarcastically. "It sounds just as if those geese are jeering," said Querida.

"They are." Derk sighed. "I bred them for intelligence and I hoped they'd talk – and I think they *may* talk, but they do it in their own language."

"Hm. I think your geese are safe from the University," said Querida, moving on. What she wanted was a griffin. She knew which one, too. But she was prepared to go about it quite slowly and very cunningly. "Why is this cage empty? The pigs?"

"No, the pigs are free-range. That should be cats," Derk told her. "I think the ones still in there are invisible, but most of them got out through the walls somehow."

Querida gave a hissing chuckle. "That's cats for you! Mine do that too, and as far as I know they're just ordinary cats. What were you breeding them for?"

"Colour," said Derk. "I was hoping for red or blue, but they didn't like the idea and it didn't work. But they took to invisibility. And the old female cat who's dead now was very proud of the fact that I took some of her cells for Elda. She used to spend hours washing Elda when Elda first hatched."

They walked past giant guinea pigs and inch-high monkeys sporting in tiny trees Derk had grown for them. "Did you use cats to make all your griffins?" Querida asked curiously, as they came to the daylight owls.

"Goodness, no." Derk unlatched the pen and let two large snowy owls hop out on to his shoulders, where they sat staring at Querida as unblinkingly as she stared up at them. "I found an old lioness who'd been wounded and left behind by the pride. I got her well again and she obliged me with cells for all the griffins before she left. And some of the other cells were from that eagle Barnabas used to have. But I used cells from myself and from Mara too. I wanted the griffins to be people, you see – but I didn't expect Kit or Callette to grow so big. I *think* Lydda and Don are going to turn out a more reasonable size, but I wouldn't bet on it. That's why I used some cat for Elda. She's definitely smaller, you may have noticed." He stroked the owls' heads and strolled on. There were always problems with the griffins. He had hoped Kit and Callette would make a breeding pair, but Kit despised Callette and Callette hated Kit. And now Kit had put on that extraordinary act with Mr Chesney – Derk wondered how he was going to pay a fine of a hundred gold without selling off half the animals.

They rounded the experimental beehives – Derk was glad Querida did not ask about those – and strolled on through the coffee plantation, where the owls left his shoulders and went ghosting off to hunt. He did not mind

Querida asking about the coffee. He was prepared to tell her quite frankly that Barnabas had taken some of his Pilgrim pay in coffee some years back. Derk had begged a few beans and was now growing coffee you did not need to roast. But there were other things over towards the stables and in the vats in his workshed he had no intention of telling Querida about.

Querida did not ask. She sniffed the rich smell rising from the bushes and wondered how many other things from Mr Chesney's world Derk was secretly growing here. Tea? Exotic vegetables like potatoes and tomatoes? Antibiotics? That stuff they made the T-shirts from that the younger wizards liked so much? – cotton, that was its name. When she finally extorted the University dues from him, she would ask for all those if he wouldn't give her a griffin. And she wondered why he was letting her know some of his secrets. There must be something he badly wanted to ask from her.

"Wizard Derk," she said, "I'm sure you didn't bring me all this way simply to sniff coffee and admire your beautiful owls. What were you wanting to say?"

Derk found he was going to have to work up to that thing. But there were plenty of others. "I didn't understand that man Addis," he said, "when he talked about expendable tourists. What did he mean?"

"Just what he said," Querida answered. "I suspect that is where Mr Chesney really makes his money. A lot of people come on the tours who are either a trial to their families, or very rich, with poor relatives who wish to inherit their money, and so on. These families pay enormous fees to make sure the person doesn't come back from the tour."

Derk pushed out from among the coffee bushes and swung round to face Querida outside the dog pen. "But that's vile! And we all go along with this?"

"And with the fact that the Pilgrim Parties kill an average of two hundred of our citizens each," Querida retorted, dry as a snake in a desert. "Given that Mr Chesney has his wishes enforced by the demon, I don't see how we *don't* go along with it. Do you?"

"No." Derk turned unhappily back to the dog run. Its door was open. The only dog still in there was the elderly houndbitch, Bertha. She came stiffly strutting out and scraped at his leg with one paw. Derk frowned as he bent to rub her ears. He knew the dogs had been shut in before the first wizard arrived. It looked as if Pretty really had learnt how to open doors, in which case *damn*! Pretty was one of the many things he did not want Querida to see. He could hear the other dogs in the distance, now he thought about it, barking and yelping over by the stables, and the pigs squealing over there too. Some game, by the sound of it. Fine, as long as they kept over there. "And how am I supposed to die one hundred and twenty-six times?" he asked distractedly.

"You have to fake that," said Querida. "As Barnabas

will tell you, it's time-consuming more than anything, considering all the other things the Dark Lord has to do. Is that dog bred for something, or just a dog?"

"I was trying for wings," Derk confessed, "but they always drop off when the puppies lose their milk teeth. See. Here's where they were." He showed Querida the two folds in the brindled fur by Bertha's shoulder blades. Bertha turned and made an amiable effort to lick Querida's face as Querida bent to look. Derk hastily distracted Bertha by walking on round the dog run to the paddock.

"You should have tried reducing the length of their tongues instead," Querida said sourly, at which Bertha shot her a nervous look and moved to the other side of Derk. So he bred them for understanding too, Querida thought. "It's all right, dog. I just hate my face wet. What are these? Horses?"

"The horses we keep for riding," Derk said. He was nervous. He was going to have to say what he had brought Querida here to say to her soon.

Querida looked shrewdly from Derk to the horses trotting eagerly over to the fence. He messes about breeding monsters out of these animals, she thought, and they still all adore him. Then she remembered the sarcastic geese. Perhaps not all of them. And none of the horses seemed anything but normal, several solid thick-legged hacks, a couple of nice desert-breds, and one truly classy brood mare, who was in foal, to judge by her bulging sides. Querida watched Derk nervously fumbling for sugar and wondered what all the dogs were barking about in the distance. "Well, Wizard Derk?"

Derk could not get round to it yet. "Did Mr Chesney really mean it about wanting a god to manifest?" he asked instead.

"You heard the man," said Querida. "And as none of the gods struck him dead, I conclude that his word is law with them too and you're going to have to produce a god for him."

"Me?" said Derk.

"Yes," said Querida. "You. The Dark Lord always sees to the novelty."

"But I can't! No one can tell the gods what to do!" Derk protested, feeding sugar to horses in distracted handfuls.

"Except, of course, Mr Chesney," Querida agreed. "This is something else you're going to have to fake, I imagine. I think it would be safest to invent a god that doesn't exist. It can be done with a simple illusion spell then. You do remember how to do illusions, do you?" Derk nodded, still distracted. Well, that's something at least! Querida thought. But she was not sure she trusted the man to invent a suitable deity. "I'll think up a plausible god for you and let you know what it looks like."

"Thanks," said Derk. The sugar was all gone. He had run out of other things to ask Querida. He wiped his hands on his velvet trousers, wondering how to say what he wanted.

"Out with it, Wizard Derk!" Querida snapped impatiently.

"Yes," he said. "It's a bit difficult. I don't like – I mean Mara's a free woman and it's not that I mind her dressing up and seducing tourists exactly—"

"I've done it for years," said Querida. "It's only more faking, if that's what's worrying you. At least Mara's not a dried-up old snake like me and she won't need to disguise herself with twenty different glamours—" Derk turned and looked her keenly in the face. Querida uneasily remembered that great black griffin of his staring at Mr Chesney. "It's a shame she's not being paid," she said.

"No. There's something else," Derk said. "You and Mara are up to something, aren't you? What's going on?"

Querida, for once, had a little trouble controlling her face. It was something that had not happened to her for years. Mara *did* warn me, she thought. He's not at all the farmerish fool he looks. Perhaps she ought to revise her plans and tell him, before he messed everything up trying to find out. "Now it's interesting you should say that—" she began cautiously.

The yelling and baying of the dogs abruptly grew louder, mixed with squealing, grunting, sounds like hysterical laughter, and the hammering of paws, hooves and trotters. Before Querida could turn to see what was going on, or Derk could move, a confused crowd of excited animals swept round the corner of the paddock and galloped straight through the spot where Querida was standing.

Derk saw, horrified, Querida's tiny dry body hurled into the air by a mixed crowd of galloping animals – and Pretty, of course. He saw her tossed aside, to land with a *thwack* against the paddock fence.

From Querida's point of view, she was suddenly in an avalanche of careering creatures. As she sailed through the air, she saw waving tails, wings, excited bared fangs, and an eye-twisting blur of black and white zigzags that puzzled her slightly. Then something slammed into her, all along one side, and she heard a snapping noise from her own body. Rather to her surprise, the old dog Bertha leapt to her side and seemed to try to defend her. And I don't even *like* dogs! Querida thought, as Bertha was pushed aside and Querida found herself lying on the ground being punched by hard trotters galloping across her. To her utter dismay, something else in her body snapped, towards the far end of her.

Derk was roaring at the creatures. The horses in the paddock galloped clear, trumpeting with dismay. Otherwise most of the noise stopped, except for Bertha's indignant snarling. In fact, Bertha had made things worse by making the onrushing pigs swerve and trample Querida. "Shut *up*, Bertha!" Derk told her ungratefully as he dashed towards Querida lying against the fence. He hoped she had fainted. He could see her left arm was broken and he rather feared her left ankle was too. He knelt down beside her to see what he could do.

Querida sat up as he reached towards her leg. "*Oh no!*" she said. She did not trust Derk an inch.

"I do know about bones," Derk pointed out. "Muscles too."

That was probably true, Querida thought, trying not to scream with the pain, but she still did not trust Derk an inch. She stared beyond him through a dreadful throbbing mistiness. The black and white thing that had bowled her over was standing anxiously some way up the path. He was all long legs and a perky little fringe of mane. His big black and white flight feathers did indeed grow in eye-twisting zigzags. So he's bred a winged horse, Querida thought. Derk made another move to help her. She pushed him off with her good hand. "I don't want to grow wings like that creature!" she hissed. "And you should have reported it to the University." It was unfair, but she did hurt so.

"Pretty," said Derk. "Pretty's only just weaned. He was playing with the dogs and the pigs. Do let me try to set those bones."

"No!" snapped Querida. It was horrible the way a person could be a perfectly sound old lady one second and a wounded emergency the next. She felt dreadful. She wanted – passionately – to have her own home and own healer and a soothing cup of her own tea, and she wanted it all *now*. "I may be injured," she said, "but I *am* a wizard still. If you'd just stay clear, I'll translocate home and call my own healer, please."

"Are you sure?" said Derk. Querida's face looked like grey-blue withered paper. He knew he could not have translocated an inch in that state – not that he could go any distance at the best of times.

"Quite sure," snapped Querida. And she was gone as she spoke, with a small *whiff* of moving air.

Derk stared at the empty place by the fence and hoped very much that Querida had arrived in the right place. He had better get Barnabas to go after her and make sure. But first, he turned to Pretty.

"Only playing," said Pretty, who knew perfectly well what he had done.

"I've told you before," said Derk, "that you have to look where you're *going* when you rush about like that. If you cause any more accidents, I shall have to shut you up in a stall all day."

Pretty tossed his head and gave Derk a resentful look over one feathery shoulder. Then he minced away sideways to where his pregnant grandmother was leaning anxiously over the fence to him. Derk thought it a pity the brood-mare could not talk. She might have talked some sense into Pretty. But all she could do was nose Pretty protectively. Pretty said to her, "Don't like Derk."

"And I don't like you at the moment," Derk retorted. "I told you not to let any of the visitors see you, and then you go and bowl one of them over. Come on, Bertha."

Most of the wizards had left when Derk and the dog arrived back on the terrace. But Barnabas was still there and the young wizard Finn, enjoying another cup of coffee with Shona and Mara. Derk was making for Barnabas to tell him about Querida, when he was brought up short by the sound of something splintering up in the roof. "Where's Kit?" he said.

"Still up there," Shona said.

Derk backed to a place on the terrace where he could see the black feathery hump across the bent gutter. He could hear rafters creaking under Kit's weight. "KIT!" he bellowed. "Kit, get down before the roof breaks!"

There was a squawky mutter from above. The politest it could have been was "Get lost!"

"What's got into him?" Mara wondered anxiously.

"I don't know," said Derk, "and I don't care. He could get hurt. Kit!" he yelled. "Kit, I give you three seconds to get down here. Then I *fetch* you down by magic. One. Two—"

Sulkily, Kit surged upright. Perhaps he meant to fly down to the terrace. Derk thought it more likely that Kit intended to take off for the hills, and wondered if bringing him back with a catch spell would damage Kit's pride too badly. But he never got a chance to cast it, any more than Kit had a chance to fly. As Kit braced his powerful hind legs for take off, the roof fell in beneath him. And Kit fell with it. He simply vanished inwards, along with the centre part of the house. With him went tiles, a chimney, broken rafters, crumpled walls and smashed windows, in a billow of plaster dust and old cobwebs. The crash was tremendous.

"Oh ye *gods*!" said Mara. "He never even had time to spread his wings!"

"Be glad he didn't. He'd have broken them for sure," Derk said. He dashed for the house, followed by the ever-helpful Bertha, followed by Finn and Barnabas.

"Derk, Derk!" Mara cried out. "The other children! They were all indoors!"

"I'll go and look," said Shona. "Mum, you look ready to faint. Sit down."

"Not indoors! Look through the windows," said Mara. "We stretched the house – *any* of it might come down! Be careful!"

"Yes, yes," Shona said soothingly as Derk scrambled in through the front door. In some mad way, the front door was still standing. A mound of rubble had shot out through it, and past it on either side. Bertha went bounding in ahead of Derk. As Derk climbed carefully through a chaos of fallen beams and bricks, he heard her start barking in short triumphant bursts.

From further inside the chaos, Kit's voice said distinctly, "Shut up, you stupid dog."

Poor Bertha. It was not her day. Derk heaved a sigh of relief.

"Lucky we're all wizards here," Barnabas said behind him. "Finn, you make sure the side walls don't fall in, while Derk and I see what we can do ahead."

As Derk crawled on through a criss-cross of rafters draped with cobwebs and sheets from the second floor linen cupboard, he felt the walls on either side groan a little and then steady under Finn's spell. They found Kit a yard or so further on, dumped in a huge black huddle and coated with plaster and horsehair, in a sort of cage of splintered roof beams and broken marble slabs. Out of it, his eyes stared enormous, black and wild.

"Have you broken anything?" said Derk.

Kit squawked. "Only the new marble stairs."

"Wings and legs and things, he means, you stupid griffin," Barnabas said.

"I'm – not sure," answered Kit.

"Good. Then we'll get you out," said Barnabas. "Where's the dog?"

"She went squirming out at the back," said Kit. "She smelt the kitchen."

"Oh gods!" said Derk. "Lydda was probably in there!"

"One thing at a time," Barnabas said. "This is going to take a separate levitating spell for each beam and most slabs, I think. Finn, can you join us?"

Finn came crawling through, white with dust and very cheerful. "Oh yes," he said. "I see. Can do. Derk, you'll now get to see some of the techniques we use when we put cities back together after the tours leave. You take the left side, Barnabas."

Derk crouched against a piece of timber and watched enviously. It was like a demonstration for students. Neatly and quickly, with only a murmur here and there, the two wizards inserted their spells under each baulk of wood or stone, and then around Kit. After a mere minute, Barnabas said, "Right. Now activate." And the entire tangle of beams and marble slabs unfolded like a clawed hand and went to rest neatly stacked against the walls. "Can you move?" Barnabas asked Kit.

Kit said, "Umph. Yes." And then, as he rose to a crouch and started to crawl forward, "Yeeow-ouch!" Derk watched him struggle forward across the rubble that had been the hall. At least all Kit's limbs seemed to be working.

"Look on the bright side," Finn said. "You're halfway to a ruined Citadel already. Want us to stabilise it?"

"Yes, but how do we get up to the bedrooms?" Derk said, looking up at the ragged hole in the roof. "And Shona's piano was up on the second floor."

"It's still up there," said Barnabas, "or we'd have met it by now. Better reassemble the stairs, Finn, and slap some kind of roof on, don't you think? Derk, you're going to owe us for this."

"Fine. Thanks," said Derk. His mind was on Kit. Kit squeezed out through a gap beside the front door and flopped down on his stomach with his head bent almost upside down between his front claws. "My head aches," he said, "and I hurt all over." He was a terrible sight. Every feather and hair on him was grey with dust or cobwebs. There was a small cut on one haunch. Otherwise, he seemed to have been lucky.

Derk looked anxiously around for some sign of the others. Mara had gone too, but he could hear her voice somewhere. In the chorus of voices answering, he could pick out Elda, Blade, Lydda, Don and Callette. "Thank goodness," he said. "You don't seem to have killed any of the others."

Kit groaned.

"And you could have done," added Derk. "You know how heavy you are. Come along to your den and let me hose you down with warm water."

Kit was far too big to live in the house these days. Derk led the way to the large shed he had made over to Kit, and Kit crawled after him, groaning. He made further long, crooning moans while Derk played the hose over him outside it, but that seemed to be because he had started to feel his bruises. Derk made sure nothing was broken, not even the long, precious flight feathers in Kit's great wings. Kit grumbled that he had broken two talons.

"Be thankful that was all," Derk said. "Now, do you want to talk to me out here, or indoors in private?"

"Indoors," Kit moaned. "I want to lie down."

Derk pushed open the shed door and beckoned Kit inside. He felt guilty doing it, as if he was prying into Kit's secrets. Kit did not usually let anyone inside his den. He always claimed it was in too much of a mess, but in fact, as Derk had often suspected, it was neater than anywhere in the house. Everything Kit owned was shut secretly away in a big cupboard. The only things outside the cupboard were the carpet Mara had made him, the huge horsehair cushions Kit used for his bed, and some of Kit's paintings pinned to the walls.

Kit was too bruised to mind Derk seeing his den. He simply crawled to his cushions, dripping all over the floor, too sore to shake himself dry, and climbed up with a sigh. "All right," he said. "Talk. Tell me off. Go on."

"No – you talk," said Derk. "What did you think you were playing at there with Mr Chesney?"

Kit's sodden tail did a brief hectic lashing. He buried his beak between two cushions. "No idea," he said. "I feel awful."

"Nonsense," said Derk. "Come clean, Kit. You got the other four to pretend they couldn't speak and then you sat there in the gateway. Why?"

Kit said something muffled and dire into the cushions.

"What?" said Derk.

Kit's head came up and swivelled savagely towards Derk. He glared. "I said," he said, "I was going to *kill* him. But I couldn't manage it. Satisfied?" He plunged his beak back among the cushions again.

"Why?" asked Derk.

"He orders this whole *world* about!" Kit roared. It was loud, even through the horsehair. "He ordered *you* about. He called Shona a slavegirl. I was going to kill him anyway to get rid of him, but I was glad he deserved it. And I thought if most people there thought the griffins

79

were just dumb beasts, then you couldn't be blamed. You know – I got loose by accident and savaged him."

"I'm damn glad you didn't, Kit," said Derk. "It's no fun to have to think of yourself as a murderer."

"Oh, I knew they'd kill me," said Kit.

"No, I mean it's a vile state of mind," Derk explained. "A bit like being mad, except that you're sane, I've always thought. So what stopped you?" He was shocked to hear himself sounding truly regretful as he asked this question.

Kit reared his head up. "It was when I looked in his face. It was awful. He thinks he owns everything in this world. He thinks he's right. He wouldn't have understood. It was a pity. I could have killed him in seconds, even with that demon in his pocket, but he would have been just like food. He wouldn't have felt guilty and neither would I."

"I'm glad to hear you think you ought to have felt guilty," Derk observed. "I was beginning to wonder whether we'd brought you up properly."

"I do feel guilty. I *did*," Kit protested. "And I hated the idea. But I've been feeling rather bloodthirsty lately and saving the world seemed a good way to use it. I don't seem to be much use otherwise. And now," he added miserably, "I feel terrible about the house too."

"Don't. Most of it has to come down anyway – on Mr Chesney's orders," Derk said. "So you were crouching in the bushes by the terrace fuelling your bloodlust, were you?"

"Shut up!" Kit tried to squirm with shame and left off with a squawk when his bruises bit. "All right. It was a stupid idea. I hate myself, if that makes you feel any better!"

"Don't be an ass, Kit." Derk was thinking things through, fumbling for an explanation. Something had been biting Kit for months. Long before there was any question of Derk becoming the Dark Lord, Kit had been in a foul, tetchy, snarling mood – bloodthirsty, as he called it himself – and Derk had put it down simply to the fact that Kit was now fifteen. But suppose it was more than that. Suppose Kit had a reason to be unhappy. "Kit," he said thoughtfully, "I didn't see you at all until you arrived between the gateposts, and when you were there you looked about twice your real size—"

"Did I?" said Kit. "It must have been because you were worried about Mr Chesney."

"Really?" said Derk. "And I suppose I was just worried again when I distinctly heard you tell me Mr Chesney had a demon in his pocket?"

Kit's head shot round again and, for a moment, his eyes were lambent black with alarm. Derk could see Kit force them back to their normal golden yellow and try to answer casually. "I expect somebody mentioned it to me. Everyone knows he keeps it there."

"No. Everybody doesn't," Derk told him. "I think even Querida would be surprised to know." Damn! He hadn't told Barnabas about that accident yet! "Kit, come clean. You're another one like Blade, aren't you? How long have you known you could do magic?"

"Only about a year," Kit admitted. "About the same time as Blade – Blade thinks we both inherited it from you – but we both seem to do different things."

"Because of course you've compared notes," said Derk. "Kit, let's get this straight at once. Even more than Blade, there's no question of you going to the University – "

Kit's head flopped forward. "I *know*. I know they'd keep me as an exhibit. That's why I didn't want to mention it."

"But you must have some teaching," Derk pointed out, "in case you do something wrong by accident. Mara and I should have been teaching you at the same time as Blade. You *ought* to have told us, Kit. Let me tell you the same as I told Blade. I *will* find you a proper tutor, both of you, but you have to be patient, because it takes time to find the right magic user – and you'll have to be patient for the next year at least, now that I have to be Dark Lord. Can you bear to wait? You can learn quite a bit helping me with that if you want."

"I wasn't going to tell you at all," Kit said.

"So you bit everyone's head off instead," Derk said.

Kit's beak was still stuck among his cushions, but a big griffin grin was spreading round the ends of it. "At least I haven't been screaming you're a jealous tyrant," he said. "Like Blade."

Well I am, a little, Derk thought. Jealous anyway.

You've both got your magical careers before you, and you, Kit, have all the brains I could cram into one large griffin head. "True," he said, sighing. "Now lie down and rest. I'll give you something for the bruises if they're still bad this evening."

He shut the door quietly and went back to the house. Shona met him at the edge of the terrace, indignant and not posing at all. "The younger ones are all safe," she said. "They were in the dining room. They didn't even *notice* the roof coming down!"

"What?" said Derk. "How?"

Shona pointed along the terrace with her thumb. "Look at them!"

Blade sat at the long, littered table. So did Mara, Finn and Barnabas. Lydda and Don were stretched on the flagstones among the empty chairs. Callette was couchant along the steps to the garden, with her tail occasionally whipping the cowering orchids. Elda was crouching along the table itself. Each of them was bent over one of the little flat machines with buttons, pushing those buttons with finger or talon as if nothing else in the world mattered.

"Callette found out how to do this," Don said.

"She's a genius," Barnabas remarked. "I never realised they did anything but add numbers. I made her a hundred of them in case the power packs run out."

Elda looked up briefly when Derk went to peer across her feathered shoulder. "You kill little men coming down from the sky and they kill you," she explained. "And we did so notice the roof fall in! The viewscreens got all dusty. Damn. You distracted me and I'm dead."

"Is Kit all right?" Blade asked. "Hey! I'm on level four now. Beat that!"

"Level six," Callette said smugly from the steps.

"You would be!" said Blade.

"Level seven," Finn said mildly. "It seems to stop when you've won there. Will the house do like this, Derk?"

The middle section of the house was there again, in a billowy, transparent way. Derk could see the stairs through the wall, also back in place. The piece of roof that had fallen in was there too, hovering slightly like a balloon anchored at four corners. At least it would keep the rain out until it all had to be transformed into ruined towers, Derk supposed.

"It's fine," he said. "Thanks." He put a hand on Barnabas's arm. "I hate to interrupt, but Querida had an accident a while ago, round by the paddock. I think she broke a couple of bones. She wouldn't let me see to them. She's gone home."

"Oh dear!" said Barnabas. He and Mara came out of their button-pushing trances, looking truly concerned.

"You should have brought her up to the house at once!" Mara said.

"She wouldn't let me do anything," Derk explained. "She translocated."

"She's done this before," Barnabas said. "Five years

ago some fool Pilgrim broke her wrist and Querida got us all fined by translocating straight home and refusing to come back. We had to do without an Enchantress for the rest of the tours. I think shock takes her that way."

Finn stood up anxiously. "We'd better go to the University and check."

Barnabas sighed and got up too. "Yes, I suppose so."

He and Finn stood there looking at Derk expectantly.

"Oh. Sorry," Derk said. "What do we owe you for restoring the house?"

The two wizards exchanged looks. "Thought you'd never ask," said Barnabas. "We'll accept a bag of coffee each, please."

"Phew!" said Shona, when the two wizards had finally gone. "I think this was the most upsetting day I've ever known. And the tours haven't even started yet!"

"I should hope not," said Mara. "There are several thousand things to do before that."

CHAPTER FIVE

✳

*F*rom Blade's point of view, the several thousand things
to be done were all learning: learning the rules in the
black book, the routes in the pink list and the green
pamphlet and the adventure points marked on the map.
He had never found anything so boring. He was used to
learning things in an *interesting* way from his parents,
among a crowd of griffins who were all good at learning
things too. If he had thought anything in the lists was
real, he might have become quite nervous, but it was only
the tours, and because he knew his own Pilgrim Party
was the very last to set off, he knew he had eight weeks
to get ready in and did not worry very much. Besides, it
was beautiful early autumn weather.

Derk of course was having to learn the same lists in just two weeks, as well as doing the other things a Dark Lord had to see to. Barnabas paid almost daily visits. He and Derk spent long hours consulting in Derk's study, and then later that day Derk would rush off, looking harassed, to consult with King Luther or some dragons about what Barnabas had told him. In between, he was busily writing out clues to the weakness of the Dark Lord or answering messages. Carrier pigeons came in all the time with messages. Shona dealt with those when she could, and with the messages for Mara too. Mara before long was rushing off all the time, as busy as Derk, to the house near the Central Wastelands she had inherited from an aunt, which she was setting up as the Lair of the Enchantress.

Parents, it seemed to Blade, always had twice the energy of their children and never seemed to get bored the way he did. It was all most unrestful and he kept out of the way. He spent most days hanging out with Kit and Don in the curving side valley just downhill from Derkholm, basking under a glorious dark blue sky. There Kit lazily preened his feathers, recovering from his bruises, while Don sprawled with the black book in his talons, so that they could test Blade on the rules when any of them remembered to. They did not tell Lydda or Elda where they went because those two might tell Shona. Shona was to be avoided like the plague. If Shona saw any of them she was liable to say, "Don, you exercise the dogs while I do my piano practice."

Or, "Blade, Dad needs you to water the crops while he sees the Emir."

Or, "Kit, we want four bales of hay down from the loft – and while you're at it, Dad says to make a space up there for six new cages of pigeons."

As Kit feelingly said, it was the "while you're at it" that was worst. It kept you slaving all day. Shona was very good at 'while you're at it's'. She slid them in at the end of orders like knives to the heart. Those days, when they saw Shona coming, even Kit went small and hard to see.

Shona knew of course and complained loudly. "I've put off going to Bardic College," she went round saying, "where I'd much rather be, in order to help Dad out, and the only other people doing *anything* are Lydda and Callette."

"But they're enjoying themselves," Elda pointed out. "It's not *my* fault I'm no good at things."

"You're worse than Callette," Shona retorted. "I've never yet caught Callette being good at anything she doesn't enjoy. At least the boys are honest."

Callette was certainly enjoying herself just then. She was making the hundred and twenty-six magical objects for the dragon to guard in the north. Most of the time all that could be seen of her was her large grey-brown rump projecting from the shed that was her den, while the tuft on the end of her tail went irritably bouncing here and there as it expressed Callette's feelings about the latest object. For Callette had become inspired and self-critical with it. She was now trying to make every object different. She kept appearing in the side-valley to show Blade, Kit and Don her latest collection and demand their honest opinions. And they were, in fact, almost too awed to criticise. Callette had started quite modestly with ten or so assorted goblets and various orbs, but then Don had said – without at all meaning to set Callette off – "Shouldn't the things light up or something when a Pilgrim picks them up?"

"Good idea," Callette had said briskly, and spread her wings and coasted thoughtfully away with her bundle of orbs.

The next set of objects lit up like anything, some of them quite garishly, but even Callette was unable to say what they were intended to be. "I call them gizmos," she said, collecting the glittering heap into a sheet to carry them back to her shed.

Every day after that the latest gizmos were more outlandish. "Aren't you getting just a bit carried away?" Blade suggested, picking up a shining blue rose in one hand and an indescribable spiky thing in the other. It flashed red light when he touched it.

"Probably," said Callette. "I think I'm like Shona when she can't stop playing the violin. I keep getting new ideas."

The one hundred and ninth gizmo caused even Kit to make admiring sounds. It was a lattice of white shapes like snowflakes that chimed softly and turned milky bright when any of them touched it. "Are you sure you're not really a wizard?" Kit asked, turning the thing respectfully around between his talons.

Callette shot him a huffy look over one brown-barred wing. "Of course not. It's electronics. It's what those button-pushing machines work by. I got Barnabas to multiply me another hundred of them and took them apart for the gizmos. Give me that one back. I may keep it. It's my very best."

Carrying the gizmo carefully, she took off to glide down the valley. At the mouth of it, she had to rise hastily to clear a herd of cows someone from the village was driving up into the valley.

That was the end of peace in that valley. The cows turned out to belong to the mayor, who was having them penned up there for safety until the tours were over. Thereafter he and his wife and children were in and out of there several times a day, seeing to the cattle. Don flew out to see if there was anywhere else they could go, but came back glumly with the news that every hidden place was now full of cows, sheep, pigs, hens or goats. The three of them were forced to go and lurk behind the stables, which was nothing like so private.

By that time, Derk's face had sagged from worry to harrowed misery. He felt as if he had spent his entire life rushing away on urgent, unpleasant errands. Almost the first of these was the one he hated most, and he only got himself through it by concentrating on the new animal he would create. He had to go down to the village and break the news there that Mr Chesney wanted the place in ruins. He hated having to do this so heartily that he snapped at Pretty while he was saddling Pretty's mother Beauty. And Pretty minced off in a sulk and turned the dogs among the geese in revenge. Derk had to sort that out before he left.

"Can't you control that foal of yours?" he said to Beauty. Beauty had waited patiently through all the running and shouting, merely mantling her huge glossy black wings when Derk came back, to show him she was ready and waiting.

"Ghett'n htoo mhuch f'mhe," she confessed. She did not speak as well as Pretty, even without a bit in her mouth.

To Derk, Beauty meant as much as the hundred and ninth gizmo did to Callette. He would have died rather than part with Beauty to the University. So he smiled and patted her shining black neck. Not ants, he thought. Not insects at all. Something even more splendid than Beauty. And when he mounted and Beauty bunched her quarters and rose into the air rather more easily even than Kit did, he felt tight across the chest with love and pride. As they sailed down the valley, he considered the idea of a water creature. He had not done one of those yet. Suppose he could get hold of some cells from a dolphin...

He landed in the centre of the village to find nearly

every house there being knocked down. "What the hell's going on?" he said.

The mayor left off demolishing the village shop and came to lean on his sledgehammer by Beauty's right wing. "Glad to see you, Derk. We were going to need to speak to you about the village hall. We want to leave that standing if we can, but we don't want any Pilgrims or soldiers messing about in it destroying things. I wondered if you could see a way of disguising it as a ruin."

"Willingly," said Derk. "No problem." The hall had been built only last spring. "But how did you know – how are you going to live with all the houses down?"

"Everyone in the world knows what to expect when the tours come through," the mayor replied. "Not your fault, Derk. We knew the job was bound to come your way in time. We had pits dug for living in years ago, roofed over, water piped in, cables laid. Furniture and food got moved down there yesterday. Place is going to look properly abandoned by tomorrow, but we're leaving Tom Holt's pigsty and Jenny Wellaby's wash house standing. I heard they expect to find a hovel or two. But I can tell you," he said, running a hand through the brickdust in his hair, "I didn't expect these pulled-down houses to look so *new*. That worries me a lot."

"I can easily age them a bit for you," Derk offered.

"And blacken them with fire?" the mayor asked anxiously. "It would look better. And we've told off two skinny folk – Fran Taylor and Old George – to pick about in the ruins whenever a tour arrives, to make like starving survivors, you know, but I'd be glad if you could make them look a little less healthy – emaciated, sort of. One look at Old George at the moment and you'd know he's never had a day's illness in his life. Can you sicken him up a bit?"

"No problem," said Derk. The man thought of everything!

"And another thing," said the mayor. "We'll be driving all the livestock up the hills to the sides of the valley and penning them up for safety – don't want any animals getting killed – but if you could do something that makes them hard to see, I'd be much obliged."

Derk felt he could hardly refuse. He spent the rest of that day adding wizardry to the blows of the sledgehammers and laying the resulting brick dust around as soot. By sunset, the place looked terrible. "What do you think of all this?" Derk asked Old George while he was emaciating him.

Old George shrugged. "Way to earn a living. Stupid way, if you ask me. But I'm not in charge, am I?"

Neither am I, Derk thought as he went to mount Beauty. The frightening thing was that there was nothing he could do about it, any more than Old George could.

Beauty, rattling her wings and snorting to get rid of the dust, gave it as her opinion that this was not much of a day. "Bhoring. No fhlying."

"You wait," Derk told her.

Next day he flew north to see King Luther. The day after he went south to an angry and inconclusive meeting with the Marsh Dwellers, who wanted more pay for pretending to sacrifice Pilgrims to their god. He flew home with "Is blasphemy, see, is disrespect for god!" echoing in his ears, wistfully wondering if his water creature might be something savage that fed exclusively on Marsh people. But the next day, flying east to look at the ten cities scheduled to be sacked, he took that back in favour of something half dolphin, half dragon that lived in a river. The trouble was that there were no big rivers near Derkholm. The day after that, flying south-east to talk to the Emir, he decided something half dragon would be too big.

The Emir was flatly refusing to be the Puppet King the lists said he should be. "I'll be anything else you choose," he told Derk, "but I will *not* have my mind enslaved to this tiara. I have seen Sheik Detroy. He is still walking like a zombie after last year. He drools. His valet has to feed him. It's disgusting! These magic objects are not safe."

Derk had seen Sheik Detroy too. He felt the Emir had a point. "Then could you perhaps get one of your most devoted servants to wear the tiara for you?"

"And have him usurp my throne?" the Emir said. "I hope you joke."

They argued for several hours. At length Derk said

desperately, "Well, can't you wear a copy of the tiara and *act* being enslaved to it?"

"What a good idea!" said the Emir. "I rather fancy myself as an actor. Very well."

Derk flew home tired out and, as often happened when he was tired, he got his best idea for animal yet. Not an animal. Something half human, half dolphin. A mermaid daughter, that was it. As Beauty wearily flapped onwards, Derk turned over in his mind all the possible ways of splicing dolphin to human. It was going to be fascinating. The question was, would Mara agree to be the mother of this new being? If he presented the idea to her as a challenge, it might be a way of bridging the chilly distance that seemed to have opened up between them.

Pretty came dashing up as they landed by the stables and Beauty almost snapped at him. She was as tired as Derk was. "At this rate," Derk told Shona, who came to help him unsaddle Beauty, "we shall be worn to shadows."

"Black shadows with red eyes?" Shona said. "Lucky you. Just what Mr Chesney ordered."

Derk felt a rush of gratitude to Shona. When the time came, he would make the human half of the mermaid daughter from Shona's cells. It would ensure excellence.

"And do you know," Shona said, "those lazy boys haven't done a thing today unless I nagged them. Elda's just as bad. I haven't had time to practise. Every time I tried, a new pigeon arrived. The messages are all over your desk. Dad, you ought to breed pigeons that can speak. It would be much easier."

"That's quite an idea, Derk said, "but it's not something I can think of just now. I shall have to go and see Querida tomorrow. There were two important things she said she'd do for me and I haven't had a word from her since she left here."

"Perhaps she hurt herself, translocating away in such a hurry," Shona suggested.

"Barnabas says she got back all right," said Derk. "Her healer told him she's as well as can be expected. But I can't afford to wait much longer, so I shall have to go and disturb her."

In fact, it was days later that Derk set off to see Querida. The messages Shona had put on his desk kept him and Beauty busy for most of a week. When he finally set off, he was determined that Querida should not set eyes on Beauty. He had seen the way she had looked at Pretty, even in shock and pain, and he was not having her claim Beauty for the University. He left Beauty grazing in a field about five miles away from University City, which was as far as he could translocate himself. He wished he had Blade's gift for it as he heaved himself onwards.

He got there, just, with a rush and a stagger on landing, at the end of the street of little grey houses where Querida lived, and walked slowly along to the right one. It looked – and felt – completely lifeless. Perhaps Querida had recovered enough by now, he thought, to get herself to the University buildings. Still, he thought he would try the door now he was here. He knocked.

To his surprise, the door moved under his fist and came open. Derk pushed it further ajar. "Is anyone here?"

There was no answer, but there was a faint feeling of life inside.

"Better make sure," Derk muttered. He walked slowly and cautiously into the house, afraid that someone like Querida would have quite a few nasty traps for intruders, and very conscious of the way the old floor creaked under his boots.

He found himself in a small, busy living room, full of feathers in jars, knicknacks, patterned cushions, patterned shawls, patterned rugs and a lot of twisted snake-shaped candlesticks. It smelt sour and furry and old-ladyish. There was a couch at the far end, all patterns and frills. Querida lay on it, covered with a patterned rug, looking less small than usual because of the smallness of the room. Disposed at comfortable intervals around her were three large tabby cats, who gazed up at Derk with three hostile looks from three pairs of wide yellow eyes. That explains the open door, he thought. The cats have to get in and out. Querida was fast asleep. Her face was white and her mouth open slightly. Her skinny splinted little left arm was laid across her chest, and he could just see it move as she breathed. He could see the outline of splints round her left leg, beside the biggest of the cats.

It seemed a shame to wake her. Derk coughed. "Er – Querida."

Querida did not move. Derk said her name louder, and then loud enough to cause the cats to twitch their ears crossly, and finally almost in a shout. The cats glared, but it had absolutely no effect on Querida. Derk was alarmed. "I think I'll get her healer," he said, feeling a little foolish, not knowing if he was speaking to the cats, to himself or to Querida.

He left the house, with the door carefully not quite shut, and set off towards the University buildings, looking for someone who might know where Querida's healer lived. Nobody seemed to be about, until he came to the square in front of the University. Here was a considerable crowd, all oddly quiet, patiently waiting around a cart pulled up in the middle, which was loaded with boxes, bundles and rolls of cloth. A tall calm lady, very straight-shouldered and seraphic-looking, was handing the things in the cart out to the waiting people and giving instructions as she did so.

"You're on the eastern posting," Derk heard her say as he pushed up closer, "so you'll need most of febrifuges and herbs for stomach upsets. Here." She briskly doled out handfuls of little cloth bags and turned to the next group waiting. "Now you people are backing up the tour parties, so make sure you have a baggage mule as well as a horse to ride. I'm going to have to give you remedies for everything under the sun. You wouldn't believe the things those Pilgrims do to themselves – everything from festering wounds to alcohol poisoning. Here. I call this my body bag." She turned to pull a sack the size of a bolster out from the cart and her eye fell on Derk. She seemed to know at once that he was not there to collect medicines. "Yes?" she said coldly. "Can I help you?"

"I'm looking for someone who knows Querida's healer," Derk explained.

"*I* am Querida's healer," the lady said majestically. "Is there a problem?"

"Well, she seems to be asleep—" Derk began.

"Of course she is," said the majestic lady. "Querida reacts very badly to pain, so I have, at her own request, put her into a healing coma until the pain has gone."

"Oh," said Derk. "But I need to speak to her urgently. Is there any chance—?"

"No chance at all," said the lady. "Come back in—" She passed the bolsterlike bag to the nearest waiting person, nearly choking Derk with the intense whiff of herbs from it, and counted on her fingers. "Come back in a week."

"A *week*!" Derk cried out.

"Or ten days," said the lady.

"But it's only four days now until the tours start!" Derk protested desperately.

"Precisely," said the lady. "This is why I am in the middle of outfitting my healers. Now do you mind going away? It is most important that every healer is in place, with the correct remedies, before the first offworlders come through."

"Yes, yes of course," Derk found himself saying humbly. She was so majestic that it never even occurred to him to suggest that the Dark Lord might be important too. He backed sadly away to a clear space and tried to translocate to the place where he had left Beauty.

To his disgust, he fell short by nearly two miles. It took him most of the rest of that day to find the field where Beauty was grazing. And he had been relying on Querida's help. While he searched, he had to keep his mind on the mermaid-daughter in order not to feel sick with worry. She was going to have to have her own pool. It would be quite difficult bringing up a child that had to be kept wet at all times. Mara and he would have to spend a lot of time in the pool with her. They would have to buy a cart in order to take her to the sea...

In spite of this, they arrived home with Beauty bright-eyed and well rested and Derk grey with worry.

"What's the matter, Dad?" asked Shona.

Derk groaned. "Querida's going to be asleep for the next ten days. I think she insisted on it. I'd forgotten what she was like. But the trouble is she promised to help me over the god manifesting *and* raise me a demon. I don't know what to do!"

"Ask Barnabas?" Lydda suggested, shuffling in with a plate of buttery biscuits.

"He's busy making camps for the Dark Lord's army,"

Derk said, absently taking four biscuits and not tasting one of them. "That's quite as urgent. They have to be ready before the Pilgrims come through. They send the soldiers in early."

"You'd better not try raising demons by yourself," Shona said anxiously.

"Or gods," said Lydda. "And Elda wants to know when you can look at the new story she's written."

"Tomorrow night," Derk said. "I think I'll go and see Umru tomorrow. Perhaps he can persuade his god Anscher to manifest – I told Umru I'd visit him anyway. But what I'm going to do about a demon, I can't think!"

"Why not ask Mum?" Shona suggested. "She said she'd be in for supper."

Derk could not see Mara helping him in her present frame of mind, but he said, "Good idea," in order not to hurt Shona's feelings. Perhaps if he were very careful speaking to Mara, and particularly careful not to mention the mermaid idea yet...

But Mara arrived late for supper, with two little creases full of her own worries above her pretty nose. She had gone very thin, and her hair had come down to hang in a fat fair plait over one shoulder. "Sorry. I can't stay long," she said. "Now Querida's had herself put to sleep, I have hundreds of things to do for her tomorrow at the latest. I'll have to get back and start moving people from the village tonight."

"From the village? Whatever for?" said Derk.

"Didn't Shona tell you?" Mara asked, and Shona looked down at her plate, not wanting to say that Derk had been too worried for her to want to tell him anything. "Well, you know I never liked the idea of them sitting right in the path of the final confrontation," Mara said. "You might be careful, Derk, but Pilgrims never are, and the village people could be hurt even in those pits. So I solved the problem by hiring them all as servants to the Enchantress."

Derk gave her an appalled look. "What *with*?"

Mara frowned the two little creases tighter yet. "What do you mean, what with?"

Derk swallowed and remembered he was meaning to be very careful and tactful tonight. She's borrowed a lot of money from someone, he thought. I have to go even more carefully. "Mara," he said, "you aren't being paid for being the Enchantress. And I've been fined a hundred gold before we even start. We haven't any *money* to hire a whole village."

Mara gave an odd little smile. "Oh, I think I can manage."

She's borrowed a massive amount! Derk thought. Dear gods! "Have you hired Fran Taylor and Old George as well? I went to a lot of trouble emaciating them."

Mara chuckled. "Fran wants to stay picking about in the ruins, but I *love* Old George! He's far too good to waste on the village. I want him to be my former lover that I've drained to skin and bone. The Pilgrims should be really impressed."

Derk watched all his plans for a mermaid daughter dwindle into unimportance and then to nothing. His chest hurt. Mara's going to leave me, he thought. She's going to leave me for this person she's borrowed money from. What shall I do? He had always been afraid of this. Wizards' marriages almost never lasted. Nearly every wizard he knew had one broken marriage, and some had more. That young Finn was on his second marriage; Barnabas's wife had walked out years ago; even Querida had been married once. Derk miserably supposed he should consider himself lucky that he and Mara had lasted eighteen years.

Mara meanwhile had turned to Shona. "Shona, darling, have you made up your mind yet? I want your help over at Aunt's house more than ever now, with Querida out of action. I'm going to need lots of silly fashionable clothes – the kind you and Callette are both so good at inventing. What does Callette say?"

"Callette's on her hundred and nineteenth gizmo," Shona said. "She'll need another day at least to do the rest. She says she might come over then. But—" She shot a look at the brooding Derk. "Mum, I don't think I *can* come. There'd be no one but Lydda to look after things here."

"I've said I can manage," Lydda said with her beak full.

"I can help here too," Elda muttered into a pile of fruit. "Everyone thinks I'm too *small*."

"Not so much small as young," Mara told Elda. "You are only ten, love, and I want you to come over to me with Callette. And why should Lydda do everything here? What's wrong with you, Don, or you, Blade?"

Don sat with a raw chop halfway to his beak, Blade sat with a cooked one on the end of his fork. They exchanged looks of panic and consternation.

"Or Kit?" added Mara.

"May I consider?" Shona asked rather hectically. "Perhaps I'll come when Callette's finished – and there isn't a piano in Aunt's house, is there?"

"Yes there is," said Mara. She got up. "That's settled then. I'll expect you and Callette and Elda the day after tomorrow. You're going to love my pink embroidered hangings!"

Breaking up the family too, Derk thought miserably as Mara rushed away.

Blade, fairly naturally, tried to rush away too as soon as supper was over. But Shona deftly seized him by one arm and dragged him through to the kitchen, where Elda was swilling plates with careless abandon.

"Blade, you really have to help me *do* something!" Shona whispered. "Haven't you *noticed*?"

"Noticed what?" Blade asked.

"Mum and Dad. They're terminally not getting on."

"They're always quarrelling. You worry too much," Elda said, shoving three wet plates into the rack.

"Wash those again," Shona said automatically. "No,

that's just the trouble – they're *not* quarrelling. Dad should have exploded just now about the money, and he hardly said a word."

Blade sighed, knowing that his carefree time was over. "I see what you mean."

CHAPTER SIX

*

*U*mru's priestly kingdom was north of Derkholm, adjoining King Luther's. Derk, riding Beauty, descended over the temple of Anscher towards midday, dazzled by the sun on the huge golden domes. Other domes of other gods caught the sun too, all over the city, but Umru's temple to Umru's god was the biggest. Anscher must surely look kindly on a High Priest who had done so much for him, Derk thought. Perhaps Umru could persuade Anscher to show himself to Pilgrims. It was worth a try, anyway.

"Bhrright!" Beauty remarked as she wheeled down towards the main courtyard.

"It surely is," Derk agreed. "Umru has to find

something to do with his money." He sighed as Beauty descended. He had been trying hard not to think of money, or of how much Mara might have borrowed, or of the mermaid daughter they would never have now. Not thinking of these things left a cold emptiness somewhere in the middle of his mind. I must think of an entirely different creature, he told himself as Beauty's hooves touched the ground.

Willing, fanatical-looking men rushed to look after Beauty. More of them rushed to conduct Derk to the presence of Umru. He was handed over to a covey of acolytes, who handed him to priests, who handed him in turn to more priests, who led him through long upstairs cloisters painted with gold leaf to where Umru was waiting, smiling, in an empty sun-filled room.

"You could have landed on my balcony, if I had known your horse had wings," Umru said to him. "Come. Sit." He led Derk to a couple of throne-like chairs.

This room was only empty after a fashion, Derk thought, settling among carved cedarwood and gold. The floor was a pattern of blocks of wood, variously scented and coloured. Astoundingly beautiful silk rugs lay here and there upon it. The ceiling was a masterpiece of marble carved to resemble a tree in bloom, and the many narrow window frames were like trees too, with fruit. In between, the walls were inlaid with more masterpieces in coloured stone. But it was still an austere room, fit for a priest. Umru was a funny mixture, Derk thought. His vestments looked simple, but the cost of them would buy Derkholm several times over. Derk suddenly noticed that his own boots had not been cleaned after milking. And one of his cuffs was fraying.

"I've come to ask you to help me," he said, tucking the offensive cuff under and doubling his feet back until the boots were under the sumptuous chair.

"And you can help me, my friend," said Umru. "As you must have seen from your black book and your maps and lists, the battles are scheduled to take place this year just beyond this city of mine, all over my fields and farms – all over this land that I have worked so hard to make prosper. What am I to do?"

"I'm not sure there's anything you can do," Derk said.

"One battle a week for the next three months," Umru added. "Everything will be trampled to mud by next spring."

"Yes, I'm sorry about that," Derk said, "but I *am* good at making things grow. I'll come back when the tours are over and make sure you have some crops at least."

"Penury and disaster will ensue," said Umru. "No seeds will be sown—"

"Oh no, it won't be that bad," Derk assured him. "If you tell the people to plant seeds anyway, I'll make as many grow as I can."

"My people too will be trampled underfoot, the women raped, the infants slain. There will be no one to sow the seeds," Umru proclaimed.

"But," Derk objected, "you must have *hundreds* of cellars and crypts for people to hide in!"

Umru sighed. "My friend," he said, in a noticeably more normal manner, "I think you are not following my drift. If the Dark Lord wishes, he can surely oblige a friend by moving the battles a few miles – say, twenty miles, bringing the site south of the mountains that border my country."

"Not easily," Derk hastened to explain. "You see the routes have been very carefully interlocked to bring several tours to the same battle—"

Umru sighed again. "How much?"

"Eh?" Derk found his fingers fiddling with the frayed ends of his cuff. He let go quickly. "If you're saying what I think you are, then the answer's—" He stopped short. Money would be very welcome, money to pay that fine, money to cover the huge sum Mara had to have borrowed in order to pay everyone in the village. On the other hand, he needed a god, or no one would get any money at all. And he needed Umru's help for that. "I don't take bribes," he said.

Umru's face dropped forward on to his stack of double chins. He looked so thoroughly depressed that Derk added, "But, as I was going to say, I'll see if I can shift the battles south for nothing. It won't be easy, because they've got everyone converging on you this year – you're supposed to hold the final clue to my weakness – and Barnabas is setting up the main camp for me. I'll have to give him the wrong map reference, tell him I made a mistake or something. But I'll do what I can."

Umru raised his face from his chins and looked deeply at Derk. "You're an honest man."

"Well, not—" Derk shifted in his carved chair until it creaked.

"And I admire you for it. With sadness," Umru said. "I really do have a great deal of money. You needn't do it for nothing."

"I will. I've said I'll *try*," Derk protested. "After all, I may not be able to do it."

"*Very* honest," sighed Umru. "So. You said I could help you. How?"

With an uneasy feeling that Umru might have been readier to help him if he *had* accepted a bribe, Derk leant forward in the carved chair and explained about Mr Chesney's idea for a novelty. And it was worse than Derk had expected. As soon as he mentioned Anscher, Umru's head tilted back and his mouth became a fat, grim line. His large face became more and more stony, the longer Derk talked. "It was in the contract, you see," Derk explained. "I know the contract was drawn up when both of us were only children, but Mr Chesney regards it as binding. *None* of us gets any money this year if we don't get a god to manifest."

"Not even for money," Umru said, very upright in his chair. "It is odd how every man has his sticking-point, Wizard Derk. You have told me yours. You have just met mine. I have done many things for Mr Chesney, for money, but this is one thing I will not, *can*not do. We do not command the gods. They command us. Any attempt to coerce the gods is vile."

This man is truly a devout priest after all! Derk thought. He was completely sure Umru meant what he said. "I see. I accept that," he said hastily. "But perhaps you could give me a hint about some way I could fake—"

"You don't see at all, wizard," Umru interrupted, "or you would not ask. No one who has known a god could even speak of faking. Let me tell you. I was not always as you see me now. I was once a slender young boy, the youngest in my family, and my family was not rich. We lived by the mountains, a long way south of this city. My father had a few cows, some goats and a flock of geese. I was only entrusted with the geese. If I lost those geese, you see, the family would not starve, and I was considered too young to watch the animals. And one day I drove my geese out to feed on a certain swelling green hill. I was sitting there as carelessly as you sit in that chair now, thinking of nothing much, rather bored, but with no ambition in the world except perhaps to guard the cows for once, when Anscher appeared to me. As close as I am to you, wizard, Anscher stood before me. And he was a god, wizard. There was absolutely no doubting it, though it is not a thing I can describe. He smiled at me. He never even asked my name. He never asked me to do anything for him. He just stood in front of me and said, 'I am Anscher, your god,' and he smiled."

Umru stared out into the empty room. Derk could see tears in his eyes.

"The glory of that appearance," Umru said after a moment, "has been with me every moment of every day, of every year of my priesthood, through everything I have done. I have always hoped he would appear again, but he never has, wizard. He never has. When I first became High Priest and started to raise Anscher above other gods, I made that hill where I saw him into a sanctuary to him. I had an altar set up there. Now I think that was presumptuous. By doing that, I tried to command Anscher to appear to me again, and that was wrong. He will not come to me again now. I am too proud, too old, too fat. No, he will not come."

Umru's voice faded away and he sat staring, with tears running down his great cheeks. Derk watched uncomfortably. He sat and watched and Umru sat and stared for so long that Derk began to wonder whether he should simply get up and tiptoe away. But Umru suddenly smiled, wiped the tears off with the sleeve of his expensive gown and said, "You know, I think it's lunchtime. Will you join me in some lunch, Wizard?"

Derk was thoroughly unnerved. "I – I'd be honoured," he managed to say.

Umru clapped his chubby hands. Instantly a group of

young boys, who had obviously been waiting outside for the signal, came hurrying in with a folding table, beakers, jugs, plates and trays of food. The trays were probably gold. The glassware was exquisite crystal. The food smelt wonderful. Derk had forgotten that the worshippers of Anscher never ate meat, but the various dishes were so beautifully cooked that he hardly noticed they were all made of vegetables. He slipped a particularly fine pasty into his pocket to show Lydda. And when the boys raced in again with bowls heaped with fruit, Derk wanted to take the strangest sort for Elda, but he did not quite like to, not after the pasty.

"Try one of these, Wizard," Umru said. "You won't have met this fruit before. I bought them off one of Mr Chesney's tour agents – we often do little deals on the side, you know. She called them oranges, I believe."

"They are," said Derk. "Orange, I mean."

Umru laughed. "You peel the outside off," he explained. "Like this. Then the inside splits into pieces, just as if one of their gods had designed them for people to eat. Remarkable, aren't they?"

"Mm." Derk was not sure he liked the sharp, definite taste, but he was sure Elda would.

"Take another home with you," Umru said generously. "I have two dozen. I only paid four gold for them, too." While Derk weighed the orange globe in his hand, thinking the thing was rather like one of Callete's early gizmos, Umru added, "They have pips. The young woman told me that they grow well in warm, dry conditions. I think they grow like apples, on trees."

"Ah." Derk looked up to see Umru smiling meaningly.

"I would buy as many as you could grow," Umru said. He clapped his hands again and the boys brought water and cloths. As Derk washed the pungent juice off his fingers, he realized that he would only need a couple of trees, at two gold for a dozen fruit, to earn the money for that fine. But they might take years to grow. Umru looked sideways at him as they dried their hands, almost uncertainly. "I – er – have another small favour to ask, Wizard, something more along the lines of what you usually do for me."

"Ask away," said Derk.

"I need forty or so newly severed heads to go on stakes all over the city when the tours come through," Umru explained. "This year I am the kind of priest who beheads heretics. Could you—?"

"No trouble at all," said Derk.

Umru looked so relieved that Derk saw the man had been truly worried in case his refusal to help with the god had annoyed Derk into refusing to work magic for him.

"I promise to move the battles if I can," Derk assured him.

Umru heaved himself to his feet. "As I said, every man has his sticking-point," he said, showing Derk he was right.

He led Derk outside and down steep stairs. It was almost like Derk's usual visits. Up to now, Derk had been feeling quite out of his depth. No one had tried to bribe him before, nor did he know how to deal with Umru's religious experiences; but there was no uncertainty when it came to putting a spell on a sheep's head or so. Then he saw what Umru had waiting for him, piled in a small courtyard below. Derk stared at the heap of old yellowy-brown human skulls and swallowed.

"Where—?"

Umru smiled. "We fetched them up from the catacombs. They were all priests once. I hope they don't worry you."

"Not at all," Derk lied.

He took a deep breath and began. It was the sort of thing he was good at and so used to that he could have done it with his eyes shut. Before long, he did have his eyes shut most of the time. The skulls, under his hands, turned back into the people they had once been, but without their bodies. None of them seemed to like the experience. Most of them stared at Derk reproachfully. If he looked away, he saw Umru nodding and smiling cheerfully. Even with his eyes shut, he felt quite ill by the end.

"Nice quantities of blood," Umru said. "Splendid. Let us hope the weather stays chilly. The usual fee?"

For a second, Derk was tempted to ask for a hundred gold. He felt he had earned it. Umru could afford it.

But he could not bear to stand beside the heap of bleeding heads, most of which were still staring at him from half-shut resentful eyes, and bargain. "Usual fee," he agreed hastily.

He took the money and fled to the main courtyard, where the fanatical men were waiting with Beauty. "This horse is for sale?" one of them asked him greedily.

"No!" Derk snapped. He was still feeling ill as Beauty took off. The surge when she leapt into the air was almost too much for him.

"Home nhow?" Beauty asked hopefully.

Derk swallowed. "No. Take a bit of a swing eastwards. I need to look at the battlefield." And to calm down, he thought. This had not been a good day.

Beauty obediently swerved out beyond the domes of the city and flapped high above the countryside there. They flew above orderly rows of orchard trees, vines and vegetables that followed the shape of the ground, green fields and stubbled ones, and some fields rich brown and already ploughed, woods, meadows, hedges. Everything was bronze-green and a little hazy in the afternoon light. Everything was beautifully kept. Through it all swung the river in prosperous curves that reminded Derk of Umru's belly, of his dragon-dolphin and then of his not-to-be mermaid daughter. He told himself sternly that Shona's idea of an intelligent carrier pigeon was a much more practical one and began to feel a little better. He could see why Umru was anxious not have the battles here. This was some of the best farmland he had ever seen. He would have to move the battlefield. That was one good thing to come out of today – and he had gained a new fruit. But he still had no god and no demon. He sighed.

"Better turn for home," he told Beauty.

She banked round, wheeling across the river, and set off south, flying much faster. She was always anxious to get back to Pretty. The blue line of the mountains came nearer with every wingbeat. Very shortly, the mountains were a line of individual hills, with craggy places pushing out into the cultivated fields like headlands, dark with heather or grey-green with rough grass. One headland over to the left caught Derk's eye because it was so green and handsomely wooded with clumps of trees. As Beauty moved nearer to it, he saw a tiny white oblong up there in the midst of the green. It could have been an altar.

"Hang on," he told Beauty. "Can you land by that white thing just for a moment?"

Beauty's tail gave a circular swish of protest, but she went obediently planing down to the left and landed softly, deep in long tender grass.

Derk dismounted in a small meadow mostly circled by trees. The leaves were a wonderful array of tinged reds, dark greens and acid autumn yellow. The grass had been mown a little, but not much – just enough to allow the growth of every kind of meadow flower. Bees buzzed among them. Beauty put her head down eagerly and moved off to graze. Derk simply stood for a while. It felt here as if peace was climbing out of the very roots of the grass, moving up through his feet to his body, and filling him with an alert kind of softness. All the worries of being Dark Lord seemed small, and far-off, and easily solved. After a minute or so, he walked over to the white thing. It was an altar, as he had thought, small and plain. Plain letters on its side said *Umru gives this to the glory of Anscher*.

"I thought this must be the place," Derk murmured.

It seemed to him that there could be no harm in asking Anscher for help. He began to explain, in an ordinary conversational way, far more calmly than he had explained to Umru, that Mr Chesney demanded a god for this year's special effect. "And if we don't produce something," he said, "nobody gets any pay at all. I know this sounds very worldly, but what it means is that there will be a lot of showy fighting over this good farming country and people will be killed for no reason at all. A great deal of effort going to utter waste, do you see?"

As he went on speaking, Derk had the feeling that he, and the small altar, were the centre of a kind of cone of attention. It was a vast cone, whose point centred on the meadow while the rest went spreading out and out, and up through the sky – or not exactly *up*, Derk thought: more like outwards, into realms and spaces beyond anything humans could reach. The attentiveness was more alive than anything Derk had ever experienced, and it was strong as a bright light. For a while, he was sure he was being heard. But there was no kind of answer.

"Please," Derk said. "Can you see your way to doing anything? *Anything*?"

There was no reply. After a time, though not immediately, he felt the cone very softly and quite kindly going away. He sighed. "Ah well. It was worth a try." He turned away from the altar and stepped through the grass. And realised he was utterly exhausted. He had never in his life felt so drained. It was an effort to get his feet through the grass.

Beauty looked up as Derk dragged himself over to her. "Nhize ghrass," she remarked. "Htasty flowers." Whatever had drained Derk had had the opposite effect on Beauty. He had never seen her eyes so bright or her coat glow so. Every feather in her great black wings gleamed with well-being.

He got himself on to her back by hanging over her, stomach down, and then scrambling. "Home," he panted and Beauty leapt into the air with a will.

They crossed the mountains. They crossed the moors and then the great magical wastes that were kept mostly for Pilgrims to seem to get lost in, and came finally, near sundown, to the more roughly cultivated land north of Derkholm. By this time Derk was recovering, but still tired enough that, when they saw a crossroads and an inn beside it, he had a sudden longing for a rest and a quiet pint of ale before he went home and faced all the new pigeon messages. He knew this inn. He knew its landlord, Nellsy, and didn't much care for him. Nellsy was a whinger. But he brewed a good ale.

"Go down by that inn there," he told Beauty.

She turned her head to fix a large blue-brown eye on him. "Nheed to hsee Prehtty."

"Soon. I'll just have one really quick pint," Derk said. She sighed and went down into the inn yard.

The two carthorses standing there backed and stamped with mild alarm. They were not used to other horses coming out of the sky. Nellsy bawled at them to stand still. He was hard at work loading the dray the horses were harnessed to with barrels, mugs and chairs. As Derk walked towards the dray, he could see a sofa and a mattress among the load as well.

"Evening, Nellsy," he said. "What are you doing?"

"Closing the inn down. Getting out," Nellsy answered. "This is my last load. The wife went with the rest of it this morning. I'm right in the path of the tours here, and I'm not staying to watch the place broken up by werewolves or some such."

"I think most of the tours are coming into Derkholm from the east," Derk said, "and the werewolves are programmed to attack in the north. You should be all right here."

"Can't rely on that. Bloody Wizard Guides get lost all the time," Nellsy retorted. "And I'm not hanging round to give them directions either. You wanted a drink?"

"Well, I *did*," Derk admitted.

"Go on in. Help yourself. There's still a last barrel set up," Nellsy said. "Sorry I can't stay and serve you, but I'm late on the road as it is. It'll be dark midnight before I get this lot to the wife's sister *and* the sour-faced bitch is going to be in bed and pretending she thought I was coming tomorrow and there'll be no food saved—"

Derk left Nellsy grumbling and went into the taproom. It was practically empty. All the tables and benches had gone and the fire was out. His boots clumped on the bare floor as he went to the bar. Someone had swept the floor, possibly even scrubbed it. Without its usual coating of sawdust and litter, it was quite handsome oak boards. Derk unhooked the last remaining battered pewter mug and managed to fill it three-quarters full from the barrel before the dregs started coming. Then he clumped outside to sit in the last of the sun and watch Nellsy rope down his load and, finally, leave. Being Nellsy, he left with a lot of shouting, hoof-battering and the squealing of under-greased axles. But he was gone at last. Peace came falling down on the yard as the dust settled. Beauty had found some wispy hay sticking out of the barn wall and was morosely pulling at it. The jingling of her tack made everything even quieter. It was such a small noise.

Derk drank, and felt better, and thought. Ideas seemed to fall through his head like the settling dust. No god then. Only three days to the start of the tours and no demon either. He was going to have to summon a demon himself. Soon. Dangerous. But he had had years of wizardry since his failure over that blue demon, and he thought he now knew enough to manage it, provided there was no one else around to get hurt. He needed somewhere totally deserted with a nice flat floor for chalking the symbols on. Like this inn. It was practically ideal. It was near enough to Derkholm that he could get here translocating in about three hops. And once the demon was there – well – Anscher had quite politely refused his help, but demons were said to take wicked pleasure in pretending to be gods. Suppose he offered the idea to the demon as a reward for guarding the Dark Lord's Citadel...

Derk poured the rest of his beer on the ground and stood up. Better do it tonight before he lost his nerve. Demons were best summoned at night. Before that, he had to get Beauty out of here and, most importantly, look up in the books exactly how you did summon a demon.

CHAPTER SEVEN

✳

"Where's Dad?" Elda asked later that evening. "He promised to look at my story."

Everyone except Callette was sitting or lying about on the still vast terrace, enjoying the warm sunset. "He's in," Blade said. "He made me rub down Beauty."

"He hasn't eaten the supper I left him," said Lydda.

Shona looked up from waxing her travelling harp. "Then he's probably in his study. I left him at least ten urgent pigeon messages there."

"I'll go and interrupt him then," said Elda.

"You do that," said everyone, anxious for some peace.

They had just settled down again when Elda shot out through the front door with shrill screams. "He isn't *there*! He's gone to call up a *demon! Look!*" She held out towards them a fruit that glowed orange in the twilight.

"Since when does an apple mean you're calling a demon?" Kit wanted to know.

"Stupid! It's underneath! I've got it skewered on my talon!" Elda squawked.

"You dipped your talon in a *demon*?" Don said.

"Ooh!" Elda yelled. She dropped to sitting position, put the orange fruit carefully down on the terrace, and held out her right set of talons with a piece of paper stuck on the middle one. "Someone get it off for me. Carefully."

Blade went and worked the paper free. Tipping it into the light from the front door, he read in his father's scrawling writing, "'Elda, here's a new fruit for you. Save me the rind and the pips and I'll look at your story tomorrow. I've got to spend the night at Nellsy's inn.' This doesn't say a word about demons, Elda."

"Come and see," Elda said portentously.

Blade looked at Don. "Your turn."

Don snapped his beak at Blade and stood up. "Where?"

"His study, stupid!" Elda said. She galloped back into the house with Don lazily slinking after her. Blade heard their talons clicking up the stairs and hoped that would be the end of the fuss. It was all typical Elda. He had almost forgotten the matter when Don reappeared, walking on three legs, with his tail lashing anxiously.

"She may be right about the demon," he announced. "He's not in the house and he's left four demonologies

124

and a grimoire open on his desk. Here, Lydda. He left this for you. It was on the grimoire making the page greasy." He handed Lydda a pastry on a piece of paper.

Lydda rose up on her haunches and took the pasty. She sniffed it. She sliced delicately into the crust with the tip of her beak. "Carrots, basil, eggs," she murmured low in her throat. "Saffron. Something else I can't make out. This is *elegant*." Then it occurred to her to look at the paper.

"First things first, eh, Lydda?" Kit said. "What does he say?"

"Only 'This seems to be High Priest Umru's favourite food. Save me supper. You have to conjure demons fasting.' Is that true?" Lydda asked. "Can't you really eat anything before you call up a demon?"

"Yup," said Kit, who had no idea really. "I don't somehow think you'd be much good at the job."

Lydda ignored him. "Where's Elda?"

"In the kitchen fussing and eating her fruit," said Don. "She's got the idea the demon's going to kill Dad. I told her not to be stupid."

"There's nothing we can do anyway," Kit said.

They settled down again in the twilight, all just a little worried. Mara had long ago told them the story of the blue demon, but as Shona said, it was a little late to stop Derk now. The pink of sunset sank away into dimness and their worry sank with it. The evening was just too peaceful.

Some time later, Callette heaved herself up the steps in the gloom and dumped a large, chinking bundle triumphantly down on the terrace. "There. Finished! One hundred and twenty-six gizmos! I said I'd finish before the light went and I did!"

"Just as well," said Shona. "I didn't want to panic you, but there was a message today to say the dragon was coming to fetch them tomorrow. May we see?"

Callette was only too ready to show off her gizmos. She proudly unwrapped the sheet around them. "Is Elda back yet?" she said.

All their heads bending to look at the glimmering heap came up to look at Callette instead. "What do you mean?" said most of them.

"She went flying down the valley while I was wiring the last gizmo," Callette explained. "She went on about Dad and a demon, but I didn't listen. It was fiddly work."

"When was this?" Kit asked tensely.

Callette shrugged up her wings. "Half an hour ago? It was still quite light."

"Someone go and make sure she's not in the house," Kit snapped. "Everyone else search the grounds."

Callette shrugged again and re-wrapped her bundle. She took it back to her shed and then, for the next ten minutes, she sat quietly on the terrace while everyone else ran about calling Elda. "I didn't think she was back," she said when they all came back panting. "That's why I asked. I'd have seen her coming from my shed."

"If she's gone to Nellsy's inn," said Shona, "that's fifteen or twenty miles off *and* it's almost dark now! Dad's not going to forgive us if she gets lost."

"Or mixed up with a demon," Blade added.

"Let's get going," said Kit. "We'll fly after her. Shona and Blade, you stay here in case she comes back while we're out."

"Oh no," said Shona. "We may not have wings, but we're going too."

"Then fetch the old swing," Kit ordered, and Don raced off. Lydda turned and galloped the other way, towards the house. "Where are you going?" Kit demanded.

"Upstairs," Lydda called over her shoulder. "I launch better from a window."

"Hey-up, look at that! Too fat to get off the ground!" Kit said disgustedly. "We're not waiting for you!" he bellowed after Lydda as Don raced back towing the old swing-seat by its attached ropes. Don dumped the swing on the edge of the terrace and Shona hastily sat herself on it. Blade sat himself on her knee. It did cross his mind that he might translocate after Elda, but then he might get lost too and cause more trouble. He held one of the ropes up for Kit and Kit wrapped it into his talons, both of them regardless of the fact that Derk had expressly forbidden this activity when Blade was ten and Kit eleven and Kit had dropped Blade into a tree. "Ready?" Kit asked Callette.

"Ready," Callette said, scraping up the rope at the other side.

Blade and Shona each gripped the ropes hard. "Don't just hang on to it, Kit. Wrap it round your wrists," Shona commanded nervously.

"Teach your grandmother," Kit retorted. "I'll count three, Callette, to keep it even. One, two, *three*."

Lydda appeared at the bedroom window just as the two big griffins took off, the wind of their wings blasting Blade's fringe about and whipping Shona's hair into her eyes. As the swing scraped, swayed and went upwards too, Lydda jumped. There was a mighty whooping of wing-feathers.

"Glory! Hark at Lydda!" Don said, rising smoothly up beyond the swing. "Are you two all right?"

"Fine," said Blade, although his hands were numb already.

Derk had the circle and the pentacle drawn on the taproom floor and was filling in the Signs and Sigils by the light of one of his lanterns. The other lantern was on the bar, pinning down his very necessary notes. The first note at the top of the first page was "TO DISMISS A DEMON IN CASE OF TROUBLE", the next "SAY THIS IN CASE OF OTHER TROUBLE", and the third "TO BIND A DEMON SECURELY". Only after that did the notes get down to the Signs and Words he was going to need.

Moving faster and faster out of pure nervousness, Derk hurried between the notes and the floor. When he was finished with the Signs and Sigils and holding the lantern up to make sure they were all exactly correct, he realised he was racing around the circle like a frightened rabbit. He made himself slow down, with the result that he nearly lost his nerve completely and could not at first bring himself to light the candles.

But he forced himself to light them, five new flames, each with a Word Spoken, and four more guardian flames. He backed away to the bar and put his lantern down beside the other one. Then, with the paper he had written it out on growing sweaty in his hand, he began on the Invocation. That went very strangely. At first it was as though each word got forgotten between his eyes and his mouth, and when he did remember and did say it, that word seemed to be dragging his brain up by the roots. Then, around halfway, as if he had passed some point of greatest resistance, it all went easy. Too easy. The words rolled themselves through his head and said themselves through his mouth as if they were something he said every day, rather than something he had not looked at for twenty years. Derk had a dim memory that the same thing had happened before, but it was too late to stop now. No one leaves a demon half conjured.

He came to the end, where he had to call out the name of the demon three times. Derk had settled on a medium-sized demon called Maldropos, which the books said was moderately obliging as demons went. He opened his mouth to say the name. And he seemed unable to say it. While he gasped and *glucked*, all the candles flickered down to sparks. The pentacle began to shine, very strongly, blue.

Oh no! Derk thought. It's happening again! What do I do *wrong*?

Still unable to speak, he backed against the bar, wishing he could back right through it and crouch down among the barrels on the other side. His eyes felt peeled open like one of Umru's oranges, unable to look away from the blueness slowly rising out from among the magic Signs. It was a beautiful blue in its way. It was dense and dark, yet it was luminous and pale too, like a night sky overlaid by a perfect spring day. And it was absolutely terrifying. It rose and it rose, and as it climbed it grew denser and thicker. Derk felt his teeth chattering. He tried to reach for his notes on the bar and found he could not move. The blueness was a star-shaped cloud, almost up to the beams in the ceiling. Derk knew he had to dismiss it *now*, before it broke loose from the pentacle. But he still could not move.

The blue cloud quivered and formed a long leg-like piece, which pulled itself free from the Signs with a jerk and stepped carefully over the chalked marks. Another leg-like piece formed, jerked, and stepped after it, followed by a third. Derk found himself waiting for a fourth one, but none came. Instead, a long blue ringed tail, like a rat's, tugged itself through the floor and swept jittering this way and that, contemptuously rubbing out the Signs.

What kept you? demanded the demon. Derk was not

sure if its voice was inside or outside his ears. *Why have you waited twenty years to call me again?*

"Terror, I suppose," Derk found himself saying. He looked up at the rest of the demon. It was all blue cloud, but he thought he could just pick out three sarcastic and pitiless eyes in a head up there. He could see the candles blazing away now, behind the demon and through it. The strength of it flattened him to the bar. Why me? he thought. Why *me*?

Because you are more easily set aside than other wizards, of course, the demon answered. It did not make Derk feel any better to find it could read his thoughts. *I don't want any of those irksome Bindings laid on me. You were going to try to set me some task, weren't you?*

"Not exactly, not you. I was hoping for a smaller demon to guard my house when I have to turn it into a Citadel," Derk found himself replying. Well, it could read his mind. He might as well say what was in it. "To appear and menace Pilgrims. You know."

Ridiculous! said the demon. *And this is why you called me to this place? To appear and make faces? Do wizards have no serious purpose these days?*

"Most of them are too busy running round after Mr Chesney's Pilgrim Parties," Derk explained.

So the lesser demons tell me. The demon's tail-appendage rippled contemptuously. It took a step towards Derk on its three lissome leg-like parts. The bar behind Derk creaked under the pressure. He felt as if he were being spread out against the wood like butter. He had never, ever met any being so strong. He braced himself to be eaten, probably by some horrible means – digested first, maybe. *No, I don't intend to eat you*, the demon said. *Yet.* Derk could tell it was laughing. The laughter came through his whole body, in pulses, shaking every nerve. Demons loved to play with humans. *Nor do I want your soul*, said the demon. *Yet. I have other flesh to boil. When I have done that, I shall come back and pay you for letting me through into this plane.*

"H – how?" Derk asked.

How? By infesting your house, of course. Isn't that what you wanted? asked the demon.

Was this a threat or a promise? Derk wondered. Did it matter? "When – when might I expect you then?"

Whenever is least convenient for you, the demon replied. *Number your days until then.*

Having said that, it began to grow again, bulging its way vastly upwards, until all that Derk could see of it were its three wraithlike legs and its constantly twitching worm of a tail. Then there was an interminable time when the tail went still and the demon's legs simply stood – for ever, it felt like to Derk. He had to stand there, squashed against the bar by its presence, between his two flickering lanterns.

And then, quite suddenly, the demon was gone. The taproom seemed darker without the blue of it, despite the benign yellow light from the candles, and felt much more ordinary. The pressure no longer squashed Derk to the bar. The relief of that made him drop to his knees, where he hawked up great gulps of air and realised that he felt utterly belittled, smaller than he had ever felt in his life.

It was not until he had knelt like that for over a minute that Derk realised that he had never once, not even at the very back of his mind, thought of asking the demon to pretend to be a god. You simply could not bring a god and a demon together in one mind somehow.

The rescue party, meanwhile, was not enjoying itself. Going down through the valley had been easy for the griffins, even Lydda. It was just a matter of a powered glide. But as the glide gathered speed, the swing seat with Shona and Blade on it swung more and more to the rear. This tipped it up, sliding both of them downwards. They clung to the ropes frantically. Only the speed of the flight seemed to be holding them on.

"I think I'd better translocate after all!" Blade gasped.

"I'd fall off for sure. Sit *still*!" Shona snapped.

Blade thought she was right. And they were high enough for Shona to be badly hurt. Then, as they levelled out and flew low over the dusky fields, Kit and Callette began to feel the strain. Neither had done much flying lately. Blade could feel them both trying not to pant as hard as they wanted to. In addition, Callette, although she was huge by human standards, was nothing like as large and strong as Kit. Kit was trying to fly slow, to level the difference out, but he kept hitting his stalling speed and having to go faster, while Callette flapped furiously the whole time – with the result that the swing wagged and dipped and surged. Blade hung on and stared at the dim grey tussocks of grass whipping by under him and hoped they found Elda soon. Out to one side, the naturally fit Don was weaving and wheeling to examine every pale place in case it was Elda's golden coat. Blade could hear Lydda out on the other side trying to do the same and sounding more like a saw horse than a griffin.

Night flying made you freezing cold, Blade discovered. Shona kept muttering, "I think I'm slipping. Gods, you're heavy! Gods, you're bony!"

After what seemed a century of misery, Kit panted, "There's the inn!"

"She must have made it there then," Don said, wheeling in from beyond Callette.

"Let's check," Kit gasped.

Because he was dangling so far below Kit, Blade could not see the inn until a short while later, when the swing rushed over a hedge and he saw the building against the sky in the distance, very black, with barely a light showing. Shona, peering round him, asked, "What's that funny blue light over its roof?"

The light grew into a blue shaft as she spoke, and they all distinctly saw three eyes in it near the top. Don let out a squawk of total terror. All the griffins, with one instinctive accord, stretched their beaks upward and pumped their wings for altitude. Flight feathers whupped and the swing soared. Blade dangled there, higher and higher, with the air round him frantic with wings being overworked and the roaring of griffin breath, and could only watch the blue thing grow and stretch higher and keep level with the griffins every foot they went upwards. The three eyes sarcastically stared straight across at them. Up laboured the panicked griffins, and up stretched the blue thing, like an impossibly long pale pole of light, and continued to stare at them in a way that said, *Do you think you can get away? Forget it*!

Then the thing seemed to lose interest. It shrank a little and stood poised on the inn roof. When the griffins wearily levelled out, heads bent down between their spread wings, ready to soar or sideslip if the thing came for them, the blueness leapt into a long flash of azure light, rushing in zigzags underneath them faster even than lightning, and disappeared into the distance behind.

Almost at once, from where the first flash had touched, there came a terrified griffin screech, followed by frantic cheepings from down below.

"*There she is*!" everyone cried out.

Don and Lydda folded wings and plummeted. As Kit and Callette circled and went down more slowly, towing the swing, Blade had revolving views of a small pale blot on the dark ground, which on the next sighting was definitely Elda crouched in a heap with her wings puddled round her and her beak wide open, cheeping terror and loneliness like a fledgling. On Blade's next sighting Don and Lydda had got there and were settling, out of instinct, head to tail on either side of Elda, each with a wing thrown across her. Elda's cheeping died down a little and turned into words.

"I was so tired. That was the demon. My wings hurt. I was so tired. That was the demon."

"Can you drop me off?" Blade called up to Callette and Kit. "I'll get her home. You three go on and make sure Dad's all right."

"Can do," Callette called down. "Round again, Kit."

The swing whirled out and lower. Blade watched the dark ground swirl near, slid off Shona's knees and landed running and stumbling in uneven grass. He almost fell to his knees because his feet were so numb. Shona's shoes whirled past his face as Kit and Callette whupped wings and gained height again. The sound receded fast as Blade stumbled over to Elda.

"It was the demon," Elda was saying from between Don and Lydda. "It came *through* me. It felt like that soda that melted your talon, Lydda. It was cold and it burnt."

Blade pushed into the warm huddle of griffins and sat down. "Can you two make it home if I translocate with her? I can't manage the four of us." He really meant could Lydda get home, but that was not the time to say it.

"I'm all right once I'm in the air," Lydda said.

"We'll just coast," Don said. "We won't try to prove anything."

"All right." Blade shoved his legs right underneath Elda's shaking body. "Elda, I'm going to hang on to you and I want you to hang on to me hard. Understand?"

"Yup." Elda fastened her talons on to Blade's shoulders, too scared to notice she was hurting him. Blade bit his lip against the pain and grasped Elda round the lion part of her body. This was a thing all the griffins hated and probably meant Elda was as uncomfortable as Blade was, but none of it could be helped.

"Ready? Here we go!"

Blade heaved them both home. Elda was nearly half as big again as Blade and it was truly hard work. For a moment, Blade got it wrong, or seemed to. He was aiming for the terrace, and he got there, but it was standing up beside them like a stone wall. Blade wrenched it straight – or maybe he wrenched himself and Elda straight, he was not sure – and, as he did so, he seemed to see a blue glimmer, behind his head where nobody ought to be able to see anything, and the glimmer was holding the terrace sideways. Elda began cheeping again.

"Don't *do* that!" Blade said to the demon, and he sat on the terrace gripping Elda's furry torso and pulling the terrace back into place for dear life. "Can't you see you're scaring Elda stiff?"

Elda had been right to compare the thing to caustic soda, Blade thought. He felt it against his mind as if he had his head in a bowl of bleach, pushing and sorting at him in a way that said, *Hm. What have we here?*

"Go away!" Blade told it.

The demon was laughing. It found both of them hilarious. The laughter went through Blade in waves and it *hurt*. He felt the demon say, *I shall go now, but I'll see you again soon.*

Blade wanted to say something like "Come near me again and I'll kill you!" but that would have been ridiculous and, anyway, he had no strength left. Sweat from holding out against the demon was running down from his hair into his eyes. He wanted to cry like Elda.

"It's gone!" Elda cheeped thankfully. Then she squawked. "What was *that*?"

It was the noise of Derk falling over a chair on the terrace and then a *twoing* as he kicked Shona's harp. "Dad!" Blade shouted.

Derk came and held up his lantern to look at them. "What's wrong?"

"The demon was here!" they told him in chorus. "And it told Blade it was coming back! Don't let it!" Elda added.

Derk had not the courage to explain how very wrong his conjuring had gone. He said soothingly, "We don't need it yet, not until I've made the Citadel. Don't worry. Where's everyone else?"

"Coming," said Elda. But it was a good hour before weary wingbeats brought Kit, Callette and Shona home, and a further half hour after that before Lydda staggered in with Don.

"You blew her into the air, leaving with Elda," Don

said to Blade. "I think she'd have had to walk if you hadn't. It was awful. She kept saying she *had* to land and I had to shout at her to keep her flying."

"And Dad had left when we got to the inn," Shona said disgustedly. "Where's he gone now?"

"Eating supper," said Elda. "It's gone all cold and horrible, but he's *gobbling*."

CHAPTER EIGHT

*

*E*lda was fit as a fiddle the next day and everyone else felt terrible. Lydda lay face down on the living room sofa, filling it to overflowing. "Someone else can see to food today," she said. "My shoulders hurt."

"Well that won't be *me*," Shona said, examining the rope burns on her fingers. "I can't even play the piano. Mum wants me to take Callette and Elda over to Aunt's house today and I'm too tired to try. Where's Callette?"

Callette was sulking in her shed, saying she was bored because she had finished the gizmos. Don's opinion was that she was as stiff as the rest of them and too proud to admit it. Don lay on his back with his wings spread all over the dining room floor, refusing to move for anyone. *He* was not proud, he said.

Blade felt strange, as if the demon had pushed something sideways in his mind. "Have I still got my soul?" he asked Kit anxiously.

Kit glared into Blade's eyes. "Of course you have! *Fool*!" Kit had got up at dawn and flown a circuit of the valley in order to convince himself he was fit. The opposite proved to be the case. Kit came home in such a ferocious bad temper that only Blade dared go near him.

Derk supposed he ought to tell them all off for taking so many risks last night – night flying, going too far, dangling Shona and Blade on the swing, and barging straight into that demon – but he was too depressed about his double failure yesterday. He sat in his study and worried, unable even to think of designing a new carrier pigeon. He found he was rather touched at the way Elda had tried to go after him. She had carefully saved him her orange peel and pips as well. He could not bring himself to scold her. Instead, he sighed and went to plant the pips.

They were all jolted out of their gloom around midday by Elda, followed by Pretty, galloping across the terrace shrieking, "The dragon's coming! The dragon's coming!"

No one except Derk had ever seen a dragon. There was instant huge excitement. Kit and Callette burst out of their dens; Lydda and Shona tangled in the living room doorway, both trying to get outside at once; Don knocked

141

over every seat in the dining room, getting to his feet; Blade raced down the wood-and-marble stairs; Derk pelted round from his workroom, and they all rushed to join Elda and Pretty at the gate, along with every one of the pigs. The dogs and the geese clamoured to be let out too, but no one could spare them any attention. The Friendly Cows and Big Hen simply clamoured, catching the general excitement.

The dragon was now halfway up the valley, and seemed to fill it from wingtip to wingtip. Blade said, awed, "I didn't know they were so *big*!"

"She's actually only a medium size," Derk said.

"They don't fly at all like us," Don observed.

"More like seagulls," Lydda agreed.

The dragon lifted her wings and came to an elegant landing on the grass downhill from the gate. She was altogether elegant, slender, glistening and lavender-coloured, phasing to a creamy colour underneath. With her wings folded as she came winding up to the gate, she almost had the look of a very large lizard.

The pigs, by this time, were snuffling nervously and backing away. Pretty was shaking all over. When the dragon arrived, towering over everyone except Kit, and emitted a delicate curl of smoke from each nostril as she halted, Pretty had had enough. He screamed and bolted, wagging his undeveloped wings frantically. The pigs broke and ran with him, squealing and soon taking to the air for speed. Pretty was so frightened that he rose into the air with them. Nobody noticed Pretty's maiden flight. They were all staring at the fine violet and green blood vessels in the dragon's wings, the way her scales refracted the sunlight like jewels, and the deep, deep look in her purple eyes.

There came a dreadful clamour from the pens and paddocks beyond the house as all the animals caught the dragon's scent. The dragon politely ignored it. "I am to collect a number of objects from here, I believe," she said. Her voice was like cellos and clarinets. Shona sighed.

"I'll fetch them," said Callette, and tore herself away the short distance to her shed.

The dragon waited, looking above their heads with such a look of great wisdom that nobody liked to say anything until Callette came back hauling the sheet with the gizmos wrapped in it.

"Here," she said, dumping it a cautious three yards from the dragon. *Chink. Chime.*

The dragon's head turned sharply down at the sound. "May I examine them?" she asked.

"Go ahead," said Callette.

The dragon's huge clawed foot delicately picked at the knot at the top of the bundle and, even more delicately, laid the cloth away to the sides. Blade had the distinct impression that the dragon was disappointed by what was revealed. But she was evidently very polite. "But these are a treasure!" said the cellos and clarinets. "My, how they glitter! And what fine work! Beautiful!"

Callette, who was not given to shyness, was overcome by this praise and put one wing over her face. "Callette made them," Derk explained. "There should be one hundred and twenty-six. Do you wish to check?"

"I shall trust you," said the dragon. "They are utterly desirable and I shall guard them with a will. What a pity that times have changed. A hundred years ago, these would all have been made of gold. As it is, I shall have to exercise enormous self-restraint not to keep them for myself. Perhaps—"

Her violet eyes turned yearningly towards Blade. "Perhaps someone should wrap them away out of sight again. I am so tempted."

With a faint feeling that the dragon was saying one thing and meaning another, Blade ventured in under the dragon's head and gingerly tied up the knot again. The smell from the dragon's breath was indescribable, hot and steamy, a little like roses mixed with rotten eggs. He had a hard job not to react like Pretty. It felt truly dangerous to be this close.

"Can I offer you something to eat?" Derk asked politely – but not altogether tactfully, to Blade's mind.

"No thank you, I ate only yesterday," the dragon replied. Blade was strongly relieved. He pulled the knot tight and backed away smartish. "I think I had better be moving along," the dragon said. "It's a long flight to the designated place in the north. A happy tourtime to you." She picked up the chinking bundle and flowed round in a turn – a dizzying sight of sliding lavender jewels – until she faced down the valley. There she gave two or three gentle, almost slow-motion, running strides and spread her wings. She was in the air as softly as a blown leaf. Lydda was not the only one who gave an envious sigh.

They watched until the dragon was a seagull-shaped speck in the distance. "You know," Shona said, suddenly and unexpectedly, "I didn't like her very much. She was so artificial."

"That's rich, coming from you!" Kit said.

"But she *was*." Callette agreed, equally unexpectedly. "I didn't like her either."

Everyone except Blade turned to disagree loudly with Shona and Callette. "Please!" Derk shouted. "No arguments! Next one to argue gets made into a statue and I grow vines up them. Dragons are strange people. These days they think of themselves as highly virtuous. I suspect this one was disgusted at having to pretend to be bad and guard treasure. I'm told they practically fight not to have to do it."

"Then why do they do it then?" said Elda.

"No idea. More of Mr Chesney's persuasive arts, I suppose," Derk said. "Now is there any chance of any lunch?"

There was a long, reluctant silence.

"I'll do it," Blade said at last.

He wished he had not said it when he was drudging in the kitchen. It was all so complicated, Kit wanting raw steak and garlic, Callette raw duck and herbs, Don raw anything and Elda wanting cooked meat for a change. That meant five lots of bacon and fried bread, the way Blade cooked. He was getting out the biggest frying pan, sighing, when he heard the dogs and the geese yelling again and Big Hen clucking her head off. Shortly, the Friendly Cows and the horses joined in. The pigs squealed blue murder. What's the matter *now*? Blade wondered.

Elda appeared in the doorway, her wings mantled with excitement. "The dragon's coming *back*! Kit says it's flying wrong – something's hurt it. Where's Dad?"

Derk was already running towards the gate when Blade and Elda reached the terrace. Shona and the other griffins were there already. Derk went out beyond the gate and stood on the grass, shading his eyes with both hands. Blade and Elda wedged themselves into the gateway.

The large black seagull shape was definitely coming towards Derkholm again, out over the plains. Even at that distance they could see something was wrong. It was sort of staggering in the sky, Blade put it to himself. One wing seemed to be damaged. The dragon would tip that way, then overcompensate and tip the other, and then right itself with much ungainly flapping, so that it came nearer and bigger in jerks.

"Distressing to watch," said Derk. "But I don't think this is the same dragon."

"Are you sure?" asked Shona.

"Yes," said Derk. "This one's a male, and I'd say it was a good deal bigger."

"How do you tell their sex?" Don wanted to know.

"The males don't have that long lizardy look," Derk said absently, staring outwards at the unsteady shape in the distance. It was odd to have two dragons here on the same day. The only explanation he could think of was that there had been some misunderstanding – or maybe even a fight – over who was to guard the gizmos.

It slowly became clear that the injured dragon was very much bigger than the first one. They kept expecting it to reach the valley any moment, only to find it was still some miles off, still approaching and still getting larger. Finally it see-sawed in across the ruins of the village.

"It's blinking *enormous*!" said Don.

It was so enormous that its ruined wings – they could see slits in them now – were truly in danger of brushing the hills on either side. The dragon had to struggle into an updraught – while they all held their breaths, expecting it to crash – in order to find room, and then manage to right itself and glide above the crests of the hills, still coming towards Derkholm. As its vast shadow blocked the daylight, everybody flinched. Then they ducked and tried to hide behind the gateposts as the tattered wings folded and the dragon came down like a meteor. It had clearly decided that a crash-landing was the only possibility in the space available. Derk jumped backwards as the mountainous body hurtled down, hit like an earthquake, seemed unable to stop and continued uphill, ploughing four large grooves in the turf. By some miracle, it came to rest quite neatly in front of Derk in a cloud of grass-bits, clods of soil and brownish, nasty-smelling smoke.

"Where's Wizard Derk?" it demanded in a further roll of smoke. It had a deep windy voice, like somebody blowing across the top of a very large bottle.

"That's me." Derk coughed in the smoke and stared up at it. It was at least as large as a house. And there was something very wrong with it. Where the first dragon had been sleek and glistening, this one was dull, jagged and stringy. Many of its dingy green scales were split, or peeling, and they hung in ridges over the sharp bones beneath. Its eyes were filmy. One wing – the bad one – was literally in tatters, with pieces of membrane fluttering loose, and the other wing was only a little better. The part of the dragon that Derk could most easily see was its underside, hollow and sagging and a queer unhealthy-looking white. There was a piece of gold chain and a bent coronet caught among the broken scales there. When Derk looked down at the nearest huge foot, he saw it was knotty and bent, with the claws growing out and upwards like the untrimmed hoof of a horse. "Do you," he said politely, "perhaps need medical aid?"

"Don't be impertinent," the hollow voice boomed. The sick-smelling smoke that came with it made Derk choke. "I've come to join your side."

"Sorry?" said Derk.

"You're the Dark Lord, aren't you?" the dragon demanded.

"For this year, yes," Derk agreed.

"Then I've come to join the forces of evil as any right-minded dragon should," the dragon boomed impatiently. "Can I put it any plainer? I've come to kill your enemies."

"Er—" said Derk. There was something even wronger with this dragon than he had thought. Possibly it was insane. He threw his head back and looked into its filmy green eyes. Under the green and behind the film, red flickered. Red in the eyes of a dragon, he remembered learning as a student, meant that it was angry. He said, very carefully and calmly, "That is extremely kind of you, but I think someone has misrepresented the position to you."

"How so?" boomed the dragon.

"Because my post as Dark Lord means simply that I pretend to be evil for the benefit of tourists who come from a world next door to this one," Derk explained. "I'm just an ordinary wizard really. And I'm only allowed one dragon, and she—"

That was as far as he got before the dragon gave way to rage. Its eyes became wholly a cloudy red. "*So it's all a stupid GAME!*" it thundered. Derk backed away from the roar with his hands over his ears, surrounded in wet brown smoke. "You've dragged me all this way to *pretend*! What are dragons coming to, letting humans make fools of them like this?"

149

"I assure you I'm not trying to make a fool of you," Derk managed to say. The smoke was making his lungs sore. He felt dizzy.

"YES, YOU ARE!" bellowed the dragon. The force of the bellow sent Derk reeling away.

This was more than Kit could take. He plunged foward. "Will you stop that!" he screamed, standing rampant under the dragon's huge muzzle. "It's nothing to *do* with him!"

The muzzle swivelled down so that the red eyes could look at Kit. "Just get out of my way, little cat-bird," the dragon said, quite mildly.

"*Little!*" choked Kit. "*Cat-bird!*" He had never been so insulted in his life.

"I don't know what else you are," the dragon said. "Move. Leave this game-playing wizard to me."

"No," said Kit. "Over my—"

The dragon swung one huge gnarly foot and simply batted Kit aside. Kit went head over heels, rolling downhill in an undignified muddle of legs, wings, tail, feathers and fur. He came to a stop sitting in a heap with his wings in two different directions, looking shattered. He had never, ever thought of himself as smaller and weaker than *anything* before.

"You'd no call to do that," Derk choked, feeling for Kit.

"I haven't hurt him. Only his pride," the dragon rumbled. "You're the one I mean to hurt."

"Now listen—" Derk began.

But the dragon opened its mouth and bellowed rage and smoke at him. Derk felt his skin begin to boil. His lungs went from sore to agonising so quickly that he could only put up the feeblest of shields against the blast. And the dragon was clearly a magic user. Derk felt the shield ripped away and more rage and smoke pour over him. He fell to the ground, trying to breathe, and trying not to breathe because of the pain. He had never felt pain like it. He wanted to scream, but that was another thing he could not do. The burning brown smoke continued to pour at him and round him and he could hear it frying the grass he rolled on. Somewhere in the distance he could also hear griffins screaming, and Shona and Blade too.

Blade began screaming at the point when the grass caught fire. By that time he had tried to put deep cold on the dragon's breath and then, when that had no effect at all, to translocate the dragon elsewhere. After that, he tried to do the same with Derk. And it was as if he was doing nothing. He felt weak and strange and belated – as if it took five minutes for him to realise what was happening anyway – and totally helpless. The dragon seemed to be able to cancel anything Blade did. It swivelled a red eye towards him everytime he tried to help Derk and then went on calmly trying to kill his father.

"Make it *stop*!" Shona screamed at him.

"I *can't*!" Blade screamed back.

There was a thundercrack of displaced air, that blew

the scalding smoke sideways over Kit – who opened his beak and made desperate noises – and Mara was suddenly standing between the gate and the dragon, wearing a dress that consisted mostly of small amounts of pink silk and black lace, which she had evidently been in the middle of trying on. "I felt something happen to Derk!" she said. "What—? Oh, ye gods!" She took one glance at Derk rolling on the burning grass and dashed in under the dragon's great smoking nose. "Stop that at *once*! Do you hear me?" She stood with her hands on her pink silk hips, glaring up at the dragon. "*Stop* it!"

There was the fizz of strong magics clashing. Then the dragon took its snout back a foot or so. Its mouth shut, cutting off the hideous smoke. "This is wrong?" it said.

"It certainly is! Don't you *dare* do that again, unless you want to be half an inch long!" Mara shouted.

"Then explain why I shouldn't," said the dragon.

"So sit down and *listen*!" Mara bawled up at it.

To everyone's great surprise, the dragon doubled its scrawny back legs under itself and sank down on its mangy haunches. "I'm listening," it thundered in a new cloud of brown smoke. "It's about time someone explained this mad world to me!"

"All right," said Mara. "All *right*! Just stop blowing smoke at me!"

"It comes out when I breathe," the dragon growled.

"Nonsense," said Mara.

Callette waited to see that the dragon did indeed stop blowing out smoke and then took off in a mighty clap of wings. "Where are you off to?" Don shrieked.

"Healer!" Callette screamed over her shoulder, making her fastest wing-strokes towards the hills.

"Oh. Gods. Yes," Don said and took off after her, going so hard to catch Callette up that he was flying like a sparrow, in swoops and furious flutters.

"Blade," said Mara, "get your father to the house."

Blade always found it easier to translocate someone if he was touching them. He did not dare touch Derk. Derk was writhing about in the cinders of the grass, blue-purple in the face and hideous red in most other places. Most of his clothes were still smoking. The way much of his skin had gone into yellow streaks and blisters made Blade hurt too in sympathy. Blade stood himself gingerly astride him and translocated both of them to the living room sofa. The dragon rolled an eye at them as they went, but did not try to stop them. Next instant, the griffin fur and dog hairs on the sofa sizzled. The translocation somehow tipped Derk on his side, which made him give a horrible hoarse yell. This so appalled Blade that he simply stood astride his father on the sofa and wondered what to do.

Lydda shot into the room. "Make him cold. Quick. First aid for burns. Freeze him!" she panted.

"Oh yes." Thankful to be told, Blade concentrated until he could feel his own feet ache with cold. Derk stopped writhing, but he was still boiled red and streaked oozing yellow, and he was not breathing properly. "Where's Mum?" Blade said desperately.

"Talking to that beastly dragon," Lydda said, sounding quite as desperate. "I suppose she has to keep it under control."

As Blade was carefully climbing off the sofa, Shona and Elda arrived. The slightest jolt made Derk utter more of those terrible hoarse noises. Blade was shaking when Shona helped him finally climb to the floor. "He's lost half his hair!" Elda wailed. "And Mum's just standing there giving that dragon a history lesson on how the tours started!"

Lydda's beak snapped. "Be quiet. We have to wait for the healer."

They waited. Shortly Kit put his head through the window, grassy and ruffled with shame. He told them that Mara was still talking to the dragon. "It turns out to have been asleep for the last three hundred years," he said. "I suppose that accounts for it. Things must have been very different when it was last awake."

"I wish it had never woken up," Elda said miserably.

Blade wished that too. It seemed unbelievable that only half an hour ago he had been annoyed with Derk for making him drudge about getting lunch. Now he would have given anything to go back to being angry with his father in the old comfortable way. "We never had lunch," he said.

Nobody wanted lunch. They waited.

About half an hour later, Callette's wings boomed as she hovered above the terrace carrying the healer slung in a blanket like a marshwoman's baby, while Don hastily landed to catch the healer as Callette tipped her out.

"Thank – thank *Anscher*!" said Lydda.

The healer, who was a thin, brown harassed-looking woman, took one look at Derk and turned everyone out of the room except Lydda. "You look the calmest," she said.

"I'm not. Really," Lydda said, but she stayed.

Soon after, Mara left the dragon for a short while and went in to speak to the healer. She came out with a shawl wrapped over her startling dress, looking grey. "She's still trying to clear his lungs," Mara said to everyone sitting or couchant on the terrace. "She says to thank whoever cooled the burns off because she can concentrate on his breathing first. But she'll have to stay the night. Shona and Elda, you run up and get her a bed ready and put clean sheets on Derk's bed, and Blade can move Derk when she's finished. Don and Kit, let me know at once when she's through, please. I want her to come and see to the dragon after that."

"You want her to see to the *dragon*!" Shona exclaimed.

Mara gave Shona one of her grimmest, chin-up looks. "That dragon," she said, "is half dead. His wings need stitching, and I think he has some kind of deficiency disease. It may have affected his mind. He needs help, Shona."

"Oh fine!" said Kit. "Fine! And has that dragon of yours killed Dad? Or not?"

"The healer *thinks* he'll be all right," Mara said, at which everyone let out large sighs of relief. "But," Mara added, "she'll have to put him in a healing coma for the next five days at least, and he'll be in bed for a while after that."

"But," said Shona, "Mum, the tours start the day after tomorrow!"

"I know. And the Dark Lord's army comes through tomorrow," Mara said. "It's a disaster. Let me know when the healer's finished with Derk." And she hurried away to see the dragon again.

CHAPTER NINE

✳

"*I*t seems rather hard on Barnabas," said Blade.

"Not nearly so hard as it would be if we told him the truth," Don muttered.

They were all clustered to the side of the terrace, watching Mara explain to Barnabas that Derk would be away for a few days. Mara was looking tired and harassed, in a coat thrown over her Enchantress finery. "Still in that awful dress, I see," Shona said, arriving after seeing the healer off on one of the horses. The healer had flatly refused to let Callette or even Kit carry her home.

"I think it's a pretty dress," said Elda.

"You would," said Callette.

"I like it too," said Kit. "And it makes her look as if she's only just got here."

There had not been much discussion about what to do. Everyone knew Mr Chesney must not find out that Derk was injured, and nobody trusted Barnabas not to tell Mr Chesney. Blade had not really understood how strongly they all felt this, until he saw Barnabas bouncing up the terrace steps this morning and jovially asking Kit, who was roosting there on watch, "Where's Derk? The soldiers have arrived." When Kit answered that Derk was away for a while, the change in Barnabas was startling. He went pale. He sagged with such dismay that even his curls seemed to droop. "But he *can't* go away!" Barnabas protested. "He's Dark Lord! It's – it's irresponsible!"

"He's afraid *he's* going to have to do it," Lydda said, while Don scudded away to alert Mara.

Mara shortly came rushing round the side of the house, coat and black lace and hair streaming. Barnabas turned to her indignantly. "What's Derk *playing* at?"

Mara was cross and out of breath and certainly looked as if she had just arrived from Aunt's house. In fact, she had spent the early morning carefully erasing the burnt patch outside the gates and had just come from coaxing the sick old dragon up into the side-valley where the mayor's cows were. According to Don, the first thing the dragon did was to eat two of those cows. "She was trying to stop it eating too much. She says its name's

Scales or something," Don reported, settling down among the others.

Mara's explanation went on for some time. "I hope she'll remember to tell us all the stuff she's inventing," Shona remarked. "It could be awkward."

"Godlike snacks," Lydda murmured. "Those will distract him. Come on, Elda. The rest of you ask her."

Barnabas turned eagerly to the tray of Umru-style pastries Lydda brought out to him. He accepted coffee from Elda. While he was occupied, Callette managed to insert herself between Barnabas and Mara, which separated them by some way. "I kept it simple," Mara whispered to Shona, under Callette's big striped wing. "I told him there's a very old dragon just woken up after three hundred years – all truth, except I told him the old dragon's up north and the younger dragons sent Derk an urgent message for help and Derk rushed off at once. After all, it's just what your father *would* do."

"But have you said we're going to fill in for Dad?" Shona whispered back.

"Several times," Mara assured her. "Barnabas was terrified he'd have to deal with the soldiers on his own. Now let me rush off and get into proper clothes before I freeze."

They saw why Barnabas was so frightened when they all arrived at the end of the valley half an hour later, the humans on horseback and the griffins on the wing. There was an enormous crowd of men just beyond the ruins of the village. Each man was dressed in shiny black and armed with a shiny black helmet and a long sword in a shiny black scabbard. Most of them were simply standing. Some were wandering in circles. A few others were sitting on the ground. And there was something very wrong with all of them. Beauty, who was carrying Shona, refused to go anywhere near. The other horses trembled and sweated.

"What's wrong with these people?" Callette asked, peering into the nearest blank face.

"It's all right," Barnabas said reassuringly. "They send them through drugged."

"Why?" said Callette.

"Er, well, you see they're all convicted criminals – mostly for murder and assault and so on," Barnabas explained. "The tours clear out the prisons once a year. I believe Mr Chesney has a contract with some of the governments in his world and they pay him to take these convicts off their hands. It's a very neat arrangement. Most of them get killed over here, but they're all promised pardons and free land and so on. All we have to do at the moment is to get them to the camp I've made for them a couple of miles over there."

Blade had spent the morning hastily reading the Dark Lord sections of the black book. "But don't we have to get them to march right across to Umru's country?"

"Burning and pillaging and trampling crops on the way," Barnabas agreed. "But your father can do that at intervals after the tours arrive. I've got camps set up for him all along the route. No problem."

Blade swallowed. Mara said, "And when does the drugging wear off?"

"In three days or so," Barnabas said. "But they'll have been promised money if they behave themselves and do just what the Dark Lord says. We don't often have trouble."

Derk's family looked at one another expressively and then back at the black shiny men. The sight was somehow even more unpleasant after this explanation. They were like cockroaches waiting to be squished.

"Ah well," said Kit. "Let's get going."

Moving the men was a little like driving cows, except, Blade thought, you had to imagine the cows were deaf, twice as stupid as the Friendly Cows, and walking very slowly on two legs. And as Elda said, even the Friendly Cows didn't get in one another's way all the time. After Barnabas got the men moving with one of his weary, practised little spells, it took most of the day to reach the camp, and it was not easy. Going through open fields, they worked out that the best way was for the griffins to walk with their wings spread, herding from behind, with mounted humans two on either side to keep the vast shuffling horde together. But getting through gates was terrible. They tried shooing the men through in batches, but that took so long that Kit decided simply to break down every hedge or wall they came to.

"They're supposed to be laying the country waste," he said. "They may as well start now."

"True," Barnabas said cheerfully. "I'll break the walls. If it's a hedge, you and Callette can just walk through it."

"But mind the thorns!" Mara called out anxiously. "Don't tear your wing-feathers."

As the drive went on, its pace slowed to a crawl. Men in the midst of the crowd kept stumbling. When that happened, one of the riders would have to force their way among the shiny black bodies and haul the fallen man up before the others trod all over him. As Beauty would not go near the army and Barnabas had to lead the way, it was mostly Blade or Mara who had to do this. Blade was riding Nancy Cobber, who was the most obliging of all the horses, so he did most of it. He hated it. Probably Nancy did too. The black armour smelt like tar and the men themselves had a nasty smell of sweat and the drug and something Blade had never smelt before which he suspected was the smell of prison. And he hated being surrounded by all their blankly staring faces.

By evening it was worse. Men were stumbling so often by then that Don and Elda were flying overhead shrieking a warning every time a man fell. And when Blade went to pull the latest fellow up, he found expressions beginning to grow on some of the faces he was pushing past. They were not pleasant expressions. They were angry, or sullen. Some were jeering or plain brutal. But a few faces were full of simple flat hatred. Blade went in and out as quickly as he could and his stomach felt odd. He was sure the drug was wearing off. And unless Derk made a truly miraculous recovery, Blade knew that he and Shona and the griffins were going to have to march these dangerous people to more than just the one camp they were making for tonight.

The camp was a large transparent dome of magic in the middle of a big field, shining a faint blue-green in the evening light. Even the soldiers seemed to be aware of it. Their stumbling steps went faster and they streamed through the opening Barnabas made in the side of the dome at what was, for them, a brisk walk. Inside, Blade could see heaps of bedding, piles of bread and barrels of other food and drink, and latrine huts at intervals.

"There. That should keep them safe and happy until Derk gets back," Barnabas said cheerfully, sealing the dome shut. Kit, to Blade's admiration, hung over Barnabas while he did it, trying to learn how it was done. Blade felt sick. He saw one man pick up a loaf inside the dome and have it instantly snatched off him by another. When the drug wore off, he knew there would be bullying, quarrels and strong ones forming gangs to terrorise the rest.

"Shouldn't we take their swords away?" he said.

Barnabas shrugged. "We don't usually bother. They have to be armed for the battles after all. I don't suppose we'll lose many in camp fights. You reckon on twenty or so, most years."

"They're criminals, Blade," Shona said, seeing how Blade was looking.

Blade was not sure even criminals deserved this sort of thing, but he had no idea what to do instead. He felt miserable. He was still miserable when Barnabas said goodbye and vanished in a cheerful clap of thunder, horse and all. He found himself thinking of that camp most of the way home.

Mara had arranged for the skeletal Fran Taylor to come up from the village and nurse Derk. Fran met them at the gate, surrounded by pigs, who were all giving out anxious squeaks and snorts and fanning their wings in distress.

"I've got the supper on," Fran said, "since you were all so late. And there's been no change. I had to spend all day chasing these pigs away from him."

"I expect they're worried about him," Mara explained, getting stiffly down from her horse.

"And the owls too. You ask Old George," said Fran. "He's had no end of bother with those birds. If he turns his back for a moment, they're in through that bedroom window and gobbing all over the bedspread like there was no tomorrow."

"Old George?" said Shona. "Mum! I thought you had Old George over at Aunt's house to be your wasted lover."

"That was just a joke," Mara said irritably. "He's here for the animals while Derk's ill. Now I really must go and look at that dragon." She handed Shona her reins and hurried away to the side valley. Shona looked exasperated.

"Wasted lover indeed!" Fran said, following them up the drive in the crowd of pigs. "Don't you let Old George hear you say that. It's bad enough being like a stick person without people passing rude remarks. We're only like this to oblige your father, Shona."

"I know, I know," Shona said hurriedly. "I apologise. It was Mum's joke."

Everyone was in a hurry to see how Derk was. Blade handed the horses over to Old George and dashed upstairs after the others. Even Kit and Callette made the journey to Derk's bedroom, cautiously crawling up one side of the creaking, magic-supported stairs and squeezing through the doorway to stare down at Derk's bed. Derk still looked terrible. His breathing rattled as he slept. It was most discouraging.

"And Mum hasn't even been to *look*!" Shona said. "She's gone to look at the dragon instead." She was angry enough to ask, sweetly and dangerously, over supper, "And how is the poor dear dragon, Mother?"

"Oh, I think he's going to be all right," Mara said, quite failing to notice Shona's sarcasm. "He'd just slept himself nearly dead, poor creature. The healer stitched the worst of his wings and told him to rest and eat once a day for the next few weeks, and I can see she was right. He's a better colour already."

"More than Dad is," Blade said.

"Lucky your father met that dragon when it was half dead, I say," said Fran. "If it had been able to breathe fire, he'd be a crisp by now. They say the fire gets into your lungs and burns you up from inside. You can go about for weeks and then suddenly drop dead."

"Wonderful!" said Lydda, sitting with her beak poised over a plate of stew which she had, for a wonder, scarcely touched. But then the stew had been cooked by Fran and was far from godlike.

"Dragons *are* wonderful," Old George observed. "They can will you into being dead. Did you know that?"

"Or they can see into your mind and twist it," added Fran. "It worries me that your poor father may have looked it in the eye. If he did, then there's no knowing what it might have done to him."

"Sometimes they can take up a wizard's own magic and use it against him," Old George said, ladling himself a third bowlful of stew. His skeletal condition made him very hungry.

"They do that by singing, you know," Fran put in. "You didn't let this dragon sing to your father at all, did you?"

"There wasn't much any of us could stop it doing," Don said.

"None of this was in the dragonlore I learnt at University," Mara said firmly.

But this failed to stop Fran and Old George remembering a host of other things that were not in

166

University dragonlore either. Most of it suggested Derk was as good as dead and it upset Elda badly. After supper she raced upstairs and opened all the bedroom windows. The pigs flew eagerly in, followed by the owls. Elda spent the night huddled on Derk's bedroom carpet among the entire herd, anxiously listening to Derk's difficult breathing, while the owls sat in a row on Derk's bedhead.

Blade had a miserable night too. When he was not dreaming, over and over, of the dragon blasting smoke at Derk – which Blade knew how to stop, except that in the dream he had forgotten how – he was dreaming of being inside the magical camp full of men in shiny black. Everyone in there was trying to kill everyone else. When Blade tried to stop them, they came for him with their swords. For once, he was quite grateful when Shona woke him early and told him to exercise the dogs.

Later that morning, Kit called a council in his shed. Kit had been very busy. Strewn on the cushions of his bed were the pink pamphlet, the green one, the yellow one, the tour map, Derk's black book, Blade's black book and piles and piles of Derk's untidy hectic notes. On the floor was spread a large map of the continent with the routes of the various Pilgrim Parties carefully marked on it; and pinned on the wall was an even bigger timetable, in seven colours. Kit had done the map and the timetable himself in that beautiful clear penmanship which only griffins seemed to be capable of. Blade thought Kit must have worked most of the night.

"I wondered where that was!" Blade said, spotting his black book.

Shona arrived last, meaningly carrying her violin. "What's all this about?"

Kit's tail slashed. He was crouched in a vast black hump in the corner beyond his map. "I've been trying to work out what we ought to be doing," he said, "and who needs to be where, and when. We've got to reckon on Dad being laid up for at least two weeks, and not too well for a month after that. It would be nice if we could have everything running smoothly for him when he's better. Don't you agree?"

"Yes," Shona said, looking soberly down at the map. "I do."

Everyone else sighed with relief. Confrontations between Kit and Shona could be terrible. Lydda quietly helped herself to a pen and some of the stack of paper Derk had made for Kit, ready to take notes.

"Right," said Kit. "Three Pilgrim Parties come through today, three tomorrow, and three the next day, and so on for the next six weeks. They each have their first confrontation with the Forces of Dark five days later—"

"Leathery-winged avians," Elda said, checking the timetable with one careful talon.

"That's right," said Kit. "And the Wild Hunt three days after that. They pick up their first clue a day later. Does anyone know whether Dad planted the clues?"

Faces and beaks turned anxiously this way and that,

mostly towards Elda, who usually knew what Derk was doing. "He did some," said Elda, "but I don't think he'd finished."

"He hasn't finished," said Callette. "He said my gizmos needed a different set of clues for each one and he was going to rack his brains."

"We'd better check on that," Kit said.

While Lydda wrote it down in large and beautiful script: *Clues. 126x10,* Don looked over her wing and exclaimed, "But that's one thousand, two hundred and sixty clues! That's an *awful* job!"

"In thirty different places," said Callette. "I'll do it."

"Then I'll invent clues," said Shona. "It seems a proper bardic activity. What else is urgent, Kit?"

"Most of it. We're going to be really busy," Kit said sombrely. "At three tours a day, by the end of three weeks there are going to be sixty-two parties of offworlders—"

"Sixty-three," Don corrected him.

"Sixty-three then" said Kit, "spread out over most of the continent, all needing to have adventures with the Dark Lord at least once a week, and a week after that, some of them might even be coming up for their Final Encounters. We may find ourselves having to provide a Dark Lord for the first ones to kill, depending on how Dad is. But the two most urgent things to work out are: How are we going to provide all the right adventures on time? and How do we get Derkholm converted into a

Citadel? There's no way Dad's going to be fit enough to transform the house."

"Yeeps!" Don said.

"Can't Barnabas do the house?" Blade asked.

"Yes, if you want him to know Dad can't," Shona said crushingly. "Kit, Mum can change the house. She's been loving converting Aunt's house. We should have asked her before she went back there."

"She'd only have time if she did it right now," Kit pointed out. "Look at the timetable. She gets a party through her Lair every day after this first week. Lydda, make a note to fetch her back."

"She won't come," Callette said.

"She'll have to," Kit insisted. "Even if Blade or I could do it, we'd be trying to be in three places at once while we do. Can anyone see how we can get to all the places the adventures are supposed to be, or do things like the Wild Hunt without Dad's magic? I can't."

Shona giggled. "Only if we dash across the country chasing Pilgrims with the dogs and the Friendly Cows!"

It was an obvious joke. Kit snapped his beak angrily at Shona. Then his beak came open again and his head swivelled to stare at the map. "I think you've got it!" he said. "If we arrange to have the dogs and the Cows somewhere central, not at Derkholm, so that we can keep crossing the paths of the tours—"

"Hang on," said Lydda. "That means us camping out somewhere. I'm going to stay *here*."

Kit's head swivelled at Lydda. "You are not. We need everyone. And if Callette's going to be flying about planting clues—"

"I'll commute," Callette said, entirely disregarding the fact that half the clues were over on the east coast, hundreds of miles away. Everyone except Lydda and Kit looked at the map and wondered how Callette thought she could do it.

Lydda raised her beak at Kit's swivelled glare. Most unusually, the crest on her head came up too, golden and fierce. "Dad needs a proper nurse," she said, "not stupid Fran. I'm going to look after him. I want to be a healer anyway."

She and Kit glared at one another and the crest on Kit's head slowly rose to match Lydda's, black and spiky and twice the size. Elda gobbled and said timidly, "I want to stay here too."

"After the other night," Shona said, "no one's going to let you camp out, Elda."

Blade had gone on staring across the map, ignoring the rest of them. It seemed to him that Kit had not mentioned the one thing that seemed most important. "I know what we need to do most," he said, "and that's get those soldiers along to the base camp in Umru's country, now, before they kill one another or anyone else. Dad's not going to be well enough to get them there before the first battle anyway. Can't we do that as well?"

"*Oh gods! More stupid suggestions!*" Kit screamed.

"It makes sense, you know, Kit," Don said leaning over the map. "We can't be in sixty-three places at once. But if we take the army and the animals and keep going north from here, we'll be able to devastate the country *and* cut across the paths of the tours to do their adventures from wherever we happen to be."

"That's right!" said Shona, rather surprised about it.

"Trust Don to find the lazy way," Kit snarled. But his beak turned towards the map and his crest slowly lowered as he saw that the idea could actually work. "I'd been wondering what Dad meant to do about the soldiers," he confessed. "And this could be how he planned to work it."

"And I promise to fly out to you from here," Lydda put in, "whenever you really need me."

"Huh!" said Kit. "I can just see you! Emergency on King Luther's borders, we send for Lydda, Lydda sets out. We cope with the emergency. Three days later here comes Lydda, smack, plomp, exhausted, useless. Too late anyway. You'd better start getting some flying practice for once."

"Leave her alone, can't you!" said Callette.

Everyone relaxed. The difficulty seemed to be over and Kit was squabbling normally.

CHAPTER TEN

✳

*F*ive days later, everyone was wishing that the dragon
had never been born, or that it had fallen out of the
sky on its way to Derkholm, or that there had been some
other way to help Derk.

"Like sending a message to Mr Chesney to say the
tours were cancelled this year," Don suggested, irritably
ruffling his neck feathers against the rain. "He couldn't
have killed us, after all, and this might."

Their great straggling procession had only got halfway
to the base camp, a whole day behind Kit's schedule, and
they had had every kind of difficulty on the way. Barnabas
had set up the camps for the soldiers what he considered
a day's march apart. Blade and Don were still wondering

how anyone made men – even men who wanted to – walk that fast. They had been many miles short of the camp the first night anyway, because of setting off late in the morning after Kit's council, and had to park the horde of soldiers in a bare field near a large village. But the villagers were not helpful. They barricaded themselves into their houses and refused to let Blade have more than one cartload of bread, and they demanded cash for it. Luckily Shona had brought every scrap of money she could find in the house. The villagers took all of it, on the fairly reasonable grounds that the soldiers had trampled over their fields, and claimed that Blade and Shona owed them for the bread. It took all Shona's bardic powers of persuasion to make them let Blade enter the debt on his machine with buttons.

"And now we simply have to get to the next camp tomorrow," Shona said as they returned to the field with Nancy Cobber harnessed to the cart.

Kit meanwhile had worked away with what he hoped was the correct magic to keep the soldiers safely confined in the field. Probably, as Kit ruefully admitted the next morning, he was more successful with the sixty or so large campfires he had made to keep the men warm. At any rate, they had to leave the lot still burning merrily when they set off again, and there seemed no reason why the fires would ever go out. But the worst of it was that they had not bothered to count the soldiers the night before. They were doing that all the time now. That first morning it was clear that nearly a quarter of the men were gone. Blade kept guiltily thinking of all the horrible things those missing men were probably doing now, but they had no one to spare to go and look for them. They just had to keep slogging on with the rest of the horrible mob. They had the tour schedule to keep to.

The soldiers were even more horrible than Blade had thought. They were inventively, jeeringly, mutinously, murderously horrible. It was probably only because the drugs took time to wear off that Blade, Shona and the two griffins got them as far as the next camp on the second day. They did not want to walk. They made this plain on the third day by all willingly leaving the camp and then just sitting down in the mud outside. Some of the soldiers now had quite severe scratches and gashes where Kit and Don had flown at them and pecked them to make them move. Those with the scratches, as far as Blade could see, boasted about them for the next two days. Pecking had not shifted one of them. Kit in his exasperation remembered the camp fires and, deciding this was one thing he might be good at, flew down and enveloped the sitting men in an illusion of fire. It looked a bit pale and ghostly, but it got most of the men on their feet. It did not get them moving. "It ain't real!" they called out, and started to sit down again. It was only when Shona, in sheer fury, turned the carnivorous sheep amongst them that they moved. They ran, some of them with charming little white sheep attached to their legs or backsides and the rest shouting about monsters.

This was the one time that the sheep had proved in the least useful. For the rest of the time, they were almost as much trouble as the soldiers. They ate everything meaty – rabbits, mice, voles, birds – and would not walk while they were eating. They had to be carefully penned up at night or they tried to eat the dogs. In the end, Shona drove them along in the same kind of magical reins that Kit and Blade had had to invent for the soldiers.

The reins were long pieces of thread unravelled from Shona's bardic robes, and they were Shona's own idea. The magic was mostly Kit's, though Blade had helped. By that third day, Shona hated the soldiers even more than Blade or Don did. They called remarks at Shona all the time. Some of the remarks could have been flattering, but even those were remarks about what Shona was like under her clothes and what ought to be done with her. The other suggestions were horrible. Luckily Shona was riding Beauty and Beauty still refused to go within more than a hundred yards of the soldiers, so Shona was spared hearing most of the remarks clearly. But she heard enough. On the third evening, she made the mistake of trying to practise her violin where the soldiers in the camp could hear her. They instantly put rude words to the music and sang them at her, very badly. The next day, their remarks were even lewder.

It was in the dawn of that day that Shona screamed that she was going *home* unless someone thought of a way to march those men until they were too tired to talk.

"*You* think of a way," Don told her irritably. None of them were getting enough sleep. "You're the bard. You're supposed to have ideas."

So Shona thought of the reins and, to everyone's relief, they worked – or they worked if they were strung across the opening in the camp where the soldiers had no choice but to walk into the reins as they left it, and if Don or Kit flew ahead, dragging.

Even so, that fourth day, the soldiers contrived to set fire to a field of grain, a hillside and a wood as they passed through. No one knew how.

"Who cares?" said Kit. "They're supposed to be ravaging the place."

Blade looked back regretfully at fine slender living trees curling and cracking in the rolls of smoke, and he felt for that wood. He could feel the trees hurting. That surprised him, because he had not realised that his magic was that much like Derk's.

To add to their troubles, most of the animals, not only the sheep, were causing concern in different ways. They lost Big Hen the first night. Everyone glumly assumed that the missing soldiers had taken her with them to eat. "I hate to think how Dad will feel!" each of them said at intervals the second day.

Then, that evening, when they had just, at last, succeeded in getting the soldiers into the proper camp they should have reached the day before, there was a whupping of powerful wings overhead. Everyone looked up, expecting Callette. "How are the clues going?" Kit screamed up into the darkening sky.

"It's not Callette, it's me," Lydda answered, gliding in a circle overhead. "I daren't land. I'd never launch again. I just came to tell you that Big Hen got home this afternoon. Do you want her back with you for eggs or not? Mum says she'll translocate her if you do."

"Leave her. I hate eggs," Kit called.

"But I like them," Don said piteously.

He was overruled, which was not unusual. "Keep her now she's back," Shona shouted upwards. "Is Mum at home then?"

"She dropped in to see the dragon," Lydda called back. "I'm supposed to tell her where you are. I'll tell her you haven't got too far yet."

She circled away and her wingbeats died into distance amid a strong silence.

"I don't *think* she meant to be rude," Blade said.

"We'll keep to schedule after this if it kills us!" Kit vowed.

So they struggled on, trying to go faster, dragging the reluctant soldiers across fields and pastures, and the third day they were delayed by having to bury one of the dogs and to tow the corpse of a Friendly Cow behind two of the horses. The soldiers had killed them both, for being too friendly. Briney the dog had simply gone up to one of the soldiers on the outside of the mob, wagging his tail and trying to get acquainted. That soldier had calmly drawn his sword and cut Briney's head off. One of the cows had followed Briney to see what was going on and run into a wall of slashing swords. Blade was nearly in tears.

"Never mind," Shona said to Kit. "You and Don will get plenty of meat tonight."

"We can't possibly eat all that before it goes bad," Kit squawked. If griffins could cry, Kit would have been near tears too.

"We can try," Don said.

After that, they had to keep the cows well to the rear of the ungainly procession – which was not difficult – and keep a stern eye on the other dogs – which was not so easy. The dogs had brains, because that was how Derk had bred them to be. They knew what had happened to Briney and they now hated the soldiers even more than Blade or Shona did. They were planning to tear out throats. Blade had to keep them leashed on more bespelled threads from Shona's robes.

That night they roasted lumps of Friendly Cow over a large fire, while the soldiers in the camp beyond chanted, "We want roast beef, we want roast beef!"

"I'm not giving them a *shred*!" Shona said. "I know it sounds mean, but they've got their own supplies in there and I don't *care*!"

They made you mean, these soldiers, that was the trouble. By the fourth day, when the soldiers still chanted that they wanted roast beef, mixed in with

179

whistles and jeers whenever they saw Shona, Blade realised that being alongside so many nasty people had a bad effect on you. Don, he discovered, felt the same.

"I don't know what does it," Don confided to him, "but they make me feel weak and depressed and vicious all the time. I don't know how Kit stands it. They really *hate* him!"

This was true. By now the soldiers had realised that Blade and Don were only young. Shona was female, so they called remarks at her. But they could not believe that four young people, one of them a girl, could control several hundreds of them. Kit was enormous. He looked savage – and behaved savagely when they did not do what he told them – and he was sinisterly black beside the golden Don. The soldiers decided that Kit must be a powerful full-grown magician of a truly evil kind who had them all enslaved. And they hated him for it. They hated Kit with such ferocious unspoken hatred that Blade could feel it, like acid on his skin, whenever he and Kit chanced to be near the soldiers together.

He felt he should warn Kit. "I can tell they're thinking up horrible things to do to you if they ever get loose," he said. "Can't you feel it at all?"

Kit answered with an open-beaked gurgle of laughter. "Perfectly well. I rather like making people afraid of me."

"It's a bit more than that," Blade said anxiously.

He would have said more, but this was the point

where Pretty disappeared completely, and they never got back to the subject again.

They had had to bring Pretty. Beauty, when she discovered that they would be away for weeks, refused to let Shona or anyone else ride her unless Pretty came too. Since Pretty could now flutter into the air quite well, whirling his dizzying black and white wings – which grew stronger every day – and he could graze and eat oats in a messy inexpert way, nobody thought he needed his mother that much and they had wanted to leave him with Old George. But Beauty insisted Pretty needed her. Pretty himself was sure he needed nothing. He was having a wonderful time frisking from side to side of the procession, teasing the dogs, chasing cows and, every so often, alarming Beauty thoroughly by just disappearing. Every time Beauty lost sight of him, she was convinced the soldiers had killed Pretty too. Since the one piece of good sense that Pretty ever showed was in never going near the soldiers, nobody took Beauty's panics very seriously, but they always caused a long delay.

This time when Pretty vanished while Blade was trying to warn Kit, he really was nowhere to be seen. Beauty soared into the air, with Shona on her back. "Sohldiers! Bhad sohldiers goht Prhetthy!"

"No, they *haven't*!" Shona said, exasperated. The reins holding the sheep were cutting her fingers, she had lost a stirrup and she had nearly fallen off. "You *know* he never goes near them. Go down!"

"Fhind Prhetthy!" Beauty trumpeted, circling higher and stretching the reins almost to snapping point.

"Oh really!" Shona was leaning off one side hanging on to the twenty feet of thread and scrabbling for her iron. "It's lucky I'm a good rider, Beauty, or you'd have lost me by now. Do go down."

But Beauty tried to go up again, neighing for Pretty, rearing in mid-air in her anxiety. Shona looked so likely to come off that Don took to the air with a clap in order to catch her, and the noise he made – maybe – disguised the approach of the people who had found Pretty. At any rate, Pretty suddenly reappeared only a few feet from Kit and Blade and the dogs, mincing joyously among the long legs of six tall fair-haired men in green.

There was a long rumble of awe from the watching soldiers.

The reason for this was that all six men, and Pretty, were surrounded in a green-blue haze of magic. The tallest man had a golden circlet on his white-fair hair. This one bowed gravely to Blade and Kit. "I come to return this small wonder-horse to the Dark Lord, our master," he said. "Can you lead me to him, if you please?"

"Er—" Blade began, but was interrupted by Beauty descending as suddenly as she had gone up. Pretty dashed to her side, at a prudent distance from the sheep, and feverishly represented himself as a poor lost lonely bewildered *stolen* little colt.

"No you aren't," said Shona. "You're just a nuisance."

Then she looked up and saw the tall man with the circlet. Her eyes went wide and black and she stared. Don landed beside her, staring too.

"I'm afraid Derk's not here at the moment," Kit said with great politeness, bending down towards the magic haze. "But we all thank you for returning Pretty. Can we assist you by taking a message to Derk?"

"I thank you," replied the man with the golden circlet. "Inform him that I must in courtesy speak with him myself. I am Talithan, eldest son of Talian Elfking."

Even Kit's confidence was shaken. This man was a very important elf indeed. Kit's throat bobbed, and he answered even more politely, "My father Derk – ah – found himself a little unwell and was forced to stay at home today." The elf prince's smooth forehead gathered into a frown at this. Kit added hurriedly, "But of course I can fly home with all speed—"

"No need," said the elf prince, to Blade's acute relief. He wanted to kick Kit. How on earth could anyone tell Derk anything when he was in a healing coma? Blade glanced up at Shona, hoping she would interrupt to stop Kit making complete fools of them all, and was exasperated to see her sitting on Beauty like a statue, staring at Talithan. Oh no! he thought. He was going to have to point out to Shona that, if Talithan was who he said he was (and he must be, because elves never lied), then he was at least five hundred years old and married already.

"I will wait upon the Dark Lord myself," Talithan

was saying. "Know that I am, only this very day, appointed to fight on his side, and these my friends with me, as Captains of his Dark Elves. This suddenness, as we must hasten to assure him, was not intended as discourtesy. Another high elf had been chosen, but is now removed, by reason of my own rash fault."

"Indeed?" Kit said, rather helplessly.

"I had the misfortune to offend my honoured father by uttering a scoffing prophecy," Talithan explained, "and for this I must regard the Dark Lord as my master for a year and a day. For this reason must I hasten to Derkholm."

"Perhaps you'd better wait for a week, Your Highness," Blade blurted out. Kit's head swivelled angrily at him.

"Your Highness," Don put in, "Dad's got no end of urgent business—" Don's beak snapped shut as Kit's head swivelled at him and Kit's tail slashed. Don knew Kit had a point here. You did not suggest to the heir of the Elfking that anything could be more important than he was. Except— "With Mr Chesney," Don added, out of pure inspiration. Kit's tail hit the ground like a whip.

"Then I will wait on his pleasure for a week," Talithan said graciously. "I do not," he said, and his chin went up disdainfully, "associate with the man Chesney, who holds my brother hostage and forces my race to do his will. But see the Dark Lord I must, if only to ask a favour of him." He half turned. It looked as if he was going, but he turned back and looked up at Kit. "Forgive me if I

184

ask impertinently, but how do two members of your race call the Dark Lord Father?"

"Because he is," Kit said, rather astonished. "He bred us from eggs."

Talithan smiled. "That explains my puzzle. I had not thought there were any griffins this side of the ocean, but if you were fetched over in the egg, the reason is clear." He bowed to the astonished Kit, to Don, to Blade and the still staring Shona. "Farewell. I must no longer interrupt your herding of this unpleasant soldiery." That left Blade almost as surprised as Kit. None of the elves had so much as glanced at the goggling crowd of soldiers.

All six elves turned as if they were about to walk away. The magic haze turned with them, like an open door shutting, and the grassy place where they had been standing was empty. Every one of the horses, including Pretty and Beauty, surged forward after them and stopped, seeing the elves were gone. Elves often had that effect on horses. Beauty's sudden stop jerked Shona out of her saddle, to land with a rush, a stagger, and a snatch at the reins round the sheep. It seemed to jerk Shona out of her daze too.

"Gods!" she said. "I had a dream about him!"

"Oh, don't go and be soppy!" Kit snapped.

"I wasn't," Shona said. "It wasn't a nice dream. There were dwarfs in it too and you'd been drowned and there was something wrong with Dad. I just couldn't believe it when he turned out to be real."

"We thought you were smitten," Blade explained.

"Of course not. He's five hundred years old and married to Malithene," Shona retorted. "I do know my Elflore, but I didn't know it was him in my dream, and it was a scary dream."

Kit prowled swiftly back to the soldiers and commenced shaking the magic reins to get the procession moving again, obviously in a very bad temper indeed. Blade thought he knew how Kit felt. Elves, when they went away, had the effect of leaving you feeling flat and ordinary and ugly. Everything seemed unpleasant. Blade found himself really noticing the way they were leaving a broad trampled trail across perfectly good farmland, littered with things dropped by the soldiers. They had no idea where the soldiers found all the rubbish they dropped, but drop it they did, all the time – papers, packets, pieces of cloth, fragments of black armour, keys, bad fruit, crusts – and after them the Friendly Cows dropped cowpats on top of that. Blade found it disgusting suddenly.

But there was more to Kit's bad temper than this. Later, when they had made it to the next camp and shut the soldiers inside, Kit said to Blade, "I never knew there were griffins on the other continent."

"Dad must have got the idea from somewhere," Blade said glumly. He felt desolated. He knew Kit was going to go away across the ocean to look for wild griffins the first opportunity he got. "It's too far to fly there," he said despairingly. "You'd drown."

"What were boats invented for?" Kit demanded.

There was a sharp frost that night. The soldiers, warm inside their camp, jeered and shouted and sang half the night, while their four supervisors shivered. At dawn, the frost melted and the rain began. The soldiers sat down inside the transparent walls of the camp, snug and dry, and refused to come out. This was when Blade began truly wishing the dragon had died before it got to Derkholm.

"*Now* what are we to do?" Shona asked. She had a tarpaulin wrapped over her head and rain was hitting it like a drum.

"Seal them in again and let them rot," Don suggested angrily. "I've had quite enough of hauling them along anyway." He shook water out of fur and feathers in gouts. It did no good. The rain was so steady and heavy that he was dark brown with it.

"No, we damn well won't seal them in again!" Kit said. He was still extremely irritable. Everyone was trying to please him without letting him know they were, because that always made Kit worse. The animals were all keeping out of his way, even Pretty. "My *timetable*," Kit snarled, raking marks in the wet earth with one long wet talon, "means that we *have* to be up near Umru's land inside a week, or we mess up at least fifty Pilgrim Parties, the gods damn them all!"

"There's no way we're going to get there by then, even if they came out now," Shona told him. "I don't think they'll move until they've eaten all the food in there."

"But we can't get to half the places in *time* from here!" Kit snarled.

"We can get to the first lots," Blade said soothingly. "They all have avians up in the coastal hills and I can translocate there easily. Just close the camp up again. I have a sort of idea about something I can do."

"What can *you* do?" Kit said rudely.

"It may not work," Blade admitted. "But I'll tell you if it does. Just shut the camp up while I'm away."

"Oh, all right." Kit sprang up in a whirl of wetness and stalked off towards the open front of the camp. "And you'd better *make* it work," he added, beak turned over shoulder.

The last Blade saw as he translocated was Kit spreading vast black wings and shaking wet out of them like claps of thunder. The nearest soldiers scooted warily back from him. They knew a bad temper when they saw one, just like everyone else.

But it was hard work translocating. Blade had always done it before with no trouble. He had not realised the effort it took. Now that he was tired from four days of travel and constant crisis, wet, and sore from riding and from a night spent mostly awake and shivering, moving himself was suddenly immensely hard work. His first effort only got him to the inn where the demon had been, where the rain was simply a light drizzle in a warm wind.

Blade stood in the empty inn yard for a moment, panting, wondering if he dared go on with his idea. Without Kit looming over him like a stormcloud to push him on, Blade found things looked far less safe and certain.

"But the dragon owes us," he said aloud. "This mess is all its fault."

That might be true from a human-griffin point of view, but Blade was not so sure now that dragons saw things the same way. The trouble was, they needed those soldiers moved and about the only creature that might get them to move was a large dragon. Blade took a deep breath and translocated onwards.

He chickened out at the last moment. He took himself home first. He told himself he wanted to see how Dad was anyway. But he fell short even there and landed in the garden, in the midst of a large bush. The first thing he saw was Prince Talithan and his five companions, sitting in a patient row on the terrace, leaning against the wall of the house in the least ruined part. They could sit there quite comfortably because it was not raining at Derkholm at all.

"Oops!" Blade muttered, and took himself to the kitchen at once, while the elves were still turning to see what the noise in the bush was.

Lydda looked up from the stove in a resigned way. "Oh. It's you now."

"Those elves—" Blade began.

"They came last night," Lydda said wearily. "They

want to see Dad, but they *can't*, not when he's asleep. I don't think Dad should see anyone until he's properly better anyway. So I told them he was in conference with Mr Chesney, but they just said they'd wait. And," Lydda added fiercely, "I told thin Fran I'd *peck* her if she told those elves Dad was ill. She's up seeing to Dad now, if Elda will let her near him. She might not."

Lydda was obviously having a fairly harassing time too. "How is Dad?" Blade asked.

"I don't *know*!" Lydda squawked distressfully. "I can't *tell* any more! You go and look and see if you think he's any different. And tell Elda she's *got* to let Fran put ointment on his burns this time, because I can't. I'm cooking for those elves."

"Godlike snacks?" Blade said.

"Godlike *dinner*," said Lydda. "And if they stay until Dad's better, that's godlike supper, dinner, supper, dinner, supper, dinner – I'm going mad, Blade!"

"Where's Mum?" Blade asked, prudently retreating towards the door.

"Back at her Lair," Lydda snapped. "Tour through any day now. She'd left before those elves turned up. At least she's not expecting Callette and Elda any more – and Callette's been away for three days now. At least I don't have to feed *her*."

Lydda was clearly not in the mood to let people hang around in the kitchen. Blade hurried away upstairs to Derk's bedroom. There, Elda was standing protectively on the end of Derk's bed, hackles, wings and crest raised, glaring at skeletal Fran. Fran was tidying away pots of ointment and bandages with her mouth pursed in a way that showed that, if she had a crest and hackles, she would have had them raised too. The room was full of hostile silence. Blade crossed the room and looked down at his father.

Some of the reason for the silence was that Derk was now breathing normally. He was almost the right colour again and most of the burns seemed to have gone, apart from a messy-looking place on one cheek. But he had gone very thin, with the beginnings of a dark beard. The black bristles hollowed his face and made him look very frail and worried.

"But he's *much* better!" Blade exclaimed.

"Do you think so?" Elda and Fran said eagerly, in unison, and then avoided looking at one another.

"Yes, I do," Blade said. "Tell Lydda. And give him my love when he wakes up."

The bedroom was not a place to linger in, any more than the kitchen was. Blade translocated himself again, rather carefully, to a place just outside the gates, where the elves could not see him. From there, he walked slowly up into the side valley. He was not going to risk alarming the dragon by appearing suddenly under its nose. He wished he knew how to surround himself in a fireproof shield, but then he remembered how easily the dragon had brushed aside his attempts to help Derk and decided that any shield would be brushed aside too. The only thing to do was to translocate at the first sign of trouble. Fast. If that was fast enough.

Blade found he was going more and more slowly. He was – he admitted it – scared stiff. There seemed no reason why the dragon should agree it owed Derk's family some help, and every reason why it should eat Blade on the spot. From what Mara had said, it was an old, wild dragon, from the days when dragons and humans were natural enemies. Or it might simply be too ill and grumpy to help. But Blade could not think of any other way to get those soldiers moving and he remembered the dragon had been prepared to listen to Mara, and he kept going. He rounded the crag that hid the side valley.

He had forgotten how big the dragon was. It filled half the valley. It was lying alongside the stream, with its head and huge talons not far from Blade, with one of the mayor's cows clasped between those talons. It was peacefully munching on that cow. Beyond, by the stream, the bent coronet and the broken chain had been carefully laid out on a flat stone. Above Blade, the dragon's wings came to two towering peaks, green as the surrounding hills. Behind those wings, Blade had glimpses of the huge body and then the spiked tail, tapering away nearly as far as the terrified huddle of the mayor's remaining cows. There were a lot fewer cows than there had been.

The thing that impressed Blade most, however, was the way the dragon had changed since he last saw it.

It glistened now, green all over, and the scales that had looked so loose and ragged had healed flat and whole again. The unhealthy white of its underside had turned a pale green. The great peaks of its wings were no longer tattered – Blade could see dark green veins in them, healthily pulsing – and the talons that were gripping the mayor's cow had been trimmed back to the proper, lethally hooked shape. Mum had been right. This dragon had been ill when it first arrived.

The dragon looked up and saw Blade. Its eyes had lost their filmy look. They were now bright green-gold. And enormous. Blade felt he could drown in one. As it saw him, the dragon put one clawed paw protectively over the remains of the cow and reached out quickly with the other paw to drag the broken chain and the bent coronet safely under its green belly.

"What do *you* want?" it said. Its voice rumbled the ground under Blade's boots and set the rest of the cows yelling with fear. "Do you people think I'm on show at a fair, or something?"

"What do you mean?" said Blade. Oddly enough, he had forgotten how frightened he was. He still knew this dragon was the most dangerous creature in the world – if you didn't count the blue demon or Mr Chesney – but all he was thinking of was how best to talk to it.

"I mean the way people keep coming to stare at me," the dragon rumbled. "I've had two little yellow cat-birds and one bigger brown one, and a stick man and a stick woman, and a little woman with yellow hair, and now you. Haven't any of you ever seen a dragon before?"

"I've come to talk to you, not stare," Blade said.

"That's what they all said," boomed the dragon. "And then they scolded me for roasting the wizard. If you've come to tell me off for that too, consider it done."

"Well, no, actually, I've come to ask you for help, Mr – er – Scales," Blade said boldly.

"Scales will do," said the dragon. "What do you mean, help?"

"You owe me. You roasted my father," said Blade.

"There. You see? You're scolding," the dragon rumbled.

"No, I'm not. I'm starting to explain." Blade braced his feet and stared up into the dragon's huge eyes. Despite the things Fran and Old George had said, this seemed the right thing to do. It had worked for Mara. "You see, because you roasted my father, we're having to do his Dark Lord work for him. We've got his army – they're six hundred murderers really, pretending to be soldiers – out in the middle of nowhere near the wastes and we're supposed to be moving them to a base camp in Umru's country, so that we can park them there while we do the Wild Hunt and so on. But they won't move. Today they just sat down and wouldn't come out of the dome."

"Leave them there then," said the dragon.

"We *can't*," said Blade. "There's a timetable – there's a whole set of battles they have to fight in. Besides, if we did leave them, they'd probably all escape and start murdering everyone."

"I thought murdering was what soldiers and battles did," said the dragon. "Why have they got to go and murder people in a particular place at a particular time?"

"Because," Blade said patiently, "Mr Chesney has arranged for the tours to have a battle each."

There was silence. All Blade could hear was the stream racing over stones. The dragon barely moved. A wisp of smoke blew from its great jaws and melted among the hairs of the carcass under its paw. There was a tinge of red in the one huge eye Blade could most clearly see. Somehow the wings above him seemed to be in sharper, crueller points, and Blade had a sense of muscles tensing all over the enormous body. He saw that the dragon had been having a joke with him, dragon-fashion, but something Blade had said was not funny any more and he had made it very angry. He got ready to translocate in a hurry.

"Some day," the dragon remarked in a croon, deep in its smoky throat, "I must meet this Mr Chesney of yours. I ought to pay my respects to the one who rules the dragons of this world, ought I not? Very well then. I shall come and pay my debt to your father tomorrow at dawn."

Blade relaxed. "Couldn't you come today?" he asked pleadingly.

"I am not ready to travel today," the dragon said. "I

am still healing. Look for me after sunrise tomorrow. Are you and your murderers easy to find?"

"Awfully," said Blade. "We leave a mile-wide trail the whole way. Thank you for agreeing – er – Mr – er – Scales, I mean."

The dragon snorted a big gobbet of blue smoke. "I won't say it's my pleasure. It sounds like a chore. I won't even agree that I owe you. It's just the only way I'm likely to get any peace here. Do you mind going away now and letting me finish my breakfast?"

"Yes, of course," Blade agreed, and found himself very nearly calling the dragon "sir", the way he used to have to call his grandfather "sir". Mara's father had been a tetchy old wizard with very old-fashioned ways. This dragon reminded Blade of his grandfather rather a lot.

He went away down the valley. Now he had time to think, he was highly surprised at how easily the dragon had agreed to help them. He hoped it was enough like Grandfather to keep its word. Grandfather always said, "A wizard's word is his bond. He should die rather than break his word, child." But the dragon could just have been trying to get rid of him. Grandfather hadn't liked being disturbed either.

CHAPTER ELEVEN

✳

*D*erk woke up quite suddenly the afternoon of the fifth day, with a feeling that somebody was calling his name. He sat up, amazed to be so weak and breathless. His face felt sore. When he touched it, he found he had almost a beard and a large weeping burn on his cheek. That brought everything back to him.

"Gods and demons!" he exclaimed. "How long did they put me to sleep for?"

He got up. His legs tried to fold. He strengthened them sternly with a spell and floundered across to the bathroom, hanging on to chairs, doorknobs, walls and finally the washbasin, where he grimly set about shaving. Elda came galloping upstairs a few minutes later to find him with his face covered with lather and smeary bandages hanging off all over him.

"Oh, *please* get back to bed, Dad!" she squawked. "Lydda's got you some broth."

"No. How long have I been asleep?" Derk said, swaying a little.

"Nearly five days," said Elda. "But you mustn't worry. Shona's gone with the boys to keep them sensible, and they're seeing to the soldiers for you. Please go back to bed."

Derk pulled a loose bandage free and used it to cover the burn on his face while he scraped hair and lather away from beside it. "Where's your mother?"

"In her Lair," said Elda. "The first tour gets to her tomorrow, and the second one goes round by the sacked nunnery and arrives as soon as the first one leaves." Elda was good at learning things. She had learnt Mara's entire programme while she sat on the end of Derk's bed, guarding him from Fran. She could have told Derk about it at some length.

Derk sighed. It had been too much to hope that Mara had been looking after him while he was ill. Probably she did not want to. "Then who is that calling me?" he interrupted, raising his chin to scrape his neck. A bristle pulled. "Ouch!"

"I don't hear anyone," said Elda.

"Magically," said Derk.

"It could be the elves," Elda said.

"What elves?" said Derk, grimly shaving away.

Elda sighed too. She could see Derk was in his most obstinate mood and she never could deal with him when he was like that. She hopped into the empty bath and crouched there while she told him everything that had been going on. Derk meanwhile hung on to the basin with one hand and then the other and managed first to shave and then to strip off most of his bandages and sponge off the ointment to see how bad the burns were. They were still quite bad.

"And Callette came back just after the elves came, and she screamed at the dragon and then went over to see Mum," Elda said. "You ought to *leave* that salve, Dad. The healer *said*!"

"What does Callette think she's up to?" asked Derk.

"Finding out what clues you'd put out," Elda explained. "She says you'd hardly done half of them."

"Then who's feeding the animals, if anyone?" Derk asked.

"Half of them are with Shona and the boys," Elda explained. "Mum got Old George in to do the rest. And she got Fran to do you – only I don't like Fran. She called me an *animal*."

"Tell Fran she's one too," said Derk. "Gods! What a mess this is!" He left the bathroom and tottered back to his bedroom to find his clothes. Elda bounded out of the bath and rushed to get her back under his weaving right hand. Derk leant on her gratefully, even though she kept trying to steer him back to bed. At least she knew what Fran had done with his clothes. He made her fetch them and sat on the bed to get into them.

"Do let Lydda bring you the broth," Elda pleaded while he dressed. "You must be starving!"

"Not really. No messages have come through from my stomach," Derk said. He was worried about whoever was calling him. They sounded urgent. He put his boots on and stood up. "Help me get downstairs, Elda. Where are these elves?"

"In the dining room eating godlike lunch," said Elda. "You could wait."

Derk knew that if he waited, he would crawl into bed again and the mess would only get worse. "No," he said and tottered towards the stairs.

Lydda had heard the activity overhead. In its present state, the house creaked mightily whenever anyone walked about upstairs. She met Derk with a mug of broth halfway downstairs and sat herself squarely in his way. "Sit down and drink this, Dad, or I'll peck your burns."

Derk sat heavily, with one arm over Elda's back. Lydda had left him nowhere else to go. He meekly took the mug. The broth in it smelt wonderful. He sipped. It was beautiful. "A poem in liquid," he told Lydda – she was sitting spread over the next four steps with her wings out to make sure he came down no further. Derk managed to grin. "Everyone should have griffin daughters to keep them in order," he said. Elda moved round to the stair above him so that he could lean against her. Derk leant into her warm feathers and sat comfortably sipping, staring out at the greenness of the garden and the valley beyond, through the magic wall Finn and Barnabas had made. "When all this is over, I think we'll keep this front wall transparent," he said. "The stairs always used to be too dark. So what else has happened since Callette left?"

"Blade came," said Lydda, "but not for long. He was soaked through because it was raining in their camp. He went and looked at you."

"He said you were much better," Elda protested, "but you look *awful*, Dad. Your cheeks are all droopy and thin."

"Sometimes," Derk said, "Blade talks good sense. I could do with another cup of this wonderful broth, Lydda."

Lydda took the mug, but did not budge. "I'll get you more when you're back in bed."

Derk smiled, sighed, and shook his head at her. Then he translocated to the person who was calling him so urgently.

Squawks of dismay were still ringing in his ears as he landed, heavily, not in the dining room, where he had expected to be, but somewhere outside. It was beginning to rain here too. Derk sat for a moment, sore and winded and getting wet, staring at steep green hillside and wishing he did not make so many mistakes in translocating. A cow bellowed nearby.

"Curses! I keep forgetting how fragile humans are!" rumbled a huge voice. Derk recognised it as the one that had been calling him. "Are you badly hurt?" the voice asked him.

Derk scrambled slowly round on his knees to stare at the enormous green dragon lying by the stream just below him. It glistened healthily in the rain. At first he thought it was a complete stranger. Then he saw the stitches in the nearest vast peaked wing. "Oh," he said. "It's you."

"And if I had not specifically called you, I would not have known you either," the dragon rumbled. "My apologies. I asked you here to make amends. Once your wife had explained the situation to me I saw that I had acted hastily and stupidly. I should never have burnt you."

"Er – thanks. Very decent of you," Derk answered.

"Not decent," boomed the dragon. "Ashamed. It was not you I should have attacked. But I was angry, very angry and shamed. I had been asleep – possibly I had settled down to die – when I was suddenly woken to find the world a different place. Dragons I had known as infants were now not only full grown but – of all things! – kowtowing to humans, taking part in a ridiculous *game*. And when I asked them their reasons, all they would do was stare into the distance and pretend to be immeasurably wise."

"Yes, they do that, the modern dragons," Derk said. "I thought it was the dragon way."

"I don't hold with it," said the great green dragon. "No living creature has the right to claim wisdom. There is always more to find out. I should know that. I imagine you know it too, Wizard."

"I've never ever felt wise," Derk said frankly. "But I suppose it *is* a temptation, to stare into distance and make people *think* you are."

"It's humbug," said the dragon. "It's also stupid. It stops you learning more. I went away from the adults and asked the fledgling dragons. There are only two of them. That's bad. Dragon numbers are badly down. They said the adults are too busy with those Pilgrim Parties to breed these days. So I asked about the Pilgrim Parties and they told me that a Mr Chesney is responsible for them and that the dragons side with this Mr Chesney because he is the chief evil in the world. Foolishness. Dragons are never on anyone's side. And they told me also that the Dark Lord represents Mr Chesney in our world. I was very angry and very shamed for my people, and I came here directly, intending, I am afraid, to kill the Dark Lord. You were lucky, Wizard, that I was tired and feeble and had no real fire."

"It was bad enough as it was," Derk admitted. "What woke you up?"

"I wish I could remember," said the dragon. "It's been puzzling me. At my age, in my condition, I should simply have slept until I died. Of course, I didn't know how bad I was. Your wife and that little healer-woman had to tell me. But I should have been too feeble to wake. All I know is that something did wake me – something that struck me like blue lightning – maybe it *was* lightning, though how it reached my cave I can't think – and that I was awake and learning from the minds around me that this world had become a small, bad place."

Derk had a notion what the blue lightning might have been. So I brought this on myself by trying to conjure a demon! he thought. But that was a small, fleeting thought beside his eager delight at discovering this dragon could read minds. It was something he had hoped the griffins would be able to do, and he had always been disappointed that they couldn't. I'm ridiculous, he thought. Here I am on a wet hillside, getting soaked in this rain and feeling too ill to get up, and all I can think of is that there truly is a creature who can read minds. "I'm quite excited to know you read minds," he told the dragon. "There aren't many who can these days."

"Nobody bothers to practise, that's all," said the dragon. "It used to be one of the first things they made you do when you started to learn magic. You could do it, Wizard, if you'd been properly taught. And be thankful that I was properly taught. I've been lying here learning things about you and about your household that I wouldn't otherwise know. If I hadn't, I might have killed most of your little cat-birds – certainly the brown one. She was most insulting. But the other two were quite rude too."

"What, Lydda and Elda as well?" said Derk. He was impressed that they had had the courage to insult a dragon. Callette was big enough to think she might get away with it – though she had seen what happened to Kit – but Lydda was only about the size of one of the mayor's cows, and Elda was smaller than that. And the dragon had eaten at least half the mayor's herd. I must pay the mayor back! Derk thought. Where do I find any *money*? "I apologise for my griffin daughters," he said.

"They were worried about you," the dragon explained, "and they rightly blamed me. They took out their temper on me. And it was the same with the two very thin people – though no doubt they hoped I would not think them worth eating. I saw my own behaviour in theirs. It is impressive the way all your people have such great regard for you, Wizard. But the skinny small boy, your son, is the one who troubles me most—"

"Did Blade insult you too?" Derk groaned.

"He was entirely polite," the dragon said. "But it was partly on his account I called you here. It seems that he and three others are engaged in marching six hundred murderers across the country."

What a mess! Derk groaned again. Apart from the danger, there should surely have been more than six hundred soldiers. Barnabas said there were to be a thousand. "Yes, I'd better see about that at once," he said. He tried to scramble up, but his feet slipped in the wet grass and his knees refused to hold him.

"Wait and hear me out!" The dragon puffed out a cloud of steam. The steam surrounded Derk in moist warmth, smelling grassy and sweet and quite unlike the smokes it had tried to kill Derk with. "I was about to say that this is where I should make reparation. Speaking as something of a murderer myself, I would say your other fledglings are in trouble."

"I *know* they are!" Derk said faintly.

"Then I suggest that, if you will give me your authority, I go and try intimidating these murderers."

"Willingly," said Derk. "Any authority you want."

"While you go back to your house and continue to heal," said the dragon.

"I'm well enough," Derk lied.

"You are not. I have been healing you as you sat here," said the dragon. "This was my other reparation. But you will need at least one more day in which to recover your strength. Meanwhile, I should perhaps tell you that you have six members of the Elder Race as they wrongly call themselves – dragons are *much* older – waiting in your house upon some footling errand of honour which they regard as hugely important."

"Oh," said Derk. "Bother, I'd forgotten those elves. I'd better see them now."

He stood up again. This time, his knees seemed stronger, although they showed a tendency to forget they had kneecaps and to try to bend the wrong way. He steadied himself with one hand on the soaking hillside and watched the dragon stand up too. It stood by stages, front legs first and then, with a roaring grunt and a long puff of steam, heaving its back legs under it. The mayor's cows belled with terror. "I know how you feel," the dragon remarked, with its huge face now level with Derk's. "I'm off for a practice flight to see if I still need the stitches in this wing. If all goes well, I shall glide gently in pursuit of your fledglings. Expect to find me with them."

Derk nodded and managed to translocate himself home as far as the terrace. While he hung on to the outdoor table there for a moment, wild cackling from Big Hen and squeals from the pigs alerted him to the fact that the dragon was now in the air. He looked up and saw it pass above the house, dwarfing everything with its huge wingspread, grass green and glittering under the rain. It was a magnificent sight, even though it did fly rather slowly and stiffly.

"And this house has to be turned into a Citadel! Gods! The things I still have to do!" Derk groaned. He let go of the table and tottered to the dining room.

The six lordly elves there sprang up from behind after-dinner cups of coffee and bowed gracefully. "My liege lord," said the one with the golden circlet. "Greetings."

They were all nearly seven feet tall. Derk found them a bit much. He hurriedly pulled forward a chair and sank down on it – and it was just as well that he did. The pigs had scented Derk while they scented the dragon. With a frenzied drumming of trotters and much excited squealing, the whole herd swept in through the open front door and on into the dining room, where they threw themselves delightedly upon Derk. The youngest porker jumped painfully into his lap. The rest stood on hind trotters to bunt him with their snouts, or surged against his knees, while Ringlet, being the oldest and the cheekiest of the sows, fluttered up on to the table where she could look soulfully into Derk's eyes. Derk busily rubbed backs or scratched at the bases of stumpy wings and bawled at Ringlet to "Get down off there, pig!"

The effect on the elves was peculiar. The one with the circlet gaped and stood like a statue. His right hand was out, with its long, long index finger pointing stiffly at Ringlet. Derk would have been afraid he was trying to turn Ringlet to stone or something, except that the other five elves were falling about with laughter, crowing joyfully, slapping their elongated thighs and hugging one another, as pleased as the pigs were. Finally, the laughing five swung the elf with the circlet round and hugged him too – at which he joined in their laughter and began slapping the others on their backs. Old George, coming in hot pursuit of the pigs, skidded to a stop in the doorway and stared. Elves just did not behave like this normally.

"Forgive us, oh my lord!" gasped one of the five lesser elves. "Talithan, my Prince, has this moment seen his prophecy come true, and we are witness to it."

"Yes, truly, my lord," said Prince Talithan. He was

panting with emotion and tears were running from his great greenish eyes. "Pray forgive me. I must tell you that my brother long ago went adventuring to our neighbour world, where Mr Chesney has him a prisoner, thus forcing all elves to do his will. And when my father lately was sorrowing at this and saying that surely one day my brother must escape and come home to us, I answered him bitterly and scoffingly, saying, 'Yea, that day will come when pigs do fly!' for which reason my father grew angry and sent me to you, to become the Dark Lord's minion. And here, where I come, behold! Pigs fly!" He pointed at Ringlet again, who was still on the table.

"Well, I've been breeding them with wings for years now," Derk said. "Perhaps you shouldn't build your hopes on it."

"I do. It was spoken as a prophecy," Talithan replied.

"Have it your own way," Derk said. "What actually brings you here? I thought I'd made all the arrangements with your people."

Prince Talithan blotted away his tears on his green silken sleeve and bowed again. "That was when others were to lead your Dark Elves, my lord. I must now pay my respects as the new leader of Dark Elves, with these my captains, Gwithin, Loriel, Damorin, Fandorel and Beredin."

They were all names famous in Elflore. Derk did his best to bow respectfully while sitting in a chair under a heap of pigs. The Elfking, he thought, must have been very angry, if he sent people like this to be Dark Elves. It was considered a great disgrace. And this made it all the odder that Prince Talithan seemed so eager to pay his respects. Derk suspected there was more to this than the matter of flying pigs. "I am honoured," he said as he bowed.

"And I am distressed, my lord," said Talithan, "that you seem not quite to be well."

"I had a little disagreement with a dragon," Derk said, "but I am honoured at your concern, Your Highness." And now let's cut the cackle, he thought, and find out what they've really come for. "Indeed, you honour me too much. What is it you were waiting here for?"

"I do, in truth, my lord," Talithan admitted, "require a boon of you."

Ah, thought Derk. "You want to be released from having to be a Dark Elf, I imagine?"

"No, no, my lord!" Talithan protested. "To be allowed to serve you, obeying your every whim for a year and a day, is all I ask!"

"What?" Derk began to wonder if the Elf Prince was mad. Maybe this was why his father sent him to Derkholm. "Why would you want to do that?"

Talithan smiled, as only elves could smile, heart-rendingly, brilliantly. "You have a small wonder-horse with striped wings," he said, "that can talk and has the power to visit the secret home of the elves."

"Pretty?" said Derk. "Can Pretty do that?"

"He can indeed, my lord," one of the other elves – Loriel, Derk thought – assured him. "We found the small horse, all of us, astray in our hidden places, crying out that he was lost."

"That was probably a lie, if I know Pretty," Derk murmured. "And?"

"I crave the small horse, Pretty," said Prince Talithan. "Give him to me, of your bounty, and I will serve you in any way you wish."

"No," said Derk.

To Derk's consternation, Talithan vaulted the dining table, dislodging Ringlet in the process, and went down on one knee among the pigs at Derk's feet. "I beg you!" he said, amidst Ringlet's irritated grunting. "My lord, I implore you! Never, for three hundred years, have I felt such joy in or longing for a living creature! Life would have meaning for me once again, were I only to own this horse and train him and ride him in the sky! I would treat him better than I treat myself. You have my word."

"Oh, do get up," said Derk. "I said no. Pretty isn't a year old yet."

"That I know," Talithan said, still kneeling. "That is why I said I would serve you a year and a day for him. I will most faithfully serve you, lord, if you will only let me have Pretty at the end of that time." He stood up, towering over Derk. "This I swear to, in front of these thirty witnesses."

Thirty? Derk looked round at the pigs, each, even

Ringlet, with his or her snout turned wonderingly up to Talithan, then at Old George, looking quite as wondering, and then over at the five elves, who each had a hand over his heart, swearing witness. Finally Derk looked over at the kitchen door, where Lydda, Elda and Fran were squeezed together, staring at him accusingly.

"I was hoping to breed more winged horses with Pretty," Derk said weakly.

"That can be arranged," Talithan suggested.

"We would like winged horses too," said one of the other elves, Gwithin, Derk thought.

"*Herds* of them!" Damorin said raptly.

Talithan glanced across at him, rather coldly. "But none to match Pretty," he said. "Well, my lord?"

There was always the other winged foal Pretty's grandmother would give birth to, Derk thought. "Look," he said, "you may regret this. Pretty can be a dreadful handful."

"He is a colt of infinite spirit," Talithan said.

Besotted, Derk thought. But this was one way of ensuring that Querida could not get her hands on Pretty. Pretty would be far happier being doted on by an Elf Prince than shut in a pen at the University. "You could put it that way," he told Talithan. "Oh, all right. After a year and a day then, Your Highness."

"Witnessed!" chorused the five captains.

Talithan flung himself down on both knees and kissed Derk's hand. "My liege! Command me as you will!"

"Command him to leave so that you can go back to bed," Lydda murmured, not quite quietly.

Derk glowered at her. "Then please go and take up your tour position," he said to the elves. "Tour number two has an expendable one of you has to kill in a surprise attack tomorrow, and after that you had better look at the ten cities you'll be besieging."

"This shall be done!" Prince Talithan said, joyously leaping up. "Let us go, my captains."

They bowed deeply and filed out of the house. Old George began shooing the pigs out after them. Derk sat watching, feeling grey, the way elves made you feel when they left.

"Upstairs, Dad. Bed," said Lydda.

Derk was just getting up to obey Lydda when Callette stuck her large brown head in through the open window. "Why did we have six soppy men in a green haze out here just now?"

Lydda spread her wings and bounded straight up from the floor, tail lashing. "*Damn* you, Callette! Why do you have to turn up and stick your beak in *now*? We'd almost got him to go back to bed!"

"I need several hundred more clues," said Callette. "Five hundred and seventy-three, in fact. And I'm exhausted. I'm mean. I'm horrible. Don't argue with me."

Derk shunted his chair across the floor so that he could lean against the wall by the window. "Just a short word," he said soothingly to Lydda. "Elda, you'll find the right number of clues in a package in the top right-hand drawer of my desk. Yellow envelope."

"Thank goodness!" said Callette as Elda scooted off. "I didn't think I *could* fly all the way out to ask Shona for any! I went and asked Mum, and she tried, but she was too busy to think straight. And I don't know what to do. I'm not as good at flying distances as I thought. I do twenty miles and then I have to come down."

"You're a high energy flier, that's why," Derk explained. Callette's eyes were dull and her feathers scrawny. He could see she had lost weight. "Twenty miles is pushing it, for you. You should be coming down for a rest every fifteen miles, at least until you're older."

"But I'll *never* get all the clues done if I have to come down every fifteen miles!" Callette wailed. Lydda sighed and sat down very upright against the far wall. Her tail, folded across her front legs, tapped the floor. Beside her, Fran stood in the kitchen doorway with her stick-like arms folded, tapping one foot in a rather similar way. "Some of the places are in the desert," Callette protested, "or right over by the far ocean! Half the tours are going to be *past* the places before I get there!"

"It's all right," said Derk. "I never intended you to do the clues, Callette. I was going to get Blade to take me to do them in my spare moments." Callette's beak opened to point out that Blade was not available now. Derk said quickly, "And by the way, however tired and cross you are, you should never call a dragon names."

"This one deserved it," said Callette. "He thought of eating me. I hoped he would. I was upset." She lifted her beak and gave a great trumpeting howl. "I was so *slow* fetching a healer to you!"

"You were not so!" Lydda called out. "Don couldn't keep up with you."

"I flew and I flew and I hardly seemed to be *moving*!" Callette wailed.

Elda came scampering back with a large yellow envelope skewered to one talon. "What do you mean?" she said. "I saw you. I never saw even Kit go that fast."

"It seemed that way to Callette," Derk explained. "Callette, I think you were in a state of shock. Things happening very fast always seem to go very slowly then. I expect you saw every blade of grass you flew over."

"I did, you know!" Callette said wonderingly. "Pebbles too. I counted them. Was that shock?"

"Yes, and the need to go unusually fast," Derk said. "I'm very grateful, Callette."

"In that case," Callette said, looking a little brighter, "I'll get on with the clues. Give them here, Elda." She put her large feathery forearm in through the window.

Derk curled the talons inwards for her and pushed her arm back outside. "Not now. You need a rest. Let Lydda do it."

"*Me?*" Lydda sprang angrily across the room.

"*Lydda!*" Callette's beak stabbed towards Derk's face.

Derk sat between two angry griffins. He did not feel equal to this.

"I can't fly worth nuts!" Lydda snarled.

"She has to launch from the *window*!" Callette squawked.

"That dragon drove him mad. I knew it," Fran put in.

"You shut up, animal-woman!" Elda said venomously.

"Be quiet, all of you!" Derk managed what was nearly a shout. Luckily they were all surprised enough to obey him. He went on hoarsely, "Lydda can certainly do it. She's a long-distance flier. I should know. I made you that way, Lydda. If you go slow and take it steady and work up gradually to longer distances, you'll be doing a hundred miles without noticing after a week."

"Are you *sure*?" said Lydda. "I thought you were making fun of me."

"Of course I'm sure," said Derk. "I built you with a double-sized heart, massive wing-muscles, slow metabolism – you've got better circulation than Callette has, Lydda. You were a special model. I hoped you might manage to cross the ocean when you were full grown. But I wasn't going to bother you with that idea until you were older."

Lydda's beak bent and she looked uncertainly at her bulging front. "I'm fat."

"Most of it's muscle," said Derk, "though some *is* due to overeating, I admit. You'll have to work the fat off as you fly. And make sure you have a high place to launch from, until your muscles adjust, won't you?"

"I'll be careful. Should I go now?" Lydda asked.

"You'd make Mum's Lair on the first stage if you go now," Elda said wistfully.

"But study the clues when you get there," Derk advised. "They're all fairly well labelled, but you'll find some of them have to be spoken by people – the Emir, for instance – and you'll have to ask to speak to those people. And I don't have to remind you that some people find griffins alarming, do I? Be very polite, but ready to dodge in case of trouble."

"Ye – es." Lydda held out her extended claws and Elda carefully stuck the yellow packet on to them. Lydda looked at it dubiously. "But what about the broth?"

"I can do broth," Fran and Elda said together. They glared at one another.

"And if I'm travelling, I shall have to eat things *raw*," Lydda said.

"I eat things raw most of the time. It hasn't killed me," Callette said. "Go away and be *useful*, the way you always are!"

Callette's feelings were very clearly hurt. As Lydda, full of thoughts and importance, paced slowly towards the stairs, Derk turned hurriedly to the window again. "Callette, I need to turn this house into a Citadel, but I won't have time to do it all at once now. Have you any thoughts on how to design it section by section?"

Callette's crest came up and her eyes were brighter.

"In black stripes, living room first?" she asked. "You want it frowning? Evil towers?"

"Exactly," said Derk. "Lots of evil towers and monsters in the forecourt."

"You'll need drawings from all angles to show how to slot the stripes together. I'll go and do some now," Callette said briskly. "When do you want the first stripe?"

"Tomorrow?" asked Derk.

"Easy." Callette turned busily from the window just as Lydda launched herself from overhead, shouting a cheerful goodbye. Lydda was clearly saving energy. There was none of the usual frantic wing-whupping. "Huh!" said Callette. "You *really* think she won't come down in the next five minutes?"

"No," said Derk.

Indoors, Elda was saying pathetically, "What about *me*, Dad?"

"You can help me get back to bed," Derk said wearily.

CHAPTER TWELVE

✳

*I*t took Blade five hops to get back to where the soldiers were – almost as many as Derk would have needed – and the only good thing when he got there was that it had stopped raining. He arrived to find Pretty galloping about in a crowd of dogs, the soldiers yelling steadily, something about their human rights, and Kit, Don and Shona gathered anxiously round Barnabas.

Barnabas had brought three heaps of what looked like large black kites. Blade gathered that Barnabas had fetched them from store in the University. "What are they?" he asked.

"Leathery-winged avians," Barnabas said cheerfully. "They don't have to look real. They attack in the dark.

Your father not back yet? Then I hope you know how to animate the things. There are three Pilgrim Parties over in the coastal hills needing to be attacked tonight. I'd help if I could, but I haven't nearly finished the base camp yet."

He departed in his usual cheerful clap of noise, leaving Kit and Blade staring glumly at the kites.

"Well," Kit said at length. "We'd better get busy."

They spent the next three hours trying to animate the kites. Kit once or twice got the things two feet into the air and sort of flapping. Blade could not move them at all. They seemed to need a magic that was quite different from any Blade could do. Don suggested tying them to some of the magic reins and towing them through the air; but when Shona sacrificed more of her robe and Don tried it, the things behaved exactly like kites and simply soared. Nothing would persuade them to look as if they were attacking anything. The soldiers inside the dome of magic pointed and laughed and jeered. Then they chanted again. This time it was "Got no food. Got no food."

"It's entirely their own fault for refusing to come out," Shona said. "They could have been nearly to the food in the next camp by now. Take no notice. What do we *do* about these avians?"

"Get the wizards guiding the tours to animate them?" Blade suggested. "If three of us each take a pile and explain—"

They decided to do that. Kit stayed behind, sitting by the entrance to the camp with his head bent, glowering at the soldiers. Don and Shona set off straight away, Don flapping laboriously with a pile of kites clutched in his front talons, Shona with her pile balanced in front of Beauty's saddle. Blade stayed to milk the Friendly Cows and feed the dogs and set off an hour or so before sunset with his arms wrapped round the third awkward bundle of kites.

He came to what he was sure was the right place in the hills. Finn was in charge of this Pilgrim Party and Blade translocated to home on Finn. Blade was rather excited, to tell the truth, at the thought that at last he might see some of the Pilgrims all this fuss was about. He set down the bundle of kites, sat on a rock and waited. And waited. There was a big red sunset. Blade watched it. When the light was almost gone, he began wondering if this *was* the right place after all. It was pretty well dark when he heard someone coming slithering and scrambling down the hillside above him.

Blade stood up. "Over here!" he called.

"Oh, there you are. I was hunting all over," said Finn. "Sorry about this. Blasted tourists insisted on getting as far as they could. We're camped on the crest up there, a good couple of miles away. Got the avians?"

"Yes," said Blade. He gave Finn the careful explanation that he hoped Don and Shona were giving to the other Wizard Guides around now. Derk had been called north to a dragon. He had sent Blade with the kites and asked Finn to animate them.

"I suppose I could," Finn agreed, grudgingly. "Hard work after a day walking, but I suppose the things only have to swoop a bit and terrify people. Let's have a look."

Blade led him by feel to the pile of kites. It was quite dark by then. Finn conjured up a little ball of clear blue witchlight, making Blade acutely envious. He wished someone had taught him how to do that. Wistfully he watched Finn loose the ball of light to hover over the pile of kites, so that Finn could see to pick one up and turn its leathery shape over, muttering. Finn stopped muttering after a while and held the kite close under the floating light. "This has got some damn queer spell on it," he said. "I can't make it do a thing. Didn't your father give you a word to activate the spell at all?"

"No," said Blade.

"Or even tell you what *sort* of spell?" demanded Finn.

"No," Blade said again, wishing now he had thought of a way to say Barnabas had brought them the kites.

"Well, I can't work it," Finn said. He combed his fingers angrily through his long grey beard. "*Now* what do we do?"

"We'd better skip them," Blade said. "I'll take them away again. The Pilgrims don't know they're supposed to be attacked tonight by avians, do they?"

"I daren't skip them!" Finn said. His blue-lit face was horrified. "I don't know what the Pilgrims know, but I know one of them reports to Mr Chesney at the end of the tour. I've seen her taking notes. I'll be in real trouble if I skip anything!"

"Oh," said Blade. "All right. Give me another hour. Wait here."

"What are they supposed to think I'm doing here?" Finn demanded.

"Meditating," Blade said, and translocated away from what he saw was going to become a long and useless argument. He went to Derkholm again, in another set of translocations, landing goodness knew where in the dark, until around moonrise he finally arrived home, somewhere near the paddock. Big Hen promptly began cackling. "Shut up," Blade said to her. "Please." He felt his way along the fences to Derk's workshop and, by the growing moonlight, managed to find one of the big wicker hampers Derk sometimes used for taking pigs across country in. A blue ball of witchlight would have been a great help, he thought, as he heaved the hamper down the path beside the cages and the pens. Big Hen cackled again as he went by. And now the geese woke up and shouted Big Hen down. "Be quiet," Blade said to them. "I've come to talk to you. Shut up and listen."

The geese understood Blade perfectly. They just did not use human speech themselves. The noise from them died down, although there was one final sound from the rear, the sound of a goose sarcastically wondering when anything from a human was worth listening to.

"This," said Blade. "You know you always want to

peck people. How would some of you like to go and fly at some people tonight and really peck bits off them and scare them properly?"

There were thoughtful, wistful croonings from the geese. It was a nice idea. But people never let them do that. Blade didn't mean it. The noises grew harsher. There had to be a catch.

"Yes, there is a catch," Blade told them. "The people have swords and they'll try to hurt you back. You'll have to be really quick and cunning to hurt them without getting hurt yourselves. Come on. Who's clever enough to hurt humans? I want six volunteers." He opened the gate of the pen. He dumped the hamper on its side just beyond and opened the lid with an inviting creak. "Anyone volunteering just step in this hamper."

The geese thought about it, with sarcastic little nasal yodels. Blade could dimly see their white heads turning to one another, discussing it. Then one goose stepped forward.

"*Blade!*" said Callette, at that crucial moment, almost invisible in the dark. The goose stopped dead. "What are you doing? I thought it was thieves."

She made Blade give such a jump that he felt dizzy. He had forgotten how cat-quiet Callette could be. "Oh, *bother* you!" he wailed. "I need them for leathery-winged avians and now I'll *never* get them into the hamper!"

Callette considered this. "Yes you will," she said. "You should have come and asked me instead of creeping about.

You have to dare them. I always get them to do things by daring them to. Watch." She leant forward with her great head over Blade's shoulder. "Come on, geese. Scaredy old geese. Daren't sit in a hamper, then? Scared to climb in a big wicker box, are you?"

There was an instant rush for the hamper. Geese fought one another to get into it. Callette had certainly got it right, Blade thought, shutting the lid down on at least eight geese. Callette hit the gate of the pen smartly with her tail so that it shut and cut off the rest of the flock. "See?" she said, above their yells of protest. "Want help carrying it?"

"I can manage," Blade said, hoping this was true. "Thanks. That was brilliant."

"You're welcome," said Callette. "Dad's a lot better, by the way. He sent Lydda out with the clues."

"You're joking!" Blade said, sitting himself astride the restlessly creaking hamper.

"No I'm not," said Callette as Blade departed.

It took him ten hops to get back to Finn. Partly he was wondering if it would take Lydda twenty years or only ten to fly round the continent, partly he was truly tired. The geese were highly annoyed at the jerky journey. Finn was not pleased either.

"What have you been doing?" he demanded.

"Getting you some avians," Blade panted. He climbed off and bent down to the hamper. "I dare you," he said to it, "to chase every human in sight at the top of this mountain. Then I dare you to come back to the hamper. Coming back will be worse, because I'll be very angry if you've hurt anyone." He got behind the hamper, prudently, and took hold of the lid. "Stand beside me," he said to Finn, "and make them look leathery as they come out."

"I can do that perfectly well from here," Finn said crossly.

"No, don't!" Blade implored him. "Come back here!"

It was too late. A goose head and neck had already forced its way past the edge of the lid. The hamper was thrown open and the geese came out fighting. Finn never got a chance to make them look like anything. He ran. He ran away up the mountain with the blue light bobbing above him, his beard flying and his robes hauled up round his knees. The geese went after him like yelling white demons, some running, some flying, and all of them with their necks stretched straight and vicious. Finn screamed once or twice. When he and the geese were well out of sight, a lot more noise broke out, somewhere above in the rocks.

"Oh well," Blade said. He sat on the hamper and resigned himself to not seeing any Pilgrims tonight, and probably no more of the geese either.

The noise stopped after a while. Blade went on sitting there, tired out. Shortly, to his surprise, the geese came marching back in a brisk huddle, uttering satisfied little noises as they came down the hillside. If they had had hands to dust together, Blade felt they would be dusting them. It was obvious even by moonlight.

"Had fun, did you?" he asked.

They made noises like laughter.

"Good," said Blade. "Now I'm very angry and I'm going to carry you off to a place full of murderers. I dare you to get in the hamper again and let me." He held it invitingly open.

The geese climbed in, making scathing noises.

"Well, I warned you," Blade said. He sat on the lid and took himself and the geese back to the camp.

Shona and Don were back already, and Shona was getting worried. She had returned first and early, because the wizard she met had simply seized the armful of kites from her and marched angrily off with them. Don's wizard had not been able to animate his kites. "He didn't even do as well as Kit did," Don said. "And he was furious. He made me swoop over the Pilgrim Party in the dark instead, and it wasn't fun. They shot arrows at me. We ought to have thought of the geese before."

"I'll go and fetch the rest of them tomorrow," Blade promised. "But oh, gods! I *wish* you could have seen Finn legging it up that mountain!"

They settled down to sleep, chuckling. The soldiers, when Blade thought about it afterwards, were oddly quiet. He saw why, when he woke in the dew-cold back end of night to bedlam and horror.

What seemed to have happened was that someone

227

among the soldiers had worked out that the magics holding the walls of their dome to the ground were only skin deep, and particularly weak where Kit had amateurishly sealed the opening. They must have spent all the previous day making plans. When they were sure that the comings and goings with the kites were over for the night and everyone was truly asleep, they started walking up the wall opposite the opening. It must have taken hours. But with six hundred strong men persistently stepping on one side of it, the dome gave way in the end. When Blade woke, the camp was a misty egg shape, filled with dark, scrambling people at the end where the bulge was. The other end was rising into the air. The dark shapes of soldiers were ducking under that end and rushing out.

It was the geese who gave the alarm. Someone fell over their hamper, just beside Blade's sleeping bag, and the geese came out fighting again. At the noise, Pretty instantly took off into the dark sky, screaming, followed by Beauty. That roused the dogs, who began rushing around barking and yelping like the Wild Hunt itself, followed by Friendly Cows, bellowing distressfully.

Blade sprang up. The geese had driven off the soldiers who had been making for him, but while he was shaking himself loose from the sleeping bag he saw a seething dark crowd round Shona and realised that the soldiers had caught Don and were using Don to catch Kit. Two soldiers were standing on each of Don's wings. Don was screaming and slashing and pecking, but quite unable to fight them off, and Kit was making thundering dives from the greying sky, trying to help. Every time he dived, a cluster of soldiers round Don hacked at him with swords. Kit was so angry he was roaring. Blade could hardly believe the noise was Kit. He had never heard Kit make a noise like that in his life. He hovered, wondering who to help. Then Shona screamed. Blade realised he just had to trust to Kit's size and strength and ran towards Shona.

There were so many people round Shona that Blade could not even see which she was. He did the only thing he could think of and turned the carnivorous sheep in amongst them. It was very faintly light by then. The sheep were easy to see in their white huddle, and even easier to hear. They were yelling to be allowed to join in. Blade fumbled them loose from the magic reins around them and drove them fiercely towards the seething soldiers round Shona. He followed them in himself with the large stake the reins had been tied to. He banged heads and whacked arms and backs with it, and he seemed to make no difference at all. And all the time more soldiers were getting out from under the dome of magic. Don was being hurt, from his screams, and Kit's great roars went on and on. Blade felt helpless and hopeless, but he went on banging away.

Then all at once there was a roaring so much louder and deeper than Kit's that it seemed to come up from the earth and down from the sky at the same time. It came from all round, as if the whole world was roaring. Something massive and dark passed over Blade's head in a surge of hot air and hit the tipped-up dome of magic. SLAP. The dome fell back into place with a wallop that shook the turf under Blade's feet, tumbling yelling soldiers in a heap down the wall with it. The massive shape wheeled above the dome and swooped down upon Kit and Don. The great roaring became words.

"GET BACK INTO THAT DOME, SCUM!" Flames flickered as if the words were on fire.

The soldiers round Don looked up, saw the gigantic dragon powering down on them, and ran.

"It's Scales!" Blade said. "Oh, thank goodness!"

Scales somehow back-pedalled in mid-dive and whirled about. Hot fumes, grass and clods of earth blew every which way in its wind. Kit was thrown out of the air and landed on his back with a grunt, a few yards from Don.

"You! Little black cat-bird!" Scales bellowed at him. "Get up and go and guard the entrance to that dome!"

Kit picked himself up without a word and limped hurriedly over there. Don gathered himself into a heap, where he crouched, whimpering. Scales glided forward to land, lightly as a wren, beside the brawling group of men and sheep around Shona. The sheep instantly struggled out from among the men and fled in bleating panic. The men had not yet noticed anything was wrong. Scales stretched out his monstrous head above them.

"I said get back into that dome, scum!" he growled.

Their faces turned up to him. It was now light enough for Blade to see individual expressions on those faces – fear, anger, bravado, horror, but mostly annoyance at being interrupted.

"It's only one of their illusions," one said.

Scales bent forward, picked up the nearest black-clad body in his jaws, and crunched. The man jerked and let out the most horrible sound Blade had ever heard. It was not even a scream. It was the noise of something in more pain than it could stand. Scales tossed what remained of the man down on the turf. "In the dome or get eaten," he boomed. "Your choice."

The rest of the soldiers untangled themselves with incredible speed and set off at a run for the dome. Kit opened the entrance there to let them in. A goose that had accidentally got shut inside the dome blasted out in a cloud of white feathers just before Kit sealed it again. After that she was forced to stand with her back to everything, preening her dignity back, too irritated even to notice the rest of the geese, who stood at a tactful distance, hooting respectfully.

Blade was kneeling by Shona. Shona's hair was over her face and her clothes were torn. She had blood on one arm, but Blade thought that was from someone else's sheep bite. "Don't touch me!" she said.

"Are you all right?" Blade asked.

"Just don't *touch* me!" Shona said.

Blade looked doubtfully up at Scales.

"Leave her be. Go and help the black cat-bird," Scales rumbled. "I want you to hold the opening shut against the ones inside, while the cat-bird lets in the ones I bring back."

It was now white dawn, light enough to see that the distance in every direction was full of frantic cows and black-clad men running away as hard as they could. Scales took off again, in another blast of hot air and flying grass. He flew low in a huge, sweeping circle, at the limits of where a man could run to in the time. Every so often, there would be a billow of fire and some roaring in the distance, and Scales would come sweeping inwards, driving a panting huddle of men towards the dome, where Kit struggled to let them in, while Blade tried to stop the ones inside from getting out.

"No, *no*!" Scales said irritably, as he arrived behind the third huddle. "Balance your magics against one another. Brace them, and then sway just a bit to make the opening. Don't people do arm-wrestling any more these days?"

"Oh, I *see*!" Blade and Kit both exclaimed. "Like that!"

"Yes. Like that," Scales growled, and swung round into the distance again.

By the time Scales drove in the last panting, exhausted crowd of soldiers, Blade and Kit had become quite good at the armwrestling style of magic. They were congratulating one another and feeling nearly cheerful again, until Scales rumbled, "Don't just stand there grinning, cat-bird, boy! You've work to do. You need to be on the march by sun-up."

They stared at him disbelievingly. "We do?" said Kit.

"I'm worn out," Blade protested. "We hardly got any sleep—"

"Got to keep these murderers busy," Scales explained, "or lose grip on them. They've no food here, they're angry, and they nearly got you once. Understand? And it's no good me trying to round up all your horses and your cows. They just panic."

"But Don's hurt," Blade objected, "and Shona's—"

"I'll see to them now," said Scales. His wings folded with a leathery, slithering, final-sounding slap. He turned and stepped delicately across the trampled grass towards Don. Kit and Blade watched his spiked green tail slide around in front of them and then followed it mournfully. You did not disagree with dragons.

"Sprained, are they, or what?" Scales was saying to Don. "Move them, yellow cat-bird. Come on!"

Don miserably flopped his wings about. "They *stood* on them!"

"More fool you, for letting them," Scales boomed. "Where're your instincts? First rule for fledglings is: Get airborne at the first sign of trouble. Didn't anyone teach you that?"

"No, sir," said Don.

"Comes of being brought up by ignorant humans, I

suppose," Scales growled. "Remember it in future. You too, little black one."

Kit glowered. "Yes. Sir. My name's Kit."

"Just remember it," Scales rumbled. "And you can be rude when you're my size, but not before." Blade looked at Kit unbelievingly. Kit was *not* going to be as big as Scales! Surely? "No, but he'll be half as big again as he is now before he's through," Scales remarked. "It's in the size of his bones. You'll be that big too, yellow one. Now get those wings moving. Nothing's broken. They're only bruised."

Don cautiously opened his wings. His neck arched in pain. He screeched.

"Flap them. Keep fanning them," Scales ordered unfeelingly. Don gave him a piteous look. "To get the blood moving," Scales explained impatiently. "I can't help you unless you help yourself."

Don ground his beak sideways with a wretched, cracking sound and managed to flap his wings, slowly, dolorously. Scales put his vast head on one side and watched. Don's wings began to move faster, and then more freely, until, in a second or so, they were truly fanning. "They're all right now! What did you do?" he said.

"Can't explain," rumbled Scales. "Encouraged nature, I suppose. Keep fanning while I see to the other one."

Blade had been worrying, at the back of his mind, at the way they had all left Shona lying beside that horrible crunched corpse. But when they went over there, there was no corpse. He wondered if Scales had eaten it in a spare moment. He felt rather sick.

"Don't touch me!" Shona cried out as they all came near.

"Sit up! Look at me!" Scales thundered.

Shona sat up as if the ground had burnt her and stared upwards, cringingly, into the dragon's huge eyes. After a moment or so, her body straightened and seemed to relax at the same time. "Oh, that's better!" she said. "Everything seems – a long time ago, somehow."

"Best I could do," Scales rumbled. He sounded slightly apologetic. "Try to keep it long ago."

"I *will*!" Shona said devoutly. "Blade, can you fetch me my spare clothes? I'm so bruised – no, I'm not! How did that happen? I'll get my clothes. You lot go and round up the animals."

Blade found himself beaming with relief. Shona was back to normal, and her old bossy self.

CHAPTER THIRTEEN

*

*I*t took most of an hour to round up the horses. Pretty, naturally, gave more trouble than the rest put together. Then they had to find the Friendly Cows, who really needed to be milked – but no one had time or energy – and then fetch back the dogs – who had in a bewildered way decided they ought to take off into the wild as a pack – and finally to assemble the geese – who refused utterly to get back in their hamper: they had decided it was dangerous in there. Nobody bothered to look for the carnivorous sheep.

"I'm glad to see the back of them, frankly," Shona said, energetically buckling baggage on to horses. "I've always thought they were one of Dad's failures."

"Dad may be upset all the same," Don said, humping his shoulders. His wings still hurt.

"Let him be," said Shona. "There. All ready to go at last."

Everybody looked at Scales. He was lying with his muzzle on his front feet, asleep. Two peaceful wisps of smoke curled from his nostrils. He was, Blade thought, very old even for a dragon and perhaps all this activity had been too much for him. Blade wished he could go to sleep too. He was so tired. Instead, he mounted Nancy Cobber and rode as near to Scales as Nancy would go. He gave a long-distance cough. Scales opened one vast green-gold eye. "Ready to leave?"

"Yes, sir," said Blade.

"Aren't we respectful all of a sudden!" Scales rumbled. He rose up. Nancy Cobber backed off and tried to rear until Blade rode her hastily out of the way. "Black cat-bird!"

"Yes?" said Kit. He was not going to call Scales "sir" again even if Scales ate him for it.

"Go and open the camp entrance as soon as I get the murderers moving," Scales ordered.

Sullenly, Kit prowled off and sat himself in front of the place where the dome opened. Scales went to the other side of the dome. It suddenly seemed a tiny, flimsy thing beside him. All the soldiers inside crowded down to Kit's end, away from Scales.

"You know, I think we've lost a few," Don said to Shona. "It was fuller than that last night."

"Too bad!" said Shona.

Scales thrust his snout at the dome where it met the ground. He worried at it for a moment, and then pushed his head and great forequarters underneath it and inside, so that the dome wobbled above his spiny back like a soap bubble. "UP, SCUM! OUT OF THE DOOR! QUICK MARCH!" Smoke came billowing from his mouth with each order.

What with Scales inside and the camp filling with smoke, the soldiers had little choice. Coughing and staggering, they crowded towards the entrance as Kit opened it and streamed outside in a great untidy gaggle. Scales took his head out from inside and trampled clean across the dome, bellowing, "FORM LINES, THERE! MARCH! LEFT-RIGHT, LEFT-RIGHT!" The last soldiers squirted out in front of him. Kit leapt aside and Scales rumbled at him, "Keep them in a line your side. MARCH, YOU SCUM!" he howled to the soldiers. "LEFT-RIGHT, LEFT-RIGHT!"

It was wonderful how quick and straight and far those men could march, Blade thought as he followed, surrounded by dogs and cows, if a huge dragon came after them and made them do it. They streamed across fields, moorlands, an arid corner of the wastelands, and then across further moors, all that morning. The geese, who liked to see humans being bullied, kept up beside Scales, alternately flying and waddling. Don was commanded to keep the line straight on the other side from Kit's. Blade wearily drove cows. He was utterly and hugely relieved when, about midday, Scales bellowed, "HALT! SIT DOWN! REST STOP!" and came gliding back towards the cows. Blade was even more surprised that the soldiers not only sat down but stayed sitting.

"Better milk those cows," Scales rumbled, stopping a tactful distance from the horses. "Give the pails to the cat-birds to give to the soldiers when you fill them."

He certainly does give his orders! Blade thought, sliding down from Nancy. Shona dismounted from Beauty, protesting, "We haven't been bothering with lunch."

"I know. They've been grumbling about it all morning," Scales said. "They've worked up quite a grievance. Do you carry any food for them?"

"Not really," Shona explained. "There's food in the camps and we've been relying on that."

"Have to make do with what we've got then," said Scales. He settled down into a great green hump halfway between the cows and the soldiers and seemed to be dozing comfortably while Blade and Shona got busy milking and handing swirling white pailfuls to Kit and Don as they were ready.

"They don't like milk. They want beer," Don reported.

"They get beer in camp this evening," growled Scales.

There were no further protests, but when Kit alighted beside Blade, clanging down his empty pail and holding his talons out for the full one, he said, "I don't understand. We'd only got the four pails, hadn't we? And all four of them are in among the soldiers full of cheese. They're guzzling it in hunks."

Blade gave a puzzled look towards the soldiers and saw one of Scales's great eyes closing in a wink. Kit was in time to see it too. "Oh," he said to Blade. "More encouraging nature."

The milking was done at last. There was enough milk left for Shona and Blade, except that the milk in the bottom of Blade's pail was in the form of a small round cheese.

"You prefer that to milk, don't you?" Scales said, when Blade looked at him. "I'll have one of those cows now."

"But—" said Blade.

"If I eat it in front of the murderers," Scales explained, "there'll be no arguing when I tell them what to do next."

Scales did just that, with horrid rendings and mooings and much blood. To add to the effect, he tore off two large lumps and tossed them to Don and Kit. Both griffins were so savagely hungry by then that they ate the pieces ravenously. The soldiers went very quiet. But Blade counted the cows and found that they still had the same number. He rather thought Kit and Don might have been eating cheese.

"I don't propose to enquire," said Shona. "But I didn't realise dragons could do this."

"Mum said some of the old ones were quite good at magic," Blade told her.

"And Scales *is* old," Shona agreed. She sighed. "If I'd gone to Bardic College when I was supposed to, I'd probably have learnt dragonlore by now. I might know all about Scales. He could have been a legend in his time for all I know."

Legend or not, Scales got them across the moors to the camp long before nightfall that evening, and the following night too. The next day they toiled briskly across much more broken terrain, filled with woods and small rivers, and arrived into camp rather later. The soldiers cheered. Inside the mist of the dome were the rows of barrels they had come to expect from the previous two nights.

"Thank goodness!" Shona said, sliding off Beauty. "We can *rest* while Blade does the avians." Blade had been taking the geese round to all three tours, because that was the easiest way to do it.

"Not much rest tonight," Kit said, groaning with weariness. "We've got the first Wild Hunts today."

"Tonight? Really?" said Don. "Have we been going that long?"

"Fraid so," said Kit.

Blade looked at the row of geese. They looked up from eating something in the grass and dared him to put them in that hamper again. "I *can't*," he said. "I'm too tired."

"Nonsense!" boomed Scales.

"Let's eat anyway," Shona sighed.

They did that. Blade fell asleep over the last of his

supper, despite rowdy noises from the soldiers around the beer barrels, and woke at sunset feeling much better. The geese, to his surprise, were sitting smugly in the hamper, waiting for him. They were not going to miss their chance to bully humans.

"All right," Blade said to them. "I bet you don't dare bully three lots again."

They made scathing noises. Easy-peasy.

Blade left as Kit was hauling himself off the ground and preparing to do the illusions for the Wild Hunts. When he returned astride his hamper of highly satisfied avians – they had sent three wizards racing up three different mountains faster than ever, and Blade had still not set eyes on a single Pilgrim – Kit was still trying to do illusions. He had given himself red eyes. He had transformed the Friendly Cows into great black horned things with ordinary eyes. Nothing would persuade the eyes of the cows to flame as Kit wanted. And the dogs kept shaking themselves irritably and losing their black coats and burning eyes in a shower of misty droplets. None of the horses would show the slightest change. Kit was looking a bit wild over it all.

"You look tired, Blade. You don't need to come," Shona said kindly.

"But I *want* to!" Blade insisted. He was dying to pretend to be the Dark Lord.

"Oh *curses!*" shrieked Kit, as the dogs all shook themselves normal again.

Scales was lying up against the dome of the camp, as he had taken to doing, to make sure the soldiers behaved themselves. He was watching Kit's efforts as sarcastically as the geese were. "If I may make a suggestion?" he boomed.

"What?" snapped Kit.

"These game-playing Pilgrims are going to see very little in the dark," Scales pointed out. "You are black. You propose to turn the yellow cat-bird black, and you have a winged horse that is black. The other flying horse, though tiny, has wings that look like the ribs of a skeleton. All you really need to do is make the rider of the black horse black—"

"That's me," Shona put in.

"—then you put yourselves in the air in front and bring the dogs along as they are to make a noise," Scales continued. "I assure you this will be enough. The cows are far too slow to keep up."

"I suppose that's true," Kit admitted.

"But what about *me*?" said Blade.

"I require you to stay here," said Scales.

Somehow there was no arguing with that. Blade had to watch, bitterly disappointed and furious with Shona for hogging the post of Dark Lord, while two black griffins with fiery eyes – Kit did not think Scales should have things all his own way – and a horned rider mounted on a winged horse all flew slowly away northwards accompanied by a posse of excited dogs and one wildly skittish flying foal. As soon as Kit was a mile or so away, the black horned monsters he had left in the camp melted into the Friendly Cows again.

"*Why* do you want me here?" Blade said sullenly to Scales.

"One of you needs to be properly rested in case of trouble," Scales pointed out. "You are the most useful, because you can translocate."

It made perfect sense, but it did not prevent Blade from feeling like Cinderella – or worse, Lydda. "What did you do with the soldier you crunched?" he asked resentfully. "Eat him?"

"What soldier—? Oh, I remember," Scales answered. "No, that was an illusion. I do not care much for the taste of human."

"Huh!" said Blade. Scales had an answer for everything. Blade hunched down by the camp fire, intending to sulk, but the sulk quickly passed into staring at flames and the staring passed into sleep, almost in no time. Blade slept for three hours or more, until he was woken by the return of the Hunt, the dogs weary but exultant, Beauty and Pretty with foam under their wings, and the rest very cheerful indeed.

"Hey, that was fun!" Don said, plumping down by the fire. "They didn't half *run*!"

"Marvellous!" laughed Shona. "I want to make a song about it."

"Me too," said Kit, mantling hugely in the shadows beyond Beauty. "A war song!"

Blade was somehow the one who had to rub Beauty down and try to get a rug on to Pretty. Glumly he handed out rewards to panting dogs and put down water, feeling more than ever like Cinderella.

"You can go tomorrow, Blade," Shona told him generously.

"Thanks a bunch!" said Blade.

But when he saw how tired everyone was the next day, he had to admit – grudgingly – that Scales might have been right. The dogs groaned and limped. Pretty hung his head and refused to eat. "Been too silly last night," he told Blade. Shona was saddle-sore and even Don was rather stiff. Blade would have felt more sympathetic if they had not all still been so cheerful. Kit might grunt every time he moved his wings, but his eyes gleamed and his crest was up cockily as he strutted over to open the camp when Scales got the soldiers walking again. "MOVE, SCUM! MARCH!"

Scales must have spiked the drink in those barrels to keep the soldiers quiet. They came out of their camp grey-faced and shambling, all with the most evident hangovers.

Shona laughed heartily. "It's nice to see so many people looking worse than I feel!"

Blade disagreed. He could feel the soldiers hating everything, the marching, Scales and Kit for making them march, this world, the people who had sent them to this world – everything and everyone. They were ready to murder someone for it. It made Blade nervous. He rode along braced for trouble.

So it happened that Blade was the well-rested and alert one who responded at once when, about the middle of the morning, there came a loud, rhythmic banging from a clump of trees over to the left of their march. He kicked Nancy Cobber and set off to investigate as soon as he heard it. Don only responded when Scales bellowed, "*Go and see what the trouble is!*" By the time Don's rather stiff loping brought him up to Nancy Cobber, Blade was halfway to the trees, and there was shouting coming from there, as well as banging.

"Some kind of fight?" Don panted.

Blade had his mouth open to agree, when an obviously terrified small pony with a large basket strapped to its back burst out from among the trees and careered towards the marching soldiers. It saw Scales. It screamed. It tried to stop and turn, but lurched and unbalanced the basket on its back. The next second it was down, rolling and kicking, frantically fighting its way out of the straps that held the basket. Blade and Don broke into a gallop. But long before they could get close enough to help, the pony kicked itself free, struggled to its feet and went racing away southwards. Blade and Don were left staring at the basket, lying in the grass, spilling gold cups, caskets, plates, bracelets, coronets and necklaces. Every object was most beautifully made and most were studded with precious stones.

"Robbers," said Blade. "Come on." He shook up Nancy Cobber again and galloped towards the trees.

There were five more ponies with baskets under the trees. Standing in a ring with their backs protectively to the ponies were six small men, whose heads only came up to the waists of the ones attacking them. The attackers wore the shiny black armour that Blade knew so well. Here were some of the soldiers they had lost three days ago.

"Uh-oh!" said Don and took to the air, remembering Scales's advice.

Nancy Cobber was hard to stop. Blade was forced to go on, into the midst of the fight. The dwarfs all had big axes, with which they were lustily hacking and parrying – except for one, who was banging for help with his axe on a large gold plate – but they were evidently losing. The soldiers attacking them were twice their size. Blade did not even have a sword. As Nancy Cobber thundered into the mêlée, all he could think of to do was to yell, so he yelled, trying to make his voice sound like a dragon's.

It partly worked. Several of the attackers turned towards him. This gave two of the dwarfs a chance to swing their axes at legs. One soldier went down. But two more came for Blade with swords. Blade had it quite clearly in his mind that he was going to be dead, when Don came crashing down through the branches overhead. He was near and sudden enough to seem huge, and black against the light, and clapping his wings mightily to stay

247

hovering. Blade thought he was Kit for a moment. The soldiers made the same mistake.

"Hell!" said one. "It's that black sod of a griffin. Get him!"

But Don got him. Don was about the size of a lion and his strength, when he cared to use it, was the strength of a lion. He seized that soldier and threw him to the ground. He threw another on top of him as the first man tried to get up. That made three attackers down and was enough to turn the fight the other way. The dwarfs became very busy swatting with the flats of their axes. The one who had been beating the plate joined in too, and within a minute all six men in black armour were rolling on the ground, groaning. Blade snatched the coil of magic reins that he always kept hung on Nancy's saddle these days, slid off Nancy and made sure that he had a loop of reins securely wrapped round each soldier.

"Foof!" said Don, landing beside him. "I thought you were dead any second there. Want me to drag them over to Scales?"

"Easier if you wait until they can walk," Blade said. None of the soldiers was badly hurt. The first one down was already trying to sit up.

Meanwhile the dwarfs were standing around making those throat-clearing sounds people make when they are embarrassed at having to say thank you. Blade could see why. They were warlike, strong-looking little men, with thick legs and big shoulders. Their hair and beards were plaited into several dozen skinny pigtails that were each woven with clacking bones and tufts of red wool, and they wore steel caps and breastplates. Their axes looked formidable. Blade could see they were the sort of folk who would think they ought to cope with six large attackers without needing help. Possibly they could have done, if they had not had to protect the ponies.

"Your other pony dropped its load out on the grass and then bolted, I'm afraid," he said, to cover their embarrassment.

The one who had been banging the plate sighed. "Typical," he said. "This mission has been a pig's breakfast right from the start. You'd think we'd offended one of the gods. We had a landslide coming out of the mountains, we spent the next day mired in the rains, yesterday was all horseflies and mosquitoes, and now this! If this tribute gets to Lord Mr Chesney in one piece at the right time, I shall be so surprised you can cut off my beard and call me a giant. I kid you not!"

Don and Blade exchanged startled glances. "Excuse me," said Don. "Why do you have to get tribute to Mr Chesney?"

"We do it every year. He requires it. He's our overlord," said another of the dwarfs, surprised and rather gruff about it.

"Then – er – where have you come from exactly?" Blade asked.

"Fastness in the Mossy Mountains. Borders of King Luther's land," said a third dwarf. "Why? You want to make anything out of it?"

"Of course not," Blade said quickly. He and Don frowned at one another, both feeling that something was not quite right. "I – er – just wondered how much further you had to go," he said.

"Oh, only as far as the nearest ocean," the first dwarf said, with angry talkativeness. "That town where the Pilgrim parties come through. They're calling it Gna'ash or something this year, aren't they? We're supposed to get there when the last tour goes out, while the demon's still got the portal open. Then the tour people take the tribute through and we leg it back home again. Just one of those little tasks that keep life interesting. If we get there, of course. I'm not counting on it this trip."

"But does Mr Chesney *own* the land where your fastness is, or something?" Blade asked, truly puzzled.

The dwarfs looked at one another. Some shrugged. The gruff one scratched among his pigtails and replied, "Don't think so. We're in King Luther's land if we're anywhere."

"Then – er – shouldn't you be taking the tribute to King Luther?" Blade asked.

All the dwarfs laughed. "No way," said the talkative one. "Tribute goes to Lord Mr Chesney because he's Dark Lord of the world. I thought everyone knew that."

Blade nodded, thinking the dwarf was probably right,

but Don said indignantly, "No he's not! My father's Dark Lord!"

The dwarfs all laughed again. "Oh yes?" said one. "I do see a strong family resemblance there."

Don's beak opened angrily. Blade kicked his front leg to shut him up. Luckily, at this moment Shona rode up on Beauty, surrounded by dogs and leading the trembling, sweating little pony. The dwarfs all started clearing their throats again. The talkative one even managed to say, "Much obliged—" before Bertha discovered that his face was just at licking height for dogs.

"Come along," Blade said to Don. The men in black were now sitting up, holding heads and rubbing legs and glowering. Blade mounted Nancy Cobber again and told Don to drag them away.

"We were happy to help," Shona was saying charmingly as Blade headed for the huge green bulk of Scales at a sharp trot.

"What was that about?" Scales wanted to know as soon as Blade was near enough.

"Six of the soldiers who escaped the other day were trying to rob some dwarfs," Blade reported. "We got them. Don's bringing them. But do you know, Scales, those dwarfs are carrying a *fortune* in golden things! They say it's for Mr Chesney and—"

"I thought I smelt gold." Scales's vast head swivelled round towards the trees. The stretch of grassy land between was now dotted with figures, Shona and Beauty in front, surrounded by cheerful dogs, and Don further back, holding the reins in his beak and ploughing forward to drag the resisting group of men in black. But Scales's head was turned towards the three dwarfs busily picking up cups, plates and bracelets and packing them back into the basket. Blade had forgotten what dragons were like about gold. He began to feel anxious. "Did they say why?" Scales asked.

"They said it was tribute because Mr Chesney's Dark Lord of the world," Blade said.

Scales went very still, with that stillness that suggested muscles making ready to spring.

"But that can't be right, can it?" Blade asked anxiously.

Scales's wings rattled in a shrug. "They must have made a mistake," he rumbled. "I think we'll feed the murderers now, since we're stopped anyway. Go and milk cows."

After lunch they pressed on again, leaving the dwarfs to go the opposite way, to Blade's relief. He had not altogether trusted Scales to leave the gold alone. The soldiers' hangovers seemed to have abated with exercise. They marched over open grassland, where trees clustered beside small streams, at quite a brisk pace, with Scales steadily crawling behind, and by evening they were beginning to see mountains in the distance ahead. By this time Blade was ashamed that he had not trusted Scales over the gold. Dragons nowadays did not have hoards – except things like Callette's gizmos for the tours – and Scales seemed to be adapting to modern ways. He had to be, Blade thought, or he would not be helping them like this.

"Helping!" said Kit, when Blade mentioned this to him. "I call it taking over!"

The next camp came into sight soon after this. Barnabas had set it up almost tastefully beside trees that were beginning to turn gold or faint orange. Everyone made for it thankfully. As soon as the soldiers were inside and Blade had taken the animals to drink at the nearby stream, Scales beckoned Kit and made Kit walk with him all round the camp, showing him how to seal the magics of the dome more securely into the ground.

"Wizard who did these camps did a rather sketchy job," he explained when they had finished. "But you should be safe for the night now. I'm off for a while. I'm getting hungry and I fancy a hunt. I'll see you soon."

He spread his wings, took three light running steps forward, and soared away into the wide evening. The soldiers, with their faces misty blue from the dome magics, lined the curving wall and made rude gestures after him. The rest stared after him in alarm.

"He's gone after those dwarfs," said Don.

"I'm afraid he has," Blade agreed.

"And maybe he hasn't," Shona disagreed cheerfully. "He gave me a sort of insight after I – when I looked into his eyes that time, and I was rather amazed at how civilized and learned he was."

"Anyway, we can't stop him," Kit pointed out.

Blade knew Shona was wrong. He knew Scales was hunting dwarfs. The knowledge took the edge off even the Wild Hunt that night, though that was splendid fun. Blade came back with his hamper of satisfied avians and took off again with a black griffin on either side of him. With the weight of illusory horns on his head, Blade rode a winged black horse in the freshness of an autumn night under a growing yellow moon. Pretty had refused to come, but, on the ground below, the dogs bayed and yelped and belled and made a wonderful din crashing through brushwood to keep up. Ahead of them, three times over, a small crowd of people made even more noise, running for their lives. The Pilgrims were never near enough to see, to Blade's annoyance, and the Hunt had to turn back each time after the tourists had pelted over a bridge across one of the rivers, because Kit said the black book said the Black Rider was not supposed to cross running water. But it was still great fun. It would have been even greater fun if Blade had not kept thinking of small pigtailed men being crunched the way Scales had pretended to crunch that soldier.

CHAPTER FOURTEEN

*

Querida sat alone in the conference hall of the University, working at the long table. Today she had managed to get from her house to this building by supporting herself on one real crutch and a magical one that she could handle with her broken arm. But it had been hard work and the stairs up to her study had defeated her. The bones were a long way from healed yet. She had become pretty weak during her healing coma, too, and the effort tired her. She wished now – as she had wished last time she had broken a bone – that she had not insisted on the coma. But she was so bad at bearing pain.

She wished she could find someone to bring her a hot healing drink. The janitor had said he would do what he could, poor fellow, but it was not really his job and he did not know where cups or kettles were kept. There was no one else about. The healers and the male wizards were all out with the Pilgrim Parties. Normally during tour-time the place would be abuzz with female wizards, who usually took this opportunity to use the equipment, but this year they were away on urgent business as well. In fact, the silence and emptiness of the University was a very satisfactory sign that the hasty arrangements Querida had made before she insisted on the coma were being acted upon.

She considered her plans. Querida's feeling had always been that Oracles helped those who helped themselves. The tours were not going to end just like that. So, in order to help the prophecies along a bit, she had all the women wizards out around the continent organising mistakes, failures and trouble for Pilgrim Parties. She was trusting Derk to make a thoroughly bad job of being Dark Lord, and it was always possible that if things went badly enough wrong, Mr Chesney might decide the Pilgrim Parties were unworkable. But there was that demon of his. Querida's plans there hinged upon the fact that demons were very legal-minded. For this reason, the women wizards were also looking for anything – any small thing – that the tours were doing which was not in the contract. Querida could then confront the demon and tell it that Mr Chesney had broken the law and it was free to go. If Mara did her part as well, then Mr Chesney would be faced with three ways the tours had broken down. Surely that would be enough to make even Mr Chesney give up.

Anyway – she pulled forward pen and paper – this accounted for the way the place was so strangely quiet and empty. Better get on. Almost the only people in town were the bards. But they had flatly refused either to join the tours or help Querida stop them. Their college was out on the edge of town and they were presumably all inside it sulking.

"And we can do without artistic tantrums," Querida murmured.

Her small dry voice rang through the great silence of the building.

"I wish I didn't talk to myself," she said. "I keep making myself jump. Heigh ho. Down to work."

She had sixty or more pigeon messages to write. She hoped the janitor was up to fixing them to pigeons – the *right* pigeons – and setting the birds loose. She had no faith in the man. But first she would have to get down to reading some at least of the great stack of messages that the janitor – after having it explained several times – had fetched from her study and piled on the long table.

Querida sorted through the stack, awkwardly one-handed. Surely one of them by now would be from a woman wizard reporting a breach of contract. *Surely*. About half the messages were indeed from women wizards, but they all seemed to be saying "We have done what you said. What do we do next?" There did not seem to be one from Mara and there *ought* to have been. Mara had promised to deliver a suitable miniature universe before the sieges started. Better write to Mara at once. And to the woman in the Emirates. Oh, here was a message from Barnabas.

Querida unfolded it clumsily. Barnabas wrote that he was worried. Derk was turning out to be much more efficient than either of them had expected. "With this in mind," Barnabas wrote, "I have jinxed the avians and made sure the containing camps for the army are really flimsy. I am putting the base camp in the wrong place and will probably jinx that too, but I have to report that so far these measures have had little effect."

Hm. Querida leant back in the large chair, considering. This was annoying. She had been *relying* on Pilgrims complaining about the Dark Lord. Perhaps it was a blessing in disguise that she had been injured herself before she could help Derk either with a demon or a god – or maybe it was the work of the Oracles, in which case it was possibly worth all the pain. She had better drag her heels a bit over demons and gods – while pretending to be helpful of course – and it might be an idea to nag and bully Derk as well. In Querida's experience, most men responded badly to bullying. It got them making mistakes. Mara's activities ought to unbalance the man too, and get him doing things wrong. Derk *had* to make mistakes. *Had* to.

"Because we have *got* to win, now we are showing

our hand," she mumured. "Once Mr Chesney realises there is a fight on, we could all be in terrible trouble."

This time her voice did not ring out entirely on its own. There were other noises too, most of it a considerable scuffling outside the hall. Perhaps the janitor had actually managed to find a kettle and was bringing her a drink at last. If so, by the sound, he was making heavy weather of it.

Querida turned enquiringly towards the doorway, just as a scrawny grey wolf, with its hackles up in a hedge all down its spine, came backing in through it.

"Oh, really, Wilkie," she said, "do please try to control yourself. What's the matter?" The janitor, being a werewolf, was always liable to change shape in moments of stress. "Assume your proper form!" Querida snapped at him. "I can't talk to a wolf."

The wolf stood humbly on its hind legs and became a man, a hairy man who did not look very bright. Wilkie hitched his trousers – a wolf's waist being lower than a man's – and said indignantly, "I told it you were sick, ma'am, I told it you were busy, I told it go away, and it won't take no for an answer!"

"What won't?" Querida snapped.

Wilkie pointed to the doorway. A huge brown bird head ducked itself down there, under the lintel, and a large round shiny brown eye rolled to look at Querida. Well I never! Querida thought. One of Wizard Derk's griffins. *My* griffin. The big female.

"Let it come in," she said. "Then you may leave us, Wilkie."

As the griffin lowered its body and squeezed its wings inwards to get through the doorway, Querida scarcely noticed the janitor shuffle warily around it and depart. She had eyes only for this huge, beautiful creature. It had caught her fancy utterly the day that Mr Chesney came. She loved the soft browns of the headfeathers and the creamy-white bars on the great wings. Now she saw there was grey in the bars too, greenish-grey, and that the same grey-green mixed with the brown in the massed feathers of the neck and outlined the alert brown eyes. The most beautiful thing about it, though, was the way the eagle-part phased so gracefully into the pale brown lion-part – a most elegant deep chested lion-part with a slim and muscular rear – so that you did not think of the creature as a mixture but as a whole. She had to admit Wizard Derk had made a fabulous beast here. This one was even more superb than the little winged colt. Querida lusted to own this creature, to bury her hands in those soft-coloured feathers, maybe even to ride on its back through the air.

"I'm not an it, I'm a she," said the griffin. "My name's Callette."

"Oh," said Querida. "I was not aware you could speak."

"Of course I can," said Callette. "How did you think I was going to give you the message from Mum if I couldn't?"

She ducked her head and removed a leather pouch that was hanging round her neck. Even in her surprise, Querida was glad to see the pouch removed. It spoiled the griffin's beautiful lines. "I – er – remember you going to considerable lengths to suggest you were dumb," she retorted. "And I assumed the message was in that pouch."

Callette wrapped her talons in the thongs of the pouch and kept it between her front feet. "This is the miniature universe you wanted," she said. "Not talking was an idea of Kit's. He often has silly ideas. It served him right when he fell through the roof. But I've got a message from Mum as well. Do you want to hear it, or not?"

Querida looked at her, sitting like a great tall cat with her tufted tail wrapped across the pouch between her shapely, taloned feet and her barred wings neatly folded. And Querida longed, yearned, lusted for ownership of Callette. "Yes, I do very much want to hear it."

Callette looked at Querida in turn, carefully, turning her head to focus on Querida first with one eye, then with the other. It was not something griffins needed to do, but Callette had the habit from her bird-ancestry and tended to do it to double check on things she felt cautious about. "Mum said I wasn't to tell you straight away," she said.

"I take it we're talking of Mara," Querida said irritably. "Why not straight away?"

Callette nodded. "Dad told me to take Elda to Mum's Lair, but he was in a hurry and he told me to *think* about the message, because Mum was sure to want me to tell you. So I thought, and I asked Mum. And she told me to tell you that if you try to own me or keep me here, either by a spell or any other way, Mum won't do any of the things you asked her to do. And the universe in this pouch will just dissolve."

Disappointment made Querida cross. Mara had her over a barrel. She *needed* Mara. What a *nuisance*! Now she would have to waste time being very cunning *and* in placating Mara. "I see," she said dryly. "What a very prudent person you are, Callette. But it beats me why you call two human wizards your mother and father. How can they be really?"

"They can be because they both put cells from themselves into all of us," Callette said. "It was the way to make us people, Dad says."

Yes, Derk had taken care to explain that, Querida remembered. Pity Callette knew. All right. Try a little wizardly pressure next. Pushing hard at Callette's mind, Querida snapped, "Very well. What was this message then?"

Callette's tail lifted from her feet and rapped once, gently, on the floor. "You haven't promised to let me go yet."

"I promise," Querida said readily. "The message?"

Callette's tail did another gentle dab at the flagstones. "That's only promising to let me go. You have to promise not to own me or keep me either, in any way."

Curses! Querida thought. That really was checkmate.

This creature was no fool. "Oh, very well, bother you! I promise not to try to own you or keep you, either by magic or in any other way. Now please can I have the universe at least, if not the message?"

Callette tilted her head for a second, checking Querida's words through. "That will do. The message is that the dwarfs from the Mossy Mountains are paying tribute of six bushels of wrought gold items to Mr Chesney every year. Dad has witnesses to confirm this. Mum says you ought to know."

Breakthrough! This *has* to be unlawful! Querida thought. It did something to make up for not owning Callette at least. But what was Derk doing, making this discovery? "Did these dwarfs have a contract to supply this treasure?" she asked, at her sharpest and snakiest.

"No," said Callette. "I went out there with Dad and I heard him asking them. They said Mr Chesney just ordered them to pay tribute forty years ago because he was Dark Lord of the world. And when the dwarfs argued, Mr Chesney told them it was to stop the dragons getting too greedy. The chieftain said he thought Mr Chesney might have been making a joke."

Ah! *Got him!* Querida's snaky smile wrapped itself halfway round her face. "I do not think," she said, "that Mr Chesney makes jokes. This was probably his true and actual reason. Did the dwarfs say anything else?"

"Yes. They said all the other tribes of dwarfs pay the tribute too," Callette answered.

Of course they would do. Mr Chesney was always thorough. Querida continued beaming, while her thoughts raced. So this was the way Mr Chesney worked, by taking care to get a hold on all the most powerful beings in the world! Neat. She wondered how he had got a hold on the demons, or if he had any bargain with the gods. That was something she must set the female wizards looking for quickly. She also wondered if Derk had the least idea of the meaning of this discovery. Mara certainly had, or she would not have sent Callette here. "And what was Derk going to do with the dwarfs after he had questioned them?" she asked.

Callette shrugged her wings up slightly. "I don't know. Nothing probably. He got in his hurry after he talked to them and told me to fly home and take Elda to Mum."

"Are you going to see Derk again soon?" Querida asked.

"Yes," Callette said. "He wants me in the base camp."

So she was making it clear that Derk would miss her as well as Mara, Querida thought. The only thing, then, was to try to make this lovely griffin stay here voluntarily. This could be managed. "Then tell him," she said, as if she were quite resigned to Callette's leaving, "to look out for any other odd thing that Mr Chesney might have arranged and let me know at once if he finds anything. Tell him it's most important."

"All right," said Callette. She rose to her four feet, carefully unwrapped the pouch from her talons and placed

264

it on the furthest end of the table. "Here's the universe. I must go now."

Querida's eyes flicked to it, gratified. It was most unlikely the spell to dissolve it would work once Callette had let go of the pouch. "You know, my dear," she said, "this has made my day. Tell Mara and Derk that I'm most grateful. It's gone a long way to console me for having to let such a beautiful creature as you go."

Callette stopped on her way to the door and looked at Querida across one glossy, barred wing. "Beautiful?" she said. "I'm not beautiful."

Ah! thought Querida. The bait is taken. "I assure you that you are," she said fervently. "You are one of the loveliest and most splendid creatures I have ever set eyes on."

"But I'm brown," Callette objected. "Elda and Don and Lydda are golden."

"Yellow gives me a headache," said Querida. "Your colouring is infinitely more subtle."

The feathers above Callette's beak jutted in a frown. "I think I'll ask Shona," she said after a thoughtful pause. "Except she may be too used to me to tell." She considered further. "But I thought you were like Mr Chesney and never made jokes?"

"And here was I priding myself on my dry sense of humour!" Querida said.

Callette continued to frown at her over one wing for a moment. Then the frown melted back into the rest of her feathers. "You're cheating," she said. "You're enticing me the way Mum entices tourists and trying to keep me here that way."

"Only a little," Querida protested – rather desperately, with a feeling she was fighting in the last ditch of her defences. "For the most part I was telling you my honest opinion. You are my idea of the perfect griffin."

"Then I will speak to Shona. Thank you," Callette said. She bent her head and squeezed her way out of the conference hall.

Querida sighed out a hiss of breath and stared at the table. Fancy being bested by a griffin! She felt ill and old and full of losses. She hadn't felt as bad as this since the day Mara's father left her for Mara's mother. Long, long ago, that had been. Still, she had coped with her feelings then and she could cope with them now. She squared her shoulders and reached for the blank pigeon slips. Now she knew what to tell the women wizards to look for, she had better tell them at once.

What she had to say to Mara took three pigeons to carry.

When those pigeons flapped wearily into their loft in Mara's aunt's house, Mara herself was hurrying through the yard below, mincing on the cobbles in stilt-heeled golden sandals, wrapped in a dressing-gown and carrying a list. The mayor of the village hurried beside her, clothed in a sort of cope made of blue and silver satin. Skinny Fran's cousin Greta was stumbling behind, trying to put the finishing touches to Mara's elaborately glamorous hairstyle, while Elda followed at a prudent distance, thoroughly fascinated.

"Flour, meat, vegetables," Mara said, "all safely delivered, thank goodness! Where is the fruit that came this morning?"

"Round here," said the mayor.

The group hurried round the corner by the new stables and stopped, daunted, in front of a small mountain of peaches, apples and pears. The gust of smells from it made Elda's beak fall open hungrily.

"Cartloads!" said Greta.

"Where do I put it all?" asked the mayor.

Mara's forehead creased even through the heavy layer of glamour on her. "It is a problem," she agreed. "Food for three hundred of us, plus twenty-odd Pilgrims every day, does add up rather." She minced up to the mighty heap and put a swift stasis spell on it. "There. That should keep it fresh." She sighed and looked at her list. "I shall have to brush up on conjuring feasts. I used to be quite good at it, but it always bothered me where the food really came from. Beer, we've got. The wine from Chell did arrive, did it?"

"Not as far as I know," Greta said, seizing the chance to arrange a long curl of Mara's hair to trail artfully down one shoulder.

"No, it didn't," the mayor said bluntly.

"Damn! And the Duchess of Chell *promised* me!"

Mara said. "We'll have to use enspelled water until it turns up, then." She made a note on her list and minced swiftly back into the house, shedding the mayor on the way. Elda followed as Mara and Greta clattered up the back stairs to the linen room. "Table-cloths, towels," Mara murmured. "That's twenty spare blue and silver uniforms. Do you think that's enough, Greta? Don't answer. We haven't time to make more. Are those my spare dresses? Have I enough?"

"If you call them dresses," Greta said dryly. "I'd call most of them strips of lace, personally."

"And someone did remember to bring some of Blade's clothes, did they?" Mara asked anxiously.

"You keep asking. I keep telling you Yes. Do stand still," said Greta. "Those top curls are wrong again." As Mara impatiently halted in the doorway, Greta added, "What about Elda? Are you going to dress her up too now she's here?"

Elda glowered at Greta for calling Mara's attention to her. "I want spangles over my wings," she said. "Shiny and all colours."

"No," said Mara. "I know you, Elda. If you had those, you wouldn't ever preen, let alone wash. You're having a tiara over your crest."

"Then strands of spangles trailing from it," Elda insisted.

"All right, but only if you go and have a bath now," said Mara.

"In a minute. I want to talk to you about Dad first," Elda said.

"Go and get a bath now," Mara replied, and looked at her list again. "Greta, is it true we've only got twenty spare pairs of sheets?"

"We'll just have to keep washing them," said Greta.

"More soap for the laundry then." Mara pushed her list against the door jamb and made a note on it. "They simply don't consider," she said, hurrying on down the corridor, "Mr Chesney, or whoever invented this Enchantress business, what it takes to put a new party of Pilgrims into freshly made-up beds every day." The two women hastened towards the grand front of the house, with Elda mutinously and silently following. "Music," Mara said at the head of the gilded stairway. "The choir has had time to practise, has it?"

"In between work in the laundry. Yes," Greta said. "They'll do better this time for sure."

"They couldn't do worse than they did yesterday, that's certain," Mara said, sighing. "How I *wish* Shona hadn't chosen to go off with the boys!"

"She needed to," Elda said, forgetting she wanted to be forgotten. "Dad needs as much help as you do."

Mara turned to her quellingly, but at that moment, the mayor came hurrying up the pretty staircase with the three flimsy squares of paper from Querida's pigeons. "These came," he said breathlessly.

"One more thing. Thanks." Mara sat on the nearest

gilded settle and bent over the pages of tiny, fine writing. "Don't go," she said absently. "They may need an answer."

Greta at once seized the chance to do further work on Mara's hair. Elda sank down on the furry floral carpet and exchanged an expressive look with the mayor, who was leaning on the gilded bannisters, panting.

"Oh, listen to this!" Mara cried out. "What does Querida think I am? She wants me to go north and make sure the pirates know to demand more money, and then she wants me to go to the Emirates and fix up with Lucia about the timing of the slavegirls' strike *and* she wants me to go and explain to the people in Chell and the other cities how to access the micro-universe. I thought *she* was going to do all that! And," she added, going on to the third tiny page, "as if that's not enough she says will I go to Billingham, Sleane and Greynash and persuade the women there not to work in the inns. I thought someone had *done* that. Does she think I'm six people in one body? Doesn't she *know* how busy we are here?"

The mayor coughed a little. "We know the drill here now. We can manage while you're away."

"And," added Greta, coaxing the curl further on to Mara's shoulder, "you can give us a bell or something so that we can ring it to warn you to come back when there's a Pilgrim Party arriving."

"It's in a good cause," the mayor pointed out.

Mara sighed. "I suppose. It's just – oh, Elda, Callette *did* get away! That's something at least. Querida says 'the beautiful griffin has outmanoeuvred me on every point' and that Callette's got a fine brain and she admires her more than ever."

"She wouldn't *really* have kept Callette, would she?" Elda asked.

"Oh yes, she would," Mara answered. "Querida's nearly as unscrupulous as Mr Chesney is. And I'm supposed to be so grateful that she let Callette go that I'll run around half the world for her!" She sat with the papers in her lap, staring down the elegant upper hallway without seeing it. "There is this," she said at length. "If I go to the Emirates, I can leave a message there for Blade, and I might even coincide with Lydda there if I go soon. And while I'm in Chell, I can make sure they send that wine."

Seeing Mara apparently reconciled to travel, Greta ventured to place the last curl becomingly across Mara's forehead and Elda decided to say what she had been waiting to say. "Mum, you've got to stop Dad going after Shona and the boys. He's still not better. He's all white and shaking."

"Elda," Mara said. Her chin was up and her voice dangerous. "Elda, did I, or did I not, tell you to go and have a bath?"

"I will." Elda stood up to show willing. "I will when you worry about Dad."

"Why should I worry?" Mara asked her coldly.

"Because he's *ill*!" Elda squawked. "What's *wrong*

with you, Mum? You always *used* to worry about him before!"

A very strange mixture of emotions crossed Mara's glamourised face, sadness and annoyance, mingled with a sort of hardness Elda had never seen in her before, a hint of worry that was covered almost instantly by scorn, and what was possibly tenderness struggling underneath sarcastic amusement. All these expressions were swiftly swamped by a sort of friendly exasperation. Elda, Greta, and the mayor too, watched Mara tilt her head and let the exasperation win. She spoke to Elda in the dry manner she used when one of the family had done something stupid. "Elda, you must know what it feels like to grow out of something. You've grown out of playing with dolls."

"I still play with the griffin lair Kit made me," Elda said defensively.

"Yes, but you don't use your baby toys," Mara pointed out. "It's the same with me and Derk, Elda."

Elda had her beak open and would have made a mighty screech of denial, had not two girls from the choir come clattering up the stair, nearly too breathless to speak. "Pilgrim Party!" one gasped.

"Just down the valley!" panted the other.

"Then what are you doing not in uniform?" Mara snapped at them, while the mayor muttered, "Got to go then," and hurried away down the stairs. Almost at once, Aunt's house erupted into a howling buzz of voices and filled with the running of feet as the entire population of the village went into its usual panic of stage fright.

"I've lost the song sheets!" somebody screamed, and someone else bellowed, "Where's the hair powder gone?"

Mara, looking as if the stage fright had touched her too, sprang up and cast off her dressing-gown, revealing a dress that was little more than a wide scarlet ribbon wrapped spirally round her. "You go and get changed," she said to Greta, who had fielded the dressing-gown. "Elda. Bath. Now. And," she added, mincing towards the stairs, "if you mention your father again, you don't get any spangles at all. I'm saving the world single-handed and I don't have *time* to think about Derk! Understand?"

Elda turned towards the bathrooms. "I understand," she said, over her left wing. "Baths and sheets and wine are more important than people!"

She broke into a gallop before Mara could get near her, walking on those high golden heels. This did not prevent Mara yelling after her, "And comb the tuft on your tail for once!"

CHAPTER FIFTEEN

✴

Scales came back the following morning, dangling two protesting hampers of geese and accompanied by a snowy, gliding echelon of daylight owls. Perched between the saw-edges on his shoulders, and looking rather the worse for it, was Derk. Shona screamed with delight and ran out from among the trees. As soon as Scales had tossed the hampers down – honk, *yatter*, SCOLD! – and made a rather heavier landing than he nowadays did, Shona hurried to help Derk tenderly down.

"Oh Dad! You've lost weight! And you look chilled to the bone!"

"Only more or less cut in half. I don't recommend

dragon riding," Derk said. "Thanks, Scales. Can I offer you a Friendly Cow?"

"No thank you," Scales rumbled. "I told you. I hunted on the way, for the first time for three hundred years. I had forgotten both the pleasure of it and what skill it took."

Derk turned as Kit and Don came bounding up, with Blade hurrying in the rear. They had all three hung back a little because they were fairly sure they were in for a scolding. But Derk beamed at them all. "You seem to have been coping rather well. Great doings. And whichever of you asked those dwarfs what they were doing did a really smart thing."

"That was me," said Don. "But Blade asked too. Anyone would. It was pretty queer."

"You're right," said Derk. "It was pretty queer. Scales came and told me about it and then we flew out to ask them some questions. Then we had to go back and send Elda and Callette to Mara. It's been a busy night. Why isn't Barnabas here? I thought he was supposed to be helping you."

"We didn't really tell him you were ill," Shona confessed.

Blade simply stood there, grinning increasingly widely as he realised that Scales could not have eaten those dwarfs after all, not with Dad there. Derk looked at him, wondering why he was so quiet. "What happened to the dwarfs in the end?" Blade asked, to make absolutely sure.

Derk laughed. "We gave them a change of destination – Scales's idea – and sent them to Derkholm. We told them, quite truthfully, that it's the Dark Lord's Citadel. They were quite pleased because it wasn't nearly so far to go." This more or less set Blade's mind at rest, although he felt slightly dubious when Derk turned to Scales and said, "I suppose you'll want to be off looking for the rest of the dwarfs with tribute now?"

"I shall help you get these murderers into their barracks first," Scales replied. "I can't see how you would get them there without a dragon to drive them."

"I expect I'd have thought of something," Derk said comfortably. "But I would be very grateful for your help."

They got ready to march, accompanied now by the whole flock of geese and with the owls riding on the bundles piled on the spare horses. Shona willingly gave up riding Beauty. Beauty and Pretty were so pleased to see Derk again that they nuzzled around him and became quite a hindrance. "You wouldn't be half so pleased if you knew my plans for you," Derk told Pretty, rubbing Pretty's forelock. "Your wings have grown, haven't they?"

The trouble was that the new arrivals had left them one horse short and with three empty hampers to carry. Derk thought briefly and then told Blade to pack all the left-over bundles into the hampers and translocate to the next camp with them. It was one of those neat solutions Dad was so good at, Blade thought, ramming things into creaking wickerwork. And he was going to have a very boring day because of it, waiting about in the next camp for the rest of them to arrive.

On the other hand, he thought, as Scales thrust his great snout under the magic dome and drove the soldiers forth with his usual roar of MARCH, SCUM!, it would be good to get away from those soldiers. As they came streaming out of the dome, Blade could feel them hating and fearing his father in a way that was beyond even the way they hated Kit. They were stark terrified of Scales, and a wizard who so cheerfully rode on Scales's back they assumed to be even more horrifying than Scales himself. It was not pleasant to feel all those minds directing hate at Derk.

Blade laid himself face down across the three hampers. Translocation might be the thing he was really good at, but he had to be touching everything he wanted to move. And, as Kit had discovered by experimenting a year ago, if the thing Blade was touching was made of iron, then Blade could not move it or himself either. Blade was glad Kit had found this out. There were two spades among the bundles. Blade had made sure they were well wrapped up, right inside everything else, before he lay on the hampers.

He whisked himself onwards and away. Scales's roaring, Kit's yells and the sound of dogs, cows and tramping feet stopped as if Blade had quite suddenly gone deaf. The sound that replaced them was that of water rushing a little way off. Blade looked up.

To his surprise, this was obviously the permanent barracks. It stood above him on top of a grey shaly hill, a very much bigger misty dome than the ones he had so far seen. Below the hill, a wide grey river rushed in a shallow slaty bed. There were fir trees growing up the hillside beyond the river and behind these Blade could see the mountains, still not very near. For a moment, he wondered if he had made a mistake in translocating. But when he looked into that part of his mind that did magical things, he knew this was indeed the next camp on the line of march. So it had to be right. Well, Kit had the map, not Blade. Blade had not attended much to how far they had gone. He got off the hampers and went down to the river, where he stood for a while chucking stones into it with loud watery *clunks* and trying to work out how he felt now that Dad seemed to be in charge again.

In a way it was a great relief. Blade did not need to feel rushed and worried any more. There was no need any longer to keep thinking of all the things that might go wrong. Derk could do that now. But Blade did not feel as carefree as he expected. The loose, easy feeling he had as he stood there throwing stones struck him as rather babyish. And Dad had made him feel even more babyish by ordering him off here with those hampers. Blade hated being pushed around. He found he wanted to think of things for himself, then do them. He wondered if Kit felt the same. Kit had been really subdued when they saw Derk coming.

Blade strolled back to the hampers with the flat river-stones clacking under his feet. Then, because he could see a wide opening in the magic dome, he went crunching up the hill to the barracks. It was always a funny feeling inside the bubble of mist, warm and windless and cut-off, and Blade found the place rather depressing with its rows of raw wooden huts, all empty. But there must be someone here. There was a horse tied to a railing outside the big hut in the distance and Blade could hear another, irritably shifting its hooves somewhere at the back of things. One of the horses must belong to Barnabas.

Blade crunched over to the big hut – where the horse gave him a glum look – and put his head in through the open door. It was raw new mess in there. The place was clearly meant to be the cookhouse and eating hall, but the huge stove had its iron chimney leaning against it, not yet connected to the hole in the ceiling, and the tables and chairs were stacked like timber at one end of the room. In between, there were numbers of big packing cases which Blade supposed must be full of cups, plates, or even food. The owner of the horse was sitting on one of these big wooden boxes eating breakfast, or possibly lunch, from a silk handkerchief spread on the knees of his green velvet trousers. He was a tall dark man, beautifully groomed, and a total stranger to Blade.

"Who are *you*?" Blade blurted.

The man looked up. "I return you the same question," he said, in a calm, unfriendly way.

"I'm Derk's son – Blade," Blade told him.

"Conrad the Bard," replied the man. "Does your presence mean that the Dark Lord has arrived?"

"They'll be here this evening. And," Blade told him, "you don't want to be inside here when the soldiers come in. They'd kill you."

"I am aware of that. My business is not with them," Conrad said coldly. "What are you doing here yourself?"

"I'm looking for Wizard Barnabas," Blade explained.

Conrad shrugged. "I know no such person. There's a drunk in a hut at the back who might know. He seems to have been here for some time."

"I'll ask him then," said Blade.

He turned to leave. The bard called after him, "This camp is in the wrong place. Did you know? It's miles too far south. I had trouble finding it."

"Nothing to do with me," Blade answered. But that did explain why he had been so puzzled, he supposed. He crunched round to the back of the cooking hall.

The horse standing tied outside one of the row of small huts there looked utterly miserable. The hut was obviously meant to be a latrine, but when Blade opened its door there was no hole dug in its floor, or any other provision. Barnabas was lying snoring inside a sleeping bag on the ground. There was a barrel beside him which, when Blade rocked it, seemed to be empty. The inside of the small hut smelt like a brewery.

"Pooh!" Blade nudged Barnabas with his toe. It was

almost a kick really. He had to do it several times more before Barnabas rolled over, sat up and gazed vaguely at Blade. Barnabas's curls and his beard looked wet. His eyes were red. His normal genial expression had turned into a senseless grin. "Barnabas!" said Blade. "You've got to get up. The soldiers are coming and this place isn't more than half finished."

"Buildings are up," Barnabas replied cheerily. "Soldiers can do the rest." He lay down, rolled over and went to sleep again.

Cold water's supposed to do it, Blade thought. But he doubted if there was any water nearer than the river. Still, there was one thing Blade was good at besides translocation. It was easier too. He concentrated. Shortly, Barnabas began to shiver in his sleep.

"Hey! Stop that!" he muttered.

Blade concentrated some more.

Barnabas abruptly rolled over and stared at Blade with his teeth chattering. His face was bluish, but this time his bloodshot eyes were looking properly into Blade's.

"Barnabas," Blade said, "how long has your horse been standing outside this hut?"

"Oh ye gods!" said Barnabas. "Is the army here already? Tell your father – be a nice lad and *explain* to him, Blade! – I don't normally binge like this when I'm working. The pressure just all got too much this time!"

"Dad won't be here till this evening," Blade told him.

"You've got about six hours to get the camp finished. You'd better get up and get going."

"I had, hadn't I?" Barnabas agreed readily. "If you'd stop freezing me to death, young Blade, I'll get up and attend to everything. I promise."

Blade did not believe him. It seemed hard not to trust a friend of Dad's who had been like an uncle to you all your life, but Blade remembered that Barnabas had given them no help at all with the soldiers, even when he knew Derk was not with them, and he said sternly, "I'll stop when you're standing up."

"Cruel brat!" Barnabas groaned and scrambled out of the bag, shaking and shivering, and got to his feet by climbing up the splintery wall. "That suit you?"

"Walk outside," said Blade.

Barnabas swayed and got himself through the doorway by pulling on the sides of it with both hands. He leant against the outside of the hut, moaning. "You don't *understand*, Blade. If you only knew how hard Mr Chesney makes us work, you'd have some sympathy for—"

"I do know," said Blade. "By now." He took some of the coldness off, but not all of it. A sort of half-chill might help Barnabas to get sober, he hoped. "There are no beds in the sleeping huts and no holes in these latrines," he said, "and the cookhouse is only half finished. I'll come and help you in a minute." He untied the unfortunate horse and led it away towards the river. As he went, he realised that he was feeling rushed and worried again. He was so used to the feeling and so used by now to thinking of more things that could go wrong that he hardly checked in his stride when he came crunching out of the dome and saw a group of cloaked and plumed young warriors waiting beside the three hampers. Wow! he thought. They look smart! And crunched on towards the river with the horse.

"The Emperor of the South to speak with the Wizard Derk!" one of the warriors called out as soon as Blade was near enough.

First things first. Blade thought. Barnabas's horse was half dead with thirst. Blade took it to the river and saw it start drinking before he turned and said, quite politely, "I'm afraid my father won't get here until this evening." By that time the warriors had unfurled the banner of the Empire. It flapped on a pole beside the hampers, huge and official and purple and white. Blade thought Wow! again as he went towards the hampers. "Excuse me," he said as politely as he could. "I need to get at a nosebag. The horse is starving. And do any of you happen to have any coffee? The wizard who's supposed to be building this camp has gone and got drunk."

They stared at him, nonplussed, but they moved aside from the hampers a little, shiny boots crunching in the shale. Golden breastplates flashed at the corner of Blade's eye as he hauled out a nosebag. Since nobody seemed to be saying anything, Blade said nothing either. He took the nosebag back to the horse, dragged it out of the river before it drank too much, and hitched it into the nosebag. When it had settled down to eat, he turned round.

The youngest of the warriors, the one wrapped in the large purple cloak, was standing only a yard or so away. Blade and he looked at one another. Shona's age. Blade thought. He looks rather nice.

"I – er – sent a runner for coffee," said the warrior.

"Thank you," Blade said, with true gratitude.

"Not a problem," said the teenage warrior. "Our encampment's only a mile away. Much too near, really. Your drunk wizard seems to have put yours in the wrong place."

"I *thought* something was wrong. It's a bit late to move it now," Blade said anxiously.

"I realise," said the warrior. "But it makes it easier to confer about the battle plans. I don't want your father to hit my legions too hard. They're nearly all new men. Most of the veterans got killed in last year's tours. I'm Titus – Emperor, you know."

"I'm Blade," said Blade, and was surprised to find himself shaking hands warmly with the Emperor of the South.

"I liked the way you saw to the horse first," Titus told him.

"Barnabas must have had it tied up to that hut for *days*!" Blade said angrily. "I very nearly kicked him. I even sort of did. But he was so drunk he didn't feel it."

284

"I'm not sure I'd dare kick a wizard, even a drunk one," said the Emperor.

"After this last week or so," Blade answered, "I didn't even think about it." He and the Emperor went and sat on the hampers, while Blade described how the soldiers tried to escape and how Scales arrived in time to stop them (or most of them). The other warriors, after a nod from Titus, sat stiffly on the shale around them. They had had a difficult time too, Titus said. The Imperial Legions had lost their way and spent most of two days in a marsh.

"And those Marsh Folk just stood around and laughed!" Titus was saying. "I thought they were supposed to be on our side, but – oh, you have company."

Blade looked round to find a small party of horsemen splashing across the river towards them. The tall gloomy one in front he recognised from the time he and Dad had consulted the White Oracle. King Luther. Definitely. He got up. Everyone round him sprang up too.

King Luther swung himself down from his tall gloomy black horse and crunched over the stones towards them. "I wondered if I'd find you here, Titus," he said genially. He and the Emperor bowed to one another like friends, but like kings with kingdoms too, Blade saw, watching with interest. Then King Luther turned to him. "And don't even think of putting the shivers on me this time, boy." Blade saw Titus swallowing a laugh at this. "Where's your father?" asked the king. "What's he thinking of, putting this camp in the wrong place? My army's not going to have time to get home between battles from here."

"I'm afraid Barnabas got drunk and probably made a mistake," Blade explained.

"Then what's Derk doing *trusting* that drunk—?" King Luther began.

"Ah, here comes the coffee," Titus interrupted.

It was in gilded picnic baskets slung on the sides of a horse and followed by a stately major domo on another horse. There was a whole feast in there, Blade saw, when the major domo grandly flipped the basket lids up.

"I suggest we all have some lunch," Titus said graciously.

Blade took a gilded and steaming flask of coffee up to the camp first, where he found Barnabas shakily slogging away at conjuring bunks into the barrack sheds. "I shall have to give up drinking," he told Blade dismally. "I've got the shivers really badly this time. Can't seem to get warm. Is that coffee? Oh *good*!"

Blade took pity on him and reduced the chill spell by half again. But he took care to fetch a chair out from the cookhouse into the open parade ground and make Barnabas sit on it before he handed him the coffee flask. He did not want Barnabas going to sleep again.

Barnabas took the flask and swigged eagerly. He puffed and wiped his mouth and swigged again. "That's better! There's still a lot to do. And *you're* not helping."

"I know," said Blade. "King Luther and Emperor Titus turned up."

"Oh. Then I let you off," said Barnabas. "Now leave them to be royal at one another or we'll never get those latrines dug out."

Blade was struck by an idea. "In a short while. I'll see to the digging for you. You finish the beds and get the cookhouse straight."

"There's some toffee-nosed bard gone and parked himself inside there," Barnabas complained. "What's he supposed to be up to?"

"I haven't a clue. Turn him out," Blade said and sped away out of the camp again.

Down near the river everyone was having a picnic, despite a few spits of rain falling. The major domo bowed to Blade and handed him a gilded wooden plate heaped with smoked salmon, corn bread and olives. "Thanks," said Blade, at which the man looked startled, as if you were not supposed to thank him. Too bad. Blade took his plate to the hamper where the Emperor was sitting. "I say, can you spare a few legionaries to dig us some latrines?"

Titus grinned. "I don't see why not. They've been doing it every day for a fortnight now. They should be rather good at it. And they're only sitting about at the moment." He said a word to one of his warriors, who commandeered the major domo's horse and rode off at a canter.

King Luther laughed so much at Blade's idea that he

nearly choked. Meanwhile, Barnabas must have started work on the cookhouse. Conrad the Bard stalked loftily out of the dome and stood on the hill above them with his arms folded, looking considerably more kingly than the monarchs having lunch. Blade was wondering again why the man was here when Titus nudged him.

"More company for you. Here's High Priest Umru now."

Umru was coming along beside the river on an extremely sturdy white horse, which he was sitting on as if the horse were a bench, with his legs dangling off one side. With him rode numbers of other priests in variously coloured robes. "Good day," Umru called and raised his hands in blessing. This seemed to be the priestly version of a bow. At any rate, Titus and Luther and their followers all bowed back, at which most of the other priests made blessing signs too. Everyone bowed again. Umru beckoned Blade with a chubby finger. "A word with you, my boy."

Blade went over to the priestly party. While he was covering the distance, two priests in black got down and helped Umru slide off the white horse. Looking at the size of him, Blade wondered how the High Priest was ever going to get back on. "Yes, sir?" he asked politely.

"You had me shivering for three hours last time we met," Umru remarked. "Has your father the wizard arrived yet?"

Blade explained that Derk would be here by the evening.

"We shall wait," Umru said. "I owe him that courtesy for putting this camp so far away on this side of the mountains. This suggests that the battles will be here too. Is this so?"

"I don't really know," said Blade.

"Then I must ask him," Umru said. "But I fear these other priests with me are coming to complain. Maybe you should warn your father." Blade looked up at them in their coloured robes, staring grimly down from their horses. "From the other temples of the other gods," Umru told him. "They do not like this idea that a god must manifest to the Pilgrim Parties."

"That was Mr Chesney's idea," Blade protested. "It's nothing to do with my father."

Umru turned to look up at the grim priests. "There, Reverences. As I told you. Will you take the boy's word and return home?"

"We shall stay and talk to the wizard," a dour priest in a red robe replied.

Umru sighed. "In that case, can you provide us with a place to wait, my boy?"

"You'd better come and sit on the hampers," Blade said.

"Hampers?" said the dour priest.

"Yes indeed," said Umru. "I see an emperor and a king sitting on those hampers. Abate your pride, Cartebras, if you must stay, and sit on a hamper too."

"Er – just a moment," said Blade. He sprinted uphill

to the camp, past the lofty bard, across the parade ground and into the cookhouse, where Barnabas was just setting up the tables and benches. Blade threw himself across as many of the benches as his body would stretch over.

"What are you *doing*?" said Barnabas.

"There are sixteen High Priests now," Blade said, and translocated with the lot back to the riverside. The priests disdainfully seated themselves and sat looking so grim that the happy chatter round the hampers died away.

"Forgive us, my friends," sighed Umru and sat, very cautiously, on the third hamper. It swayed sideways, but luckily it held his weight.

Blade began to see that it was one of those days. And here he had been, expecting it to be a day of empty waiting. The next person to arrive appeared so suddenly and quietly behind him that Blade thought he must have translocated there. But it seemed not. He was a gaunt man dressed all over in leather, who looked nearly as grim as the priests. "Chief Werewolf," he said abruptly. "This camp is in the wrong—"

"I *know*," said Blade. "And I'm afraid my father won't get here until this evening."

"Then I'll wait," said the werewolf. "This camp has got to be moved or the werewolves won't be able to manage. We have to attack Pilgrim Parties sixty miles away between battles."

"And I have to hold evil court for them eighty miles

290

away," King Luther called out. "It can't be done. Come and join us, my friend."

The werewolf glowered at Blade as he stepped over towards the hampers. Blade was rather glad that the next people to arrive were only a squad of legionaries, each carrying a spade and all running briskly in step, while a fierce officer ran behind them chanting, "One-two, one-two, one-two." Blade jumped up from the shale and showed them where the huts were in the camp. "No problem at all," said the officer. "These lads do this twice a day before breakfast, don't you, boys?"

"More like three times," a legionary said ruefully.

"Then jump to it!" shouted the officer.

We could do with a few officers like him, Blade thought as he came out through the camp again. He wondered if Titus could lend him a few – except that it did not seem to be quite in the spirit of the rules. Blade was wondering if there was anything about it in his black book – which he hoped Kit still had safely – when he looked up to see the next arrival just dismounting from the most splendid horse he had ever set eyes on. Even the bard deigned to give a slight whistle and remark, as Blade went past him, "Now *that* is horseflesh."

This latest person, as Blade saw when he was near enough, was female. She was tall enough to be an elf, but probably, Blade thought, she was something else. Her hair was brownish and her eyes slanted a bit. Her skin was brown as well and, though she was dressed from head to foot in soft white doeskin, the doeskin was the only soft thing about her. She was as tough and stringy and fierce as dried curried meat. He watched her put her hands on her narrow hips and look ferociously over the crowd around the hampers.

"Which of you is Wizard Derk?" she snapped.

Blade prudently hung back, out of trouble.

"None of us is, madam," King Luther replied politely. "We're waiting for him too."

"I'm Wendela Horselady and I want Wizard Derk *now*," said the lady. "He may be Dark Lord, but as far as I can tell, he must be the only person in this *world* who has the *least* consideration for animals. I've *got* to talk to him about my horses. I've absolutely had *enough*!"

"But Wizard Derk is not here yet, my daughter," Umru said.

The Horselady looked slowly around the space by the river. By this time there were not only a large number of people there, but two dozen horses too. "You're all using my horses," she said. "I'll talk to you first and then to Wizard Derk when he comes. I've had trouble enough finding this camp – someone's put it in *quite* the wrong place – and I may as well make it worth my while. Now, listen. So many of my horses got killed last year that I had trouble meeting my quota for *this* year. I've had to send out some of the breeding stock. And that means fewer foals next year – a *lot* fewer, because those darned Pilgrims are so *careless*. Six tours have lost *all* their horses *already*, and I'm not providing them with new ones just to have *those* broken down—"

"Madam," Umru managed to interrupt, "I assure you I cherish my horses, particularly the only one that can carry me."

"—by stupid *fools* who think they're just some kind of walking *chairs*," the Horselady swept on. "And now you're all coming up to this ridiculous round of *battles* and there's bound to be absolute *carnage* amongst the horses, because there always *is*, and I shall have practically none *left*, and most of those will be hurt in some way. Why you people can't be more *careful*—"

"This really isn't Our concern," Titus said stiffly. "Our legions mostly fight on foot."

"Yes, I know they do!" the Horselady retorted. "Your lot is the worst of *all*. Your beastly legions go for the horses every *time* in order to get the riders off. Well, I'm warning you, if they do that this year, if a *single* horse gets maimed or killed—"

"Look," said King Luther, "you can't have a battle without any horses being hurt—"

"Yes, you *can*, if you fight on foot!" the lady contradicted him. "And you're going to *do* that, because, as I said, if one *single* horse gets hurt, I shall simply recall the entire lot."

"That's surely easier to say than to do," King Luther said. "For a start, you'd have to—"

"I'd just do this." The Horselady put her fingers to

her mouth and gave a long, warbling whistle. The heads of all the horses turned towards her. Then they all, even Barnabas's horse, and Umru's, and those that had been tied to stakes by King Luther's men, trotted eagerly towards her over the shale. The bard's horse came out of the dome at a canter and reached her first. The noise, for a moment, of hooves crashing on stones, was horrible. "You see?" the Horselady said, out of the crowd of horses. "Nothing simpler." She patted necks and rubbed noses. "There, my loves. Go back to your borrowers for now. I'll call you again when I need you." All the horses obediently turned and went back to where they had come from, except for the bard's horse, which the bard caught on its way up the hill and made to stand beside him.

By this time, it was dawning on Blade that he must go and warn Dad that there was a pack of trouble waiting for him when he arrived. But there was a camel now, coming round the dome of the camp. The man on its back asked the bard something and the bard pointed to Blade. The camel came down the hill, splay-legged and knock-kneed, and stopped with a snarl beside Blade.

Blade found this arrival very hard to understand, but he gathered that this man was a personal servant of a Vizier and his message was something about "the Emir acting strange". He told him to go over to the hampers and wait. At least the Horselady, who was now walking about haranguing everybody whom she happened to be near, could not possibly worry about a camel, or so he hoped. Nor, he thought, could she have anything to say to the next two, who were coming splashing up the river on foot.

These two climbed up the bank and accosted Blade. "This camp is in the wrong place," the first one to reach him said.

I shall scream! Blade thought. "Tell me your complaint or message and I'll tell my father when he gets here."

"We're not really together," said the one behind. "I'm from Chell City. Something's seriously wrong with the arrangements for the siege there."

"And I'm from the north," said the one in front. "I've come about that wretched mauve dragon. Who gave it permission to roost right in the middle of our fur-trapping drove?"

Blade persuaded them both to come and sit down with the grim priests.

"Do you use horses?" the Horselady demanded, looming up behind them.

Blade fled down to the river in a clatter of stones, where he intended to translocate at once before anything more happened. A large dark shadow sailed above him as he ran. He looked up and saw, to his surprise and joy, Callette coming in for a neat landing by the river. "Hey!" he shouted, joyfully crunching towards her. "I thought you'd gone to Aunt's house!"

Callette settled her wings and took a drink from the

rushing water. "I did," she said, "and then to the University. I can go much faster if I come down for a rest every ten miles. Dad said to meet him here, but I got here first. But he's only about half a mile or so away now. They were chasing some soldiers who were trying to run away when I went over. They won't be long."

"Thank goodness!" said Blade. "You wouldn't believe how many people are waiting here to complain to him!" He meant to go on and pour out to Callette all the events of the day, but he stopped because he could see Callette was upset about something. Her wings kept rising and her tail lashed on the gravel. "What's the matter?"

Callette looked up and around and ruffled her crest feathers. "Blade, can you do me a favour? Can you get two of those people who've never seen me before and bring them over here? I need to ask them something." It was an odd request, but Blade supposed Callette had her reasons. She had reasons for everything she did. He nodded and started back for the benches and the hampers. Most of those waiting there had clearly never seen a griffin before. They had all turned to stare at Callette. "*Honest* people!" Callette called after him.

That probably cut out at least half of them, Blade thought. And King Luther had met Kit, when Kit and Dad took the pigs over to perform at his palace last year, and although the Chief Werewolf looked honest, Blade did not like him at all. Nor that bard standing up there on the hill. Blade chose the Horselady, on the grounds that this would stop her going on at the man from Chell City, and Titus, because he liked Titus.

He was astonished at their reaction. When he interrupted the Horselady by taking hold of her fringed doeskin elbow, the lady said, "*Really*? I'm *honoured*!" and clearly meant it. Titus said, "Oh, marvellous! I've always wanted to meet a griffin!" Both of them crunched downwards towards Callette with Blade as if he had offered them a real treat.

Callette examined them with one eye, and then with the other. "Good choice," she told Blade.

"How can we help?" asked Titus.

"I want to know if you think I'm beautiful at all," said Callette.

"You certainly *are*. You're *superb*!" the Horselady said, even more vehemently than usual.

"You're quite the most beautiful being I've ever been privileged to meet," said Titus.

"And you're a *lovely* mover! Trust me!" added the Horselady.

"Thank you, both of you," Callette said happily.

Blade was even more astonished. Callette was just familiar brown Callette to him, his more-or-less twin sister, who had hacked her way out of her egg while Blade was being born. Mara always said she never knew which of them had eaten most or cried loudest. But the Horselady seemed quite sure, and Titus must have been surrounded by beautiful things all his life. Callette was beautiful. Fancy that!

He had to leave the three of them talking beside the river, because the first of the soldiers began arriving then, streaming among the trees that grew between the riverside and the moorland with a terrible crunching and clattering. Blade had to move the benches, the hampers and the people, and get some of the people to move the horses and the camel, to give the soldiers a free passage to the camp. By the look of them, the soldiers were in an even meaner state of mind than they had been that morning. Blade was afraid someone could get hurt. But before any accidents could happen, Kit came swooping in over the trees to make sure the front ranks behaved. The waiting people stared at Kit, and stared again at Don flying back and forth to herd the soldiers who came next. The air was full of wingbeats and the clacking of feet on stones while the soldiers streamed on up into their camp, where Kit swooped down to seal them in. The dogs, cows and geese arrived next, herded by Shona, who was also leading the horses, including Beauty and Pretty, while the owls flew in above. This all caused more staring. When Derk finally arrived, he caused the greatest sensation of the lot, because he was riding Scales again. It was quite impressive, even to Blade, who knew Derk was only doing this to frighten the soldiers.

The sensation lasted only moments. After that almost everyone surged towards Derk, shouting to be heard.

Barnabas went past Blade at a rolling run, crying out, "I can explain! I can explain everything!" The bard too mounted his horse and rode that way with the rest. But instead of joining the crowd round Scales, he turned aside and rode up to Shona. As Shona dismounted from Nancy Cobber, he handed her a scroll with a large seal dangling from it and then rode away without a word to anyone.

Shona put Nancy's reins under her arm and unrolled the scroll, looking mystified. She looked at what was inside. She went pale. Then she dropped Nancy's reins and threw herself on to the shaly ground, screaming and crying.

CHAPTER SIXTEEN

*

*B*lade wondered how his father did not scream and cry too. As Blade rushed across the shale on his way to Shona, everyone round Derk was shouting and the Horselady's voice was coming out over the top like a descant. She had hold of Beauty by her halter. "*And* this mare is overtired! *Look* at her!"

"'M all rhight! 'M fhine!" Beauty was protesting as Blade got to Shona.

Kit got there at the same time, in a spurt of stones. "What's wrong? What happened?"

Shona's face was in her arms, buried in her hair. Shaking with sobs, she simply held the hand that was clutching the scroll up to Kit. Callette and Don arrived as Kit read out:

"'The President of Bardic College hereby informs ex-student Shona that she has broken our express command not to assist in any way with Pilgrim Parties or Pilgrims. Had the ex-student condescended to attend at our College, she would have learnt that all bards are now forbidden to have any dealings with these tours. She is accordingly hereby expelled from our College and forbidden to perform as a bard in any manner henceforth.'"

"I didn't *know*!" screamed Shona. "No one *said*! What shall I *do*? I don't have a career any longer and I can't *live* without music!"

Kit was shaking with rage. Feathers and hair stood up in a ridge all down his back. "I've a good mind to go after that fellow and pull his head off!"

"That won't help," said Callette. "Come and comfort her."

Kit raked the shale furiously with all ten front talons, but he moved round opposite Callette and settled head to tail with her, enclosing Shona in a warm feathery nest. Shona just lay there between them and cried desolately. Blade had never seen her – or anyone else – so horribly unhappy. It stunned him. He could not think what to do.

"Horses," Don said to him. "Feed dogs, quick supper, avians in hampers."

Blade nodded. It was a relief to have things to do.

By the time they were daring the geese into hampers, Derk's face was hanging in harassed folds, but he had sorted out most of his visitors. Barnabas was sitting sulkily over a mug of coffee, Scales had flown away north to speak to the purple dragon, and Derk had assured the priests, with complete honesty, that he had made no arrangements whatsoever to have a god manifest, even a fake one. He had assured Umru that they would not have battles in his country. He had promised to discuss the whole matter of battles with Titus, King Luther and the Chief Werewolf tomorrow, and he had agreed to go to Chell and to take a look at the Emir later. But the Horselady was still at his elbow, haranguing him.

"*I said yes!*" Derk told her loudly on his way over to Shona.

The lady stopped and stared at him.

"You don't listen, you know," Derk said. "I said yes when you began. We'll fight on foot. I've been worried about the way the Pilgrims treat horses for years. That's why I'm breeding ones with wings. I thought they'd survive better."

"Oh," said the Horselady, almost faintly. "Thank you." She went hurriedly away to the riverbank, where Pretty was making the bad mistake of trying to flirt with the camel. "Get *away* from it, you stupid little horse! Do you *want* your leg broken?"

"Now what's the matter here?" Derk said wearily, shoving in beside Kit. Kit held the scroll out to him. Derk took it and frowned at it in the growing dusk. "Oh dear. Oh my poor Shona! This is ridiculous. I'll speak to the Bardic President as soon as I can, I promise." He sat down and put his hand on Shona's back. "It'll be all right. I won't let this happen. Lords, I'm tired. Is someone seeing to the Wild Hunt tonight?"

"Me." Kit sprang up, lashing his tail. He was still extremely angry. Derk stayed sitting beside Shona, saying comforting things, but it was fairly clear to him that Shona was not believing him.

Derk sighed. "I wish Mara could talk to her."

"Shall I go and get her?" offered Callette.

"No, no. She's busy." Derk did not want Callette going all that way and seeing Mara refuse to come near him. He was fairly sure Mara had not even come near him when he was lying half dead from dragon smoke. But he did not want to think of this mystifying rift between himself and Mara just now. He was not sure he could face it. He sighed again.

"Eat something," said Callette. "Do I sound like Lydda?"

Derk managed to laugh. "Not really. Let's find some food. Barnabas ought to eat too."

"Everyone's saying he put this camp in the wrong place," Callette said severely.

"He did," said Derk, "but it was where I wanted him to put it, so it doesn't matter. Shona, will you get up and eat something, please."

"No," said Shona. "I couldn't."

She was still not eating next morning. She sat wrapped in a blanket, staring at nothing with her cheeks white and sucked inwards, and did not seem to notice all the comings and goings around her. The Emperor and King Luther arrived back for a conference, and so did the Chief Werewolf. Derk thought for a moment and then put Kit in charge of everything to do with the battles. The Horselady and the man with the camel left, but the man from Chell City hung around anxiously, insisting that the Duke of Chell needed Derk, while Derk followed Barnabas about, arguing with him.

"I think you could have made an effort."

"I did, Derk. I do. I've tried healers and I've tried spells, and none of it stops me breaking out and bingeing. But I did take care to set all the battle spells in the dome before I touched a drop this time. Those are important. You ought to let me activate them."

"You know I hate spells that force people against their will!"

"Yes, but you'll never get them to behave like real soldiers without. Look in that dome. They're just lying about or beating one another up."

"I know," Derk said sadly. "I'd hoped to appeal to their reason, but I'm not sure they've got any. All right. Activate those spells then. Why are you shivering?"

"Withdrawal," said Barnabas.

Derk looked at him closely and said, "Blade!"

They were standing right beside Shona while Blade took the cold spell off, but Shona did not seem to see or hear them. Kit's head kept swivelling to her as he sat by the river with the Emperor and King Luther. Each time he looked at her, he shook with rage. Blade did not understand.

"Don't be so dim!" Kit growled at him. "You know how *you* felt when Dad said you couldn't go to University."

"Yes, but I feel better now, after the Oracle," Blade said.

Kit glared. "Thickhead. Nobody took *me* to any oracle, did they? I feel for her. I know what it's like not to have any future."

Blade decided to go quietly missing after that. Kit had made him feel guilty and he was not sure that was fair. Unfortunately, Callette had noticed him slipping away among the Friendly Cows and Derk easily caught up with him. "Don't vanish, Blade. I need you. I'm leaving Kit in charge here while we do some translocating."

"Where do you want to go?" Blade said, rather sulkily.

"University first. I have to see Querida."

Blade sighed and took them both there.

They found Querida at the conference table again, with pigeon messages spread out all over it. There was a small stove on the table too, and a kettle singing on the stove. The room was full of the scents of several herbal teas. Querida looked up from the elegant cup in her little dry hands.

"Oh, it's you," she said, rather guiltily. Most of the time she felt no guilt at all for anything she did, but to see Derk standing there looking drained and unwell, and the boy – Blade, that was his name – in torn and grass-stained clothes, made her slightly ashamed of what she was doing. Well, it's in a good cause, she told herself. On with the bullying. "I suppose you've come here wanting me to conjure you a demon," she hissed.

"A demon has been conjured," Derk said carefully, and Blade looked at him, wondering why he put it like that. "But I'd be very grateful if you could do something about a god or so. Some of the tours have got quite far by now. We're running a little short of time."

"You can see I'm up to my eyebrows in work here!" Querida took a hand from her teacup and fluttered her fingers across the mass of papers in front of her. "But I shall give it serious thought as I work. How do you fancy a snake god with feathers on its head?"

"I think there *is* one of those – on Tecahua Island," Derk said.

Querida knew there was. He was her favourite god. "So there is," she agreed. "Bother. It is so difficult to think of a god that someone hasn't had somewhere. But I'll keep thinking. I'll let you know in a week or so. Meanwhile, as you're here, I'd like to ask you about a couple of these messages." She put down her cup and searched across the spread of papers, finally selecting two from opposite corners. It was like that memory game where you find pairs of cards, Blade thought. It was not a game he was fond of. The griffins always won. "Here we are." Querida held up the first paper. "This is from a farmer in the central plains, complaining that his flocks are being attacked by small carnivorous sheep. Any comments?"

"I've no idea how that happened," Derk said, with perfect honesty. Blade uncomfortably studied the flagstones in the floor.

"And this," Querida said, waving the second paper, "states that a party of men in black armour attacked a monastery near Blendish, but were beaten off by magic. Fortunately the abbot is an ex-pupil of mine. Have you been *losing* people, Derk?"

"No, I have," said Blade. "They try to escape all the time."

"Scales is going to try to round them all up," Derk said. "Is that all? We've got to get down to the Emirates today too."

"Well—" Querida's hand hovered over the message slips again. This was something quite different and rather worrying, which had only come in this morning. She was in two minds whether to keep it secret or not. But, probably because of that slight guilt she felt, she thought she would mention it to Derk anyway. Her hand darted to a paper that she had set aside from the others. "There's this. Do you know a wizard called Betula?"

Derk nodded. Blade said, "She's a friend of Mum's."

"Then you'll know that she is reliable," said Querida, "and probably that her field of study is the nature of magic itself. She says she's finding a steady decrease in the ambient magic over quite a large area north of Costamara. What do you make of that?"

Derk looked perplexed. "I don't see how she can. I always thought magic was part of the very earth itself."

"So did I. But it appears to be leaving us," Querida said. "If Betula is right, this is going to panic everyone, including Mr Chesney, so I must ask you not to mention it. But just keep your magic senses peeled as you go about, will you? You might discover what's going on. Now, if you'll forgive me—"

They left Querida sitting in front of her papers and went out into the deserted forecourt, where Blade said, "You want to go to the Emirates? I've never been there. I don't—"

"It'll be like going to the Oracle," Derk explained. "I'll show you on the map. But I thought we'd go to Bardic College first and see if we can do something to help poor Shona."

Blade took them to Bardic College, where they drew a complete blank. Derk hammered on the great locked door repeatedly, but no one answered, not even to tell them to go away.

"They knew you'd be along, Dad," Blade said.

"So they stuck their bone-filled heads into the sand," Derk agreed angrily.

"*Do* something to them," said Blade. "Make them forget the words of all the songs. Untune all their pianos. They deserve it."

"Yes, but it wouldn't help Shona. Let's get to the Emirates," Derk said.

Blade thoroughly enjoyed the Emirates. It was wonderfully hot and dry there, which was a treat in itself after camping in frost and rain, and he liked the Emir's palace. It was one of the hugest and silliest buildings he had ever seen. Derk chuckled as Blade stared at its ninety-four twisted towers, its red dome and its green and yellow chequered cupolas. "I wonder if Umru has ever seen this," he said. "He'd be green with envy. Tear yourself away, Blade. We have to find the Grand Vizier."

The Grand Vizier was a large man, with the look of someone who had suddenly gone thin – rather like Dad, Blade thought, looking from one to the other – and he was feverishly glad to see Derk. He led them at a trot through halls and passages, gasping out as he trotted, "It is terrible! You must see – see for yourselves. Here. Stand here. Watch that cross-corridor. Here he comes now."

A tall thin man in a red hat crossed the end of the corridor where they were standing. He was walking very upright in a sort of stiff strut, holding both his arms bent rigidly at the elbows. "I am a pup-pet," he was saying in a blank, toneless voice. "I have no mind."

"There," said the Grand Vizier as the Emir stalked out of sight. "Did drugs do this? A spell? Is it the red hat? The tourists all stare at him strangely. We try to keep them away from him. It will not do."

"I'm afraid," Derk said, panting rather from trotting in the heat, "that he's pretending to be hypnotised. It's my fault. I didn't know he couldn't act. I'll try and sort him out, but it's going to take a bit of time and tact. Have you got anywhere my lad here can wait while I try?"

"Certainly, certainly!" said the Grand Vizier.

Blade was slightly offended that Dad did not consider him tactful enough to help talk to the Emir, but he was entirely interested – though rather shy – when servants showed him to a room full of highly beautiful slave ladies, whose aim seemed to be to make Blade the centre of their universe. They sat him on soft, sweet-smelling cushions, fanned him, brought him water to wash in with flower petals floating in it, combed his hair, and gave him a silk shirt because the one he had on was torn. Meanwhile, six more ladies played music to him, almost as well as Shona might have played it, and another lady took his socks away to be washed. Instantly, some of the others pounced on his dirty feet and washed those too.

"Oh, you needn't bother!" Blade kept saying, slightly to the side of each new lady. It was hard for him to look at them. Their clothes were so very gauzy that he knew he would stare and gape quite rudely if he once started looking properly.

"No trouble," they answered, laughing. "Now you've arrived, this is our last day here, so we don't mind a bit."

Another pair of ladies came to Blade with a tiny cup of very sweet coffee and a wide tray of sticky cakes. "Take the green ones," the lady with the cakes advised him. "Those are the ones the griffin said were godlike."

Blade forgot to tell her she needn't bother. He even looked at her. "*Lydda* was here?"

"Oh yes!" they all said. "And we want you to tell us all about her. Did your father really make her?"

Blade enjoyed himself even more after that, telling them about Lydda and the other griffins, while they sat round him in a half circle with their hands clasped round their gauzy knees – except for the lady who had washed Blade's socks, who was now darning them – and stared at him with wide, beautiful eyes. He felt as godlike as the cakes.

And then they suddenly all stood up. "We have to go now," said the one with his socks. She passed the socks to him, neatly mended. "Tell the Emir that there are going to be no more slavegirls from now on, here or anywhere else."

"I – ah—" Blade began, thinking he ought to explain that the Emir was not behaving as if he would listen.

But they were all gone. They had not left by any of the doors. The room was simply empty, apart from somebody's silk scarf slowly fluttering to the tiled floor in a warm blast of scented air. It felt like a mass translocation to Blade. He was still wondering where they could have gone when the scarf reached the floor and became a folded piece of paper, lying on the tiles. Blade padded over and picked it up. It was, to his astonishment, a note from his mother.

Dear Blade,
Please give the Emir the message about slavegirls. It's important. I'm thinking of you a lot and looking forward to your visit here with your Pilgrim Party. And tell Derk that I've remembered about the dragon.
All my love,
Mara

"Where are all my slavegirls?" thundered the Emir, just as Blade had finished putting on his socks. The Emir seemed quite normal now. He came rushing into the empty room with Derk behind him and stared about irately, more or less as anyone might who was suddenly minus twenty pretty ladies.

Blade, rather hesitantly, told him what the sock-darning lady had said.

"*But there are always slavegirls!*" the Emir howled. "The tourists *expect* them!"

Derk was looking weary. "This is something you have to deal with yourself, Your Highness," he said. "We have to go to Chell. Perhaps you could, consider hiring some girls." At this the Emir began shouting that hired girls were not slavegirls and Derk turned wearily to Blade. "Blade, if you would."

Blade took hold of his father's sleeve and brought them north a long way to where Derk had said Chell was. "They translocated," he said as they arrived. Chell was perched in front of them on a hill, crowned with a castle and surrounded by vineyards. "Hey, it's beautiful!" Blade said. "Are they really going to destroy it?"

"Chell and nine others," Derk said. "That's the tours for you. Who translocated?"

As they walked uphill between the vines to the city, Blade told Derk about the ladies. "I think the one who darned my socks must have been a wizard," he said. "She had the feel – oh, and she left a letter from Mum." He passed the note to Derk.

Derk's face sagged as he read it. "So your mother remembers that Scales burnt me. Good of her." He passed the note back.

He looked so strange that Blade said, "Are you all right, Dad?"

Derk just grunted and took hold of a bunch of grapes hanging out over the path. "Ripe," he said. "Looks like a good vintage too. I suppose they're leaving them because of the siege. Barnabas would cry at this waste. I'll see if I can save the grapes."

"Don't you want to talk about Mum?" asked Blade.

"No," said Derk. "I want to see what's wrong in Chell."

But they could find nothing wrong in Chell. Inside the walls, everyone was going cheerfully about the business of preparing arrows and making armour, just as they should have been. Derk and Blade were shown up to the castle, where they were met by the Duchess of Chell, who seemed quite resigned to losing her city and her grape harvest.

"It's the way it goes these days, Wizard," she said. "I'm sorry the Duke's not here to meet you himself. He'd tell you the same. Can I offer you any refreshment?"

Derk refused, on the grounds that they were both full of the Emir's sticky cakes, and they went away again, through the city and downhill among the vines. "There *is* something wrong," Derk said, "but I'm blowed if I can see what. Could you?"

"I thought," Blade said doubtfully, "that they all seemed a bit too cheerful."

"Me too," Derk agreed. "No regrets even about these grapes. But it's nothing you can pin down. Let's see if Prince Talithan's noticed anything. He's doing the besieging. He must have been and talked to them too."

"How do you get hold of him to ask him?" said Blade.

"He's an elf and he's sworn allegiance," Derk said. "He should come when I call him. I hope." He stood still in the dusty rutted road between the vines and called out, "Talithan! Prince Talithan, I need you!"

After a short while, during which Blade was certain Derk was just making a fool of himself, a blue-green misty light swung towards them in the road like a door opening, and Prince Talithan stood there bowing. "Forgive me, my lord. I was far to the south, discussing the siege of Serata."

"That's all right," said Derk. "If you're on Serata, you must have been to Chell and made all the arrangements here already."

"A week ago, lord," Talithan said. "All seems in order, I have my list of expendables, and my elves are armed and ready. We shall sack each city between the battles at your side in Umru's land."

"Er – you'll find the battlefield is actually about fifty miles south of where it should be," Derk said. "But how was Chell? Did everything strike you as in order here?"

"I found nothing wrong." Talithan was clearly puzzled to be asked. "Methought the Duke seemed depressed, but that I understood. He was about to lose a city and a good vintage."

"Ah well," said Derk. "It was worth a try. See if you can save these vines if you can."

Talithan bowed. "I had that thought myself, lord."

When Prince Talithan had retreated away through his misty door, Derk shrugged. "Maybe that man from Chell was an alarmist. Back to camp, Blade."

They returned to a chillier, greyer climate and a great deal of bustle. High Priest Umru had made them a thank-you present of a set of tents. Don was galloping about showing the young priests who brought them exactly where each tent should be set up. Very priestly tents, they were, white and embroidered with the emblems of Anscher.

"Not exactly right for a Dark Lord," Derk said, "but I won't grumble."

Inside the magic dome on the hill, the battle spells now seemed to be working. The men in black were exercising, doing sword practice, or marching off to the cookhouse, almost as if they were real soldiers. Derk nodded to Barnabas, who nodded cheerfully back.

The main activity, however, was around Kit. Kit was in his element. He had maps, plans and lists spread out and pinned down with flat stones near the river, and he was surrounded by people, all listening to him attentively. "Your fanatics are lined up here," Kit was saying to a priest. "Keep them back in the trees until midday." Blade saw King Luther and Titus and the werewolf among Kit's listeners, but there were many others he did not know, including some elves, several dwarfs, a sturdy man holding a helmet who was probably a mercenary, a group of strange white-faced people almost as skinny as Old George, and numbers of men in gold earrings, each wearing a fur draped across one shoulder. Around them, less important people came and went as Kit sent them off on errands. A mercenary came in at a run as Blade watched.

"That stream does run north and south."

"Damn," said Kit and made a note on a map. "Someone – you in the fur – go and find out all the places it can be crossed. I don't want to waste strength defending fords. The legionaries may have to dig it deeper."

"They can do that," said Titus. "But what's the timing of my attack on the Dark Elves?"

Derk watched with a broad smile. Kit's eyes were bright and his neck eagerly arched. "You know," Derk said to Blade, "I think getting Kit to plan the battles may have been an inspiration. How's Shona?"

Shona could not have been more of a contrast to Kit. She was still sitting staring at nothing. She did not seem to notice Callette crouching protectively beside her, nor did she look up when Pretty scampered past, showering them both with gravel as he played tag with the dogs. Blade went over to her, but she did not look at him either. He sat down beside Callette.

"Who are the people with the white faces?"

"Vampires," said Callette. "I don't like them. They look at your forelegs and say 'Juicy wrists'."

"Whose side are they on?" Blade asked.

"Ours, I think," said Callette. "They look quite wicked."

CHAPTER SEVENTEEN

✴

*F*rom then on, it was all bustle, preparing for the first of the battles. Blade could not understand how his father found time to make drawings and calculations for carrier pigeons in the midst of it all.

"It keeps me sane," Derk said mildly. Or drives me mad another way, he added secretly. The trouble with pigeons was that they had no brains to speak of, and no room to add any. Derk experimented, in between crises, with putting an extra brain somewhere in the middle of the pigeon, but that seemed to mean that the poor creatures would have even more trouble getting airborne than Lydda did. Perhaps they should fly by magic, somewhat in the way dragons did, he thought, as Scales flew in to report that he had moved the purple dragon six miles and one furlong to the south-east, and then took off again to search for dwarfs and missing soldiers.

At dawn, two days before the battle, Talithan revolved abruptly out of his misty doorway, looking pale and distressed, and crunched hurriedly to Derk's priestly tent. Pretty careered over to him, whinnying with pleasure, but Talithan put him gently aside. "Lord, I have failed you over Chell," he said, as Derk came to the tent-flap.

Derk was in the middle of shaving and not wholly awake. "Lost the grape harvest, did you?" he said. "Not to worry."

"No, no. We saved the grapes. Indeed," said Talithan, "the city of Chell stands in every way whole and entire, save for its people. That is my failure."

"Been a massacre, has there?" Derk asked. His heart sank.

"Oh, no indeed!" Talithan cried out. "There were no people there at all – no citizens, that is, lord. We found streets, halls, markets, houses all empty, and not one soul to be discovered. Thinking they must be crammed within the castle, we stormed our way thither – setting the illusion of fire on houses as we went, for appearance's sake – but within the castle were only ten parties of Pilgrims, and the wizard with each party hardpressed to conceal his own group from the rest in all that emptiness. And right angry they were, for their orders are that each party should believe the town besieged for its benefit alone. And upon the urging of these wizards, we stormed our way downwards into the bowels of the dungeons, pretending to pursue the tourists. There we found the Duke of Chell locked in a dungeon, but no other soul besides. The wizards are seething angry, lord."

"I'd better go and calm them down," Derk sighed. "Blade! Saddle Beauty for me. Don't worry, Prince. I consider you did everything you could to retrieve a very peculiar situation. But I'd better find out what happened in Chell. Does the Duke know?"

"He says he found himself seized and imprisoned, but he knew not by whom," Prince Talithan said. "He had been in the dungeon for days. But where the citizens went, he knew not. Is it true I have not failed you, lord?"

"It is true," said Derk. He repeated this that evening when he came back totally mystified. Chell was completely empty, except for the Duke, gloomily sitting in the castle. The townspeople had gone. They had taken all the food and most of their belongings, but they had left no tracks. Derk spent most of the day flying Beauty in wider and wider circles round the city, hoping to locate the people, but there was no sign of them. "I don't understand it!" he told Prince Talithan. "You wouldn't think we could mislay several thousand people, but we surely have."

Beauty was too tired that night for Blade to ride her out on the Wild Hunt. Blade let the geese out of the hamper after they had performed as leathery-winged avians and sat on it beside Shona. He had promised Callette he would look after Shona until the Hunt got back. She was still pale and wretched, although she ate a little and even talked sometimes. Blade wished Lydda was back to look after Shona. Everyone else was too busy. Callette was doing her best, but even she was swept up in the mounting bustle and excitement as Kit prepared to stage the battle.

The night before the battle, Blade hardly slept. Everyone got up before dawn, and Blade felt sick, empty and giddy with nerves, as he watched other people arriving or getting ready. Kit was galloping from one end of the camp to the other, a huge speeding blackness, squawking orders. Barnabas was hurrying around in the near dark, chinking in black chainmail, putting the final touches to his battle spells on the soldiers.

"These spells won't last more than twelve hours," Barnabas said repeatedly to Derk and Kit. "Make sure you call a retreat before they wear off, or I won't be answerable for the consequences."

Around the camp, half-seen people kept arriving. Blade saw a band of white-faced vampires, but most of the figures milling about were entirely strange to him. Some of them had a demonic look.

"Not really. We're from ordinary villages," one demonic person told him. "We agreed to look like this. It keeps you out of the way of the tourists."

When it got lighter, Blade saw that quite a number of the new arrivals had the brown robes and leather satchels of healers. Derk grabbed one of them and told her to stay in the camp to look after Shona. "That girl needs a mind-healer, not me!" the healer grumbled. "But I'll stay anyway. I detest battles." Blade wondered how anyone could.

Then came the marvellous moment when the sun came up and Barnabas opened the soldiers' dome. Drums beat. The soldiers came marching out in ranks with black banners overhead. A pipe played somewhere and Derk wheeled Beauty to march at the head of his army. Derk was all in black silk. Blade's clothes were largely black too and he marched beside Beauty carrying a black banner with a strange device, invented by Kit. His job was to plant the banner by Derk and then act as a messenger, translocating with Kit's orders to wherever they were needed. As Kit had pointed out, someone who could be in another place as quick as thought was very useful indeed. "And I wish you weren't going to leave so soon," Kit said repeatedly.

Don and Callette marched with Derk and Blade. Kit had made Don inky black with red eyes, but Callette had totally refused any alteration. "I want to stay beautiful," she said.

"Well, you look quite black from underneath," Kit said at last, forced to give in.

As all the people behind the soldiers got into motion,

carts of ammunition creaking, horses protesting, feet rhythmically crunching, Blade gave himself over to the sheer excitement of marching with an army on a crisp autumn morning – it was cold enough that everyone's breath steamed in rolls above the march – to the sound of drums beating and pipes playing. When they reached the site of the battle, his excitement was boundless.

The place was one of a chain of valleys. "When we wear one valley out, we move on to the next," Kit had explained. For the moment, this first valley looked perfect, with its meadows below, through which wound the little river that had so bothered Kit, and its sides filled with green and gold trees. There, on the opposite wooded hill, the forces of Good had gathered. They had coloured flags, bright uniforms and trumpets sounding. They looked resplendent. But Derk's forces were majestic in their own way too, in their sombre blacks, with the dark banners flapping and the drums solemnly beating. There were also at least twice as many of them, because of the tour rule that the forces of Good should be heavily outnumbered but still win. Blade looked searchingly over at the bright ranks, trying to pick out the Pilgrim Parties. He knew that there should now be at least twenty-one parties embedded in that army, each kept carefully apart from the others by their Wizard Guides, but he simply could not pick them out.

Blade dithered with eagerness. The horses were being led away and the various divisions of their army were taking up their correct stations. Derk on Beauty was the sole rider there. He was looking from side to side with a sort of weary calmness Blade just could not share, seeing that everything was ready. And, seeing it was, Derk raised his arm in the signal.

A deep, deep horn bellowed. The soldiers in black began to advance and, as they moved, Kit rose into the air majestically from the rear. There was a gasp, even from his own side. Derk, in these battles, had cheerfully agreed to pretend to be one of his own minions. Kit was Dark Lord. He had made himself twice the size and worked hard on his power of illusion until he was able to make it look as if a huge shadowy figure was riding on his back. The size and power of the figure made the air dark. And Kit could also see everything that went on below in the battle.

"Blade," his voice sounded more or less in Blade's ear – Kit had been working on this too – "Blade, go and see why the Dark Elves aren't moving with the rest."

Blade shot himself over to the left wing of the army, but as he got there Prince Talithan hastily took up his position and the elves began to advance. Kit's voice said, "That's all right then. Go and tell the Good dwarfs that they're supposed to stay back in the woods." Blade whirled himself across the valley. While he was arguing with the dwarf captain, the two armies came together in the meadows below with a sound like a great metallic grunt, and thereafter Blade lost all sense of what was going on. He supposed that Kit, grandly circling above, must still know. He had to, because he kept sending Blade to different places. But down in the meadows it was just seething desperation, shouting, clanging, feet braced and sliding in the mud, faces that were resigned, or businesslike, or fierce, arms chopping and hacking, and always mud. Blade saw arrows arcing in the sky, but he did not know whose. The marvel of it was that it made no difference to the excitement. Blade was near screaming with the excitement. There was a place where people were charging forward with spears, and another – or maybe the same place – where spears were planted with points slanting and people seemed to be fighting a last stand. Everything he saw was muddled in the vast, dull, brangling din that filled the valley, and the oily smell of armour mixed with the smell of people sweating. His excitement got muddled in it too. Down by the river there was a charge through the water, feet labouring and splashing in sheets of water. Blade saw someone slip over, by the far bank, and everybody else go running and climbing over the person's heaving, muddy body. Then it happened to someone else, as the charge came rushing and howling in the other direction.

In spite of the excitement, Blade wanted to shout at them to be careful.

There were rousing warcries, yells and grunts, but not much blood or screaming at first. The screaming began when Don and Callette went winging across the valley to drop brown bundles on the forces of Good. As each bundle hit, it went off with a *boom* and a ball of rich red flame. And screams. The screaming sounded so much in earnest that Blade found it hard to remember that Don and Callette were dropping the bundles where they would do least damage. He wanted to shout to them to be careful too. Some of the trees caught fire and the valley filled with smoke.

Kit sent Blade to Prince Talithan. Blade found him just at the moment when a bearded wizard carefully pushed a sweaty, middle-aged man forward and nodded at Talithan. Prince Talithan said, "Forgive me. You are down as expendable." He batted aside the man's waving sword and pushed his own sword neatly into the man's chest. The man thumped down on to the mud just by Blade's feet. Blade looked into his bluish, twisted face and thought, Funny. The first Pilgrim I've seen is a dead one. "Kit wants you to advance now," he told Talithan, and then whisked away into the woods to tell the fanatics to join the battle.

Another funny thing, he thought as he whisked. I'm hating this battle quite as much as I'm enjoying it.

The fanatics were crouched among the trees, bent over their curved swords, polishing them while they waited. When Blade told them they could attack now, they sprang up with yells of fervour, lofting those swords, and rushed forward in a gaggle. "Anscher, Anscher, Anscher!" they screamed. Their eyes glowed staringly. Their faces were full of devout rage. Blade realised that they truly were fanatics, and the excitement of the battle nearly choked him. The excitement rose and rose as the black-robed crowd raced downhill with the curved swords flashing over their heads and exploded into horror as they entered the battle. The fanatics clearly did not care if they lived or died. They sliced everyone in their way. There was a lot of blood about from then on. Blade saw a line of legionaries trot forward in good order and go down like dominoes as the fanatics met them. He met King Luther wading grimly away from the front line, holding a dripping red cloth to one arm. He met increasing numbers of people who died just as he met them, just like the Pilgrim. None of them died peaceful. They were in undignified sprawls, or curled up, and their faces showed the pain of their last moments. Blade hated it. But he also wanted to cheer the fanatics for killing them. He hated the heavy brangling din of the battle, and yet it still excited him enormously. Before long, he was thinking he was being pulled in two by these different feelings. And he was ashamed of hating the battle almost as much as he was ashamed at being so excited by it.

After the fanatics charged in, it seemed impossible that the forces of Good could win. But Kit had things well under control. Shortly he sent Blade to Derk, where Derk sat on Beauty at the head of the soldiers in black. Beauty was splashed with mud and blood and not at all happy. Derk was looking incredulous. "These men are survivor types," he told Blade. "Tell Kit we've hardly lost one."

"Kit says you can start retreating now," Blade said.

"Oh ghoodh!" said Beauty.

It took some time for Derk's men to disengage. By that time Blade felt that the noise and the double feelings were never going to stop. But when the afternoon light was slanting across the valley, there was a gap in the front line where the soldiers had been and Kit had almost no need to send Blade to tell the various captains to pretend to flee. Most of them were hurriedly withdrawing anyway, except for the fanatics, and there were almost none of them left. Bundles of dead black robes lay everywhere in the muddy floor of the valley.

Blade watched the forces of Good gather triumphantly under the burnt trees. Healers were coming quickly out of the surviving woods and hurrying to those of the people lying around who were still moving. A fresh, neat line of legionaries trotted out after them, carrying spades.

At that, Blade could not stand any more and took himself away, back to the camp. Don was standing by the river with his head hanging, golden again, but draggled.

"I hated that!" he said to Blade. "The trouble was, I enjoyed it too. What's wrong with me?"

"I felt just the same. I wish there wasn't another one next week," Blade said.

They leant together, exhausted. "And we've still got the geese and the Hunt again tonight!" Don groaned.

Shona came out of her tent. She walked down towards them in that strange way she had lately, as if the air was thicker for her than for other people and made moving an effort, but she looked rather better. "Both of you come to my tent," she said. "The healer's got some brandy and we're cooking steak."

Don and Blade went gratefully – and quickly, because Kit and Callette were coming in to land and both of them looked almost unbearably cheerful.

After that, Blade found he was dreading next week's battle. He buried himself in the work around the camp and forgot about it as much as he could. But he envied Kit and Callette for their uncomplicated feelings about it. They enjoyed battles, both of them. Then Blade found he envied Don too. Don had managed to have a heart-to-heart talk with Derk, in which he told Derk all about the double way the battle made him feel, and Derk had said that in that case Don could take charge of the geese and the Wild Hunt and not go to any more of the battles. Blade tried to catch Derk then and say the same, but Derk had left. Prince Talithan had tried to sack a second city and found all the citizens missing from this city too. Derk was hunting for them.

"Because they all have to be *somewhere*," he kept saying.

"They're lying low," Barnabas said. "They know there'll be trouble with Mr Chesney."

"Yes, but *where*?" said Derk. In the end, since it was

time for the next battle, he sent the daylight owls to find Scales, each with a message tied to its leg asking Scales to look for the missing townsfolk.

The battle took place without Don, and Blade found it worse than the first. His excitement, and his hatred of it, seemed twice as strong, now he knew what to expect. It made him feel like two people in one body. He wondered, in the evening when it was over at last, whether he could stand another time.

The next morning, Derk was gone again. Barnabas came up to Blade after breakfast carrying a bundle of clothing with a cardboard folder balanced on top. "You've got three days to get yourself down to the coast," he told Blade cheerfully. "Your Pilgrim Party starts the day after that. Here're your wizardly robes and the list of your Pilgrims is in this folder. Got your black book? Map and pamphlets? You'll need those. And do remember there's bound to be someone who'll be reporting back to Mr Chesney. Pilgrims pay a reduced fee if they do, so there's always someone. Make sure you always do exactly what's in the black book, won't you?"

It was a tremendous shock to Blade. He was thinking of his own tour as still in the distant future, and here it was, on top of him. It was almost equally a great relief. He did not need to stand another battle after all. Otherwise, he felt rather frantic. He had not learnt much of the black book, and what he had learnt had gone all vague in his head. Kit had the map and the book and was not pleased.

"But you've made at least a hundred copies!" Blade protested. "And I need them."

Kit grudgingly gave up the rather battered black book and the dog-eared map. "I was reckoning on having you for another battle at least," he said. "I can't believe we've been out here nearly six weeks. Callette's not going to be half as quick with my orders. She'll have to fly everywhere. I'll have to rethink my plans. And we'll have to have Don back. All right. You go. I'd better call a meeting of my captains. Those werewolves didn't pull their weight in either battle and I want to talk to them anyway."

Kit paced away, muttering in his beak and swinging his tail. Blade turned to take the map and the book to his tent and nearly ran into Shona.

"I've decided to come on this Pilgrim Party with you," Shona said. "I can be your tour bard."

Blade had a moment when he was really pleased, and then another moment when he was furious at the way Shona never let him do anything by *himself*. These were followed by a third moment when he was afraid that Shona's mind might have gone strange. The three things together caused him to say doubtfully, "But won't the Bardic College be awfully angry if you do?"

"*Let* them be angry," Shona said. "They've expelled me from their college and forbidden me bardic status. There's nothing else they can do to me. And I hate sitting around in this camp so close to those awful soldiers.

You *will* let me come with you, won't you, Blade? Please."

"It will be nice to have someone I know with me," Blade conceded.

They settled that they would leave after Derk came back, so that they could say goodbye to him.

CHAPTER EIGHTEEN

✳

When Derk returned from soothing angry Wizard Guides and heard the news, he had mixed feelings. In one way he was pleased that Blade would have Shona with him to keep him sensible. On the other hand, he was afraid that Shona was so upset at losing her career that she was thinking of getting herself killed somewhere along the way. But he had no time to argue. Tomorrow, unless Finn was badly behind schedule, the first Pilgrim Party would be arriving at the Citadel to kill the Dark Lord, and Derkholm was still not a Citadel. So he simply implored Shona to be careful and watched Blade take hold of Shona's arm. Shona was clutching a bag, her violin, her harp and her flute. Blade only had his bundle of robes and the folder.

"Black book?" said Derk.

"In my pocket," said Blade. "Don't fuss, Dad." The two of them disappeared with the strong inrushing of wind that always went with a translocation.

"Kit, you'll have to fly the Hunt tonight with Don and Callette," Derk said to Kit. "I have to get to Derkholm."

"But I've called a conference!" Kit protested.

"Then make it brief," said Derk. "You haven't time to enjoy yourself tonight."

Kit was extremely offended, mostly because Derk was entirely right. Kit loved holding conferences. He was always thinking of reasons for calling them and ways of making them go on as long as possible. Derk left Kit scowling with his crest-feathers right down on his beak and went to where he had left Beauty still saddled.

"Htake Phretty htoo," said Beauty. "He ghoes to bhad elfh ahll the htime."

Derk knew this was true. Talithan had only to beckon and Pretty vanished. But it was time Beauty got used to this. "Pretty can't fly that far," he said as he mounted. "Why is it I can't do a simple thing like leaving camp without at least two arguments?"

Beauty whisked her tail crossly as she took off. But she was a good-hearted creature and she made good speed. They were over the ruins of the village well before sunset. Derk went down there to check that skeletal Fran was now back, picking through the debris for the benefit of the tourists. She was. "Have you got everything you need?" he asked her.

"A sight more comfort than I would have up at your house!" she retorted.

Derk flew on up the valley wondering what Fran meant by that. Had a row with Old George, he supposed – though there was always the possibility that Lydda had come home and turned Fran out. It was certainly high time Lydda returned. She had laid all the clues. Derk sometimes felt that the clues were the one thing the Wizard Guides did not complain to him about.

Before he took Beauty to the stables, Derk stood looking ruefully at the house. So far, he had only had time to do one of Callette's carefully designed transformations. About half the end where the living room was soared into half a black crooked tower. The result was peculiar.

"And I'm not going to have time to follow the plans properly, I'm afraid," Derk murmured. "Sorry, Callette. They were brilliant."

Here the pigs found him and rushed jubilantly across the garden, pursued as usual by Old George.

"I thought I asked you to keep them out of sight," Derk said. On his last visit, he had experimented with the pigs as servants of the Dark Lord. But as soon as he put the illusion on, they had stared at their bloated black bodies in such horror that Derk took pity on them and decided just to keep them where the Pilgrims could not see them.

"I do, I do," said Old George, "but they get wind of you and they're out before I can turn round. It's as much as I can do to stop those damn dwarfs putting them in their pot. Can't do more than that, not if you paid me every basket of treasure they've got."

At this, Derk left Beauty with Old George and hurried to investigate. He had been afraid that the dwarfs would change their minds, once Scales was not there to intimidate them, and go on to the coast instead. But it seemed not. He found them, ponies and all, camping in the kitchen. Lydda would have fits, Derk thought. Perhaps Lydda had indeed come home, seen what six dwarfs could do to a kitchen, and left to live with Mara. He must ask Old George. "I'm glad to see you got here," he said to the dwarfs.

"Been here for days now," said the surly one, whose name was Galadriel. Derk had been wondering, ever since he discovered this, what Galadriel's parents had been thinking of. "What do you want done with the tribute, then?"

"We'd like to see it properly stowed, have you sign for it, and be on our way home, you see," the talkative one explained. His name, more aptly, was Dworkin. He was some kind of sub-chief.

Derk looked at the six huge baskets taking up the half of the kitchen that the dwarfs and their ponies were not using. Kit's den, he thought. Kit would not be pleased, but according to these dwarfs, there were twenty more bands of them from all over the continent, making their way to the coast with tribute. If Scales only found half of them, Kit's den was the only place big enough to hold it all. "I'll show you where," he said. A thought struck him, possibly because of the mess in the kitchen. These dwarfs might stand in for the pigs. "Would you," he asked, "consider staying on a month or so and acting as the Dark Lord's servitors? The tours would pay you, of course."

"How much?" said Galadriel.

"Well," said Dworkin, pulling his braided beard, "we would have been travelling for the next month anyway, in the normal course of things, so I suppose it's no skin off our nose, so to speak. It depends, really, on the money and on what you want to ask us to do."

Derk consulted his black book. "This year's fee is twenty gold each. I'd need to change you a bit – you have to look swart, you know – nothing radical, though, there's no time. And the job is to pretend to stop the Pilgrims from getting near me. Make a show of violence, hack at their ankles, that sort of thing. Would that be possible?"

The dwarfs looked at one another and grinned a little. "Could be fun," one suggested. Simpse, Derk thought this one's name was.

"Make that forty gold each," said Galadriel, "and it's a bargain."

Derk took out the calculator and entered on it: *Servitors 240 gold*. It rather pleased him that Mr Chesney should pay the dwarfs for once, instead of the other way round. "Done," he said. He showed them to Kit's shed and watched wonderingly as each of them heaved up a tremendous basket and trudged off with it as if it weighed nothing at all. But it did not improve the state of the kitchen much. He would have to move those ponies.

For now, he spread Callette's drawings out on the dining-room table and studied the work he needed to do on the Citadel.

There was no time for anything but skin-deep changes. Other wizards who were more practised in this kind of work might have done it, but Derk had worked with animals and plants all his life and he was slow with buildings. And first things first. The dwarfs needed the kitchen and the animals needed protection. Derk went and led the dwarfs' ponies out of the kitchen and shut them in the paddock with Pretty's grandmother. "They'll be much safer and happier here," he told the dwarfs, when they caught up with him and protested. Then he went round all his crops, tobacco, cotton, tea, coffee, nylon plants, the new orange trees and many other things, most still experimental, shutting them inside a strong dome of magic that made them invisible. After that, he did the same for the animals. There was no guarantee that the pigs would stay inside this dome, but Derk implored them to try. And the cats. Now the village was a deserted ruin, all the cats had come home in disgust. Derk told them to stay in their pen. They just looked at him.

"And how do I feed them now they're twice as

invisible?" Old George demanded, looming at Derk's elbow.

"I'll do it," said Derk. "You just haunt the garden, wailing."

"What do you mean? I never wailed in my life!" Old George said.

"You get forty gold for it," said Derk.

"Ah," said Old George.

By the light of the setting sun, and with Callette's drawings anxiously in his hands, Derk concentrated on the house and garden. The garden became a desolate forecourt with pitfalls and chained monsters in place of the flowerbeds. The bushes and trees were broken black pillars or mazes of evil black walls. For the house itself, Derk followed Callette's design drawing for the completed Citadel and made it a tortured black façade, full of weird sharp angles, twisted arches and impossibly jutting towers. It looked highly impressive against the sunset. But since it was only an inch thick, Derk could not have any Pilgrims going inside it to confront him. Fortunately, Callette had left the enlarged terrace almost as it was. All the griffins liked it this way, because it was so big. Derk added broken black archways along the front of it, twisted like the towers, and tormented low walls. Then to prevent anyone going in through the front door, he constructed a long trench of illusory balefire just in front of the doorstep. This looked surprisingly impressive, flickering white and wraithlike in the growing dark. Derk considered a moment, and then added an impression of untold depth to the trench. Like that, it made the perfect place to be done to death in. The Pilgrims could think they were hurling the Dark Lord down into a bottomless pit.

Quite pleased with his evening's work, Derk walked through the trench and entered the house, where the dwarfs were making rather appetising smells. "What are you cooking?" he asked.

They looked just a little shifty. "Your walking skeleton kept giving us eggs as big as my head and we got rather sick of them," Dworkin explained. "So we – er – "

"Went foraging," said Galadriel.

"He wouldn't let us touch the pigs or the monkeys and we don't eat cat," Simpse added. "But we found a herd of cows in that side valley and they didn't seem to belong to anyone, so— "

"We're roasting an ox," Galadriel said, jutting his plaited beard aggressively.

"Ah well." Derk sighed. "I owe the mayor for twelve others anyway."

"You can have some too," Dworkin said politely. "And we've got egg of course, and we found the cabbage patch and the place with those round brown roots."

"You mean my experimental bread-potatoes," said Derk.

The dwarfs gave him wary looks. "They cook down just like dumplings," Simpse said. "Aren't they digestible then?"

"They were designed to be highly nutritious," Derk said. "I hope you left some for seed."

"We didn't pick quite *all* of them," Simpse said.

Derk sighed again and joined them for a filling supper of roast beef, roots and huge slices of hard-boiled egg, after which he slept better than he had been doing lately. In the morning he went anxiously outside, munching a leftover slice of egg, to see if his transformed Citadel looked convincing by daylight.

Not bad, he decided, as long as the dwarfs kept the Pilgrims too busy to look closely. It had a flimsy sort of look, if you stared at any of it for long. But he was a little startled by the flowerbed monsters. He had not realised that a griffin's notion of a monster would be something made up of bits of human being. Still, they were unusual. And they stirred their many misplaced legs and wagged their several shaggy heads in the breeze in a horribly lifelike way. The balefire looked a little pale by daylight. Derk strengthened it to a brighter white and added another wall or so in the way, so that the Pilgrims would not see it straightaway. Then he went into the kitchen to shake the dwarfs awake and turn them swart.

By the time he had done that, fed the animals and induced Old George to wear the fluttering shreds of garments – "I'm not *decent*!" Old George protested, to which Derk replied, "No, you're a walking corpse and you're beyond that!" – the first Pilgrim Party was actually making its way up the valley. Derk groaned. The valley was green, whitened by morning frost. He had forgotten to make it a waste of cinders. Well, it was too late now. He hurriedly assumed his disguise as Dark Lord and waited for them on the terrace.

There were sixteen tourists, led by Finn, men and women who all looked battered, grubby and tired. They toiled their way up to the gates, which Callette had designed beautifully as a pair of great clawed hands, and stood looking through doubtfully. Finn stepped forward and threw a ball of witchfire at the gates. Derk obliged with a shower of sparks and allowed the clawed hands to swing apart. Finn urged the Pilgrims inside. None of them seemed keen on the idea. They hurried in and halted in a huddle, staring in extreme horror at the flowerbed monsters. Finn urged them on again. Two steps later, Old George crossed their path, uttering muted cries. It was not exactly wailing. It sounded more like "Ho, ho, ho!" The Pilgrims backed away from him. Finn shoved them forward.

Old George, pleased with the effect he was having, stopped and faced them. "I was once a prince like you," he announced.

"Oh shut up and go away, George!" Derk murmured, pacing the terrace.

Finn obviously felt the same. "Avaunt!" he said, and threw witchfire at Old George.

Old George retreated, huffily muttering, "I was only doing it to oblige!"

Finn pushed the Pilgrims forward again. They got halfway up the garden and then it was the turn of the dwarfs, who sprang gleefully out of hiding, shouting warcries and whirling their axes. They looked spectacular. Derk congratulated himself. As well as colouring them blue-black, he had had the idea of converting all their braids into writhing snakes. And this part, he was pleased to see, went with a swing. The Pilgrims were used to fighting by this stage in their tour. They drew swords and hacked at the dwarfs. The dwarfs, with great artistry and much enjoyment, hacked back. They swung and wove and menaced the Pilgrims, but allowed themselves to be slowly driven backwards through the transformed garden, until, after about ten minutes of fierce and bloodless fighting, the Pilgrims had almost reached the terrace steps.

And those steps were a sudden zigzag of acid blue light.

With a noise like the sky splitting, a vast blue three-legged being loomed above the fighting. Its rat tail toyed and slithered among Derk's black archways. The blueness of it pulsed nastily and the nearness of it scalded everyone's mind like salt water on a fresh graze. Old George was suddenly wailing in earnest in the background. The dwarfs fled screaming, and the Pilgrims only stayed where they were because Finn slammed a quick immobility spell on them. In the distance, Derk could hear the pigs shrilling. He was quite at a loss himself. He simply had not expected the demon to appear.

The demon had two eyes glaring greedily upon the transfixed Pilgrim Party and the third swivelled to look sarcastically at Derk. He felt the bleachlike burn of it on his mind. *That's why I'm here. I warned you. I shall appear like this to every tour party.*

But why? Derk wondered. Demons were never this obliging.

The demon's laughter flooded against his brain, making him sick and dizzy. *I have my reasons. Be sure I don't do it to oblige you, little wizard.*

And it was gone, in another zigzag of blue light, just as Finn, white as a sheet and shaking all over, had nerved himself to raise a hand and quaver, "Avaunt!"

How do I manage to follow an effect like *that*? Derk wondered irritably. It took him a second or so to pull himself together and muster his Dark Lord illusion again. Luckily, it took Finn an equal time to remember to take the immobility spell off his party and even when he had, the Pilgrims were slow to move. By the time they came hesitantly among the black arches, Derk was a vague black shadow with burning eyes, outlined against the flickering balefire of the trench.

The Pilgrims stopped dead again at the sight of him. Finn kicked the nearest one in the ankle. "We know your weakness," the man said uncertainly. "Your time is up, Dark Lord."

The next part was truly difficult. Try as he might, Derk could not get the Pilgrims even to attempt to kill

344

him. He bellowed with sinister laughter, he loomed over them uttering threats, he adopted a toneless chilling voice and explained that he was about to toss each of them into this bottomless pit flaming with balefire. This pit. Here. Then he went and stood invitingly beside the trench. But they simply stood and stared at him. It was not for nearly a quarter of an hour, until Finn managed to cannon into the woman who happened to be in front, causing her to stumble against Derk with a scream, that Derk was able to consider the deed done. In the greatest relief, he threw up his arms and toppled sideways into his trench.

From there he heard the woman burst into tears. "That's horrible!" she wept. "Whatever it was, it was entitled to life, just like we are!"

"It will come back to life soon enough," Finn said truthfully. "And you've saved the world and the tour's over. Look. The portal's just opening now."

Derk had always been curious to know how the Pilgrims got home once their tour was finished. He rolled over and, with his chin on the edge of the terrace, he watched among his illusory flames as a pointed oval opening appeared, floating in nowhere above the flagstones. He could feel, distantly, the presence of another demon who was making the opening.

A pretty, smiling lady appeared in the space. She was wearing a smart uniform with a peaked cap. "Congratulations, ladies and gentlemen," she said. "You may now return home. On behalf of Chesney Pilgrim Parties, I hope you have had a most enjoyable tour."

The Pilgrims turned and shuffled eagerly towards the opening and the lady. "Well, it was interesting," one of them said carefully.

"I could use a bath!" said someone else.

The woman who had pushed Derk wiped her hand along under her eyes. "But we don't approve of the way you exploit this whole world for—"

Another woman took hold of her arm. "Not *now*! Wait until we get outside Chesney Building. Then we can go to a newspaper office." She pulled the first woman through the opening.

They were the last to go through. The pretty lady smiled and nodded and the distant demon closed the opening. And that was all. Derk climbed out of his trench.

"Thank the gods!" said Finn, sinking down on to a nearby wall. Luckily it was the outdoor table in disguise and supported his weight. "Sorry about that. These were a really slow lot. Total wimps. You always get some, but these were the worst I've ever known. You couldn't manage a cup of coffee, could you, by any chance?"

"It's about the only thing the dwarfs don't like. There should be some," Derk said, and led the way across the balefire to the kitchen. Finn shuddered at the sight of it and retreated to the dining room.

"Forgive me. I've been living rough for nearly six

weeks," he explained, when Derk brought the coffee. "Phew! That party was hard work. And I'm afraid none of the gods did manifest, did you know? I made my tour one down in your village, in the end – a sort of smiling child, promising them success. I hope you don't mind."

"I hope the real gods don't." Derk turned one of Callette's drawings over and wrote on the back of it, "*Fran. To tell wizards smiling child in village*," as a reminder to himself to make sure the other wizards faked a god too. Querida had really let him down there.

"Nothing struck me down," Finn said. "There are two more parties waiting in the village. I'll drop a hint to them on my way back, if you like, and they can have their gods before coming on up here. By the way, whatever went wrong in Chell? I arrived to find the place deserted. I had a real job to keep my party from seeing the other ones, and a lot of fast talking to do when we found the Duke in a dungeon. Your elves managed quite well, considering. But where did all the people go?"

"I wish I knew," Derk said.

Finn gulped the last of his coffee and sprang up. "I have to go. My next tour starts tomorrow night. I want to get some sleep, a proper meal and a hot bath – in that order – before I set off again. See you again in six weeks."

Finn left and, while Derk waited for the next Pilgrim Party, he wondered how Blade and Shona were getting on.

CHAPTER NINETEEN

*

*B*lade and Shona arrived to find bunting hung out in the town and a large banner over the main street saying GNA'ASH WELCOMES YOUR TOUR. The inn where the Pilgrim Party was to assemble was just up the street. It was large, empty and quiet. The landlord, who seemed to be all on his own, showed them to two sparse little rooms overlooking the main street and pointed out the bathrooms down the corridor.

"A bath!" said Shona. "Let's get *clean*!" It was clear Shona had been right to come. Blade could see that she was instantly much more cheerful.

They had baths, blissfully, and washed their hair. Blade had truly meant to spend all the rest of the time studying the black book and the map. Instead, he went to sleep. So did Shona. It was so marvellous to be in a real room with a bed. Every so often, they were woken by the landlord for a meal, after which they staggered upstairs and fell asleep again.

The third time they were sitting dozing over their food in the empty taproom, Shona remarked, "This is the same as the last meal. Or have we only had one?"

The landlord looked long-suffering. "Don't blame me, blame the wife. She joined this Women Against Pilgrim Parties they're all joining this year and walked out a month ago. Took all the barmaids with her and left me on my own. Bread and stew is all I know how to cook."

"Well, it's filling," Blade said, and they went upstairs to sleep again.

On the morning the tour started, Blade woke up in a panic. The Pilgrim Party would be arriving that afternoon and he knew there was absolutely no way he was going to learn all the rules and the route in time. He spread the black book and the map and the pamphlet out on his bed and tried anyway. But it was no good. He was still half asleep. By the end of the morning, all he had really learnt was that his tour was one of those which went north-east to the Inland Sea, so that his party could be captured by pirates and rescued by dragons while the other tours were busy down in Grapland and Costamara. He was just going to have to look each day up in the pamphlet as it came. As for the black book, there were whole sections of it he had not even looked at. He leafed through them. "*Rules*," he read. "*1. Wizards are to grow beards, wear their hair below shoulder-length and carry a staff at all times.*"

"Help!" said Blade. He leapt up and rushed to the mirror. After half an hour of trial and error, he found a way to grow himself a long white beard and a bush of white hair. Out of it, his face stared, rosy and rounded and young. He looked like an albino dwarf. Hopeless. He found how to turn all the new hair dark. This time he just looked like a dwarf who had forgotten to do his plaits, but it would have to do. Now, staff. Blade rushed out of his room and tore down to the inn kitchen, where there was a rack of wooden spoons. He snatched the largest and was racing upstairs with it when he ran into Shona.

She actually gave a gurgle of laughter, the first laugh he had heard from her since the bard handed her that scroll. "Blade, you look *ridiculous*! Like a dwarf on a bad day. And why are you waving a *spoon*?"

"Staff," panted Blade. "Rules. Better in robes." He pushed past her and hurried to his room, where he spent another twenty minutes trying to persuade the spoon to look like a wizardly staff. Whatever he did, the staff grew a broad flat part at the end that was a spoon. And the robes, when he put them on, were too big. Even when he hitched them up with his belt and rolled up the sleeves, they were too big. He waded down to lunch, treading on hems and trying to disentangle his beard from his belt-buckle. As for eating stew through all this hair, he was not sure it was possible.

Shona watched him struggling. Before long she had both hands over her mouth to stop herself giggling. Finally, she took pity on him and went upstairs for her scissors. "Hold still," she said and carved him a hole in the beard for his mouth. After that Blade could eat – though he still found himself chewing hair from his chin from time to time – and when he had finished, Shona made him stand on a chair while she cut the robes down to the right size. She prised the spoon out of his hand and fetched him a walking stick someone had left in the inn hatstand. "There," she said. "Wasn't it lucky I decided to come with you? Come upstairs and I'll hem the edges."

Hemming the robes took a while. Shona was only halfway done when they heard confused rhythmic shouting out in the street. Blade wrestled open the window and they both leant out. The main street below was lined with people, mostly women and children. As far as they could hear, some of them were shouting, "Go home, Pilgrims!" while the rest chanted, "Ban the tours!"

"There really is strong feeling!" Shona remarked.

Blade could not be bothered with that. Between the crowds, he could just see the heads of other people coming up the middle of the street. His stomach did some strange diving about as he realised he was about to meet his first live Pilgrims. *His* Pilgrims. He snatched up his list and ran for the door. Shona was only just in time to grab the back of his shirt.

"Don't be silly! I haven't finished your robes. Anyway you should give them time to get settled in their rooms. *Then* go down to the taproom and meet them. Remember you're a wise and stately wizard and you don't need to run after them."

Blade supposed she was right. Besides, it was soon clear that not all the Pilgrims arrived at once. Every so often there was a new outbreak of chanting in the street and, when Blade craned from the window, he saw another few heads moving slowly up the middle. He sat nervously twisting his list and watching Shona sew.

Shona had just bitten off the last thread when the landlord knocked at the door. Blade jumped up again and Shona hastily got him into the shortened robes. "Man from the tours to speak to the wizard at the kitchen door," the landlord said, when Shona opened the door.

Rather puzzled, Blade followed the landlord down the back stairs and through the kitchen, which was now full of the smell of onions being chopped for tonight's stew. The man waiting at the back door wore a casual version of the kind of clothes Mr Chesney and his people had worn. "Sorry about this, Wizard," he said. "I oughtn't to be here, really, but there's a bit of a crisis at the portal. We're ten parties of dwarfs short. Only one lot came through. You didn't happen to see any others on your way here, did you?"

"Er – with ponies and baskets?" Blade asked.

"That'll be them!" the man said, obviously relieved. "How far off were they?"

"Quite a long way," Blade said truthfully. "They grumbled about the way they were delayed." He felt so dishonest that he was forced to stroke his beard and look wise.

The tour man pulled his own chin in a worried way. "I don't know *what* to do then. The last pair of Pilgrims just came through and the portal's due to be closed in an hour. There'll be a right stink if the dwarfs aren't here by then. I could lose my job. Look, if you see them on your route, better tell them to make for the Dark Lord's Citadel instead and we'll take the lot through from there. And I'll ask the other Wizard Guides to tell them the same. All right?"

"All right," Blade agreed, and he went upstairs again, rather sobered to think that someone was going to be out of work just because he and Don had rescued six dwarfs.

"Nothing's ever simple," Shona said when he told her. "Wait another hour and then go to the taproom."

Blade could not wait that long. He went down after half an hour. By that time, at least half the twenty people on his list were sitting about on the benches awkwardly drinking tankards of beer and getting to know one another. "I *know* it's expensive," a woman was saying as Blade came in. "Dad and I sold our house to come on this tour. But we wanted to do something really interesting before we got too old to enjoy it."

"That's right, Mother," agreed the man beside her. "Nothing ventured."

They both looked immensely old to Blade, and rather fat. He wondered if they would survive the tour, let alone enjoy it. At that, he realised that his nervousness had vanished and he was simply interested. All the Pilgrims had their hair cut in a way he was not used to and carried foreign looks on their faces. This made them seem to be wearing fancy dress, even though they were dressed in the sort of clothes Blade thought of as normal himself. One of the rules was that Pilgrims should dress in the clothes of Blade's world. He went towards them with his list.

"Ooh!" shrieked a small fair girl. "It's our wizard! Look, bro, a real wizard! Isn't he small!"

"I have dwarven ancestry," Blade lied, rather crossly, as he looked for the girl on his list. Why couldn't he grow, the way Kit did?

The girl was Susan Sleightholm on the list, and down as a late entry. She had big blue eyes and her hair hung in masses of not-quite-real curls, like wood shavings. She squealed excitedly and hung on to Blade's newly hemmed sleeve. "Call me Sukey," she said, staring fixedly up into Blade's eyes. She was even shorter than he was. "I'm Sukey and this is my brother Geoffrey."

Sukey was about Shona's age, Blade thought. She was

wearing a baby-blue tunic and trousers. He did not like her at all. He pitied her brother for having to put up with her. Geoffrey was tallish and fairish and he looked nice. Blade dragged his sleeve away from Sukey's spiky fingers – she had red nails, like Don's talons when he was eating meat – and went to the people who had sold their house. They were Mr and Mrs Poole, but they insisted that he called them Dad and Mother.

More Pilgrims were coming downstairs all the time now. As they sat down and the landlord brought them tankards, Blade went among them trying to fit them all to the names on his list. It was bewildering. Although they were young, old, fat, thin, serious, jolly, dark, mid-brown and fair, they all had that foreign look and he could not tell them apart. For a start, there were six intense-looking younger women with long straight hair, four men with rugged, far-away gazes wrinkling their eyes, and two more couples just like Dad and Mother Poole. One of them must be supposed to report back to Mr Chesney, Blade thought, but he simply could not tell which. He was polite to all of them, in case.

Almost the last Pilgrim to arrive was a shortish, fair-haired young man, who came sauntering down the stairs with an air. He was obviously rich, rich enough not to have to sell anything to afford the tour. Blade could tell he was, both from his air and from his clothes, which were stylish and made of very good cloth. And he was almost the only Pilgrim who wore those clothes as if they were not fancy dress. Blade looked at him with relief, because he knew he would remember this man. In fact, as he hurried over to him, Blade had a feeling that he *did* remember the man, as if he had seen him before somewhere. But that was obviously a stupid idea.

"I'm Blade, your Wizard Guide," he said. "I'm small because I have dwarven ancestry. And your name is—?"

The man smiled charmingly. "I'm Reville Townsend."

I like him, Blade thought, as he hunted for the name on his list. He missed it somehow, but as he started at the beginning again, he was distracted by the arrival of the last two Pilgrims. The woman came first, pushing past Blade and Reville and marching towards the nearest free bench. She was very tall and rather lean and she wore glasses. Her hair was white, cut in a sort of scalloped helmet. It looked more like a majestic sort of hat than hair. But the most notable thing about her sent Blade scurrying after her, forgetting his list.

"Excuse me, lady. Excuse me! You're not supposed to be wearing those sort of clothes!"

The lady smoothed her neat maroon-coloured trousers and patted the pearls round the neck of her fluffy white sweater before she looked at Blade. It was a totally immovable look. "Young man, I see no reason at all to masquerade in silly clothing like yours. What I have on is respectable and practical, and I shall continue to wear it." She looked past Blade and called out, "Come along, Eldred. Don't dawdle."

The man with her came forward vaguely. He was tall and thin too, with deep creases down his cheeks and deep hollow eyes, and he had a lot of fine white fluffy hair. As Shona said later, he looked like a dandelion seeding. And he was wearing otherworld clothes as well, though his were tweedy and shabby. Blade looked round for his list to see who these people were. Reville Townsend came up with a smile and handed him the folder. "You left me with this."

"Thanks." The only two people not yet accounted for were down as E. and S. Ledbury. Oh yes, and here was Reville down at the bottom, R. Townsend, a late entry like the awful Sukey. "Look, Mrs Ledbury, the rules say—"

The lady looked at him chillingly. "*Miss* Ledbury, if you please, young man. Professor Ledbury is my brother. He is a very learned man and naturally a trifle vague. You cannot expect him to bother with your rules. He is above them and I disregard such things. Sit down beside me here, Eldred." She turned her back on Blade and fetched some crocheting out of her bag.

Reville grinned. "Leave her. You get people like that."

Blade nodded ruefully. He and Reville sat on a bench together, but where Blade sat with his robes twisted and had to get up again to put them straight before he strangled, Reville sat with his silk-lined cloak thrown back and his rapier elegantly in a convenient position, all in one smooth movement. He saw Blade look. "I practise a lot," he explained. "I spend an hour every—"

He broke off as Shona made her entry. Shona came down the stairs carrying her harp and wearing her green bardic robes and she came with such an air that Blade could have sworn that not one Pilgrim noticed that the robes were creased all over and ragged where they had been unravelled to make magic reins. "Good evening," she cried ringingly. "Ladies and gentlemen, I am the official bard to your Pilgrim Party."

Everyone's head turned, even Miss Ledbury's waved helmet, and there were cries of admiration, interrupted by Mother Poole calling out, "Oh, do come and sit with me and Dad, dear!"

Shona did not leave the stairs straightaway. She stood three steps up, staring across the taproom, and seemed to Blade slowly to come alight. It was as if the life in her, that had not been there since the bard handed her the scroll, came welling back into her, and then welling up further, until Shona was twice as alive as she had been, brimming with life, glowing with it. Miss Ledbury's lips pursed. Her head turned to look in a certain direction, disapprovingly. Blade turned to look the way Miss Ledbury and Shona were both looking and saw Geoffrey Sleightholm on the end of both gazes. He was looking back at Shona with the same sort of dawning of life.

Oh dear! Blade thought. I wish it had been Prince Talithan now! It was not just that Mr Chesney's demon did not allow anyone to leave this world, or any Pilgrim to stay here. It was worse. As Shona crossed the taproom and went to sit beside Geoffrey – just as if there was no one else there beside the two of them – Blade surreptitiously unfolded his list again. Yes. There it was. "*G. Sleightholm X, P or E.*" The X meant that Geoffrey was expendable and the other letters meant that Blade was to arrange to have him killed either by pirates or by elves. Blade could only hope that Shona got over Geoffrey, or they found they didn't really like one another, or quarrelled, or something, before the expendable part had to happen.

Blade did not sleep well that night. It was not just Shona, although she was part of it. To his terror, Shona and Geoffrey clearly liked one another enormously. Blade kept thinking of the way Shona had been after the bard handed her the scroll and realising that she might be worse after Geoffrey was expended. And there was no Callette here to help her, either. But there were many other things on his mind too.

Some of it was the way all the Pilgrims seemed to rely on him and keep asking him things, even how to eat their suppers. He was not sure he could stand being in charge to this extent. The worst was when he had to show Dad Poole how to use the toilet.

Another difficulty was Geoffrey's sister Sukey. Maybe it was because her brother was suddenly only interested in Shona, or maybe she was going to do it anyway, or just because they were both small, Sukey attached herself to Blade. She sat by him, she smiled at him, she stroked his arm, and his beard, and she wriggled herself up to him saying, "I've *always* wanted to know a real wizard!" Apart from the fact that Blade knew he was not yet a real wizard, quite apart even from the fact that he did not like Sukey, she offended and embarrassed him. And other people. Dad Poole kept giving him troubled glances, and Miss Ledbury looks which raised her eyebrows up above the steel frames of her glasses.

By this time anyway, Blade hated Miss Ledbury even more than he disliked Sukey. She had a notebook in her crochet bag. Blade knew she was the one reporting to Mr Chesney. She made notes on everything, unclipping a pencil with efficient mauve fingers and scribbling it down whenever anything new happened or got mentioned. She scribbled in code or shorthand. Blade had looked and found he could not read a word.

"Don't pry, young man," Miss Ledbury said. "It's not your place. Eldred, that's enough beer tonight. It's too sour. It'll disagree with you."

Blade hated the way she ordered her poor vague brother about, and he heartily resented the way she treated Blade himself like a servant. "Young man, fetch the landlord. This stew is uneatable."

"You may well regard this as the best meal of your tour before it's over," Reville told her cheerfully.

Miss Ledbury raised eyebrows over steel glasses at Reville. "I do not intend to indulge in privations just for sport." And she made Blade fetch the landlord and the landlord provide bread, cheese and fruit. After that, she brought out a special jar of coffee from her bag and made Blade get her a kettle of boiling water and some cream. "No, Eldred, not for you. Coffee keeps you awake."

Miss Ledbury keeps you awake! Blade thought, tossing fretfully in bed. And Shona and Sukey, not to speak of Dad Poole peering anxiously into the earth closet. But in addition to all this, he kept finding himself doing sums as well. Mother Poole had set him off by telling everyone again that they had sold their house to afford the tour. Someone replied to this, "And I suppose you had to find another thousand credits each for the insurance?"

"*Two* thousand each," said Mother Poole, "because we're older, you see, dear."

From what the others said to this, Blade was astonished to learn that all the tourists had had to pay Mr Chesney from one thousand to six thousand credits each in case of accidents, even expendable Geoffrey, and that they did not even get it back if they arrived home unhurt. As he tossed and turned, Blade found himself adding up what Mother Poole had sold her house for – he did not know what a credit was worth, so he called it a gold piece – multiplying that amount by twenty for the rest of the Pilgrims… then by one hundred and twenty-six, for the other tours… adding in this insurance-thing… multiplying that by one hundred and twenty-six… then remembering that people paid more thousands of these credits to have Prince Talithan put his sword through Pilgrims… adding

that in too at an average of two expendables a party…
then putting a value on all that gold eleven parties of
dwarfs brought in each year… and the answer came out
with so many noughts on the end that Blade thought he
must have gone to sleep in the middle and multiplied it
all by a thousand by mistake.

He turned over on his pillow and did the sum again.
And it was the same huge number of gold pieces. Then
he compared this figure with the money that wizards and
kings got paid, and remembered that Mara was not getting
paid at all. It did not take much thinking to work out
that Mr Chesney was making more money in a year than
there was in Blade's whole world. And Blade's people
were the ones who did the work.

"But that's not *fair*!" he murmured and went to sleep
at last, as if his mind had been waiting for him to arrive at
saying that before it would let him stop thinking.

CHAPTER TWENTY

❋

*I*n the morning Blade had to run after kettles for Miss Ledbury again. Then he consulted the pamphlet and discovered they were supposed to be leaving in two hours. But all the Pilgrims had rushed off to look at the market. "How am I going to get them back in time?" he asked Shona despairingly.

"If we have all the horses waiting for them when they get back, we can set off the moment they turn up," she said. "Why does the exact time matter?"

Because Miss Ledbury is taking notes, Blade thought. "Because we're travelling with a merchant until the bandits attack," he told Shona, "and we have to meet him at midday."

"Let's go to the horse market then," Shona said.

The horse market was an enclosure on the edge of town. The banner hanging over the main street now read GREYNASH HATES THE TOURS, Blade noticed as they went. There was another banner saying the same nailed to the fence of the horse market. Otherwise there was nothing much there except a huddle of horses in the middle of the enclosure and Geoffrey and Sukey Sleightholm leaning on the rails looking at them. Shona's face lit. Blade's heart sank. Sure enough, Sukey gripped him by his sleeve and stared into his eyes so intensely that he wished he had grown his beard all over his face.

"Oh, Wizard—" Sukey began in the sweet voice she used specially for Blade.

To Blade's relief, she was interrupted by the Horselady, who came striding out from among the horses. "Here, Wizard – Oh, it's *you* under all that hair, is it? Twenty horses for you."

"Well, really we need twenty-three," Blade said. "My sister's here as bard."

He had to wrestle his sleeve loose from Sukey and show the Horselady his list before she would believe him. "Two more than *I* was told, even without your sister," she said, when she had counted the names. "Why can't they get it *right*? Very well. I'll bring them round to the inn. *With* feed. And the reason I'm doing this *myself* is that I want to make it quite clear that if anyone mistreats a horse or hurts one in *any way*, I shall call them *all* in and you can do the rest on *foot*. Have you got that? I'm going round all the tours saying this. I'm giving *warning*."

"Right," said Blade. "By the way, how much do they pay you for the horses?"

"Not enough," the Horselady replied over her shoulder as she strode away.

It wouldn't be, Blade thought. He went back to the inn with Sukey skipping beside him as if she was half her real age. The other Pilgrims straggled happily back an hour or so later. They had all, except Miss Ledbury, bought themselves swords. Even Professor Ledbury had acquired a mighty old twisted iron broadsword which he would keep whirling round his head. Blade winced every time he heard it whistle.

"Harmless high spirits," Miss Ledbury said. "Much better exercise than weighted clubs, young man."

With Sukey dogging his steps and Shona concentrating on Geoffrey and being no help at all, Blade got them all to load their horses and buckle everything where it should be. This led to another set-to with Miss Ledbury. The tour had provided each person with a rolled blanket, a cloak and two leather waterbottles. Miss Ledbury would have none of these. Instead, she and the Professor had scarlet sleeping bags, neat windcheaters and backpacks to carry plastic waterbottles and Miss Ledbury's coffee.

"I do not care what your black book says, young man," she told Blade. "I am not on this tour to do penance and my brother is in poor health. Our equipment is far more efficient."

The trouble was, Blade rather agreed with her. But he did not like to see good blankets and waterbottles wasted. He strapped them on his own horse instead.

"Oh, Wizard, take mine as well," Sukey said. "They're such a nuisance."

"You'll be cold," Blade said.

"You can give me them tonight," she said, archly smiling.

The result was that when everyone finally mounted up, Blade was strung about with bundles and not in the best of tempers. When he realised he had forgotten his walking stick staff, he ground his teeth and decided to leave it behind. But Reville hurried out of the inn, carrying it. Bracelets flashed on his arm as he held it up to Blade, smiling. "Oh, you needn—" Blade began.

Here Mother Poole fell off her horse. She did it with a wild shriek and a laugh and lay on the ground gasping, "Every picture tells a story!" It was, in fact, only the first of many, many falls, and Mother Poole always shrieked and always laughed and always said, "Every picture tells a story!" but Blade did not know that then and he felt dreadfully anxious and responsible.

"Let's get moving, shall we?" Geoffrey suggested in a calm, carrying voice.

Everyone, to Blade's mortification, instantly obeyed Geoffrey. Mother Poole floundered aboard again, Reville got on his horse, and the procession straggled out of town, pursued by barking dogs and children shouting, "Go home, tourists!" and "Piss off Pilgrims!" Miss Ledbury managed to make a note about this as she rode.

The merchant, waiting in the highway with his line of covered waggons and mounted guards, received them impatiently. "About time too! Thank the gods this is the last party! I'm real sick of going from here to nowhere and pretending to run away from bandits. And I don't envy you having this lot for another six weeks, Wizard. They look a right bunch of idiots."

They did too, Blade thought, surveying his party, what with Sukey's baby-blue outfit, the Ledburys' outlandish gear, and the innocent, eager looks on all the faces except Reville's and Geoffrey's. Those two at least looked as if they knew what they were in for.

They journeyed on rather slowly, with frequent pauses to collect Mother Poole off the ground, and everyone seemed in high good spirits. Even old Professor Ledbury rode beaming vaguely around at fields and woods and the distant hills. Blade was glad that the bandits were not going to attack until the next day. His Pilgrims seemed to need time to take things more seriously.

They were very merry that night around the campfire, listening to Shona sing. The exceptions were Miss Ledbury, Sukey and Blade. Miss Ledbury had gone round asking the merchant and the guards all sorts of searching questions about where they were from and how much they earned and how they felt about their work, and now she was writing it all down by the light of an efficient little electric torch on a stand. She had a little black cassette thing whirring, too, that she said was recording Shona's songs. Blade knew he should tell her that the black book said she should use a candle and not have the recorder at all, but he knew she would take no notice. Besides, he was gloomily wondering what to do about Sukey.

Sukey had come up to him while he was unloading his horse, beguilingly shaking her wood-shaving curls. Blade thought she had come for her blanket and turned round to give it to her. He found the baby-blue tunic pressed against him and Sukey once again staring into his eyes. "Oh, Wizard, is it true that a special magic happens when a wizard kisses you?"

Blade felt hot under his beard and wholly trapped. He did not know what it was about Sukey – a smell, or a look, or something – but every time she came close to him she seemed to remind him of someone else he disliked very much, though he could not for the life of him think who. "Wizards are forbidden to kiss," he told her sternly. "Here's your blanket. Now leave me alone."

Sukey took the blanket and turned to look over her shoulder at him. "I don't believe you. It's not in any of the rules I've seen."

"It's a secret rule for wizards. Go *away*!" Blade barked at her. To his embarrassment, his voice came out like a griffin's squawk. His hairy face felt hotter than ever.

"There's no need to be rude," she said huffily. He watched her go up to her brother Geoffrey and tell him how rude Blade had been. But Geoffrey was helping Shona unload her horse and he simply said something brief and sarcastic. Sukey had been sulking ever since. Blade stared at her pouting profile in the firelight and wondered what to do about her.

Miss Ledbury snapped off her torch. "Bedtime, Eldred. Don't forget to remove your rainproof trousers before you get into your sleeping bag."

"Up the wooden hill to beddie-byes!" laughed Mother Poole.

"Down on the stone floor, you mean!" someone else joked.

The Pilgrims began unrolling blankets and preparing for the night. Blade watched Professor Ledbury obediently climbing out of his trousers and was glad to see the poor old man wore long white woollen pants underneath. Reville was watching too, and at the sight of those long skinny legs in white wrinkly wool, he turned to Blade with his eyebrows up humorously.

At that, or maybe at the set of Reville's head as he turned round in the firelight, Blade almost recognised Reville. He knew – even more than he knew over Sukey – that he had seen someone exactly like Reville not so long ago. Blade lay awake on the damp and lumpy ground, wishing he had dared to bring his sleeping bag like the Ledburys, going doggedly over in his mind everyone he had met in these last crowded months. Reville was not tall, so he could not be that obnoxious bard, or the man on the camel. But some of the Emir's ladies – could Reville be a woman? No. There were hairs on his chin that had picked up the firelight as golden bristle. Was he a wizard? No, most of the wizards were tall too, and so was King Luther. But some of King Luther's men – no. So why was he thinking of the times he had seen King Luther? Then Blade had it. He chuckled incredulously and went to sleep.

In the morning, he took Reville aside, well aside and out of hearing from anywhere, a hundred yards up the road. "What's all this about?" Reville laughed. "Make it quick. I want my breakfast."

"You're an imposter," said Blade. "You're from this world. You shouldn't be a Pilgrim at all."

To Blade's secret relief – because he suspected Reville was rather good with that rapier of his – Reville was simply amused. "And how do you make that out?"

"I've seen you before. You were with Querida and King Luther and High Priest Umru when Dad and I visited the White Oracle," Blade explained.

Reville's brows went down and his lips pursed, though – again to Blade's relief – he was still amused. "Score one to you!" he said. "And here was I, trained never to forget a face, and I'd clean forgotten you! After you put that cold spell on us too! I'm slipping. Blame that awful beard. What do you want from me?"

"What are you doing here with this Pilgrim Party?" Blade asked.

Reville grinned and pulled up his left sleeve. Fastened all the way up his arm was a row of wristwatches, nearly twenty of them, as far as Blade could tell. "Thieves' Guild," Reville explained. "These little clocks can fetch as much as a thousand gold each. People don't have them here. The Pilgrims take them off with their other offworld gear and give them to the landlord to put back across the portal for them. He leaves them in his strong-cupboard until he's got the lot. I walk in pretending to be another Pilgrim and pay the cupboard a visit. Bingo. Boringly easy – except that this time you gave me a bad moment looking me up on your list. I had to do some quick faking while your back was turned. And then I spot those two who refuse to be parted from their offworld stuff. She's got that torch and that recorder, and a hot flask, and I *think* she's got a weapon too. I haven't discovered what *he's* got yet, but you can understand the challenge, can't you?"

"Yes," Blade admitted.

"She watches all her stuff like a hawk as well. I can't resist. But I'm here with Querida's permission. If you want a deal to keep your mouth shut, it won't be worth much," Reville warned him.

"That depends," Blade said cunningly. "Do you *want* me to tell Miss Ledbury who you are?"

Reville winced slightly. "It looks as if I don't get

breakfast today," he said regretfully, "unless you want something I can – I tell you what! Suppose I offer to pry your bard away from that Geoffrey?"

Blade shook his head, equally regretfully. He knew Shona when she had made up her mind. He was going to leave that to Mum, when the party reached her Lair. "No," he said. "But I won't say a word to anyone if you can take Sukey off my hands."

Reville stared at him as if he thought Blade had gone mad. After a moment, he said, "Let's get this straight. Did I hear you correctly? You – don't – want – Sukey?"

"Yes," said Blade. "I don't."

"But wizards *always* get themselves the most gorgeous – it's part of the perks. You should see some of the other wizards!" Reville said distractedly. "Ye gods! Are you *sure* about this?" Blade nodded vehemently. "This has made my day!" said Reville. "All right. It's a deal." He wrung Blade's hand and, with a beaming smile on his face, set off at a run for where the Pilgrims were gathering round the campfire for breakfast.

Blade followed slowly, slightly bewildered. Reville was probably only about six years older than he was. Did six years really make that much difference to the way someone looked at Sukey? Blade hoped not, or not where he was concerned himself. If it did, then something obviously went seriously wrong with your mind in those six years.

"I can't eat stew for breakfast, young man," said Miss Ledbury. "I shall be ill."

Blade sighed. Back to business. "It's traditional," he explained. "Ask the merchant." Old Professor Ledbury was still in his long wrinkly underpants, he noticed. "I think your brother may have forgotten his trousers, Miss Ledbury."

He escaped behind one of the merchant's carts while Miss Ledbury bullyingly dangled the trousers in front of her brother and the Professor blinked and said, "What trousers? Whose trousers are those?"

They went on after breakfast. The bandits did not attack that night.

The merchant was very irritated. He took Blade aside the next morning and explained that he was a busy man and, because this was the last tour, he had some real trading fixed up and due to start the following day. "With winter coming on, I can't hang about here on these bad roads. I'd be mired down until spring. I've got to leave today and turn south."

Blade consulted the black book. "It says 'within three days' here. They're probably going to do it tomorrow morning as a surprise."

"One more day then," the merchant agreed grumpily.

The caravan journeyed all that day, into wooded, hillier country. It rained slightly most of the day, which made the merchant grumpier still. It rained again in the night, forcing the Pilgrim Party to sleep under the carts, but there were still no bandits. The Pilgrims got up wet and crotchety, except for the Ledburys in their waterproof bags. In fact, Professor Ledbury was the liveliest of anyone there. He swung his great old sword and invited Reville to a fencing match. Reville looked at the wide, rusty blade wavering in the Professor's hand and said politely, "Perhaps some other time, sir," and turned back to Sukey. Blade was utterly grateful to Reville. Sukey barely looked at anyone else now, and certainly not at Blade.

"What do these bandits think they're doing?" the merchant hissed, grabbing Blade by the sleeve and pulling him behind one of the carts. "They're still not here. And they get paid enough."

"Perhaps they've forgotten there was one more tour," Blade was suggesting, when Geoffrey and Shona came in great leaps down the slope at the side of the road. Geoffrey was pale and Shona was chalky.

"Blade, you'd better come up there and look," Shona whispered.

"You stay. I'll go with him," Geoffrey said quietly. "It's not nice."

Puzzled and cross, Blade followed Geoffrey up through damp grass and sopping bushes, into woodland where he caught hair and beard and robes on low branches while Geoffrey strode irritatingly freely ahead. They went a long way to kiss one another, he thought angrily. Then they came to the place. Blade stopped being annoyed with Geoffrey and was glad he was there.

It had been the bandits' ambush, certainly, but the bandits had been ambushed themselves. There were nearly thirty people lying in ungraceful attitudes under the trees, with rain trickling on their clothes and pattering upon their white, unfeeling faces. Blade felt sick when he saw the wounds on some of them. The attackers had been brutal.

Geoffrey pointed at a broad trampled swathe of grass and bushes, leading away uphill. "Looks as if the attackers were after their horses, whoever they were."

One of the dead people, and only one, was wearing shiny black armour. Blade knew who the attackers were. They were some more of the escaped soldiers. "Don't tell anyone," he said hoarsely.

When he thought about it later, Blade realised that this was the moment when his tour started to go wrong. Entirely wrong. The fact was, he panicked. At the time, he thought of himself as behaving rather well. Although the one thing he wanted to do was to translocate far, far away from there *at once*, he knew he could not do that alone, nor try to bring all the Pilgrims and their horses with him if he went. He thought he controlled his panic. He told himself he was quite calm. But he knew what those soldiers were like, and now, looking at the dead bandits, he knew what they could do to people. His one thought was to get everyone as far from those soldiers as possible.

He returned solemnly to the road. He stuck his hands

into his sleeves in what he hoped was a mystical posture and cried out in what he hoped was a mystical voice, "Danger! I have foreseen danger! We must leave this place at once."

The merchant shot him a shrewd look. "Well, in that case I'll love you and leave you," he said. "It's mostly beets and apples at this time of year, but I do have a living to make." He trotted away to the lead cart, calling orders to his guards and drivers. In less than a minute, the train of five carts and six outriders was in motion. In a minute more, they had the carts turned round, and in another minute, they had gone, hell for leather, back down the road. The Pilgrims watched uncertainly.

"Everyone get on your horses," Blade called.

"Yes, mount up, all of you," said Geoffrey, and everybody did, including Shona, who was looking rather the way she had the morning the soldiers broke out of the dome. "I'll make sure you're all right, my love," Geoffrey said to her. "They won't come near you again. Where to, wizard?"

It seemed to Blade that the road they were on wound off in the same direction as the trampled track the attackers had made. And the high banks on either side of it made it perfect for an ambush. Blade forgot the road and trusted to the instinct by which he found places when he translocated. He pointed in what he thought of as the right direction. That way was towards the next tour-event, which was the attack by leather-winged avians in two days' time. Geoffrey nodded and gestured. The Pilgrim Party rode up the bank on the other side of the road, shed Mother Poole at the top, retrieved her, and set off across country.

For the next two days Blade struggled to get to the rendezvous with the avians. It was very confusing country, all ups and downs, and little wooded ravines where deep streams rushed. Blade was so busy trying to get his Pilgrims in the right direction to the right place, that he forgot that the black book said he was supposed to be telling the Pilgrims that they faced the menace of the Dark Lord. Shona reminded him once or twice, but Blade was too anxious about the journey to attend.

"But they have to be told, Blade," Shona protested. "They have to know where to pick up the clues. Where's the first one?"

"I don't know. I'll look it up tonight," Blade said.

He had forgotten again by that evening. Everything and everyone was so miserable. It was still raining, and because they had left the proper tour-route they had to make their own camp. There was very little food. According to the black book, the bundles everyone carried behind their saddles were full of food for the horses. Food for the pilgrims was to be found in the camps along the route, carefully bespelled to keep it fresh, but of course they were not at a proper camp. Luckily most of the Pilgrims had brought some things to eat, filched from the inn, but it was only the sort of thing you could slip into your pocket. That night they had oatcakes, apples, a few lumps of cheese and a lot of bad temper round a smoky, fizzling fire. Most of the bad temper was directed at Miss Ledbury, who sat with her waterproof hood snugly up round her face, sharing a large slab of chocolate with her brother.

"I haven't enough to go round," she stated. "You should have thought of bringing some yourselves." She fetched a small self-heating kettle from her backpack and rattled her coffee jar at Blade to show him she needed some water.

"I'll fill it," said Reville, looking at the kettle even more greedily than he had looked at the chocolate. Blade was surprised when Reville came back with the kettle full. But Reville seemed determined not to leave Sukey. Blade could understand that even less. Among all the Pilgrims' grumbling voices, Sukey's was raised highest and loudest and most peevishly – and most often.

"Why can't we all have some coffee at least?" Sukey demanded.

There was such an outcry of agreement from the other Pilgrims that Shona said hectically, "Listen, and I will tell you the bards' tale of the menace of the Dark Lord."

Blade thought she told it much better than he would have done. Shona's tale was full of spine-shivering phrases and snatches of songs, and her description of the horrors of the Dark Lord's Citadel was masterly. "But it is said that the Dark Lord has one weakness," she said, staring meaningly at Blade, "and that there are clues to be found as to what this is."

Clues! Blade thought. Help! "I must meditate," he mumbled for the benefit of anyone who was not riveted by Shona's tale-telling, and scrambled away into the wet bushes. There, with rain plopping off his beard and his long hair damply trailing across the pages, he managed to read the dog-eared pamphlet in the last of the daylight. Shona, still describing the terrible creatures that inhabited the Dark Lord's Citadel, looked at him expectantly as he came crawling back. "Mum's Lair," Blade mouthed at her.

She nodded. "To go back to the matter of clues to his weakness," she said, "it is told that an enchantress holds the secret. If we wish to defeat him, we shall have to brave her clutches."

The rain stopped during the night. Everyone was a little more cheerful when they set off again. They spent that day ducking under wet trees and splashing through streams and, around sunset, very hungry, they toiled up a rocky rise and did reach a camp of sorts. It did not look as if anyone had used it for some time.

"I think it must be one from last year," Shona whispered to Blade, pretending to help him with his horse while Geoffrey was organising people to gather firewood.

Blade thought the same. But he went to the food cache and hopefully took the stasis spell off it. The large cauldron of stew inside it had dried to a sort of cake over the year or so it had been there. Blade thought that they could cut it into lumps and pretend it was steak, or something. The bread was awfully stale, but they could toast that. And the cheese was – well, better leave the cheese. He took the rest to Mother Poole.

"Don't ask me, dear," she said. "Ask Dad. He's the cook in our house."

Dad Poole did his best, but it was not wonderful. Miss Ledbury meaningly fetched out another slab of chocolate. When they had all eaten what they could, Blade stuck his hands mystically in his sleeves again. "I feel danger near," he said portentously. "I think it best if we build a very large fire tonight."

"Won't that attract the attention of this Dark Lord?" someone said anxiously.

"Fire keeps all magical ills away," Blade said firmly.

"Start gathering more firewood," Geoffrey commanded. "The wizard knows his job."

Everyone did so. Blade was annoyed at the way everyone did what Geoffrey said, and he was even more annoyed at having to be grateful to Geoffrey for it, but a large bonfire got built. When it was blazing nicely on top of the rise, Blade stuck his hands in his sleeves again. "I must meditate," he said. He went downhill to wait for the person who saw the large fire and brought the geese there. He hoped it was Kit. He was missing Kit badly. Kit had so many ideas about what to do and he organised people even better than Geoffrey did. Blade realised that he had relied on Kit to organise him all his life, and he felt quite lost without him, out here in the middle of nowhere.

But it was Callette who came. She ghosted down about two hours later and wearily thunked a hamper beside Blade's feet. "Why are you in this place? I've been looking all over the hills for you."

It was so dark by then that all Blade could see of her was a curve of beak, a gleam of eye and the paleness of the bars on her wings. He was delighted to see even that much. She was Callette. She was family and home. "You wouldn't believe, Callette!" he said. "We got lost because the bandits were murdered by some escaped soldiers and one of them keeps falling off her horse and one of them isn't even a Pilgrim!"

"Yes, but I have to get back," Callette said. "I spent hours looking for you. I'm supposed to be doing the Hunt."

"Sorry," Blade said. "Is everyone all right? Kit, Dad, Don?"

"Don nearly lost all the dogs last night," said Callette. "Even Kit's tired. He keeps being nice to me. Do you want these geese or not?"

"Yes, I suppose," said Blade.

He got behind the hamper as Callette tipped it up and opened it. No geese came out. Instead, two large pale pigs, sleepily grunting, stuck their snouts up to stare at Callette. Callette stared back in almost exactly the same surprised posture she had used when she brought Mr Chesney the barrel of blood, beak poised downwards, wings curved up. But Blade could somehow see her surprise was real. "How are they here? What have those geese done now?" she said.

"Translocated two pigs? Callette, they *can't* have done!" said Blade.

"They can," Callette said. "They do all sorts of things at night at home. They got bored being avians. Last night I only managed to get one into the hamper. I put her in and she pecked me."

"And now they're showing you. I see," Blade said. The pigs recognised him and ambled amiably round to him. They were Ringlet and Bouncer by the feel, he thought.

"Do you want to use the pigs instead?" Callette asked.

Blade, with an arm round each of two warm, tubby, bristled bodies, found himself horrified at what the Professor's whistling sword or Reville's rapier might do to them. "They'd get killed. Dad would have fits."

"I suppose I could swoop over your bonfire a bit," Callette offered.

Blade found himself horrified at that too. "No, you'd get hurt. Then you couldn't do the Hunt. Put them back in the hamper and go. I'll think of an illusion or something."

"If you're sure," Callette said, obviously glad to go.

"I am sure," Blade said. "You get going."

Ringlet and Bouncer were only too pleased to resume

their interrupted snooze in the hamper. Callette took them up with a jerk and a slight whop of wings and ghosted away. Blade felt sad. Too sad and much too tired to think of illusions. He had no idea how Kit did them anyway.

"I have averted the evil," he announced to the Pilgrims. "You may sleep in peace."

Shona naturally wanted to know what had happened. Blade took her some way down the hill and explained. "Those geese have funny minds," she said. "Dad says they always want to fly south really. Maybe they did."

"They'd better not fly near me," Blade said. "I'll – I'll – actually it's hard to think of something to do to geese that are probably wizards, but I'll do *something*."

He took the Pilgrims towards the Wild Hunt the next day. They missed it entirely.

Blade could not understand it. He had led everyone through the confusing hilly landscape, not confused at all and quite confident that he was converging on the place near the river where the Hunt was to find them, and instead they came out above the wide green vale where Mara's Aunt's house was. Three days early. Blade was almost as astonished to see it as Callette had been to see the pigs.

CHAPTER TWENTY-ONE

*

*B*lade looked at the distant clump of trees hiding Aunt's house, and the inviting spire of smoke rising up from it, and decided that it would be silly not to go down there. Besides, he doubted if the Pilgrims would let him lead them away from it.

Dad Poole said, "Hey, that looks inviting!" and most other people said thankfully, "Civilisation at *last*!" while Sukey said, "I'm cold, I'm hungry and I'm *tired*. I'm not going a step further on this stupid tour unless I can have a bath and wash my hair."

"You shall, you shall, my lady," Reville assured her. He was looking at the spire of smoke as eagerly as anyone there.

Blade looked them over, uncomfortably. Most had that pinched and withered look you get from being out in all weathers with too little food. The women drooped. The men nearly all had slightly villainous beginnings of beards. They clearly needed a rest. As Blade looked, Miss Ledbury met his eye. For a wonder, she did not say anything, but Blade knew what she meant. They were to go down to that house, or Mr Chesney would want to know why. Professor Ledbury just smiled. He was the only one who seemed to be thriving on the tour. He actually looked younger than when he had first arrived, sort of boyish, Blade thought.

The trouble was, Mara was not expecting them yet. Blade cleared his throat and stroked his beard importantly. "Our first clue lies within that hidden house," he said, "and we must go there. But great danger lies within as well. It is the Lair of an evil Enchantress. Perchance she is away from home. I will go ahead and scout. The rest of you follow slowly – Geoffrey, make sure they do." Geoffrey nodded cheerfully, and Blade knew his orders would be obeyed. "Be prepared to flee if I shout," he warned them as he set off.

He rode down the vale at a canter, throwing up divots of moist turf, and only slowed up when he came to the little gate into the wood. The village mayor met him there, looking most magnificent in a sort of priestly cope of silver and blue.

"It's all right. We saw you coming," he told Blade.

"You're not the only ones to come at the wrong time. The last lot are just leaving, so she says you might as well bring yours in now. But bring them this way, so they don't see the other lot."

"Right. Thanks." Blade turned and made glad beckonings. The group of people cautiously approaching across the pastures broke into an eager gallop, even Mother Poole, who actually stayed in her saddle, so anxious was she to get to civilisation.

The mayor solemnly bowed each of them through the gate and led them among the trees to spacious stables that Blade did not remember ever being there before. Here boys and girls from the village, also dressed in blue and silver, led the horses away. Every one of them was trying not to laugh at the sight of Blade in his beard. Blade glowered as he followed the mayor into— He looked up at what had been Aunt's house. Wow! he thought. The place was a small fairy palace with tinsel towers.

His mother stood in the hallway in a dress that made Blade ashamed to look at her. Everyone else goggled. He heard Shona murmur, "Honestly! *Mother!*"

Mara smiled and welcomed everyone. And, as Blade could feel as a sharp, headachey tingling, she bespelled every soul who trooped in past her, except Blade himself. "Why did you do Shona too?" he whispered.

"She was going to give trouble. I could see it in her eye," Mara said. "What's the matter with her? Why is she here anyway?"

Blade explained about the scroll from the bards. "But I think it's Geoffrey Sleightholm who's the matter with her now," he said.

"Ah. Well, I can look into that while she's here. Poor Shona!" Mara said. "And you look damp and tired out, my love. Go upstairs and get dry and clean and rested, and come down when you're ready for something to eat. Then you can see what all this is about. You can take that beard off if you want. No one's going to notice."

Blade went without thinking to the room he usually had when they stayed in Aunt's house, and it was still there, looking just as usual in the midst of the fairy palace. Fran's cousin Greta from the village was just finishing changing the sheets on the bed. "It's like running an inn, this," she told Blade. "One person out, next person in, and hardly time to get sheets washed in between. But it's all in a good cause. Your mother's a wonderful woman, Blade."

"Yes, but that *dress*!" said Blade.

Greta laughed. "That! That's her *modest* one! She said to me, she said, 'Oh dear, Blade's on his way here now,' she said, 'and I don't want him to see any of the usual dresses. Where's the one that covers the top of me got to?' And we couldn't find it at first. We had a right panic on, I can tell you!"

"Oh." Blade could not help wondering about Mara's other dresses then.

After Greta left, he fell on the bed and slept. It was

early evening when he woke. His first act was to get rid of the beard. That was such a relief that he almost decided not to have a bath – until he realised that his reason was that Sukey had whined on about needing a bath, and knew that this was childish of him. So he got clean and dressed in the ordinary clothes that Greta had hung over a chair for him. They were some of his own old clothes that Mara had obviously brought along here specially. Blade was pleased that she had remembered, but a bit rueful that the clothes still fitted him. Two years ago, when Kit and Callette were growing so big, Mara had promised Blade that he would shoot up to be taller than Derk when he was fourteen. But this still had not happened.

Feeling very hungry by then, he went downstairs. Down here, the whole house was different. Blade made his way towards the place where, by the sounds, there seemed to be a party going on. He could hear a continuous, humming roar of voices, mixed with singing and someone playing the flute, and the clinks of glasses and plates. Blade thought he recognised the flute-playing as Shona's and, sure enough, as soon as he entered the vast, draped, glittering saloon that had once been Aunt's drawing room, the first person he saw was Shona. Shona was standing on a dais, looking flushed and happy and very pretty in her best dress, playing her flute as if nothing else mattered in the world. The village choir, in blue and silver, was on the dais behind her, doing the singing. The rest of the room was full of people sitting in pairs at little gilded tables, talking and eating.

One of the village girls grabbed Blade's arm. "Here you are. This table's you. Your mum says eat first and then go round and listen to what they're all saying. It's a scream, really. They don't notice a thing, with all the spells she's got on them. But I wish you'd kept that beard. I wanted to see it."

"You'll see it tomorrow." There was a huge meal steaming on the little table, all Blade's favourite foods. Blade sat on the one little gilded chair and became very busy for a while. He could tell as he ate that Lydda had not cooked this food – though someone had done it quite well – which saddened Blade, because it meant that Lydda was still not back from planting the clues. But he could hear Elda's voice ringing out from somewhere across the saloon.

Elda was the first person he looked for when he was finally satisfied. The days of travelling had left him hungrier than he had thought possible. But he was done at last. Elda was right on the other side of the huge room, couched opposite one of the straight-haired serious Pilgrim girls that Blade still could not tell apart. Elda was very pleased with herself. She had a small twinkling tiara fixed across her crest and other long twinkling threads streaming across her wings and her back. Her coat and feathers gleamed with care, rich gold and smooth, right down to the tuft on her tail which, with Elda, was usually a mucky blob, but was now an elegant fluffy tassel. Blade could see it whisking excitedly above Elda's gleaming back.

To get to her, Blade had to go past most of the other tables in the room. There was a Pilgrim at each table, facing someone from Mara's household. Most of them were people from the village, but some were people Blade had never seen in his life. The nearest table held a rather majestic lady in crimson, sitting across from Miss Ledbury. At first he thought he had never seen her before. But as he passed, he heard her say, "Oh no, my dear. I'm afraid I was more ruthless than that. When I realised that my husband was going to let the city be destroyed and keep all the money himself, I put him in a dungeon and took over."

Miss Ledbury seemed quite unusually bemused. Her notebook was lying beside her plate, but she seemed to have forgotten it. She leant forward and asked anxiously, "Is he still in the dungeon?"

The lady in crimson picked the notebook up and put it into Miss Ledbury's hand. "No, my dear. The elves let him out. Do remember to take notes, won't you? We want this all down in black and white. He's not Duke any more and I don't think the people will have him back."

The Duchess of Chell! Blade thought, edging past. Well I never!

Miss Ledbury was scribbling industriously and the

Duchess was saying, "But it was quite an operation to make sure all the citizens were safe," as Blade moved on to the next table, where the mayor was describing to Dad Poole how they had had to dismantle the village in order to meet Mr Chesney's requirements. Mother Poole, at the next table, was listening to Old George's son, Young George, who was telling her exactly how much everyone who assisted with the tours got paid. "It's not equal pay by any means," Blade heard Young George say, "when you think that King Luther is getting two hundred gold this year and the dragons are only getting their one gold goblet each every five years." Beyond this, Blade edged past Sukey, who was listening to a lady dressed in the same sort of doeskins as the Horselady describing what happened to horses in the battles. To Blade's surprise, tears were pouring down Sukey's face. At the table after that, Reville had his face wryly twisted as he listened to the death-rate among the legions. By now, Blade had seen what was going on, so it did not surprise him, when he reached Elda, to hear Elda saying to the long-haired girl, "No, you still seem to think Dad keeps me like something in a zoo. I'm a *person*, not a teddy bear or a savage beast."

Elda shot Blade a friendly, talk-to-you-later look, and went straight on talking. "Anyway, I was telling you. Kit had just got over the top of the big tree when he yelled out that his strength had gone and he let go – just like that. And Blade and the swing fell straight down into the tree." Blade shot Elda a look at that. He remembered this only too well. Elda swung her beak round defiantly at him and continued. "I was ever so small then – I was only six – and I yelled, but there was no one else anywhere near and Blade was coming down through the tree, sort of bouncing on his back and screaming, and I had to do something. So I flew up into the tree and tried to catch him. And then we both came down through the tree, but much slower, and my wings didn't seem to help much. Dad said that was because they weren't properly developed yet. He was furious with me as well as Kit and Blade. And Kit made an idiot of himself going up and down over the tree howling out that it was an accident all afternoon, and Dad told him to pull himself together, but he couldn't. Anyway, we were two griffins and one human, and Dad treated us just the same, that's what I'm trying to tell you."

Blade made another face at Elda. "Just the same?" he asked. "You got off lightly compared to Kit and me."

"Hush," said Elda. "*I'm* telling it." She tossed her tiara-ed head at him and turned back to the Pilgrim girl.

Beyond Elda, Mara was reclining on a couch. Geoffrey was perched on a stool beside the couch and Mara and he were talking, very seriously. Blade did not want to interrupt them, any more than he wanted to listen to Elda's memories. He went over to the dais and listened to the music.

But it an went on for hours. Every so often, Shona

and the choir took a rest, sitting on the edge of the platform with filled rolls and drinks. Whenever they did, the Pilgrims all got up and changed tables. By the end of that long, long evening, each Pilgrim had listened to all the speakers, Miss Ledbury's notebook was three-quarters full, and every one of Blade's party had had a talk with Mara herself, though none for so long as Geoffrey. Blade's head ached, and he was sick of the rumble of voices and the sweet scents that seemed to come from the draperies. They *are* working hard, he thought, if they do all this every day.

Finally, however, the Pilgrims and Shona suddenly got up and went to bed, moving like sleepwalkers. Everyone else stretched and relaxed. Mara fished a dressing-gown from under her couch, wrapped it round her and came to hug Blade. Elda bounded up and pressed against the back of him.

"That was exhausting!" Mara said. "It's the double spell that makes it so tiring. You have to make sure they go away thinking they've been thoroughly seduced but still remembering all the things we've told them. It was a great help that you've got one who takes notes, Blade. Querida reckons that if we send everyone home knowing the real facts, some of them are going to make trouble there for Mr Chesney. And I really think that some of this lot of yours might, Blade. You've got some rather interesting people here. Do you understand what we're trying to do?"

"Yes," Blade said, although he still did not think it justified the clothes under Mara's dressing-gown.

"And it's fun," Elda said.

"I had a long talk with the young man Shona seems to have fallen for," Mara said.

"Geoffrey. I saw," said Blade.

"He's fallen for her too. He seems very nice," Mara said, and hesitated, as if she was wondering whether or not to say something else.

"But Mum," Blade protested, "it's not just that he's a Pilgrim – he's down as expendable!"

"Oh," said Mara. "That – makes a difference. Then I think, for Shona's sake, you'd better make sure he survives."

Blade thought of Prince Talithan efficiently running his sword into that Pilgrim during the battle. "How *can* I, Mum?"

"Do you know how to put protections round a person?" Mara asked.

"No!" Blade said crossly. "Nobody's taught me anything useful – you know that!"

"All right. I'll do it. I'll go and do it now," Mara said wearily. "And I suppose while I'm at it I'd better do the same for his odious little sister."

"Sukey's not expendable," Blade said. "I wish she was."

Mara sighed. "Yes, but from what Geoffrey was telling me, she shouldn't be here. Her parents think she's on holiday in her own world. She seems to have twisted Geoffrey's arm to make him bring her with him."

Blade went to bed thinking that this was entirely typical of Sukey. He could not understand why Reville seemed to like her so much.

In the morning, Blade glumly regrew his beard while he was consulting the black book and the pamphlet to see where he was supposed to go next. Round by the Emirates on the way to the Inland Sea, he discovered. All right. He put his robes on and went to the kitchen, where Elda found some scissors and Mara cut him a hole in the beard for his mouth. Then they hung over him, making sure he had a large breakfast and enough food packed in his blanket to last a week. Mara told him what to do next. Blade said a reluctant goodbye and went out into the paddock, where all the horses were waiting, ready saddled. There, as Mara had told him, he raised both arms in a dramatic, wizardly gesture.

That side of Aunt's house rolled up like a blind, revealing the saloon, where all the Pilgrims and Shona were just finishing breakfast.

"Be thankful I am here to rescue you from vile enchantment!" Blade shouted.

They sprang up as if he had pricked them and came streaming sheepishly outside.

"Get mounted," Blade told them. "We must hurry away." And he rushed about making sure of everyone's girths, trying to avoid Shona. But it did no good. She waited by Blade's horse and grabbed his arm before he could mount.

"Was *I* enchanted too? *Mother* did that to me?" she whispered angrily.

Blade could not think of anything to say but the truth. "She said you were going to make trouble."

Shona was furious. Her cheeks coloured, her mouth pursed and she looked round into the opened-up saloon as if she had half a mind to storm back inside. But for some reason she changed her mind and marched away to her horse in a manner Blade knew was ominous.

He watched her anxiously all that day. He knew what Shona was like. She had waited weeks once to revenge herself on Don, and by the time she did, Don had forgotten the quarrel entirely and felt very surprised and injured. But this time Shona seemed to do nothing but chat happily to Geoffrey and sing songs for the Pilgrims. It never occurred to Blade that Shona might have grown up since then. By the end of the day, he had decided that Shona must be plotting a long-term revenge of some kind. Maybe she was waiting until she saw Mara again, but she was quite as likely to be angry with Blade too. Blade knew he had to be very wary. So he went on watching, and made plans for what he would do in case Shona pushed him into a river, or gave him something horrible to eat – or worse, told the Pilgrims what age he really was.

The trouble was that Blade was so preoccupied with Shona that he had very little attention for the route. He relied on the way he knew where to go when he translocated. It never occurred to him that this might be an entirely different sort of sense of direction. He led the Pilgrims towards where he thought the Emirates were, with the result that he led them steadily in the wrong direction for the next three days. True, they arrived at a camp on the first two nights, but, as later became evident, these were almost certainly the camps that were intended for tours on the other two routes. By the end of the third day, they were crossing country that no Pilgrim Party had ever crossed before.

Some days after that, Scales came coasting down into Derk's camp by the river and told him that Blade had disappeared.

CHAPTER TWENTY-TWO

*

Nothing seemed to be going right for Derk. He was now so busy that he had not thought about his new homing pigeon for days.

Prince Talithan had found three more cities deserted when he tried to sack them and he was, to Derk's mind, being extravagantly upset about it. "I have failed you, lord," he kept saying. And three angry wizards translocated in. One said that the pirates had demanded higher pay before they captured a single Pilgrim more, and the second wanted to know why the dragons had deliberately dropped his Pilgrims in the snow a day's walk from the dragon with the gizmos. The third complained that the Emir had no slavegirls. "And my

Pilgrims were *expecting* them," he said. "They're talking of suing me."

"How did they know what to expect?" Derk asked wearily. "Unless you told them."

"They'd heard things from last year," the wizard defended himself. "I may have dropped a hint or so, but they knew what I meant."

"I'll take it up with Querida." Derk promised. He sent the daylight owls to Querida with a message about it and also, hopelessly, asking whether Querida had invented a god yet. He came back from interviewing pirates and arguing with dragons to find, as he had half expected, that the owls had returned with a note signed by someone else, saying that Querida was very busy just now and would get in touch later. Derk glumly faced the fact that Querida had no intention of helping him.

He was tired. Any spare time he had was taken up with journeys to Derkholm, where at least two Pilgrim Parties arrived every day to confront him and push him into the balefire. The day after a battle, there were often as many as seven parties waiting for him. Derk was sick of falling backwards into his trench, but he never had time to invent a different way of being killed.

The griffins were tired too, and Pretty was bored. Pretty was so bored with the Wild Hunt that he started leading the dogs off in the wrong direction. Don got quite hysterical about it – even worse than Prince Talithan over the empty cities, Derk thought. But he forgave Don because it was borne in upon him that Don was too young really to be in charge of anything. He put Callette in charge of the Hunt instead and Don wretchedly agreed to have another try at helping with the battles.

Then the geese replaced themselves with six pigs and vanished. Now not only was Callette furious, but they had six puzzled pigs getting under everyone's feet in the base. Every time he tripped over Ringlet, Derk hoped savagely that the geese had gone home and the dwarfs had eaten them. But when he flew Beauty to Derkholm to get tipped into his balefire, Derk found no sign of any geese, only increasing numbers of dwarfs. Scales seemed to have rounded up almost all of them. Look on the bright side, Derk thought. Kit's den was packed full of treasure. Old George was being quite a convincing wailing skeleton these days, and the demon turned up faithfully to terrify the Pilgrims at every confrontation. Derk gave up wondering why the demon was doing it. He was simply almost grateful.

He flew back to the base to find more things going wrong. The Emperor Titus came apologetically to report that half his younger legionaries had resigned and gone home. "They all say their mothers are ill," he said. "We sent to check and it seems to be true. There's some kind of illness that only affects older women. We had to give them all compassionate leave." And after the Emperor came the mercenary chief of the Forces of Good, swearing and cursing because every one of his female soldiers had deserted in the night.

Kit's brow jutted and Kit's tail lashed at this news. Derk could hardly blame him. It was a real puzzle how the Forces of Good could win convincingly when half of them were missing. Kit, Derk sometimes thought, was the only one not being a problem. Now he had stopped feeling so important, Kit had settled down and become almost sunny. Kit was the one who tried to joke Callette out of her fury over the geese. It was not Kit's fault, Derk thought, that this had only made Callette angrier.

But behind all this, Derk was increasingly anxious about Lydda. She ought to have come back from laying clues long ago. He kept hoping she had gone to Mara. In the end, he sent Prince Talithan to find out. Mara would talk to Talithan, and it would take Talithan's mind off the disappearing citizens. But Talithan came back within the hour to say that Lydda was not with Mara and Mara was as anxious as Derk. "She says she will cause other lady wizards to search, lord."

Derk sent the daylight owls off to look for Lydda too. Lydda was too young, just like Don, and he knew he ought not to have asked her to fly so far. He never would have asked her if he had not been ill.

He had just sent the owls off when Scales arrived with the news that Blade had disappeared. Derk's stomach twisted and he was nearly sick with worry. At first he thought that the whole party, Shona included, had gone missing. "No. You misheard me," Scales rumbled. The reason he knew Blade was missing, he said, was that while he was checking for dwarfs from the Eastern Range, he had flown across a Pilgrim Party wandering miles from anywhere a tour should be. "I dropped down and spoke to them," he said. "Your Shona seemed to be in charge and she told me. Some crisis in the night. Young Blade seems to have vanished in a clap of noise, taking two of the others with him."

Blade now! Derk thought. Blade was too young, just like Don and Lydda. He ought to have refused to let Blade be a Wizard Guide, whatever the Oracle said. "Show me where they are on the map," he said.

He unrolled the map and pinned it down with stones. Scales's great head bowed over it and one long claw very delicately made a tiny prick mark, right in the middle of nowhere. "There," said Scales. "Nothing else for miles."

"Hm," said Derk. If he got the balefire fallen into quickly tomorrow, he would be able to get to that region and still be back for the battle the day after that. "Thanks," he said to Scales. "Could you spare time to look for Blade at all?"

"Be glad to," said Scales. "I was getting bored hunting dwarfs."

Before he left for Derkholm the next day, Derk checked up on the soldiers in the dome. This was another worry nagging at the back of all the others. It was hard to pin down, but years of spells not going quite right, from the blue demon on, had given Derk a feeling for magic that was not acting as it should, and he was sure that the spells Barnabas had put on the dome were not holding in some way. The men in black were behaving as soldiers should, drilling, exercising, queueing at the cookhouse, resting, caring for weapons, but Derk was sure that something, somewhere, was not quite right. He could not place it. He went round and looked carefully at all Barnabas's workings. But they seemed to be correct. He would have liked to consult Barnabas, but Barnabas was not there to consult. Barnabas spent less and less time in the camp. Sometimes he only turned up at the last minute before a battle, in a strong gust of beer-smell – which was the main reason why Derk was sure something was wrong. But he could not find it. Besides, Beauty was ready and he was in a hurry. He left.

At Derkholm, he fell into his balefire three times in quick succession and did not wait to chat with Serklid, the third wizard, at all. "Blade's missing," he explained. "I have to go. Could you do me a favour and ask the dwarfs if they've eaten goose lately?"

He left Serklid murmuring, "Goose? Why goose?" and took off in a whistling of Beauty's black pinions.

Beauty was as glad as anyone to have a change from routine. She flew with a will, circling high above the hilly, trackless region that Scales had pricked out and searching as earnestly as Derk did. It was she who found the Pilgrims. "Smhell hhorses," she announced, and she began descending long before Derk spotted the group of riders straggling across a grassy upland. When they were low enough, Derk saw the one in front was wearing bardic green.

"That's them!" he said joyfully. "Clever of you, Beauty!"

The riders all looked up as Beauty came swirling down. Most of the horses spooked, and so did some of the riders, to judge from the way at least four of them fell off. Derk landed a prudent distance away. Shona swung down down from her bucking horse and came racing over, followed by a tall male Pilgrim.

"Oh, Dad! I *am* so glad to see you! We thought you were another dragon for a second. This is Geoffrey," Shona said.

She looked wonderful, quite her old self, and prettier than ever, Derk saw. He examined this Geoffrey who was clearly so important to her. What a pity the man was a Pilgrim. What Derk saw, he liked. A nice person, an honest one, with a commanding look to him. "What on earth are you all doing so far off the tour route?" he said.

"That was Blade," Shona said. "Oh, Dad, he never looked at the map once! I'm not sure he knows how to read a map even. You know how you always think he *must* know because of the way he translocates, but I think that must be something quite different. So he's been leaving maps to Kit, because Kit's good at them, and we were quite lost long before he vanished."

"Yes, but what happened to Blade?" Derk asked.

"*And* my sister and her latest boyfriend," Geoffrey

said ruefully. "They're gone too. We don't quite know what happened, sir. Our camp was raided in the night, we do know that, by quite a lot of people on horseback. Professor Ledbury over there woke us up, shouting and swinging his sword about, and we all jumped up. But it was dark and pretty confused, sir, and all I can work out is that my sister was wearing pale blue, which made her the easiest to see, and the raiders grabbed her and rode off at a gallop with Sukey screaming blue murder. We think Reville – he seems pretty taken with Sukey – went chasing after them on foot and that Blade went after them both. But it's only guessing. There was a sort of bang anyway, and Shona says it makes a bang when someone translocates fast, and the three of them have been missing ever since."

"We've been trying to carry on," Shona explained. "We did follow the riders' tracks for a day, but we lost them the next day, and now we're trying to go on with the tour. But Blade had the map and we don't really know where we are."

"Is that what you think we should do, sir?" Geoffrey asked, polite but anxious.

Difficult question. Derk thought about it. They were days of travel from anywhere except Derkholm here. By the time they reached the Emirates, the Emir would not be expecting them any more. If they cut out the Emir and made straight for the Inland Sea, the pirates would have gone home for the winter. The pirates had been very firm about when they would stop. If the party went the other way, it might just arrive in time for the very last battle – or it might not. "Do you all want to carry on?" he asked.

By this time, most of the other Pilgrims had dragged their resisting horses within earshot. Derk's question caused Miss Ledbury to come striding forward. "My good man, are you suggesting we have any choice in this matter?"

Dear, dear, what a dragon! Derk thought. She must have been quite a match for Scales. How does she keep her hair so neat? "Of course you have a choice, madam," he said. "You are the customers and customers are always right. I was simply thinking that if you were to turn round and travel due south – *that* way, Shona – you would eventually reach a road. You'll know it, Shona. It goes to the University one way and Derkh—er, the Dark Lord's Citadel – the other way. You could all get home quite quickly from the Citadel."

"Oh, thank *goodness*!" exclaimed a straight-haired girl. "I am so sick of this!"

"On the contrary," snapped Miss Ledbury. "I have by no means completed my surv – er, tour."

A fierce argument broke out. It sounded as if half the party agreed with Miss Ledbury and the rest had had more than enough already. Derk said quietly to Shona, "I'm afraid I shall have to leave you to sort this one out. I must go and look for Blade and the other two."

Geoffrey smiled at him. "Don't worry, sir. I'll let them argue and when they're tired of it I'll tell them they're going south."

"And they'll do it," Shona said, "believe me. See you soon, Dad. Find Blade quickly."

But Derk could not find Blade. Beauty went round and round in ever enlarging circles centring on the place Derk guessed the Pilgrims had been when they were raided, and there was nothing. No sight, scent, feeling of Blade or anyone else – nothing but broken, hilly landscape and no roads, no people and not even a solitary house. Blade could hardly have chosen a more deserted area to disappear in. In the end Derk had to give up and return to base, or Beauty would have been too tired for the battle the next day.

The three griffins came anxiously to meet him. "Any luck?" asked Kit.

Derk sighed and explained.

"We'll all go looking when the battle's over," Kit said. "If I give us each a sector on the map—"

Don rolled his eyes. "You and your maps. Barnabas is back, by the way."

"He's drunk again," said Callette.

Derk sighed even more heavily as he led Beauty over to the horse-lines and unsaddled her. "I can't stand much more of this," he said to Pretty, who came cantering over to greet his mother.

"Why do you?" Pretty asked brightly.

"Good question," said Derk. The sight of Pretty

soothed him. He was now a splendid colt, almost as big as Beauty, bright-eyed and strong, and those striped wings of his were showing signs of being twice as efficient as Beauty's, just as Derk had hoped. He patted Pretty's neck and went to discuss tomorrow with Kit. Naturally he fell over Ringlet on the way.

Kit had a problem. "I didn't think we'd wear the valleys out so quickly," he said. "We're on the last one already. We can't use the one beyond that. It's full of lake. And beyond that there's nothing but thick woods. I think we may have to go out into the moors for the next battles, and that would be difficult even with the Forces of Good up to proper strength."

Derk sat on a treestump with the map draped over one knee and Ringlet's snout affectionately on the other. He saw what Kit meant. This last valley, the one Kit was using tomorrow, was quite steep and small anyway. The next one, over a wooded ridge, was almost entirely a lake. "How many more battles have we?"

"Six. We're almost halfway through now." Kit sighed a little as he saw the end of his planning and conferring coming closer. He did love it so. "If we don't move out to the moors, we have to go back and reuse the earlier valleys, and I don't see how we can. The first valley we used is still only trampled mud. I flew over and looked."

"Grass doesn't grow back at this time of year," Derk observed. "Ask Barnabas to go and green it up."

"He's asleep. Snoring," said Kit.

"I'll do it then," Derk said wearily. Callette silently handed him a cheese sandwich. Derk took it, moved Ringlet and the map, and translocated to the site of the first battle, eating as he went.

The valley was an awful, desolate mess, worse now the leaves had come off the trees. The autumn rains had swollen the stream into a muddy marsh, and the place was full of crows, picking over the bare ground. Derk drove the birds off and got down to work. He felt better as he set the spells for greening. Making things grow was what he was good at, clean, absorbing, refreshing work. He was ankle-deep in marsh and the ground was already spiked with grass blades, bright green in the setting sun, when Don came hurtling in.

"Dad! All the horses have gone!"

Derk looked sadly at the four skidding, muddy tracks Don had made landing. "What?"

"Beauty, Pretty, Nancy Cobber, Billy – all of them!" Don said breathlessly. "Kit and Callette have flown off after them, but I'm not sure – It was more like magic. They left all their bridles behind."

The Horselady, Derk thought. Some Pilgrim somewhere had mistreated a horse. She had carried out her threat and recalled every horse there was. "She'd no call to take Beauty and Pretty too!" he said. He was quite hurt that the Horselady had done that. "Anyway, fly after Kit and Callette and tell them to come back. It's specialised magic. They can't do any good."

Don dithered. "But you need Beauty tomorrow!"

"I'll have to do without her, won't I?" said Derk. "I'll speak to the Horselady after the battle."

The battle started several hours late the next day. Almost the only people who were in place in the last valley at the right time were the legions and the werewolves, who did not use horses to get there. King Luther was over an hour late. The fanatics and the mercenaries were an hour later still. It was possible that some Pilgrims never got there at all. Agitated wizards kept appearing all through the night and during the dawn, imploring Derk to hold the battle up because their parties were still ten, or twelve, or twenty miles off and were going to have to walk all the way. Nobody but Barnabas got much sleep.

At least the delay meant that Barnabas could be sobered up. While Kit paced up and down beside the river in black impatience, slapping the shingle with his tail, Derk marched to Barnabas's tent and hauled the sleeping wizard out. When Barnabas did nothing but curl up on the stones and moan, Derk took the bucket of riverwater Callette handed him and poured it over Barnabas. Barnabas sat up with a yell, dripping twirls of water from every curl on his head.

"Have a heart, Derk!"

Derk took the flask of coffee Don handed him and passed it to Barnabas. "Drink this. Then check the battle spells on the soldiers, please. They don't seem right to me."

Barnabas glanced up the hill to the dome, where the

soldiers were dimly to be seen forming up in ranks on the parade ground. "They're fine, Derk. Promise."

"Check all the same," said Derk.

Barnabas swigged down the coffee and got up, dripping and dismal and grumbling, and trudged his way around the dome. Derk went with him to make sure. As far as he could see, the spells were indeed in place and all correct – but yet he was still not happy about them. When Barnabas opened up the dome and the army marched out, Derk watched the men narrowly. They all *seemed* just as usual. By this time, the black armour, though brightly polished, was battered and rather worn and a lot of the soldiers had got themselves extra weapons – bows and arrows mostly, but some had morningstars, dwarf axes or a second sword – picked up from dead enemies. But they had had those for several battles now. That was nothing new. Their faces inside the black helmets looked grim and unfeeling, just as usual. And yet— Derk was frustrated. Nothing was obviously wrong, but he was sure something was. He sighed and took his place at their head, on foot for a change, with Callette beside him carrying the black banner with the strange device. Drums beat, trumpets sounded. They marched to the valley.

It was just as well this was a much smaller valley, Derk thought when they reached it. Now half the legions and a third of the mercenaries were gone, the Forces of Good, up among the trees opposite on the hill that hid the lake in the next valley, were small indeed. Kit had had his work cut out to plan their victory convincingly. Their own side was smaller too, but this was because people had been killed. Kit called this "natural wastage". Derk wished he wouldn't. He gave the signal to advance.

Both sides shouted and began moving downhill. As the front lines closed on one another, Kit as usual rose majestically from behind Derk's lines, twice the size and with the illusion of a dark shadow riding on his back, and circled above the fighting, uttering dreadful screams. It was always awesome. Derk stared upwards admiringly. Kit looked almost as big as Scales. He blocked off the light.

Movement caught the corner of Derk's eye. He turned sharply to the right. Half the soldiers there were down on one knee on the hillside, bending longbows, aiming upwards. The glimpse he had of the nearest face did not look bespelled in the least. What the—? Derk slapped a hasty and ragged stasis spell out there. Bowstrings twanged and most of the arrows looped harmlessly around the hillside. But almost at the same time, Don screamed a warning from Derk's left and, behind Don's scream, Derk heard the breathy *whuff* of a flight of arrows truly aimed. He whirled that way to see arrows storming into the sky and the soldiers on that side punching the air, capering about waving longbows and pointing triumphantly.

Above the valley, Kit screamed even more dreadfully and lurched in the air. Two black stalks were sticking out of his chest. Another black stalk was slantwise into one wing. As Derk stared, scarcely able to credit this, the shadowy figure vanished from Kit's back and the mighty black illusion shrank. Kit was suddenly a black griffin half the size, tumbling and shrieking and turning in the air. One wing was flailing uselessly, whirling Kit upside down. Then he fell like a stone and plunged out of sight beyond the opposite trees. Only some big black flight feathers were left, twirling above the hill. All around, the soldiers cheered and shouted their hatred and joy. They had been out to kill Kit and they had.

Beside Derk, Callette spread her wings. "Stay where you are!" Derk snapped. "And you, Don."

He translocated himself, messily, and so jerkily that half of him seemed to be still in the valley for a second, among a battle that was breaking up into chaos. His own side was fighting itself. The werewolves, the monsters and King Luther's men threw themselves upon the soldiers in black. Groups of Pilgrims, cheering lustily at what they took to be the death of the Dark Lord, raced across the valley to join in, while the legions and most of the dwarfs and mercenaries hung back, bewildered by this. It was not part of the plan. They only moved when the fanatics stormed out of the woods and began attacking everyone impartially. As Derk arrived among the trees at the top of the opposite hill, the valley became full of a seething free-for-all. He knew he should have told Don and Callette to get to safety. They were going to be killed too.

But the lake was below him, long and blue-brown.

He was in time to see the reflections of trees in it tossing and breaking in the great ring of waves where Kit had gone down. Bubbles came out of the centre for a moment and then stopped. By the time Don and Callette arrived, Derk was staring at the very last ripples lapping the shore.

"I told you—" he began. Then he gave up. "What's the use? Did either of you see Prince Talithan?"

"He went into that green haze," Don said. "All the elves did when the fanatics came out."

"Barnabas went too," Callette said sourly. "He knew I was going to pull his head off."

Derk looked at her and saw blood on her beak and her talons. But it did not seem to be her own blood, so he did not let it worry him. His mind seemed to have closed down into a very small space. There was only one thing in it. "Follow me back to camp, both of you," he said, and translocated again.

In the camp, he collected the dogs, the pigs and the Friendly Cows into a huddle and called Talithan. As Callette and Don landed by the river, the green haze swung and Talithan stood on the shale beside them. He was pale and breathing heavily, but he bowed politely to Derk. "You have need of me, lord?"

"Yes. Come over here," Derk called to the griffins. "Talithan, do one more thing for me. Then you can collect Pretty from the Horselady and I won't trouble you again."

Talithan looked puzzled. "But, lord—"

"The Horselady had no business to take Pretty," Derk

414

said. "Tell her from me that he's yours. What I want you to do is to put all of us here into your green haze and move us back to Derkholm."

Talithan's eyes moved dubiously from Derk in his huddle of animals to the two griffins. "So many," he murmured.

"Can't it be done?" Derk asked.

Talithan looked at his face. His manner changed. "I was merely thinking," he said gently, "that very few have ever walked through our country. Of course it can be done. I shall take you through my own lands, lord, all of you."

When King Luther and the Emperor Titus panted into the camp half an hour later, blood-spattered, exasperated and wanting an explanation, they found the place deserted.

Chapter Twenty-three

*

*I*t was a big mistake, Blade discovered, to translocate in among a troop of galloping horsemen. It would have been a mistake by daylight. In the dark he was lucky not to be killed. Sukey's kidnappers did not even know Blade was there. They simply galloped on. Reville, pounding up on foot around dawn, found Blade lying in the clump of gorse he had been kicked into some hours before.

"Are you all right?" said Reville.

"*No!*" said Blade.

In fact, he was only very badly bruised. In the days that followed, he kept finding new black horseshoe shapes on new, unlikely parts of his body. But no bones were broken. Reville assured him of that. It seemed that all

Thieves' Guild members learnt quite a bit about healing. And about making other people do what they wanted, Blade discovered. As soon as Blade was sitting up, moaning, Reville said, "Good. Now translocate us both to where those riders are."

Blade shuddered. "No. I can't. I'm not going to get ridden over again."

"Just take us to a hundred yards behind them," Reville said. "You can do that."

"Why?" said Blade.

"Because I want to catch up with them before they do anything to Sukey, of course," Reville said.

"But there's about half a hundred of them. What can we do?" Blade protested.

"Only twenty or so. I'll think of something," Reville replied. "Come on. Think of Sukey."

Sukey, in Blade's opinion, was not worth thinking about. He had only gone after her because, what with the dark, and the way she was screaming, he had woken up and thought it was still that morning when the soldiers tried to escape from the dome. Sukey's screams had been very like Shona's. He had realised it was Sukey and not Shona while twenty horses – only twenty? Well, that made eighty hooves – were each individually treading all over him. Now he did not want to move. But Blade was low and aching and feeble, while Reville was well and strong and worrying about Sukey. Reville won.

They translocated. A hundred yards ahead, a tight

little group of horsemen trotted over the moor away from them. All of them were in black except for one rider in the midst of them who was in pale blue. Blade's heart sank. He knew who these were. Escaped soldiers. They could be the same group who had ambushed the bandits. Reville was right to be worried about Sukey. "There's nothing we can do!" Blade moaned.

"We keep following. They have to stop sometime," Reville said.

Blade could still hardly walk. He let the riders get well ahead and then translocated himself and Reville again. They did that all day until, finally, in the evening, the group stopped and made camp. Blade sat in an exhausted, aching heap and let Reville creep away to investigate.

Reville was gone nearly an hour. "This isn't going to be easy," he said, arriving back suddenly in the twilight. Loaves, pieces of cheese and a winebottle thudded down in the heather beside Blade. "They're keeping Sukey right in the middle. They've got ropes tied to her ankles and her wrists and each rope is round a man's wrist the other end. But they don't seem to be hurting her. They seem to be arguing with her most of the time. I got close enough to hear her telling them all the bad things that would happen to them if they didn't let her go, but that was all. Lucky they don't keep any kind of a guard on their provisions. Let's have supper and think."

Blade ate ravenously. Reville ate dutifully, to keep his

strength up. He really was wretchedly worried about Sukey, Blade realised. "Are you in love with her or something?" he asked Reville incredulously.

"Don't sound so astonished. She's wonderful," said Reville. "Yes, I am in love with her, if you must know. I never thought I could be before this. Ice cool, I used to call myself. Cynical. I was all set to marry an heiress for her money. But now I'm going to marry Sukey or die."

"She's a *tourist*!" said Blade.

"So?" said Reville. "I don't hold it against her. And she's promised to stay here with me."

Blade found this hard to believe. He thought Sukey must have been leading Reville on. It would be like her. So, the sooner they got Sukey back from those soldiers, the sooner she could disillusion Reville and the sooner Reville could return to sanity. "What are you planning to do?" he said.

"Go in there as soon as they're asleep and cut the ropes," Reville said. "Obviously. I'll do it alone. You're like a dragon with corns. I suppose it's those bruises. You wait here."

"For transport," Blade said bitterly. "Thanks."

But Reville's plan did not work. He came back disgustedly at dawn with more food. "One of the four on watch all the time," he said, moodily tossing Blade a loaf. "I think they may have spotted us following them. Try keeping us further back today."

They tried that for the next two days. Blade's bruises

hurt more and Reville became almost too tired to steal food. The evening of that third day, Blade pointed out that, amazing as it was, no one had tried to hurt Sukey yet and the two of them were not going to be much use to her as they were. He explained that he could catch up with the soldiers, even carrying Reville along, from anywhere up to fifty miles away, and he suggested that they had a day's rest. Reville did not agree. He and Blade had a nasty argument. It only ended when Blade burst into tears, tore his beard off and threw it at Reville.

"Oh," said Reville, staring at him. "I was forgetting you're only young. And I tell you, it wouldn't take much to make me cry too. All right. A day's rest. We move in when we're fresh."

That was the evening the Horselady called in all the horses.

This time it was Reville who got trampled. After the argument, both of them fell asleep, close together for warmth, with heather pilled on them for further warmth. The last thing Blade heard was Reville demanding to know who the stupid fool was who decided that the tours always started in autumn, until, even from a deep sleep, Blade heard and recognised the drumming of eighty hooves. He translocated without properly waking up, and settled down to sleep again a hundred yards away. He found Reville in the morning by the groans.

"Gods!" Reville howled. "I tried to get up and run! A mistake." After a long pause, he added, "You know, I don't think I was sympathetic enough when this happened to you."

"Look on the bright side," Blade said. "The kidnappers are walking now."

Unfortunately, Sukey's captors seemed to have decided that someone had stolen their horses. For the next few days they were so watchful that Reville did not dare limp too near them. They sprang up at the least noise and stabbed their swords into bushes. And they guarded Sukey as if she were the most valuable thing in the world. If they had not been forced to abandon quite a heap of provisions when the horses left, Blade and Reville would have starved as they hobbled along behind. As it was, they had more stale bread than they could carry.

The kidnappers were clearly going somewhere. They crossed the moors in a steady straight line and eventually struck a road, a well-used looking road with high bushy banks and wheelmarks on its stony surface. Blade and Reville pursued mostly by letting the group get out of sight and then translocating to where they could see them again. In between, Reville was too bruised to do much except sit and look gloomily at the ruined wristwatches on his arm and worry about Sukey. He thought there must be an outlaw stronghold that the men were making for. He told Blade that the Thieves' Guild knew of hundreds of people who had been kidnapped for no apparent reason, over in the east, and that nobody ever found where they had been taken. "We must rescue her before they get wherever they're going," he kept saying.

The road made things a little easier. The soldiers seemed to relax once they were on it, and Blade found that the high banks made it possible to get quite close to them. Whenever the trudging group stopped, Blade took hold of Reville's skinny, muscular arm and brought them behind a clump of gorse or some small trees on the bank, where they lay flat and listened to Sukey's high voice, arguing.

"This is not going to do any of you the slightest good, you know. Where do you think I'm going to run to, anyway? You've all got great long legs. You could catch me at once if I ran away."

None of the men seemed to attend much to Sukey. They treated her more like a valuable animal than anything else. But during the second day of sneaking after them along the road, Reville nudged Blade as they lay behind some dead blackberry bushes, and pointed. Blade saw that Sukey now had only one rope on her, round her waist. It was also clear that the men had expected to get wherever they were going before this and were running out of food.

"We can manage one more day, with luck," one of them said. "How far is it now?"

"Take us at least two days more," replied another, who had a tattered map. "More like two and a half at the rate she walks."

Blade felt he had known these two men for a long time. He had first seen both of them when he and his family had helped Barnabas get the newly arrived army to the camp near Derkholm. He had pushed past them on Nancy Cobber and noticed that they seemed less drugged than the rest. Meanwhile Reville was plucking at Blade's sleeve in an alarmed way. After the party had heaved to its feet again, cursing and grumbling, and hauled the arguing Sukey off down the road, Reville said, "We're running out of time. As soon as they get to their hideout, we'll have *no* chance."

This was certainly true. "What do you suggest?" Blade asked.

"I think," said Reville, "that I've got the hang of this translocating now." Blade stared at him. Reville grinned. Despite the big yellow and green bruise on his face, it was almost his usual jaunty smile. "I'm a magic user," he told Blade. "Most thieves have to be. I've been watching fairly closely what it is you do when you translocate. And if I can do it too, then we can both jump in among them, cut that rope, grab Sukey before any of them can stop us and jump out again with her. Mind if we practise a bit?"

They spent the rest of that day practising. At first Reville could only move himself a few feet and his direction was unpredictable. Blade got used to dodging fast. But Reville's face set in stern, determined lines. "It'll come," he panted. "I was like this over picking pockets and now I'm up with the best. I'll fetch up by that rock over there by this evening, you'll see." And he did. Blade was impressed.

At sunset, Blade took himself to the bank above the place where the kidnappers were camping in the road. After a pause, Reville arrived too, muddy down one side. "Slight mistake. Ditch," he explained. "Where is she?"

To their disgust, Sukey was once more attached to four ropes for the night. They waited anxiously for daybreak. At dawn, they shared a hard, greasy end of cheese and watched the kidnappers share much the same between themselves and Sukey. Then someone tied a rope to her waist and the band moved off.

"Thank *Wiksil*!" whispered Reville.

"Who's Wiksil?" Blade asked.

"God of Thieves. Are you ready?" said Reville. Blade supposed he was. "Then *go!*" Reville cried out.

He went. Blade went a scared instant later and found himself in amongst black armour, sweaty smells and startled, unpleasant faces. Sukey was partly behind him. He grabbed her by her travel-stained blue silk and, as his fingers met in it, he heard Reville shout, "And *go!*" So he took off again. After that, it was highly confusing. Sukey screamed all the time, which made it even more confusing. Blade rather thought that he tried to translocate in one direction while Reville went in another. However it happened, they went in a set of wild zigzags. Blade saw moor, mountainside, different moor, a sucking marshy place and – for one terrifying instant – the men in black all round him in the road again. He and Reville leapt frantically away from that – road, bank, more bank, another stretch of road – bundling and wrenching the screaming Sukey between them. And at this point Blade sorted out that it was no good expecting Reville to get it right and tried pushing the next time Reville pulled. He pushed hard, to get as far away as possible.

They ended up staggering and splashing in the edges of a barren little mountain lake, high in a cup of khaki-coloured hills somewhere. Blade realised he had hold of Sukey by the seat of her trousers and let go quickly. Sukey stopped screaming and flung herself on Reville.

"Oh, Reville *darling*! I *knew* you'd rescue me!"

"I was behind you all the way, my love," Reville said. "Now I'll never let you go."

The two of them stood kissing passionately in the water, regardless of wet boots.

Well, well, thought Blade. Perhaps she wasn't just leading him on after all. Feeling rather let down, he waded and squelched among spiky rushes until he reached drier turf, where he stood and looked round the barren lake for some clue as to where they might be.

It was not so totally deserted as he had first thought. A low green spit prodded out into the water just below a place where the mountains formed a kind of saddle. There was someone fishing from the end of the spit. He must have been very much engrossed in his fishing, because he had not even turned round to see what the screaming and splashing had been about. Blade squelched along the lakeside towards him. It was, he found, one of those confusing landscapes where everything is smaller than you think. He reached the spit of land quite quickly, and the mountain rearing above was only a hill really.

"Excuse me," he said.

The man fishing turned round with an enquiring smile. He was wearing huge wading boots and clothes the colour of the hills surrounding them. He seemed young and good-natured. "Good morning," he said cheerfully. "Can I help?"

"We're a bit lost," Blade explained. "Can you tell us the best way to go?"

"The nearest big place is Costamaret," the fisherman said. "It's more than a hundred miles south-east of here."

"Oh," said Blade. He thought about translocating there and realised, just by thinking about it, that his ability to translocate had been completely drained for the moment by the mad zigzag struggle with Reville. "Is there anywhere nearer than that?"

The fisherman shifted his rod carefully into his left hand and pointed with his right at the khaki saddle of hill above them. "Up there. You'll find somewhere on the other side of that." He smiled, obviously feeling for the dismay on Blade's face. "It's the only way really. I'm sorry."

Blade looked up along his pointing hand. It was not

so far to that lower part of the hill, though it looked steep. He looked back at the fisherman.

He was not there. There was not even a ripple in the water or a footprint from his waders. Whoever the man was, he was clearly a very powerful magic user. Blade had not even felt the power it must have taken to vanish like that. Meanwhile Reville was towing Sukey along the lakeshore to the spit. Both of them were pink and happy and full of energy. "Up there to that low part then?" Reville said to Blade.

"Did you see anyone?" Blade asked.

"No," said Sukey. "But that's where you were pointing, wasn't it? You know, you look a lot younger without your beard."

She and Reville set off at a joyous run up the hill. Blade plodded after, still wondering about that fisherman. But before long he was thinking more about the energy being in love seemed to give to Sukey and Reville. The hill was not only steep, but covered with the kind of mountain grass that is nearly as slippery as ice, but they were at the top before Blade was two-thirds of the way up. He was thinking that being in love might just be worth trying, when Reville threw himself flat and made urgent motions to Sukey to do the same. Blade came up the rest of the way on his hands and knees.

"What's the matter?" he asked.

Reville motioned him to stop talking and crawl to look over the top of the hill. Blade wormed his way there, expecting to find the road again and the kidnappers standing in it, waiting.

He saw the road, certainly. It curled round beneath him and led into a messy sort of hole in the mountainside, below and to the right. He saw men in black armour, too, but not the ones who had carried off Sukey. These had on armour so old that it had mostly gone back to brownish-black leather. Blade only recognised it as soldier-wear from the style. These men – ten or so of them – had nasty-looking whips with which they were threatening three groups of ragged, skinny people who were bowed down and straining to push three large covered metal trucks along three lengths of metal rails. Each set of rails came out of one of three more messy holes in the mountain, then ran for a hundred yards before it just stopped. Blade puzzled about this. He also puzzled why the struggling people did not just turn on the men with whips, until he saw they were chained.

As he saw the chains, the puzzle about the rails was solved too. Each truck had now struggled its way to the very end of of the rails and stopped. A cheerful figure in a billowing robe sauntered up to stand level with them, ran a hand through his grey curls and then made the sort of weary, practised gesture that Blade knew rather well. Three curious slits appeared in front of each truck. They seemed to be slits in the very nature of things, because they ran through the moors, mountains and the road and yet seemed to float on top of the landscape at the same time. The slits writhed about a bit, settled, and became openings into somewhere else. Blade peered, but all he could see beyond the openings were more metal rails continuing the ones the trucks were on. The men in old soldier armour shouted and cracked the whips. The bowed people in chains heaved. And the trucks ran through into somewhere else. The openings vanished and the overseers urged the prisoners back to the mountain again, where, if Blade craned, he could see three more trucks waiting.

He did not wait to watch any more. He slithered down the hillside to join Sukey and Reville on a sort of ledge. They stared at one another. "That was Barnabas!" said Blade.

"I know. Does Querida know?" Reville said. "That's quite an important question, because it could be that everyone at the University is in on this. In that case, where's the money going?"

"What money? What do you mean?" Sukey and Blade asked, almost together.

"That's a mine, more or less inside this hill we're sitting on," Reville explained, "and it's run nice and cheaply on kidnapped slave labour. Whatever they mine is going offworld. By the ton truck. *Someone* is making money out of it, and I don't think it's only Wizard Barnabas." He dived round on Sukey. "What's in those trucks? Any idea? What does your world get?"

"I haven't a clue," she said. Her eyes were wide and

worried among her tangled curls. She suddenly looked older and shrewder and more like Reville. "And I want to know," she added.

"Then we'll go and find out." Reville stood up, looking very determined.

"Why?" Blade objected. It was unexpectedly warm on the hillside ledge. He wanted to sit there and rest.

But Reville turned to him in a way that surprised Blade, because it was like Titus or King Luther when they were being royal. "Someone," said Reville, "is robbing my world. I want to know who, why and what. Because it's illegal. *I'm* the only person around here who's allowed to steal stuff. Guild rules. So how do we best get a look at what they're stealing? Ideas?"

Blade stared at him, feeling glad that he had not happened to tell Reville about the dwarfs. Sukey looked round thoughtfully. Then she pointed behind Reville. "There may be an opening up there. We could sneak in that way."

As Reville swung round to look, it occurred to Blade that Reville and Sukey were a good match for one another. Sukey looked – and was – a girlish sort of girl. Yet she had hardly turned a hair at being kidnapped and now she was as cool and collected as Reville, and far cooler than Blade was at the idea of sneaking into a mine full of illegal robbers with whips.

"Yes. A sort of cave, maybe," Reville said, and set off for the dark dent in the hill that Sukey was pointing to.

Sukey scampered with him. Blade slithered reluctantly after.

There was a hole in the mountainside there. It was hard to tell if it was natural or someone's early attempt to dig a mine. It was rocky and earthy and it led a way inwards in a passage high enough for them all to walk upright. Before it grew too dark to see, Reville snapped his fingers and, to Blade's envy, caused a blue tuft of witchlight to sprout from his left hand. He held it up to guide them.

"Reville, you're marvellous!" Sukey sighed.

"Just go carefully," Reville whispered. "I can feel a big drop somewhere ahead."

The drop was simply a hole in the earthy floor. Beyond it, the passage came to an end. Reville knelt down and shone his left-handed light into the hole. There was an insecure-looking old ladder bolted to the near side.

"Old mine shaft," Reville whispered. "Excellent." He swung himself on to the ladder. It creaked like a dead tree in a gale. "Once at a time," he said warningly. "It won't carry three."

Blade had to wait in the dark while Sukey followed Reville down. After that, there was no question in Blade's mind where he was going. He was going with Reville and the light if it killed them all. He arrived at the bottom of the rasping, swaying ladder with his teeth chattering. Just the cold, he told himself. Just the cold in here. He turned thankfully towards the blue light.

It was bigger than he had thought. He could see Sukey and Reville through the sheet of blueness, on the other side of it, staring as if they had been put under a stasis spell. There were three eyes in the blueness, all of them watching Blade sarcastically. He understood why he had been feeling as if he had been plunged into a bath of icy acid.

"Oh," he said. "It's you."

Me, agreed the demon. *I said we would meet again. Why are you here? Have you come to steal demon food like the other humans?*

"Demon food?" said Blade.

They dig it out of the mountain and they take it out of the world, the demon told him. *And they set the place round with wards and demon traps. Take just one ward off for me. I will make you rich.*

"I – I'm afraid I don't know how to," Blade said.

Or I could kill you if you don't, the demon suggested.

"But that wouldn't help you," Blade answered through clenched teeth.

Then what reward would persuade you? wondered the demon. *Let me see.* Blade felt it pressing all over his mind, sickeningly. He could not think of any way to stop it. He just had to stand there, shaking all over, until the demon seemed to have finished. Then he felt its laughter pulsing through him. *He wants Deucalion to teach him magic! I could arrange that.*

But the White Oracle said Deucalion would teach me

anyway, Blade thought. That was a comforting thought, until Blade realised that the Oracle had not said how it would be arranged. Sweat came popping out all over Blade at the idea that Deucalion actually might be a demon. He opened his mouth to protest again that he had no idea how to take demon wards off. And he realised the demon had gone. Strange.

"Phew!" said Reville. "That was nasty! What *is* demon food?"

"I really don't know," Blade said.

"I think the poor thing was hungry," Sukey said. "It wasn't going to do anything to Blade. It was just letting him know they were stealing its food."

"Poor thing – nothing!" said Reville. "Don't ever get sorry for a demon, love. It will eat *you*."

"Then are *people* demon food?" Sukey asked. "It's not people in those trucks, is it?"

"No, they just eat souls usually," Reville said. "We *must* get a look in those trucks."

They hurried along the earthy gallery the ladder had brought them to. Shortly, there was another hole and another ladder, this one in much better repair, with dim light shining from below. Reville dismissed his tuft of witchlight and they all clambered quietly down. Halfway to the next earthy floor, the demon wards began, strung across the shaft like cobwebs made of nearly nothing. At least most of them were warding against demons, but Blade saw others that seemed to be warding the mine against being found by other people. Sukey found all of them fascinating. She stretched a hand out to the nearest.

"Don't *touch* them!" Reville and Blade whispered, both at once.

Sukey snatched her hand back and climbed on down, looking chastened. Reville went very cautiously from then on, because the ladder brought them down into what was clearly a side passage in the main mines. At the end of the passage, trucks were being pushed past in a much wider space that was properly lit by electric lights in wire cages. Chains clinked. Ragged people grunted and strained, and the lighted part was filled with the rumble, rumble, squeak of heavy wheels moving on metal tracks. After one cautious look, Reville led them along the passage the other way.

"Too many overseers out that way," he said.

Blade lost touch with where they were after that. As Shona had pointed out, his sense of direction was not the same as other people's. He simply went where Reville went. He thought they might have gone parallel with the main part, until they came to a slanting place, where smaller trucks were squealing slowly downhill under a raw-looking ceiling propped up by girders and beams. To Reville's delight, these trucks were not covered. Each one seemed to be heaped up with earth and broken rocks.

"What is it?" Reville wondered. "Some kind of ore?"

He and Sukey both took a handful and went upslope to the nearest wire-caged light. The place where it hung was probably weaker than the rest. The walls and ceiling here were entirely lined with iron girders, making it rather narrower than the rest of the sloping track. When Blade squeezed up beside them, Reville and Sukey were sorting knowledgeably through their handfuls of dirt. Sukey seemed to know as much about minerals as Reville did. But they were both puzzled.

"Bit of iron ore, shale, limestone – a lot of nothing really," Sukey was saying.

"Not even gold-bearing," Reville agreed. "Not volcanic. So no diamonds."

"It could be some kind of valuable chemical," Sukey was suggesting, when they all heard the squealing rumble of another truck coming. They pressed themselves against the iron wall to let it go past and Sukey said, still inspecting her handful, "If I didn't know better, I'd say this was just what it looks like – any old earth and stones."

"It must be *something* valuable," Reville said as the truck came rumbling past.

Blade understood then. Sukey was right, right about the demon and right about the stuff in the trucks. The demon had been trying to tell them, in its demonic way, and no demon could ever do anything without threats or laughter. But he never would have realised what it had been trying to say if they had not been standing inside the narrow place surrounded by iron. As the truck came through, rumbling the walls and the tracks, with its pile of cold earth almost brushing Blade's face, he found himself receiving a blast of solid magic – magic that seemed like part of the very smell of the heaped-up earth and stones. And he remembered that iron insulated magic. "Got it!" he said. "It *is* just earth and stones and it *is* valuable! Our whole world's magic. The magic's part of the earth. That's what they're stealing – magic!"

Reville gave a little whistle. "So demons eat magic!"

"They must do," Blade was saying, when Reville's whistle seemed to be taken up from further down the passage, loud and shrill. Someone along there shouted.

"I see them! Intruders in shaft twenty! Up there in the arch!"

Sukey and Reville threw down their handfuls of earth and they all three ran. And ran, and ran, with whistles and shouts urging them on to dodge round corners, whisk up side passages, or double back the other way, stumbling on stones, splashing through at least one underground river, stubbing toes on iron tracks, tripping over spades, and racing bent over behind rows of big metal trucks. Reville was good at this. He was *trained* for it, Blade thought, struggling to keep up, with his robe flapping around his knees and getting in his way. Deeper and deeper into the mines they went. They pelted through wet yellow mud in front of rows of chained people, who all leant on their spades to watch them.

"Tried that. Been there," Blade heard as he splatted past. "Bet you my next meal they'll be caught in gallery five."

And Blade was. He was not sure if it was actually gallery five or somewhere else. He only knew that he somehow lost Reville and Sukey, turned down the way he thought they had run, and ran full tilt into a pair of overseers. He was grabbed in an instant and his arms were twisted behind him. Blade struggled and fought and tried to translocate, but his ability to do that was still not there. All he could do was put his cold spell on them, but they were used to the chill of the mines and hardly seemed to notice. They ran him along the wide earthy tunnel to a metal door and shoved him into a small room like an office. The door clanged shut behind him. Blade, half dazzled by the much brighter light in there, found himself blinking at Barnabas.

Barnabas was blinking too and breathing heavily. "You can't be allowed to leave, you know," he said, in his usual jolly way. "Sorry about this, but this is a highly secret operation, Blade. It beats me how you ever got inside the secrecy spells over this area. They were some of my best."

The only thing Blade could think of was to play stupid. "I don't understand," he panted. "What are you doing here?"

"Mr Chesney had to have an agent this side," Barnabas said, "and he chose me. Or did you mean the earth-mining?"

"That," gasped Blade. "Just *earth*. I mean—"

"It's full of magic," Barnabas said. "Everything in this world is." And while Blade was thinking *I was right!*

Barnabas went on, "But it doesn't endure very long in the world it goes to. It does marvels while it does last, of course. I believe they market it as the new super fuel and use it to run all their machines, but they have to keep getting more."

"Don't they pay for it at all?" Blade asked.

"Why should they? It's just earth," Barnabas said. "They pay me and the overseers rather well for our help, naturally, but who else would they pay?"

"Then why do you keep it secret?" Blade demanded.

"Patriotic people like Querida or your father would be bound to object," said Barnabas. "I suppose there may even come a time when this world gets short of magic, but that won't be in our time. It won't be for hundreds of years. Meanwhile, you wouldn't deny Mr Chesney and his world all the obvious benefits of massive amounts of cheap power, would you?"

Why is he explaining to me like this? Blade wondered. As he wondered, he realised that Barnabas was keeping his jolly, crinkled, bloodshot eyes entirely on Blade's face. As if Barnabas was carefully not looking at something behind Blade. Blade whirled round. But it was too late. The overseer behind him reached round with a long arm and jammed a pad with something smelly on it against Blade's nose and mouth. Then he held Blade's head hard against his chest until Blade was forced to breathe the smelly stuff in. Blade did not even manage to put his cold spell on Barnabas, although he tried.

CHAPTER TWENTY-FOUR

*

When Prince Talithan's green haze swung outwards and let Derk and his companions out into the garden of Derkholm, Derk almost understood how it was done. At any other time he would have been fascinated, but now, when Talithan asked gravely, "Do you require anything more, lord?" Derk said, "Only to be left completely alone, thank you." Prince Talithan understood and stepped away into the haze again.

Derk had only vague memories of what he did for some while after that. He supposed he must have put the dogs, the pigs and the Friendly Cows in the right places and given them food. But maybe Old George did that. Derk recalled Old George jogging beside him like a skeleton out for a run, protesting, while Derk was sealing Derkholm off from the rest of the world, but Derk was putting out his full power to do that and he had no attention to spare just then, even for Don, who galloped anxiously at his other side, saying, "Won't you even let Mum in then?"

"She won't be coming here," Derk said, and almost lost his magics in the terrible, bitter grief at the way Mara had left him. "Go away, Don."

"Shona, then?" said Don.

Shona, Derk remembered, was probably on her way here. "All right. I'll leave the back gate," he said and made a small, almost invisible passage to it, that you could only find if you knew where the back gate was. Lydda, if Lydda was still alive, could come in that way too. The rest of the grounds Derk sealed with a strength he did not know he had. Then, as far as he remembered, he went and camped on the terrace. He must have put out the balefire and filled in the trench when he made himself a hut out of the tables. But he did nothing else. He simply could not be bothered to take the rest of the Dark Lord scenery away. He sat in the hut. After a while, cautiously and kindly, the pigs came along and settled in with him. Derk scratched between wings and rubbed backs from time to time. It was the only comfort there seemed to be.

Blade was gone. Mara was gone. Lydda was gone. Kit would not be coming back.

It was wrong to have let Kit have charge of the battles.

Kit had been too young, just like Blade and Lydda. And the soldiers had hated Kit. And I knew they hated him, Derk thought, and I still let him fly up there where they could take a shot at him, merely because I was finding it all so difficult being the Dark Lord. It should have been *me* they shot.

He did not know how many times he relived that awful moment when Kit dwindled and tumbled in the air with three arrows sticking in him. He relived himself staring at the surging ripples in the lake where his first, best, cleverest, most successful griffin had gone down. He knew exactly where Kit's body would be, under the water. He would go and fetch it up when he had got over hurting about it so much.

But the hurt went on. Derk sat in his hut on the terrace and hurt and wished people would leave him alone. There were constant interruptions. Everyone came on tiptoe, and terribly *kindly*, which irritated Derk. Don came at least once an hour. Don was growing, Derk noticed after a vague number of days, bidding fair to be nearly as big as Kit. Seeing Don made the hurt worse, even though Don usually just looked at him and then went away. Old George always came with some gloomy news or other.

"Quite a crowd outside the gates by now. Wizards with them look pretty impatient."

"Go away," said Derk.

Next time he came, Old George said, "Bigger crowd

still. Been trying to get in, but the wizards can't seem to manage it."

"Go *away*," said Derk, and he reinforced the magics round Derkholm.

"Never seen a Dark Lord they can't get at before," Old George said another time. "Don't seem to know what to do. Must be several hundred tourists out there now."

"*Go* away!" sighed Derk.

"Them dwarfs," Old George said, reappearing some time after, "got their beady eyes on your cows. You can't expect me to keep them off single-handed."

"Get Don to help you guard them then," said Derk. He was so irritated that he took the emaciation off Old George.

Old George was not grateful. "Now I haven't got a rag to my name that fits me!"

"Borrow mine. Upstairs somewhere," Derk said.

"If the dwarfs left you any. Into everything, they are," said Old George.

"*Go away!*" said Derk.

The dwarfs interrupted nearly as often. There seemed to be swarms of them now, from several different clans, each distinguished by the objects plaited into their braids. They told Derk what each bead and colour meant. They seemed to feel that Derk needed to chat. One of them sat and told him stories of ancient dwarf feuds and battles, until Derk implored him not to. All of them seemed to feel Derk ought to eat. They kept bringing him food. Derk had no interest in any of it until the time Dworkin brought him a crispy fowl's leg.

"Goose?" Derk enquired hopefully.

"No, well, actually it's one of a flock we found penned up in the hills. Just ordinary hens, you know," Dworkin explained. "But they seemed to be going begging, so we brought them here the morning before you came back. Lucky, that. They make good, tasty eating. Try it."

"No thanks," said Derk, listlessly wondering who in the village he owed money to now.

Don ate the chicken leg, as he had eaten all the other food the dwarfs brought to Derk. Derk himself might have starved but for Prince Talithan. Talithan took to appearing, very softly and tactfully, every day. He said nothing, for which Derk was grateful, but simply stood and surveyed Derk and the pigs in the hut. After a while, he began to bring a succession of tall, grave elfin ladies along with him too. Each lady brought something with her – a flask of glowing liquor, a shining fruit, a box of melting biscuits, a plate of enticing shellfish – which she put down beside Derk before bowing and leaving. Everything they brought smelt and tasted so heavenly that Derk often ate or drank it before he had time to think. Possibly it made him feel better.

The demon kept putting in an appearance as well. It would bulge up from between the terrace paving stones, fix all three eyes wonderingly upon Derk, and then subside away downwards. It never said anything. But Derk could feel it around much of the time, puzzling over him, and he wished it would go. He had a notion that the demon was being tactful too, in its way.

There was one other set of people whom the magics surrounding Derkholm would not prevent from appearing, but they had so far not appeared. From time to time, Derk wondered what he would do when they did. Mostly he was too miserable to care.

Meanwhile, here was Don again, tiptoeing up with a clack of claw and a rattle of feathers that said *I am being tactful* in a way that made Derk want to scream.

"Dad, Callette's been in her shed for *days* now and she won't come out. She's worse than you, even. She hasn't eaten a thing since we got back."

Callette was still growing. This was serious. Derk actually got up and shambled down the garden, past the fading, tattered remains of the human monsters, to Callette's shed. He stood outside it and called.

"Go away," said Callette.

"You can't stay there," said Derk.

"Yes, I can," said Callette. "I'm not sorry Kit's dead and I know I ought to be, so I'm staying here until I *am* sorry."

Derk thought of Callette misbehaving when she was small and of himself saying, "Go to your room until you're sorry." Oh dear. "I don't think it works like that, Callette," he said helplessly. "I know you didn't get on with Kit. You can't help that." Silence from the shed. "I'm sorry enough for two," Derk said. "Won't that do?"

"Go away," said Callette.

Taste of my own medicine, Derk thought, and went back to his hut on the terrace.

Querida came the next day. To a wizard of her powers, Derk's defences were – not exactly child's play: they nearly defeated her – possible to overcome with a severe struggle. She arrived on the terrace, leaning heavily on the stick she now used instead of crutches, and not quite so calm and strong as she would have wished.

Good gracious gods! she thought.

The smell of pig and person from the hut was appalling. Behind it, the house was almost as bad. Since Derk had stopped caring about the Citadel magics, parts of it had frayed or fallen off. The house was now a patchwork of dark archways and black half-towers mixed in with ordinary windows and walls. Barnabas's transparent repaired part shone out above the sinister black carvings round the Citadel door. But the door was open, showing an indescribable mess inside, horse droppings and chewed bones, among which dwarfs came and went – more and more dwarfs, as they realised that someone new had arrived. Querida did not blame the big golden griffin sitting protectively beside the hut for looking so unhappy.

"Really, Wizard Derk, this place is like a pigsty!" she said.

Derk settled more comfortably among the pigs. "It *is* a pigsty," he said.

An old man wearing clothes far too tight for him arrived on the end of the terrace in a crowd of panting dogs. "You want her thrown out?" he asked.

Really! Querida thought.

"No, no," said Derk. "She'll probably go when she's said what she wants to say."

"*Really!*" said Querida. The old man and the dogs settled down on the terrace steps, preparing, like the dwarfs crowding the sinister doorway, to listen to everything she said. Querida sighed in exasperation. "I suppose there's no chance of anyone bringing me a chair?" Apparently there wasn't. Nobody moved. "Very well," Querida said, leaning on her stick. "Wizard Derk, are you aware that there are now thirty-nine Pilgrim Parties waiting outside your gate?"

"They'll go away in the end," Derk said.

Querida thumped her stick on the flagstones in exasperation. "But there is no way they *can* go away except through your Citadel!" When Derk did not reply to this, she added, "And the only reason there aren't more parties out there is because all the horses have disappeared. Did you know that?"

"Yes," said Derk.

"And all the dragons have vanished," said Querida.

"They're angry," said Derk, "about the gold." This was important. Scales had explained why. Derk came up on one elbow and explained to Querida. "Dragons sit on gold because they get vital vitamins from it. They haven't been allowed enough gold for years."

"Oh," said Querida. "I wasn't aware of that." Seeing that Derk might now be attending, she went on quickly, "And there's been the most dreadful chaos up on the battlefield. I had to send for High Priest Umru to sort it out. The Empire and King Luther declared war on one another and the mercenaries were killing everything that moved. I don't think there's a single offworld soldier surviving by now. What are you going to do for an army?"

Derk did not want to hear about battles. He came off his elbow and lay back among the pigs. "Ask Barnabas," he said bitterly.

Querida pursed her lips. She was not getting through to this man. "In fact," she said, "there is hardly a single tour-event *anywhere* that hasn't broken down in some way. They depend on the Dark Lord to keep them organised."

"I know," said Derk.

Querida hissed with annoyance. It was true she had meant the tours to break down. She had done a great deal of work to make sure they did. But not like this, with more than half the Pilgrim Parties stranded here. "Wizard Derk—" she began.

Something heavy shuffled behind her on the terrace. "Leave him alone," said Callette.

Querida whirled round. Her mouth dropped open. Callette's eyes were dull and reddish. Her lion coat was sticky and staring. Under the disordered feathers of Callette's wings, Querida could see every one of Callette's ribs. The feathers stuck this way and that from her scrawny neck and her whole body drooped despairingly.

Callette said to Derk, "I've found out I am sorry about Kit after all."

Querida went on gaping. It began to dawn on her that she was intruding on real grief here.

"So am I, Callette," said Derk. "So am I."

"I've no one to fight any more," Callette explained. Her bloodshot eye swivelled to Don. Don backed away.

As he backed, a hole appeared in the universe. It occurred with a smart popping noise, more or less where Don had been sitting, writhed a bit, and then settled to a neat arched shape. Querida was probably the only one who noticed the sudden blue light that bulged alertly from between two stones in the terrace and then faded quietly away to a thread. Everyone else was watching the hole in the universe, where Mr Addis straightened his tie and stepped down in front of Derk's hut.

"Good morning," Mr Addis said cheerfully. "There seem to have been one or two hiccups in our choreography. I'm here to sort things out."

"Just go away," Derk said wearily.

Mr Addis stared down at him and straightened his tie again. "For a start," he said, "Mr Derk, you were required to manifest as a dark shadow, not as – er – an extra pig." He looked up at the house and he frowned. "This simply will not do as a Citadel. The illusion is not convincing. And—" His eye fell on the dwarfs. "There seems to have been some mix-up over the tribute as well. Mr Derk, Mr Chesney is already seriously displeased and this will displease him further. We're talking extensive fines here, Mr Derk. Why have only one third of our Pilgrim Parties returned home?"

"Because I've stopped them," said Derk.

"*Stopped* them!" exclaimed Mr Addis. "You can't do that!"

"Yes, I can," said Derk. "I have."

"But you're under contract!" Mr Addis cried out. "Mr Derk, I am here to tell you that Mr Chesney will enforce that contract with the utmost severity if you fail to comply with our terms. We're talking more than *extensive* fines now. We're talking *crippling*." Derk did not answer. Mr Addis said, slowly and loudly, as if he thought Derk had become stupid, "Mr Derk, where are our remaining Pilgrim Parties?"

"Sitting in the valley outside here, I suppose," Derk said. "Until they show some sense and go and find something better to do."

"Those are nine hundred and eight people," Mr Addis told him, slowly and sternly. "Mr Chesney will not countenance the loss of nine hundred and eight people."

"Oh, go away." Derk turned his head and stared at Ringlet.

"Shall I throw him out?" Old George offered.

"You'll do no such thing, my good man." Mr Addis held up a hand as if it were a dam to stop Old George and looked sternly down at Derk. "Mr Derk, we are talking the loss of nine hundred and eight people here."

Derk came up on to his elbow again. Then to his knees. Finally he stood up. Mr Addis backed away from the filthy, unshaven mess that Derk was. "Loss?" said Derk. "People? I've lost my wife and my son. I saw the griffin who was a son to me shot down by *your* soldiers. My daughter and my griffin daughter are missing. And you talk to me of nine hundred tourists who aren't even dead!"

Mr Addis put up his hand again, damming Derk this time. "Come, come, Mr Derk. I'm sure we can settle this in a friendly way."

"You don't understand," Derk said, heavily and expressionlessly. "Kit. Is. Dead. Now go away."

"I think Mr Chesney's interests are best served—" Mr Addis began.

But this was where Callette lost her temper. "You heard him," she said. "He said go away. So go." And she tramped towards him with her neck out like an angry goose.

Mr Addis eyed her critically. "I don't think your talking monster is in very good condition, Mr Derk."

Callette spread her dishevelled wings. "No. I'm not. I happen to be very hungry. I think I shall eat you. You're nice and fat." She crawled forward another step.

"Call her off!" Mr Addis said. His voice had gone shrill and uneasy.

Derk simply folded his arms. Callette lunged. Mr Addis realised just in time that she meant what she said and ran for his hole in the universe with Callette's angry beak a mere inch from his backside the whole way. "Mr Chesney will hear of this! Mr Chesney will hear of this!" Mr Addis babbled as he ran, and leapt, and landed on hands and knees inside his hole.

"Food!" shrieked Callette. Her beak ran hard into some invisible barrier just in front of the hole. It hurt her. She backed off and rubbed her beak with her wing, while Mr Addis scrambled out of sight and the hole shut with a *clop*. "I meant that about food," Callette said to the nearest dwarf. "Perhaps I shall eat you."

"Wouldn't you prefer cooked food, madam?" the dwarf said anxiously. "We have a roast just ready to serve."

"Bring it here," said Callette. She swung her evil, scrawny head round at Querida. "And if *you* bother Dad, I'll eat you too."

"I don't think I'd taste very good, my dear," Querida said.

"I can kill people. I killed the ones who shot Kit," Callette remarked. "Didn't you think I could?"

"I'm sure you can – but I'm also sure you should never have been put in a situation where you thought you had to," Querida replied. "Derk, this child needs looking after."

"I can see that," Derk said. He unfolded his arms and wrapped them round Callette's thin neck. Callette's head flopped on his shoulder. "My brave Callette," he said.

Querida watched. She watched Don crawl unhappily up to Derk too, and Derk realise that Don was feeling as bad as Callette. She watched him spare an arm from Callette to wrap round Don. Querida watched a hurried group of dwarfs bringing what looked like half a roast cow on a huge platter out on to the terrace. She watched Callette's beak swing eagerly towards it. Querida murmured to herself, "I must see Mara. I made a mistake there." She rapped her stick sharply on the paving stones and vanished.

CHAPTER TWENTY-FIVE

❋

*B*lade woke up from the unpleasant, blank sleep caused by the smelly stuff, feeling ill. He rolled on his face and discovered that the hand he was trying to pillow his cheek on had a thick iron cuff on its wrist, attached to a cold length of chain. There was iron underneath him, rumbling and juddering with what seemed to be impossibly speedy movement. This made him feel so much worse that it was a while before he could move his eyes around to see where he was. There were iron bars all round him and, beyond those, high banks going by so fast that they looked blurred. The sight nearly made him throw up.

An hour or so later, he was well enough to realise what this all meant. He was in an iron cage, only tall enough to sit up in and only long enough to stretch out in if he lay from corner to corner. This cage was roped to the bed of a cart and being towed very fast down a sunken road by the horseless carriage Barnabas had made for Mr Chesney. To make quite sure that Blade could not translocate out of this mess, his wrist had been chained to the iron cuff. As to where he was being towed, Blade preferred not to think. You got to hear of places where— No.

Blade shut his mind and just lived. He was usually quite good at this, but he had never had to do it before while being constantly reminded by the jarring and juddering underneath how fast he was being dragged off to— No. He felt as if he was covered with little bruises. The wind of the movement blew through the bars and made him deeply cold. And as if that was not enough, it was becoming harder, every time he tried, to fit into the wretched cage from corner to corner. At first Blade thought it was just because he kept losing the exact right position. But by nightfall he had changed his mind. He was growing. His body had chosen this moment, of all moments, to shoot up from boy size to man size, just as Mara had promised it would. Of all the stupid things! Blade tossed and shifted and still found his head and his toes jammed ever tighter against the bars. He began to fear he would end up bigger than Kit.

Well, at least I'd burst the bars open, he thought, and tried not to panic.

About the time darkness fell, the towing stopped, with a sort of croak. Blade almost went to sleep in the blessed peace. Then doors banged and voices woke him up, in the middle of an argument.

"Just no damned good!" said a man. "What's the hurry?"

"I've told you," said Barnabas's voice, sounding breathy and frightened, "I need this cargo delivered to Costamaret tonight."

"Well, it's not going to be," said another man.

The first man said, like somebody explaining to an infant, "This wizard glow of yours doesn't light up the road enough. Not a rough road like this, going so fast, and towing. You want to risk a spill? Break all our necks?"

"So we wait out the night here and go on in the morning," said the second man. "I could use some sleep."

"I want a guard on the cargo then," said Barnabas. "One of you sleep in the trailer."

Cargo, thought Blade. That's me. It was not good to know that someone who had been like an uncle to you all your life could talk of you as cargo. And mean it. Costamaret was even less good to think of. It was one of those places— No. Blade listened to one of the men climbing up beside the cage, snorting and grumbling as he wrapped himself in layers of coats against the cold. Don't offer me one, will you? Blade thought. He listened and waited. The man in the cart fell asleep quickly, but

Barnabas wandered in the road for a while, smoking a cigar. At last he climbed inside the horseless carriage and there was silence. Get drunk again, why don't you? Blade thought. Very cautiously, he reached up with his free left hand and began trying to undo the cage.

It fastened with a long bolt that had a padlock on the end of it. For a moment Blade thought he could undo it easily. Then his fingers closed round the padlock and were flung off by a feeling like an electric shock. A spell on it. An iron padlock, too. It took real wizard skills to bespell iron. Yet again, Blade cursed the way Dad had refused to let him go to university. He crouched with his face on the floor, wondering what to do.

Light feet landed on the roof of the cage, two pairs of them. Reville and Sukey? Blade thought, in a surge of hope he had not dared feel before. But there had been the faint *ting* of a claw on iron as the second pair of feet came down. "Blade?" whispered a well-known voice.

Blade nearly hit his head on the roof. "*Lydda!* Lydda, what are you doing here?"

"Ssh!" The man by the cage was stirring. Lydda waited until he had settled down again and then stuck her beak between the bars. It was an advantage griffins had over humans. They could direct a whisper with their beaks so that only one person could hear it. "I've been following you for hours," Lydda whispered. "I smelt you in there."

Lydda had always had the most acute sense of smell

of all the griffins. What luck she was near! "But what are you doing here?" Blade whispered. "This is the road to Costamaret. I heard them say."

"Flying about. Having fun," Lydda replied. "I'd never been on my own before. I like it. Making campfires, cooking things I caught. Fun. But how do I get you out? There's a spell on this padlock."

"Try. It's a bit like a stasis spell," Blade whispered. "You could undo the ones in the kitchen."

"Usually. Elda's better at that than me. But I'll have a go." Lydda, by the faint sounds, sat back on her haunches and took a look at the padlock. At last, Blade heard a tiny scratching as Lydda put out one cautious talon and plucked at the spell. He felt the spell yielding.

And Barnabas exploded out of the carriage, shouting, in sheets of wizard fire.

Lydda screamed. Her wings whupped. And whupped again. Then she was gone, but whether she was safe or badly burnt Blade had no idea. He touched the roof of the cage and his fingers fizzled. He snatched them away. Oh damn. Poor Lydda. Poorer me.

"What was *that*? What was that creature?" the man in the cart was demanding.

"I didn't see. A small dragon, I think," Barnabas said. "I just felt it fiddling with the lock-spell. While you snored. Get up on top of the cage and sleep there."

"No fear," the man said earnestly.

"Do it, or I'll burn you too," Barnabas said. "You've

457

got a gun, haven't you? Then get up there. Shoot the thing if it comes back."

Blade listened to the man spreading coats on the hot roof and then climbing up there himself. There was no chance of anyone undoing the padlock now. He almost cried. He wished he knew where Lydda had gone, but there was no sign of her. Perhaps she had been very badly burnt. He waited, hoping she would come back all the same, and fell asleep in the end out of sheer misery.

At dawn, the vehicle started off again. The men were complaining they were hungry and saying they could get breakfast in Costamaret. Barnabas said, "You could have been back in the mine by now," as he checked to see if Blade was still crouched inside the cage. He did not speak to Blade. Just cargo, Blade thought.

The juddering and jolting were worse this time. The driver was going fast, causing the cart to slew about sick-makingly. Blade went back to just living again, with his chained arm wrapped round his head. It seemed to go on for hours.

Then suddenly there were houses whipping past outside and people getting out of the way. None of them seemed troubled at the sight of Blade rumbling by inside his cage. He got the idea that this was something they were quite used to seeing. But this part did not go on for long. The vehicle surged into a huge chilly shed, where a crane of some kind swung the cage off the cart and clanged it down on a stone floor.

"—so he can't translocate," Blade heard Barnabas saying breathily, not far away. "And I want this one dead as soon as possible. Understood?"

"Perfectly, lord wizard," someone answered oilily. "We have the very thing."

Barnabas left then. Blade was hauled out of the cage by cheerful brown men in loincloths. He was so jolted and cold and cramped that he could hardly walk. But they supported him expertly and rushed him to a small cubicle with a high bed in it, where one of them snapped the end of the chain into a fastening on the wall, and they left Blade alone there.

But not for long enough. Blade was still trying to get either his hand out of the cuff or the chain out of its lock, when he was interrupted by another cheerful man in a loincloth. This one was twice the size of the first two.

"Oh no, you won't get loose like that!" this one told him jovially. "Stop wasting your strength, boyo, and turn over on your front."

"Why?" Blade asked suspiciously.

"Because I've got to massage you to get you combat-fit. You go in the arena this afternoon," the man told him. "This is Costamaret here, where we love to watch a proper fight. And we love the Pilgrim Parties for bringing us the idea. Of course we've improved on it. Got contests you'd never dream of. You're booked for one of those. So lie flat, boyo, because I've only got four hours, and by the look of you, I'm going to need every minute."

Blade looked at the man's size. He sighed and wriggled flat on the high bed. "I've not done anything wrong," he said. "I was kidnapped."

"They all say that," the large man said cheerfully. "Makes no difference to us. They all go in the arena, just the same."

He set to work spreading Blade with oils until Blade felt like a salad – which made him think yearningly of Lydda again – and then pummelling and squeezing and bending Blade. It was not unpleasant. Blade could feel every single one of his muscles being made to work without using any energy. A bit later it was punishing. Then it got pleasant again. But the worst part was the way the man talked.

"Only two ways for you to get out of here, boyo," he said, swatting at Blade's stomach with the edges of his hands – bang, bang, bangbangbangbang. "Get carried out in a bucket or get the other man carried out. Kill enough of your opponents and they let you go free." Bang, bang, bangbangbang.

"How many?" Blade managed to ask.

"They keep putting the number up. Not sure what it is this week. Fifty?" Bang, bang, bangbangbang.

I am dead, Blade thought. He felt strange, as if he were not really present in the body the big man was so carefully kneading into shape.

"Starting your growth-spurt, aren't you?" the man remarked as he pulled and bent at Blade's legs. "Lucky we got you at this stage. Much more impressive if you're small in front of someone big. Much better show. Do well at it and we put a plaque up on your grave."

At long last, the kneading and pummelling was finished. "There," said the man. "Now you get a good meal. It's up to you whether you eat it or not, but I advise you to try. More strength, better show."

Blade was, in a remote, indifferent way, extremely hungry. When they brought the food, he propped it on his knees and ate it all. Then, rather to his own surprise, he fell asleep.

"Well done, boyo," the large man said, waking him up. "Done everything right. Time to go. Get into these clothes."

The clothes were of shoddy cloth, but very bright, scarlet breeches and crimson vest. Blade put them on, with the large man holding the chain and threading it through the vest for him, and then he was taken by other people down a corridor smelling of illness to a huge iron door. Just beside the door was a long coil of very thin chain attached to a sturdy staple. Blade watched, feeling depressed, while his own chain was fastened to the end of the thin chain. Beyond the door, he could hear the noise of a large crowd of people chattering cheerfully. The audience, he thought. If I kill fifty opponents, he thought. No.

Another man came up with a list. "You're down as expendable. You don't get a weapon," he told Blade. "But you're allowed to use the chain. And remember. You fight, or you get a squirt of the fire-hose. Ready?"

Blade shrugged. The list-man took that as an answer and opened the iron door. When Blade did not move, two people took him by the shoulders and pushed him through.

There was quite a big oval space beyond, floored with sand. Benches went up all round, full of happy, chatting people. When they saw Blade stagger through the iron door, unreeling chain behind him, they cheered and clapped and gave catcalls. There were much louder howls for Blade's opponent, who was being pushed through the door opposite on the end of six pitchforks. Blade's stomach sank as he saw what he was supposed to fight with just a chain. It was a huge black griffin. One of its wings trailed and it limped from a fire-hose burn on one flank, but it was utterly formidable all the same.

I shall just walk to the middle and let it kill me, Blade thought. Then he recognised the griffin. It was Kit. But Kit so ragged, red-eyed and shamed that Blade still hardly knew him.

Blade raced across the sand, dragging the chain as he ran. The crowd got very excited, thinking Blade was going for a head-on attack. "Kit! Kit, what are you doing here?"

"Oh gods!" said Kit. "How do we work this?"

"But—" Blade could see Kit was not chained the way he was himself. "But why don't you just fly away?"

"One broken wing, both clipped," Kit snapped, more

thoroughly shamed than Blade had ever seen him. "Shut up, Blade. They burn you for not fighting. I'm supposed to kill you. What do we *do*?"

"False fight?" Blade suggested. "The way we used to frighten Mum?"

Kit brightened. "That might work. All right. One, two and *three*!"

They jumped towards one another. False fighting, as they had perfected it when Kit was eleven and Blade ten, involved a lot of yelling, even more quick movement that meant nothing, and a great deal of rolling around. The crowd loved it. But it took Blade only half a minute to see it was not really working. He kept getting tripped by his own chain. Kit was even more hampered by his broken wing. When they tried the rapid roll over and over, Kit screamed and actually slashed at Blade in his pain. The crowd thumped feet on the wooden benches and roared. Blade rolled hurriedly away, as far as he could with the chain which had somehow got wrapped round Kit's right hind leg, and found that his crimson vest was split diagonally down the front to show a long, bleeding gash. He and Kit lay panting on the sand, staring at one another.

"Sorry," Kit gasped. "I was going to let the next person kill me. Get the chain round my neck next time."

"No," said Blade. "Get this handcuff off me somehow. Then I can translocate us."

"I'm too big."

"I'll do it somehow. I did Elda easily."

"But I'd have to bite your hand off."

The slash down Blade's chest began to hurt fierily. He clenched his teeth. "If that's what it takes, then bite it off."

The crowd began a slow handclap. At the sides of the sandy arena, men in loincloths took the clips off the ends of hoses fastened to barrels and others stood up ready with tapers to light the gas that came out. Kit rolled an eye at them.

"We have to keep moving or they'll burn us."

"Let's do the savage chase then," Blade said. "Ready, steady, go!"

He got up and ran, sprinkling blood on the sand to the crowd's great pleasure. Kit kicked his back leg free of chain and came after Blade with his neck stretched out, one wing spread and the other raised as far as it would go, moving his legs very fast almost on the spot. It looked spectacular. Shona always used to scream when they did it. This crowd screamed too, and clapped, while Blade ran in an arc at the full stretch of his chain and the men with the fire-hoses relaxed.

"Going to spring," Kit warned Blade. "Now!"

He leapt, high and mightily. Blade ploughed to a stop, fell on his back underneath Kit as Kit jumped, and ended up clinging to the underside of Kit's body with his legs and arms. Kit yelled. Blade hastily moved so as not to hurt the broken wing any more than he had to. Kit began running back and forth in short charges, pretending to worry at Blade, with his head down between his own forelegs.

"What now?" he asked, looking upside down into Blade's face. "I really don't want to bite your hand off. The man I did that to – he bled to death."

"But the cuff hasn't got a lock," Blade panted. "I think Barnabas put it on by magic. Can you get it off by magic?"

"No," said Kit. "All the cuffs are fastened by a spell I don't understand. That's why I bit—"

Blade saw him look sideways and then upwards. He rolled his head against the sticky, sandy fur of Kit's chest and saw the fire-hoses being lighted.

"Drop," said Kit. "We may be lucky. I think it's going to rain. Drop and run."

Blade thumped to his back on the sand. It had certainly gone very dark, he saw, as Kit jumped aside. The crowd was bawling and screaming and the men with the hoses were, for some reason, pointing their streams of fire up into the air. Perhaps the gas did not go out quite at once. Blade jumped to his feet, into a tremendous roll of fire. Both sides of the arena vanished in it for a moment. There was a sound that seemed to be thunder. As Blade staggered a few steps, fairly sure that the arena had been struck by lightning, the blaze cleared to show the exploded remains of barrels, shrivelled hoses and charred benches with little flames flickering on their edges. At the narrow ends of the arena, people were fighting one another to get out. And the thunder was louder than ever.

An enormous voice boomed out of the thunder. "Can't you fly, cat-bird?"

"No, sir," Kit shrieked. "Broken wing."

"And I can't land. Place too small. What's wrong with the boy?"

"*Iron!*" bellowed Kit. "Stops his magic."

"Stupid little beasts. Get beside him and keep still then."

Blade collected his wits enough to look upwards. Scales was hovering over the arena, filling the whole sky with the booming of his webby green wings. As Blade looked, Scales extended both gigantic forelegs and scooped Blade and Kit up in his talons. They might have been dolls. The great wings cracked like whips as Scales fought for height to get out of the burning arena, clutching the two of them to his hot, scaly chest. There came a painful jerk as they got to the end of Blade's chain. Blade felt the cuff leave his wrist and craned out to watch it fall, chain and all, back into the sand, and wondered for a moment if his hand was down there with it. He held it up, in front of a whirling, diminishing view of a town with a huge pile of smoke rising from somewhere in the middle, and found he still had a hand after all. Then they were going up again, to level out. Kit, dangling like a kitten being carried, shot Blade a look, a mixture of shame and delight. Blade knew how Kit felt. You felt stupid, being carried by something this large, and very uncomfortable. Scales's horny claws bit in around you, and Scales's great voice came rumbling through the enormous, hard, bellows-like chest the claws had you clamped against.

"Stupid. One of them can't heal himself, the other one can't do iron spells. Any hatchling dragon would be better off than that."

Though it was plain that Scales was simply grumbling to himself, Blade and Kit both squirmed. "Nobody *taught* me iron spells!" Blade called out.

"Even if I did know how to heal myself, it wouldn't have helped!" Kit bellowed. "They clipped my wings!"

"Quiet," Scales grunted. "Got to find the place – oh, there she is."

They were now well out over grasslands, faded creamy with the autumn. Blade saw the pale stretch of the earth tilt and rotate beneath them as Scales wheeled in against the wind. The great wings above and behind him cupped with a sound like a storm. The ground came rushing in towards them. It was much rougher than Blade had thought, and full of rocks. Scales's voice rumbled, "Letting go now."

Blade and Kit found themselves dumped on the grass, sliding. While they staggered and bumped into one another. Scales glided in to land beside a tall boulder which had a small golden shape dancing on top of it. "There you are, girl. No problems. Got you the black cat-bird too while I was at it. I thought you'd want him. No accounting for tastes."

"Lydda!" Kit and Blade screamed.

Lydda rose into a ramp to wrap both forearms round Scales's huge neck and rub her beak delightedly against his great muzzle. "Thank you, Scales. I love you." She looked tiny beside him.

"My pleasure," grunted Scales. "I like you too." He had a preening sort of arch to his neck, as if he meant it.

Lydda laughed, leapt down from her boulder and bounded to meet Kit and Blade. They did the griffin dance none of them had done since they were small, circling and jumping, wings spread, arms waving, all of them laughing their heads off, until Blade ran out of breath and left the other two still at it. Lydda looked small to him, even now. This was a new Lydda, he realised, slender and sleek and bright-eyed, with a deadly look to her talons and an even more deadly look of power to the glistening sweep of her long bent-up golden wings. She was batting Kit joyfully on the beak with them, but they still looked deadly.

"Hey! Doesn't she look tremendous!" Blade said to Scales.

"Good hunter too," Scales agreed. "I met her out hunting yesterday. That's how she knew where I was, after she'd trailed you down to that sandpit. How did you get into that mess? Eh?"

"Barnabas. He's being paid by Mr Chesney to mine for magic," Blade said. As he said Mr Chesney's name, Scales once again went lizard still. "But I don't know how Kit got there," Blade added.

Kit and Lydda were now jumping over one another by turns, wings spread and beating. The contrast between Lydda's spread of golden feathers and Kit's clipped ones was painful.

"Grow some more feathers, cat-bird," Scales boomed. "It's unsightly."

Kit stopped prancing. He spread out the wing that had been broken and stared at it. His head swivelled accusingly at Scales.

"That's right," said Scales. "I could mend that. But I don't grow feathers."

"But," said Kit, "I can't. They won't."

"Stupid," growled Scales. "Like *this*."

Blade was not sure what Scales did. Kit stood for a moment with his head bent and then looked up at Scales in a startled way. "Is that *all*?"

"That's all, unless you want to grow scales, spines and spikes as well," Scales answered. "Sit down while you're growing them and explain how you got into that sandpit. All this prancing about is making me hungry."

"He doesn't mean most of the grumping," Lydda murmured to Blade. "But I think dragons have to keep sort of half-angry most of the time. Did you know you'd torn your vest?"

Blade looked down at the slash Kit had made. His vest was hanging open over goose pimples and blood-stains, but there was no sign of the cut. "Thanks," he said to Scales.

"She wanted you in one piece," Scales said, with a flick of his tail towards Lydda. "Well, Kit?"

Kit was crouched facing the wind, as griffins did to keep warm, concentrating in some way. "It was the geese," he said.

"*What?*" said the other three.

"After the soldiers shot me and I fell in the lake," Kit explained, "I lay in the mud at the bottom and thought I was dead. Then a goose dived down beside me and dragged the arrows out with its beak. And I realised then that I was holding my breath and thought I'd better come up for some air. So I shoved up and floundered and gasped at the surface. By that time the whole flock of the geese was round me, pushing and pecking and getting my blood on their feathers. I tried to get away – I mean I can't swim, but they kept pecking until I arrived at the shore. There was a man there telling them what to do, but they couldn't get me out of the water, whatever he told them. The man pulled me out in the end, by my beak. Then he told me that he was very sorry, but he thought I really had to learn that killing people wasn't a game, and he went away with the geese and left me lying there. It was odd. I wasn't bleeding any more, but my wing was broken and I felt awful. And after a bit, the hunters from Costamaret came with a cart. They'd been hunting lions for the arena, but they didn't mind catching me instead. They tangled me in a net and cut my wing feathers, then they heaved me on to the cart and brought me along to Costamaret."

"I know how that feels," Blade said, shivering.

Kit looked at him broodingly. "Only partly," he said. "You were the fourth person I had to fight. What do you think happened to the others? It's *horribly* easy to kill a human. Lions are much more difficult. I had six lions. But lions and people were just the same. They all wanted to stay alive. So did I, at first. That was the awful part – them or me. And I had no more right than they did to be alive. I just had a beak and talons and they didn't."

"Yes, well, no need to get morbid," Scales interrupted. "Dragons have that problem too. Ah. Here comes that priggish mauve chit at last, being useful for once in her smug little life, I hope." He lunged to his feet, suddenly dwarfing them all, and spread his wings with an impatient blatting. The mauve dragon circling in the distance snaked round into a long U-turn and glided towards him. "Short-sighted as well!" grumbled Scales. "Hurry it up, woman!"

The mauve dragon landed, rather awkwardly, at a safe distance. She looked quite small beside Scales, and lizardly slender.

"What's the news?" Scales barked at her.

The lady dragon released the claw she was holding awkwardly against her chest. Two white daylight owls sprang rather hastily out of it and glided, one to Blade and the other to Lydda. While they were detaching the message-tubes from the feathery legs, the mauve dragon disdainfully shook free the padding the owls had been riding in. It proved to be Blade's clothes that he had left in Mara's Lair, and a thick coat. The messages were from Mara too. Blade read:

"Blade, darling, for goodness sake try to get to Derkholm as soon as you can. Your father needs you badly. I'll meet you there and explain."

Lydda's message said the same, except hers began, "Lydda, my love, I'm afraid your holiday's over…"

Dragons, it seemed, did not need to speak in order to exchange news. Scales rumbled, "Let's get going, if you're up to flying, cat-bird. She says we have to get to Derkholm."

CHAPTER TWENTY-SIX

✳

"WHY ARE WE WAITING?" sang the Pilgrims outside the gate. There were so many of them by now that Derk could hear them like a massed choir, even through his defences. The noise was the last straw to skeletal Fran. She had grown tired of sharing the ruins of the village with more and more Pilgrim Parties anyway, and now they had taken to walking up the valley every day, singing. The Wizard Guides with them just shrugged when Fran objected – she had an idea that the wizards had put the Pilgrims up to it in the first place – and so the morning came when she had had enough. She walked up the valley ahead of the Pilgrims, where she found Derkholm hidden behind a white shiny substance that hurt her knuckles when she pounded on it. So she ducked round to see if the back entrance was open at all. There she had a considerable shock.

"Did you know there's dragons roosting all over the hills out at the back?" she demanded as she arrived on the terrace.

"Nothing to do with me," said Derk.

Fran took in the hut on the terrace and the pigs. This was quite a shock to her too. "I hardly know you from the pigs," she said. "Are you coming out of there?"

"No," said Derk.

"*George!*" screamed Fran. And when Old George arrived at a run, thinking someone was being killed, she said to him, "Hose. Now." Then she rounded on Don. "And what are you doing – a great big creature like you – sitting there letting him get like this? Go and fetch your mother this instant. What are your wings for?"

Don gulped. "You said dragons—"

"That's your problem," Fran told him, as Old George trotted back, unreeling hosepipe and surrounded by leaping, barking dogs, who were all looking forward to some fun for a change. "Fetch your mother this instant, or I'll hose you too!" Don fled in a squeak of talons and a rattle of wings. "Now," Fran said to Derk, "I'm going to count up to three—"

"Count to a hundred if you like," Derk said.

Fran snatched the hose from Old George, opened the nozzle to full and turned it on the hut. Pigs squealed and squirted out from it, glistening. "Go back to where you belong!" Fran screamed at them, hosing mightily. They fled in sprays of water and the dogs pursued them. By the barking and squealing, a royal chase shortly developed, round and round the plantations. Derk stood the hosing until he was soaked through and sitting in liquid pig-manure and then crawled out on to the terrace. "Now get upstairs and get bathed and changed before Mara gets here," Fran commanded.

"She's not coming," said Derk.

"Oh, yes, she is, if I have to fetch her myself!" Fran announced and hosed Derk away in front of her, into the house.

There Fran encountered the dwarfs. Derk owed it to the dwarfs that Fran did not follow him upstairs and hose him into the bathroom. All the time he was bathing – and it took a while: he was rather astonished at how filthy he was – he could hear battle raging downstairs. Fran passed the hose to Old George, who was glad enough to use it, and took up a broom herself. Derk heard the repeated *crack* of it hitting dwarfish heads. There was a great deal of yelling, screaming and protesting, mingled with the hissing of the hose. But by the time Derk had dried himself and put on clean clothes that had all somehow grown too loose everywhere, most of the yelling had stopped. As he came downstairs again, he could hear Fran and Old George doing mighty works with hose and broom in the kitchen. The dwarfs were all out on the terrace sullenly cleaning out the hut. Callette was couched there among the broken remnants of black walls, with a grin at the ends of her beak, keeping the dwarfs up to their work.

"I didn't think I liked Fran," she said to Derk, "until now. The dogs are still chasing the pigs, by the way."

Derk could hear them. "They needed the exercise," he said.

"*We* don't," Galadriel said pointedly.

"Too bad," said Callette. "Fran says you owe the mayor and the blacksmith for a herd of cows each, and the tailor for all his chickens and six other people for goats. And Dad for several tons of vegetables of course. Can you pay, except by working?"

"We could dock it from the tribute," another dwarf suggested hopefully.

"I don't think those dragons out there will let you," said Callette. "Keep working."

Feeling weak and too clean and sad, Derk went to sit on the ruins of a black wall that had once been a chair. He was nearly knocked off it by Elda. Don was with her, looking rather pleased with himself. Elda came bounding up, flashing in the sunlight from several hundred stray sequins that had somehow got lodged among her feathers. Derk suspected she had left them there on purpose when she last preened. "Steady on!" he said, swaying.

"Sorry, Dad. I'd have been here ages before this, only I didn't know what to do about the dragons," Elda explained. "And you've made it so I couldn't fly in. So I sat and wondered what to do until Don came and helped me. You bow to dragons and say 'Good morning'. At least, Don did." She rose up with her front feet on the wall and looked closely at Derk. "Dad! What's the matter with you?"

"Overwork," said Derk. "Among other things. Elda, why—?"

"Mum says she'll be here as soon as she can," Elda rushed on. "I was supposed to say. Querida fell over again, you see, and Mum has to help her put the people back in the cities, because they're in one of Mum's miniature universes and need to be made big again first."

"Is *that* what she needed it for?" Callette said. "Why?"

"To prevent needless slaughter," Elda explained rather pompously.

"I don't think I dare tell Talithan this!" Derk was murmuring, when Mara herself walked on to the terrace. She was very much her usual self, in her ordinary clothes, with her hair in a big blonde plait over one shoulder. Derk stared at her and felt weaker than ever.

Mara had overheard Elda explaining. "Elda, does this mean you've only just got here? I *trusted* you!" And while Elda was protesting about the dragons, Mara turned and took a big golden armful of Don. "My love," she began, and then her nose wrinkled. "Don, you smell of dirty lion. Go and get a bath at once, and then *preen*. You look as bad as you smell." As Don galloped off, Mara flung herself on Callette next and hugged her. "Goodness,

Callette, you're far too thin! I can see it's high time I came back!"

The dwarfs took advantage of Callette's being hugged to stop work and stand in a long row, bowing. Mara looked at them bemusedly and bowed back. "Would you care for something to eat, madam?" Dworkin said wistfully. "There's a witch with a broom in the kitchen at the moment, but I hope she'll leave if we explain that we need to cook for the lady of the house."

Mara laughed. "Then please tell her." And as the dwarfs scampered into the house, she mouthed at Callette, "Who?"

"Skinny Fran. She hit them with a besom for making such a mess," Callette said.

Mara turned, laughing, to Derk. Derk slid rather shakily off his wall-chair and wondered whether to smile at her. Mara threw both her arms tightly round his chest, almost stopping his breath. She leant her head against his shoulder and said, "Oh, Derk, I'm so *sorry*! I didn't even realise I was being unkind. It was all Querida's fault. I told her she was to come here and explain. Where *is* she? If she's let that healer put her into a coma again, I shall pull her beastly leg right *off*!"

"I'm here, I'm here!" Querida croaked. She hobbled out from behind a broken black archway, propped on her magic crutch. Mara barely looked at her. She was stroking Derk's face now, saying, "You look quite good in a beard now your face is so thin, love! Oh, I could *kill* Querida!"

"I think she means it, too," Querida said to Callette. "I've never seen her so angry. It's my miscalculation. I used to be married to Mara's father, you know, and I've never felt Derk was good enough for the daughter of a man like that."

Mara said to Derk, "But what possessed you to shut yourself away among all this mess?"

Derk was surprised to find he was grateful to Fran that the mess was not twice as bad. "Kit," he said, and choked. "Blade. The last straw."

"Oh, I heard, I *heard*!" Mara said. "But I think Blade's all right."

She and Derk seemed set to stand looking at one another all day. "Tchaa!" Querida hissed disgustedly to Callette. "Do they want me to explain? Or not?"

Callette's response was; "This wall's really a chair." She lifted Querida up and dumped her on the wall. Querida went stiff all over with outrage, until she discovered that she was quite comfortable. The black stones felt like cushions.

"Thank you, my dear," she said. "Wizard Derk." When Derk at last tore his attention from Mara, Querida said, "I apologise. Apologising is not a thing I'm good at, so I'm only going to do it this once, and you'd better listen. You see, we wanted to put an end to the way Mr Chesney is exploiting our world and we hoped, by making you Dark Lord, that you'd make such a hash of it that the whole organisation would fall apart. I thought that's what the Oracles meant. But as soon as we arrived at Derkholm to meet Mr Chesney, I realised that you were going to be rather efficient after all, and cast about for some way to take your mind off the task. And I'm afraid I put a spell on Mara, to make her decide to leave you. I don't suppose it did much good."

"Well, it didn't exactly help," Derk said. "Was letting me down over the demon and the god part of it too?"

Querida nodded her little dry chin. "But I *was* very busy. I was organising the women wizards to send everything wrong that they could think of, you know."

"So," Derk asked, hoping, "might it have been you who lent Mara money?"

"I *gave* her money," Querida replied. "I can afford it, and she was working on my plans, after all."

"And are you satisfied now?" Derk asked.

Querida looked a little glum. "I'm not sure. I didn't in my wildest dreams ever think you'd shut the Pilgrims out. I really don't know what's going to happen about that. I've done my best to exploit the situation by putting the women wizards out there waving placards that say 'Go Home Pilgrims', but I really don't know where we go from here. I think we may be in bad trouble. You wouldn't consent to open your gates again, would you?"

Derk smiled down at Mara. "No. Not yet."

Querida sighed and watched the dwarfs hurry back with hastily carved plates of chicken and beef and a stack of bread. Evidently Fran was not having them in the kitchen for long. Some knelt down on the flagstones and made sandwiches, while others went round with mugs of beer.

"You owe for the beer too," Callette said to Galadriel. "I'm keeping a list." She reached over and took all the sandwiches that had been made so far. Don dashed out on to the terrace, a much paler gold, with pearls of water hanging on his feathers, and saw her eating them. He squawked indignantly. "Wait your turn," Callette said calmly. "I'm still bigger than you."

"Oh, *food*!" someone cried out. "Let me at it!"

Shona came limping up the terrace steps. She was followed by Geoffrey, the Ledburys, Dad and Mother Poole, and everyone else in Blade's Pilgrim Party. The dwarfs exchanged looks and sped back to the kitchen for more. Fran could be heard as soon as they got there, making as much noise as the pigs and the dogs.

"We've been walking for over a *week*!" Shona said, flopping down on to the flagstones. "I am so tired! When I saw the hills were full of dragons, I simply thought, I don't *care* if they eat us, I just want to get home! But all they did was stare at us. Dad, I hope you don't mind me bringing everyone in through the back way."

"Not at all," Derk said vaguely, as all the other Pilgrims flopped down too. Most of them thankfully hauled their boots off. Geoffrey took his socks off as well and ruefully showed Shona some very well-developed blisters. So he's not totally perfect! Derk thought with some relief. He wondered who the small blonde girl was and the rather ragged young man, and why they did not seem as footsore as the rest. He watched these two help themselves to a sandwich each and come over to him.

The young man bowed. "Lady Mara, Wizard Derk. I am Reville and this is Sukey. We've got some rather unpleasant news for you, I'm afraid. Your son Blade was with us when we discovered that Mr Chesney was stealing magic by mining earth here and taking it into his own world. Wizard Barnabas was in charge of the mining, and I'm afraid he caught Blade."

"Barnabas!" said Derk.

"Are you sure?" said Mara.

"I saw him myself," said Reville. "Sukey and I tracked them all the way down to Costamaret—"

Sukey smiled adoringly at Reville. "He learnt to translocate. He took us both."

"With a few side-trips," Reville said. "I haven't got it perfect yet. That's part of the reason we were a bit slow getting here. The other reason is that Costamaret has a Thieves' Guild—"

"What's all this? What is this about?" Querida cried out, leaning down from her apparent wall. "You did say *Barnabas*, did you – Regin, isn't it?"

Reville bowed. "I didn't see you there, ma'am. It's Reville really. Thieves' Guild policy is to give a false name for all public meetings."

Querida disregarded this and hissed at him to tell, tell,

tell. The dwarfs handed them all sandwiches and mugs of beer and stood by listening while Reville and Sukey gave the history of their adventures in the mine. Querida shot Derk a quizzical look when they mentioned the demon, but she did not interrupt until Reville was saying, "And the Thieves' Guild in Costamaret was very sorry about it, but they say the arena is protected by magic and there's nothing they could do for Blade—"

"So *that's* why magic was draining away!" Querida interrupted. "What we must do—"

Reville interrupted her. "No need to do anything, ma'am. Stealing is the business of my guild. We deal with non-guild thieving. Costamaret Guild has gone in to close the mines down – they're doing it at this moment. Sukey planned the operation. She's a wonderful planner." He put his arm round Sukey's blue silk shoulders and squeezed proudly. "I don't think anyone will get away."

"But I insist on dealing with that traitor Barnabas myself!" Querida said, loudly, because Mara was saying to Derk, "No, I know Blade's all right. Scales—"

"No," Derk said grimly, around Mara. "Whether Blade's all right or not, I'm the one who's going to deal with Barnabas." He put his head up and bellowed, "*Talithan!*"

Silvery music swept across the terrace. Several dwarfs carrying plates backed hastily away from the greenish haze that was opening by the front door. When Talithan stepped out of it, he was evidently in the middle of some kind of celebration. His clothes were gorgeous even for an elf prince. He had a harp on one arm and the other arm draped over Pretty. Pretty gave everyone a coy look and bent his neck to nuzzle Talithan. "You called, lord?" Talithan asked.

The Pilgrims stared at him yearningly. Mother Poole was in tears, sobbing, "But he's so *beautiful*!" while Professor Ledbury got up and stood staring.

"Sit down, Eldred," said Miss Ledbury. "Finish your sandwich."

"Sorry," Derk apologised. "Caught you at a bad moment, Prince?"

Talithan smiled. "Merely that the Horselady has given me Pretty, lord, after some negotiation. I take pleasure in seeing you look better than erstwhile. What is it I can do?"

"Find Barnabas, wherever he is, and bring him here, if you would be so good," Derk said.

"Ah," said Talithan. "Then you noticed the man deliberately botched the magics on the unpleasant soldiery? I had been wondering if I should inform you of it."

"Er – that was on my orders," Querida admitted. "The man was on both sides."

"Just bring him," Derk insisted.

Prince Talithan bowed and swept Pretty and himself away inside the magic haze. Everything at once felt drearier. The Pilgrims sighed. Shona said angrily, "He's welcome to Pretty! Silly, fickle little horse!" and then burst into tears.

"There, there, my love," Geoffrey said with his arm around her. "I've heard this is the way elves make you feel, that's all it is."

"Right. Oh, right!" agreed Professor Ledbury. "As if one had lost something precious."

I have, Derk thought. I've still lost Kit.

CHAPTER TWENTY-SEVEN

❋

*K*it, to his shame, could not keep up with the dragons, or Lydda. There was nothing wrong with his new pinions as far as Blade, sitting wrapped in his thick coat waiting to translocate, could see, but he was making no speed at all. When even the daylight owls passed him, Kit landed and howled with misery. Blade ran after him.

"It's all right, you fool. You're just terribly out of condition."

"I feel weak and small and useless!" Kit groaned.

"I'm like that all the time," Blade pointed out. "Look, would you let me sit on your back? I can move us both in stages then, I think."

"*Anything!*" Kit said abjectly.

Blade climbed astride him, clamped his knees on Kit's great wing muscles and shoved off towards Derkholm. He managed to move them about ten miles.

Kit dug his talons into the wintery grass. "You're going in the wrong direction," he said. But at that moment, Scales and the mauve dragon, with Lydda winging hard to keep up, went sailing over about half a mile to their left. "I let you off," said Kit. He let go of the grass and Blade took them another ten miles or so. "I could have sworn—!" said Kit. "You know, I think you go in zigzags, like that blue demon did." He became very interested in the process of translocation after that and nearly forgot his misery. They arrived on the hillside above Derkholm well ahead of Lydda and the dragons.

Below them, Derkholm and its grounds were covered with a dome of magic so thick and strong that it looked milky white. Frost had formed on it, making it wink in the slanting autumn sunlight. In the valley in front of Derkholm was an extremely large crowd of people, most of whom seemed to be angry. Blade could see fists being shaken and placards being pitched this way and that. DOWN WITH CHESNEY, he saw, just before somebody threw it down and jumped on it. There was angry tussling around THIS IS OUR WORLD and BAN PILGRIMS, and someone was hitting someone else with UNITE AGAINST THE TOURS. Those not brawling were chanting. Blade could hear "Why are we waiting?"

counterpointed against "Go home Pilgrims!" He climbed off Kit and put his hands over his ears.

"Help!" Kit muttered.

The dragons on the hills had been sitting so still that Blade had vaguely taken them for piles of rock. But as soon as he moved, huge dragon heads swung their way. Enormous green or yellow eyes inspected them disdainfully.

Kit cleared his throat and trumpeted across at the nearest dragon, "Excuse us. We're on our way home. Do you know if it's possible to get in there?"

"People have been coming and going through a little hole at the back," the dragon sang back, and yawned. Smoky breath poured down the hillside around them.

Blade and Kit hurried downhill out of the smoke, coughing. "The back gate must be open then," Blade said.

"I hope I can fit through it," said Kit.

The hole in the dome was a very tight fit indeed. Kit stuck in it at first, until Blade prodded Kit's straining hind-quarters and hissed, "Hurry! There's a dragon after us!" Kit shot inside as if the hole was suddenly greased and glared at Blade when Blade popped through after him. "Well, you'd have been all day if I hadn't said it," Blade said.

Kit muttered, and muttered some more when they passed his shed and found it stacked full of baskets with golden goblets and crowns spilling out of them, but Blade could tell that Kit was too glad to be home to be truly annoyed. They came round to the terrace steps, where they stopped and stared at the patchwork of house and shredding Citadel. They came up the steps into a crowd of dwarfs and Pilgrims, who were all gazing at Prince Talithan, towering out of a blue-green haze near the front door and looking surprisingly grim. Talithan had one long elfin hand clamped on the shoulder of Barnabas.

Inside his ring of grey curls, Barnabas's face was an unhealthy blue-red. He was shaking. "You must see how it is, Derk," he was saying. "You have to understand. I have a drink habit to support. And the mines don't do any harm. We only export earth."

"Secretly, without anyone getting paid for it except you," Querida said from her seat on what looked like a ruined black wall. "And the earth you export happens to be full of magic."

"Yes, well, I believe Mr Chesney does sell it for quite a lot on the other side," Barnabas conceded, "but that's nothing to do with me. I can explain—"

"There's no possible explanation that can satisfy me," Reville said. He was leaning beside Querida with his arms folded, looking as grim and lordly as Talithan. "You were stealing and you are not a member of my guild. Wizards, I demand that this man is handed over to the Thieves' Guild for trial. By our law, he should have both hands cut off."

Barnabas shuddered and looked piteously towards Derk. "Derk, you're my *friend*!"

"Not any more," Derk said from beside Mara. Kit

and Blade exchanged glances. They had never seen Derk look so stern. "Why did you take the spells off the soldiers?" Derk asked.

"I *had* to," Barnabas explained. "Fifty of them were under contract to the mines. Last year's overseers were getting impatient, because they couldn't go home until the new ones arrived, you see. They were *pressuring* me. And the new overseers were all stuck in the camp having to fight a battle every week."

"Some of them weren't," Reville said. "They kidnapped Sukey."

As Reville said this, an acid-bath chill began to wash across Blade's mind. It was a feeling he had had twice before. He looked to see where it was coming from this time and saw blueness swelling up from the cracks round the paving stones where Barnabas was standing, cunningly mixing with Talithan's haze. Blade wondered whether to shout.

Be silent or I shall eat you too, the demon told him.

"Well, how was I to know that?" Barnabas demanded. "All I knew was that they hadn't—"

The blueness rose up around him. Barnabas's voice became a long, thin, bubbling noise. Talithan jumped backwards as the demon began to spin. Its blueness spun faster and faster and Barnabas became a twisted dark swirl, spinning inside it. The swirl grew longer and thinner as it spun and shreds threw off it, but Barnabas did not stop screaming until the darkness had faded into the blueness completely. It seemed to take a century, though it lasted only for seconds. So that's how demons eat, Blade thought, swallowing hard and very queasily. Everyone was pale and still as they watched the blueness sink back into the terrace again.

"*Yik!*" said Kit.

Geoffrey stood up barefoot beside Shona, looking as if he were trying not to be sick. "I want to know more about those mines."

"So do I, young man," said Miss Ledbury.

Elda looked towards the Pilgrims and saw Blade and Kit standing behind them. She sprang across the terrace, shrieking, bouncing from one pair of feet to the other in the spaces between dwarfs and Pilgrims. "Mum! Dad!" she shrieked. "*Blade's* back! *Kit's* here!"

Dwarfs had to scramble out of the way as Mara, Derk, Shona, Don and Callette surged after Elda. Blade found himself in the middle of a happier reunion than he would have believed possible that morning. Shona kissed him, kissed Kit. Derk barged Shona aside to hug him and then collided with Mara who was in the middle of turning from hugging Kit to hugging Blade and crying out, "Oh, Blade! These clothes I sent you are too small!"

"I started to grow," Blade told her, as well as he could from under Callette's massive wing and being bumped about between Elda and Don, who were trying to griffin-dance with him in spite of Derk, who was now trying to hug Blade and Kit at once. Beaks stroked Blade's face and clacked on Kit's beak. Three sets of arms tried to fold on them. Feathers swiped and caressed them. *And I used to think we had no family feeling!* Blade thought. He wished Lydda was here to share in it too.

And Lydda was there, almost as Blade thought this, dropping neatly from above on a truly magnificent wingspread, screaming to join in. "Oh, thank the gods – I was so worried!" Derk said and Callette said, "That's good. Now it's everyone."

Blade glanced upwards to see where Lydda had come from. He was in time to see the tip of one of Scales's huge claws slicing through the rest of the magic dome. For an instant or so, Scales could be seen as a mighty shadow above the milkiness. Then Derk's defences crumpled away and folded downwards, letting in a burst of extra light from under Scales, who wheeled about and landed on most of the garden monsters. He sat up, rearing higher than the dome had been.

"Forgive the intrusion," he rumbled at Derk. "We need to talk."

Scales was wearing the battered coronet. At least, Blade realised, it was the coronet that had *seemed* to be battered, until you noticed that a coronet had to be a strange, irregular shape in order to fit the head of a dragon. Now it looked more like a crown. And what everyone had thought of as the broken gold chain was hooked to the spikes of Scales's neck to dangle gleaming and complete on his chest.

Mara went to the edge of the terrace with her arm over Lydda, still smiling from the reunion, and turned the smile up to Scales. "Forgive me, I only realised who you were a while ago. You're Deucalion, who was once king of the dragons, aren't you?"

"I hope I still am!" Scales rumbled. He raised his crowned head to look at the other dragons crouching along the hills over Derkholm. "How say you, dragons?"

The other dragons lifted their heads in reply and hailed their king in a musical roar, each dragon crying a different note in a massive bugling chord. A number of the dwarfs crouched down and covered their ears. The house, the ground, the terrace and the whole valley shook. Blade thought, deafened and astonished, The Oracle said a *dragon* would teach me magic! Why?

Meanwhile, the angry Pilgrims outside and the extremely irritated wizards with them had seen the dome collapse and surged towards the gates. They stopped short when Scales landed, started to surge forward again, and stopped once more when the dragons roared on the hills. Nobody could move during a sound like that. But as soon as the great cry stopped, the Pilgrims in front began edging on, through the gate and into the space by Deucalion's great right wing. Most of them were shouting that they were going to *kill* that Dark Lord, but they stopped yet again and all backed into one another when the demon rose high on its three legs in front of the terrace.

Scales rose up to meet it. "Tripos!" he growled. "Demon king. Go!"

If you exorcise me, you'll regret it, Deucalion, the demon replied. *You need me.*

The bleach-burn of its talk was enough to cause utter silence, except for a woman Pilgrim near the gate who said, "Is that the Dark Lord? But I thought—" and stopped with a gulp when one of the demon's three eyes turned to look at her. Or maybe it was the thunder of Scales's answer.

"Need YOU?" the dragon roared.

The demon, rather slyly, untwisted its tail from around its three legs. The tail went snaking out across the terrace, and stabbed the air with its wormy blue tip, somewhere between Querida's wall and Prince Talithan's magic haze. The air there writhed about and split apart with a *pop*. The split became a neat arched opening. Mr Chesney stood in the arched space, staring around the terrace with his mouth set into a grim, upside-down smile. He nodded at what he saw there, as if it was even worse than he had expected.

"Ah, I see," said Scales. "You were holding it shut." And he added, most unwillingly, "Thank you."

Mr Chesney shot Scales an irritated glance for speaking out of turn. He did not notice the demon towering nebulously behind him. His eyes travelled stonily from Querida on her wall, with Elda now crouching at her feet and Reville leaning beside her, on to Mara, Lydda, Callette,

Don, across forty dwarfs or so, to Blade and Kit, and stopped at Derk.

"Wizard Derk," he said in his flat voice, "you are facing a great deal more than bankruptcy for this."

Derk could only manage a shrug. Mr Chesney was having the same effect on him as he had had before. Derk so hated the man that all he seemed to be able to think of was ideas for new and fantastic animals. They came pouring through his mind: the carrier pigeons – easy – and vegetarian eagles with pouches for messages, centaurs, talking elephants, manticores, kangaroos with hands and human faces, chimeras, walking mushrooms, winged goats. Or how about creating a unicorn?

Luckily, Mr Chesney did not seem to expect an answer. His eyes travelled coldly on, across the Pilgrims, over more dwarfs, on to Talithan, and then, with a jerk, back to the Pilgrims. "You two," he said. "Come here."

Miss Ledbury stood up. So did Dad and Mother Poole. The Pooles sat diffidently down again when Mr Chesney snapped, "I didn't mean you."

Miss Ledbury stayed standing up. "But I mean to talk to you," she announced. "I am a plain clothes detective attached to the Police Bureau, Missing Persons and Unsolved Murder Departments. I was sent to investigate the reason why so many people who go on your Pilgrim Parties never come back."

"Do you think I haven't taken legal advice?" Mr Chesney asked her, flatly unconcerned. "Anything that happens on this world is outside the jurisdiction of your Bureau. But you can arrest Wizard Derk if you like. He was the one who closed the portal here, not me. Speak to my lawyers. You'll find I've done nothing illegal."

"Ah. Then I'd better put a word in here," Mother Poole said cosily. "I work for Inland Revenue. And my enquiries suggest that the money for your insurance fraud *and* the fees for bumping people off here *are* paid in our own world. The tax owing on both must be in the millions by now, not to speak of the fact that most of it is illegal income. Don't talk to me about arresting this nice young bard's father, my dear. I can't wait to get you home. And Dad here's licking his lips."

Dad Poole cleared his throat. "I'm from the Monopolies Commission," he said. "I *was* looking into the way you're the only one who runs tours to this world, but I've since been hearing about a certain mining operation you have here."

Mr Chesney waved a cold hand. "I said speak to my lawyers. You'll find I'm clean. Now if you don't mind, I'd like to talk to my daughter and my stepson. Sukey, Geoffrey, I said come here."

Shona dashed forward and seized Geoffrey's arm. "He's not going back with you!" she said.

"No, indeed he isn't," Mr Chesney agreed. "I want to speak to the wizard who had charge of his party. I marked Geoffrey down as expendable myself."

"You did? You unfeeling—" Shona began.

Geoffrey said, "I can speak for myself, love." He turned to Mr Chesney. "So it was all lies about my getting experience of the tours, was it? And the ski-lift and the car crash were intentional, were they? I did wonder. I can think, you know."

"I didn't want you taking a share of Sukey's inheritance," Mr Chesney said, shrugging a little, as if this was the most natural thing. "It's a considerable sum, these days. That's all. And I'm not at all pleased with you for bringing Sukey here with you."

"She was dying to come," Geoffrey said, "so I arranged it for her."

"You'd do anything to spite me, wouldn't you?" Mr Chesney said.

"No," said Geoffrey. "You just think I would."

Mr Chesney turned aside from him disgustedly. "Sukey."

Blade had been watching Sukey as she edged round past Mara and Lydda to stand next to Reville. Now he understood why the escaped soldiers had carried her off and then treated her as if she was so valuable. They knew who she was. They must have been hoping for a reward from Mr Chesney. Blade also knew why he had disliked Sukey so much. She was quite like Mr Chesney to look at, although even Blade had to admit that she was a great deal prettier. He still thought she was quite like Mr Chesney in personality. She seemed very like her father as she grabbed Reville's arm and said, "I'm not coming,

Daddy," in the same sort of flat voice Mr Chesney used. "I'm staying here. I'm getting married to Reville."

Mr Chesney was so angry at this that he almost looked human. "What?"

Sukey nodded. "Yup. Reville's ever so rich. He's got a lovely house for me. And he's a thief. You should be ever so pleased."

"Well, I'm not. It's plain ridiculous," Mr Chesney stated. "It's not going to happen, and that's my final word, Sukey."

Reville gave one of his smoothest bows. He looked round at the large numbers of people all watching and listening and said ruefully, "I intend it to happen, sir. And – this is a fact we don't like generally known but it may help to change your mind – I am actually the richest person in this world. Hereditary Head of Thieves' Guild, at your service, Mr Chesney."

"It's still ridiculous," Mr Chesney snapped. He turned to Sukey, almost pleadingly. "You don't understand," he said. "He's not real life. None of these people are. They're all just the way they are because I turned their world into a theme park. If they didn't happen to be under contract to me, they'd be nothing – just rough types in a world that happens to have some magic to it."

"Dear me," Querida put in from her perch on the wall. "And now we all come fluttering down like a pack of cards, I suppose." She cocked an eye up at the demon, still towering behind Mr Chesney.

I can't eat this one, the demon told her. *The demon in his pocket prevents me. It is my mate and he keeps it half-starved. Set it free. Then I will eat him very slowly.*

Querida glanced at Reville. "Regin – Reville – what's your name?" she murmured.

"Need a diversion," Reville whispered back.

Elda nodded and slipped away round the wall. Don saw her go and slipped off after her.

Sukey said to Mr Chesney, "They're people just like you are. I'm staying."

"I don't understand," said Mr Chesney, "how you can be so unfeeling."

"Look who's talking!" Sukey said.

Sukey was standing by Reville and Mr Chesney was looking at them both. Querida looked round for some way to make Mr Chesney look away from Reville and found Scales's enormous head looming above her. "Unfeeling indeed." Scales boomed. "My dragons are being killed by inches because you keep them too short of gold."

Mr Chesney barely glanced at Scales. "There's no suffering involved. I had an expert assess the exact amount they needed."

"I don't think much of your expert then," Mara chipped in. "Who was it?"

Professor Ledbury stood up shakily. "It was I, madam. I remember I told him it was only a guess."

Prince Talithan seemed to realise that they were trying

to make Mr Chesney look somewhere else. He stepped forward. "There is no lawfulness, sir, in the manner you took my brother and held him hostage to force the elves to your bidding."

Still looking at Sukey, Mr Chesney said, "Nonsense. He came of his own free will."

"But I didn't!" Professor Ledbury protested. "You tempted me with promises of strange sights and when I came to see, I found I was seized and held in a place where I lost my magic and grew old. Only when I lost all memory of who I was did you turn me loose."

Prince Talithan strode up to the professor and stared into his haggard old face. "Eldreth?" he said. "Can you be my brother Eldreth?"

"I fear so," Professor Ledbury said sadly.

"Then pigs do fly!" Talithan cried out and flung his arms round the professor.

"Well done, Eldred," Miss Ledbury said, fetching out her notebook. "We can close the file on you at least."

Querida felt Reville tense, hoping to use this reunion as a diversion. But Elda's diversion arrived at that moment and it was much more effective. She said afterwards that she and Don had met it coming anyway and simply encouraged it a little. Ringlet came first, flying a jeering half foot too high for the dogs to reach her, with the whole pack of dogs beneath and around her, jumping, barking, yelping, and being pursued themselves by the rest of the pigs, some on foot, some in the air, and all squealing mightily. Pretty, who had clearly deserted Talithan for this game, came cantering after them, neighing with laughter, and after Pretty, flapping and angry, with their necks stretched out, rushed a number of geese, home at last, but only about half the usual number. Old George sped after them, shouting uselessly. After him lumbered the Friendly Cows, mooing and bewildered, dropping cowpats into the confusion, driven on by Don and Elda. And after them – Don explained later that it was pure coincidence – came galloping a herd of the dwarfs' ponies, anxious to be reunited with their masters, followed by Nancy Cobber and all the Derkholm horses. Last of all came Beauty, flapping, neighing and dragging the Horselady who was hanging on to her bridle and trying to stop her.

"See Prhetty! See Prhetty!" Beauty screamed.

Almost everyone on the terrace was forced to roll, dive or dodge out of the way of the stampede. The demon did not move. It just let all the animals flow through it. Mr Chesney did not move either. Blade watched him being shoved this way and that by the racing crowd of animals and trying to pretend, just as he had before, that nothing was happening. While Blade was shoving himself and Kit aside to make room for Ringlet and the dogs, he kept his eye on Mr Chesney and saw a blur beside him, and then the same blur again, beside Querida. The hammering of paws and hooves and trotters had been too much for Querida. She had drawn herself up into a crouch on the wall, with her face hidden. As the Friendly Cows thundered past, Blade saw the blur become Reville. While the ponies streamed across the terrace, Reville nudged Querida and handed her what looked like a paperweight filled with yellowish fog. Blade found himself impressed by Reville's skill.

The Horselady gave up the struggle and let Beauty chase the rest on her own. "I was only bringing her *back*," she explained to Derk. "When I call, they *all* come, you see."

As the stampede went rushing away round the house and Don and Elda came loping back to the terrace, grinning, Querida sat up on her wall and waved the paperweight.

"I've got your demon here, Mr Chesney!" she called.

Mine, said the demon Tripos, snaking down a luminous blue hand-thing.

"No, mine," Scales said, grabbing for it with an enormous clawed foot.

Mr Chesney strode towards Querida, holding out his hand imperiously. "I'll have that here, if you please."

Querida clung to the glass globe with all the might of her withered arms and all the strength of her magic. This was going to be difficult.

Then a great stillness came over everything. This was followed by a faint stirring in the air which gave the feeling of music. Everyone looked up and saw that Anscher was there.

Blade thought the gods probably came out through

the front door, but perhaps they came from somewhere else entirely. There was absolutely no doubt they were the gods. They all had such a strong stillness about them that it almost gave you the feeling they were in violent motion, and there was a faint light on them that came from somewhere where the rules were different.

Blade had no doubt who was Anscher. He was the same person as the man he had met fishing. Beside Blade, Kit stirred and muttered, "He's the one who told me to learn—"

No one had any doubt. Prince Talithan and his brother went down on one knee to a tall goddess with dark hair. The Horselady bowed almost to the paving stones to another goddess with an arched neck and flowing hair. Wizards and some of the Pilgrims knelt to others. Reville bowed deeply and elegantly to a small, smiling god. Even Scales bent his crowned head to a mighty dragon in the background.

Anscher smiled and came forward. The rest of the geese came stepping proudly around his feet, as smug as if they had brought him themselves – as maybe they had.

"Why have you waited until now to manifest some gods?" Mr Chesney asked Derk. "There have been quite a few complaints, wizard. I want an explanation."

"You shall have one," said Anscher. "We manifest by our will, not yours."

He still seemed to be only a step or so beyond the

front door, but he reached down and plucked the paperweight from among the hands and talons reaching for it at the other side of the terrace. The demon Tripos gave a soundless scream that made everyone's mind throb.

"Be quiet," Anscher said mildly. "You shall have your mate back shortly." The noiseless noise stopped at once. "The gods have been forced to wait too," Anscher continued, "until people of this world asked to be able to rule their own affairs. The gods need to be asked. And for forty years the people of this world found it easier to do what Roland Chesney told them than to ask for this world for themselves. Roland Chesney, you have not used this world well. We now remove it from you. We give the wizard Querida the task of making this world into its own place."

"But," Querida whispered, "won't that take ages?" Her dry little voice could hardly be heard.

"At least another forty years," said Anscher. Querida, assured by this of a very long life, sat up straight and seemed much less frail. "And, as the Oracles warned you," Anscher said, "it will not be easy. Slaves have to learn freedom. But we give you the children of Wizards Derk and Mara to help you in this. And for the same forty years, while this world mends, Roland Chesney shall live as he forced this demon to live."

Anscher held up the smoky paperweight. It was now clear glass. Small as it was, everyone could clearly see the little dark figure of a person inside it. Mr Chesney was no longer standing on the terrace. Anscher stowed the paperweight in the fisherman's pouch at his belt. He smiled in a way that struck everyone as if he were smiling personally at them. "Do well," he said.

Derk sighed as Anscher smiled at him. It seemed hard, he thought, that High Priest Umru had not happened to be here. But later, when he heard that Umru had died at almost that precise moment of a massive stroke, with a look of intense delight on his face, it seemed to him that Umru had indeed seen Anscher just once more. He always hoped so, anyway.

Everyone was distracted then by all the dragons on the hill hastily jumping or flapping out of the way of two madly zigzagging demons, one luminous blue, the other smoky yellow, who shot along the hills and around the hills and finally streaked over the top and out of sight. There were no gods any more by then. The dragons were already crawling and winging down to Kit's shed, where each of them seized at least two baskets of treasure.

"Hey!" said Galadriel to Scales. "We didn't come all this way to pay tribute to *dragons*!"

"Then take it back from them," suggested Scales.

"Doh!" said Galadriel. And all the dwarfs tried angrily to get Derk's attention.

Derk was with Querida, surrounded by angry Wizard Guides. "How are my Pilgrims supposed to get home now?" demanded Finn.

"Easily." Querida looked over their heads at the steady

stream of grubby, footsore Pilgrims coming through the gates and edging round Scales. "There are over a hundred wizards here, male and female – enough to riddle the place with portals, now there's no demon to keep them closed. Go and open one yourself."

"I don't know how," Finn confessed.

Querida sighed. "Very well. I'll do it myself."

Blade watched her stand up on the wall and do it, interested. It didn't seem very difficult. Derk waited until the weary, travel-stained people were climbing eagerly through and then went to talk to Shona. She was with Geoffrey, Reville and Sukey, talking with Miss Ledbury and the Pooles. Neither Geoffrey nor Sukey seemed at all bothered to be without Mr Chesney. In fact, Derk thought they both looked relieved.

"We'll be taking this tour business apart on the other side," Dad Poole was saying, "and all the subsidiaries."

"You won't have much when you get home," Miss Ledbury said. "I take it you *are* coming home really?"

Sukey and Geoffrey both shook their heads. "No. We're staying."

While they were talking, Derk took hold of Shona's arm. "I'm going to Bardic College tomorrow," he said. "I'll make them take you back even if I have to bespell the lot of them."

"No need, sir," Geoffrey said, swinging round from Miss Ledbury. "*I'm* going to do that. They'll do it."

Derk had to admit that if Geoffrey told the bards,

they were likely to stay told, but he felt the smallest bit hurt, all the same. Shona was still his daughter.

Here they were all shoved out of the way by the mauve dragon, who came crawling up on to the terrace to drop a chinking bundle by Callette's front feet. "Here," she said, towering over Callette. "I didn't let the Pilgrims have any of the good ones. I thought you'd want them back."

In the bundle were more than half Callette's gizmos, including the fabulous one hundred and ninth. Callette bent over them, entranced. "Thanks!"

"You're welcome. I've got real treasure now," the mauve dragon said and snaked round off the terrace, causing another stumbling rush of people trying to get out of the way.

"My goodness!" Querida said, standing on her wall and gazing down at the gizmos. "I'll buy those from you. I'd like to exhibit them at the University."

"Not till I've finished admiring them," Callette said.

Blade looked up from the gizmos to find himself, and Kit, being beckoned by one of Scales's massive talons. They looked at one another and went to the edge of the terrace, about level with the talon. "I'm going to be living in your side valley for the next decade or so," Scales told them. "I've taken a fancy to it. While I'm there, I'm going to teach you both wizardry if it kills us all. We'll start with mind reading. Turn up there tomorrow morning, both of you. Boy, cat-bird, got that?"

"My name's Kit," Kit said. "Is this because of what the god said?"

"Only partly," said Scales. "Mostly it was the sight of the pair of you in that sandpit, with all the ability to get out of it and not knowing how to. That irritated me." He turned himself slowly around, causing Pilgrims to scamper right and left, and marched away through what used to be garden, trampling false walls, real bushes and fraying monsters as he went.

Kit looked at Blade. They both had mixed feelings. "Let's have some fun first," Kit said. He called out, "Griffin dance, anybody?"

All the other griffins, even Callette, bounded to join the dance.

"Do it in the garden then!" Mara bawled. She was distractedly counting dwarfs, elves, wizards and stray Pilgrims and healers. "Hundreds," she said. "Must get rid of the cowpats first. And then there's us. Call it three hundred?"

The dwarfs had descended on Derk and were arguing with him. "Then if they've left seven baskets, you can give them to us," Galadriel was saying.

Derk was distracted too, thinking of how you made unicorns. But he had been counting on those seven baskets of treasure to stay solvent with after all this. "I don't think I owe you quite that much," he protested.

"You don't owe them nothing!" Old George said, rather red and breathless after chasing animals. "They ate the little monkeys and the big hen and had a try nibbling your nylon plants. And ask Fran what they did in the kitchen. She's got supper started," he added.

"Oh, tell her not to bother," Mara said. "I'm going to be conjuring a feast."

"Can you do that?" Derk asked her, wishing it was something he had the knack of. He meant to go on to ask her what she thought of a unicorn in the family, but instead, the perfect idea came to him at last. "Mara, what do you think to us having a winged human?"

"Derk!" said Mara. "Oh, yes, well, why not?"

MAGICAL BOOKS FROM
Diana Wynne Jones

... Magic rules the worlds!

Spells are the hardest things to get right...

No magic allowed here!

Follow your dreams...

'Always perfectly magical' Neil Gaiman

'The best writer of magic there is.' Neil Gaiman

Four tales of Chrestomanci